UNSTOPPABLE

A **KATE PREACHER** THRILLER
BOOK 2

MICHAEL MALOOF

*Join my VIP Reader's Club
for all things Kate Preacher.*

ALSO BY MICHAEL MALOOF

RELENTLESS

A *KATE PREACHER* THRILLER *BOOK 1*

Winner of the Clive Cussler Grandmaster Award
Adventure Writers Competition

Praise for Relentless

"Taut and energetic, Relentless lives up to its name in action and suspense. An engrossing first-rate thriller."
— Dirk Cussler

"The title says it all. Relentless is an overdose of white-knuckled action and suspense. Guaranteed to keep you turning pages far into the night."
— Jeff Edwards, Bestselling author of Steel Wind and The Damocles Agenda

"Michael Maloof's Relentless is a heart-pounding thriller that grabs you from the very first page and doesn't let go until the explosive conclusion. Kate Preacher is a heroine for the ages—smart, tough, and relentless in her pursuit of justice."
— Ryan Steck, The Real Book Spy and author of Out for Blood

"Maloof has created a sharp, witty, and competent protagonist who can hold her own in a world of ruthless killers. Fans of strong, intelligent female protagonists will root for Kate and find in her a heroine they won't soon forget."
— Booklife Reviews

*"The world is a dangerous place to live,
not because of the people who are evil, but because of the
people who don't do anything about it."*
—Attributed to Albert Einstein

*"Vengeance may be the lord's
but beware the woman with nothing left to lose."*
—Katherine Preacher

PROLOGUE

FOUR DAYS BEFORE JAKE'S FUNERAL

MONDAY, APRIL 20th
2:00 PM EDT

MANHATTAN INTERNATIONAL TRAUMA CENTER (MITC), NY

IN THE LAST FORTY-EIGHT hours, Kate Preacher had killed seven men. *The count doesn't matter. That's what Jake would say. The message did: Come at me, and it's the hospital or the morgue—I don't care which.*

The helicopter's rotors clawed at the Manhattan sky, lifting Kate into the air and away from the carnage. She was safe—for now.

From the hospital rooftop, Vitali Moshenski watched her ascend, his expression almost fatherly. But Kate didn't trust him—too many secrets, too much left unsaid. Still, he was useful—opening doors, managing chaos, cleaning up the fallout at Moore Tower

When Kate asked for somewhere to go, Vitali's first suggestion had been to seek the company of friends. But when she insisted on solitude, he relented, arranging this flight to his Hudson Valley estate—a place to think, to work, and to plan her next move.

Alone in the helicopter, a roller-coaster of emotions and thoughts collided. She was startled to realize it had only been four days.

Four days ago, Jake was in Paris. Smiling. Bragging about an anniversary present. Promising he'd make it home—this time.

That was a promise Jake couldn't keep. While Kate watched and listened, her world turned upside down. Tires screeched. Cries of "Allahu Akbar!" rang out. She could still hear the continuous explosion of automatic gunfire and the collision of screams and shattered glass. Jake's phone laying at the edge of the road caught flashes of the terror, while Kate's screams for her husband vanished amid gunfire and chaos.

The world was shocked by yet another Paris terrorist attack—the senseless murder of thirty-six, and the heroics of a man the French media dubbed l'Américain, *the American*. It seemed Jake was the right man in the wrong place. Kate knew better—Jake was executed. She didn't know why, not yet—but she wouldn't stop until she did.

The helicopter banked east. City lights vanished, replaced by forest and water—but the noise in Kate's head remained. She closed her eyes, her fingers pressing against the NanoVault beneath her shirt as if the touch might summon Jake's voice.

She pulled it free, turning the device over in her fingers. The cool metal was familiar now—like a well-worn chess piece between moves. But the board was still a blur. The opponent, unseen.

Jake left her the first move.

She just had to see it.

"Find this," Jake said in the recording, lifting the device from under his shirt. His voice was steady, but she saw the tension, the clenched jaw. *"And do your thing. See what everyone is missing. What I missed. Solve the puzzle. And take them down."*

Kate exhaled slowly, her grip tightening around the device.

Devin Moore never took it off—not until the moment he had no choice.

His throat crushed, gasping for air. He ripped it from his neck and thrust it into her hands. Bargaining for his life.

She let him die.

A marketing ploy. That's all it was supposed to be. The Golden NanoVault. A high-stakes challenge to hackers around the world—break its encryption, claim a fortune. Fifty million in Bitcoin.

No one ever cracked it. Not even Nomad.

But it wasn't just a game.

Devin's encrypted storage wasn't just a gimmick—it was a vault of secrets, shielding something so dangerous that he killed to keep it buried. A French mathematician—gone. Nomad—next on the list.

And now it was hers.

Jake's files were inside, somewhere beneath layers of encryption. But what else did Moore hide? He built this empire on privacy, selling the illusion of security to the world. But what was he protecting for himself?

She exhaled again, gripping the NanoVault tighter.

The helicopter jolted slightly, catching an air pocket. Kate opened her eyes, swallowing the ache in her throat, and glanced at the co-pilot.

He gestured toward the window, his voice cutting through the roar of the rotors. "Almost there."

Kate tugged at her harness, then leaned forward, her gaze following his hand. What she saw was a picture of old-money grandeur—a relic of America's Gilded Age. She guessed the estate was easily 200 acres, or more, of rolling hills and forest, the kind of property built by families whose names adorned library wings and hospital foundations.

The helicopter touched down on a pad set just beyond the main house. Everything about the man who greeted her, from his posture to the way he clasped his hands behind his back, radiated an unshakable confidence that came with a lifetime of service.

"Mrs. Preacher," he began, his voice as polished as the rest of him. "Welcome to Deerfield. I am Langdon, the estate manager. Mr. Moshenski asked me to ensure your stay is...uninterrupted."

Kate raised an eyebrow, her curiosity piqued. "Langdon," she repeated, testing the name. "Do you have a first name?"

"No, ma'am," he replied with the faintest hint of a smile. "Langdon will suffice."

Her lips quirked, a faint smirk escaping. "Alright, Langdon. Lead the way."

Langdon gave a small nod, his expression betraying the barest trace of amusement. "I understand you're traveling light," he continued, "so a few essentials have been selected and placed in your suite. Additionally, Mr. Moshenski has arranged for a personal stylist to assist with anything else you may require. Discreetly, of course."

Kate's smirk deepened, and she allowed herself a wry glance at him. "Of course."

***

THE HIGHLANDS SUITE WAS a picture of understated elegance. A central seating area. A plush gray couch. A large picture window framed a view of rolling hills and a shimmering lake below, its surface reflecting the golden hues of the late afternoon sun. Beyond the lake, groves of ancient trees stood like sentinels.

By the window sat a small dining table with a setting for one. A bowl of perfectly arranged fruit and an assortment of artisanal snacks—a small plate of cheeses, crackers, and chocolates.

Langdon gestured to the table. "The chef thought you might appreciate a few light refreshments after your journey. Dinner can be served here, should you prefer, or in the main dining room."

Kate glanced at the table, already certain this was where she would dine. "This is perfect," she began. "Are there any other guests?"

"No, ma'am," Langdon replied. "And none are expected."

Thank God, she thought. *No introductions, meaningless chit-chat, questions, or condolences.*

"In the master closet, you'll find an estate robe and slippers, along with a few additional items procured for your stay. Should you require anything further, your stylist is scheduled to meet with you tomorrow morning at nine, but she's at your disposal should you wish to adjust the time."

Kate nodded, but her attention was captured by the executive workstation positioned near the far wall. "Floating high-res monitors. Herman Miller chair," she began. "Power and network ports, cable management, and task lighting—this setup was designed by an expert."

Langdon nodded and smiled. "The card on the desk provides details on accessing the estate's network." He paused, a hint of humor threading his voice. "I suspect, given your expertise, you'll find the setup adequate. Mr. Moshenski has asked that you refrain from exploring the estate's network security. He suspects you would have little difficulty circumventing our defenses but would prefer you not test that theory."

Kate allowed herself a faint smile. "Understood."

When Langdon left, Kate dropped her bag onto the couch and plopped down alongside. For the first time in days, she felt a flicker of calm. Just a flicker, but for now, it was enough.

***

WHETHER CONSCIOUSLY OR NOT, everything about her arrival at the estate had been in slow motion. Bathing, changing, dinner in the room—even setting up her devices—each step had been careful, methodical, and calculated. But beneath it all, she knew the truth: she was afraid.

Moore's NanoVault was a Pandora's box. At the last possible moment, Jake's files had been transferred to the device, but their condition was a mystery. She suspected some files would be corrupt. But how many? And how important? She was afraid of what she might find—and might not. She was afraid to fail.

She sat at the workstation, her fingers cradling the device, hesitating as the weight of its history pressed down on her.

Jake's files weren't just answers to his final riddle—they were a reckoning. And now, with his files tucked inside Moore's one-of-a-kind device, Kate wondered what else was on Moore's NanoVault. *What secrets might Devin have secured on the vault*, Kate wondered. *What did he think was so valuable, so important, he never took this off—except to bargain for his life?*

Kate took a deep breath, steadying herself. *You can do this*, she thought, echoing Jake's words from the video. *Solve the puzzle. See what everyone else missed.*

She pushed the fear aside, connected the device to her system, and considered Moore's passcode.

Hardly unique, she thought. *He must have believed the code's irrelevance added security*. In that regard, he wasn't wrong. Most passwords, phrases, and codes had a personal connection, and with enough time and background information, they were relatively easy to break.

Kate recalled Moore lying on the floor, his trachea crushed, the image of him gasping for air and pleading silently for her help burned into her mind. With trembling hands, he tore the device from the chain around his neck and pressed it into her palm. His right hand lifted weakly, flashing three fingers, then one, then four, repeating the sequence over and over—three, one, four.

She turned to the NanoVault and set its mechanical dials to the first seven digits of Pi:

3-1-4-1-5-9-2

The lock clicked open.

***

10:47 PM EDT

THE FIRST FEW HOURS of exploring, mapping, and decrypting files were tedious but not unusual. Years of digital forensics work, first as a CIA analyst and more recently with a Richmond law firm, stressed the value of patience—and the rewards of progressing methodically.

Including rewards she hadn't expected.

Kate's breathing was steady but shallow as she launched the encrypted video chat. When Nomad's avatar appeared on the screen, she sighed and relaxed.

"I didn't think I'd be hearing from you so soon," Nomad said, his voice laced with curiosity. "Is everything OK?"

"Sorry," Kate replied, brushing off his concern. "Did I wake you?"

Nomad laughed. "Carpe Noctem, *seize the night*," he said. "Besides, I'm still too wired from this morning's near-death experience. What's up?"

"I connected to Moore's NanoVault—"

"Are Jake's files intact?" he interrupted. "I didn't have much time—I wasn't sure..."

"Relax. So far, many—maybe most—are intact," Kate replied. "They'll take time to untangle and understand. But that's not why I called."

"You want me to have a look at the corrupted files?" Nomad asked. "There's always a chance I can recover some of them."

Kate arched a brow, her tone firm. "If you'll stop interrupting me, I'll show you what I found."

"Oh. Sorry. What did you find?"

"Here," Kate said, sharing her screen. "Take a look."

"Holy crap on a cracker."

"That's not quite what I said," Kate replied dryly, "but you get the idea."

"How much is it?"

"At market value...almost *two hundred fifty million*," Kate said, her voice steady, though the size of the number lingered in the air. "This is way more than the bounty."

"A lot more," Nomad agreed, his tone cautious. "Moore's key wasn't just his metaphorical *Swiss Bank Account*—it was the real deal. How many times did we hear him use that analogy?"

"We all assumed he meant privacy and security," Kate said. "Turns out he meant it literally."

"Right, but don't forget, Moore was a multi-multi-billionaire," Nomad said. "In the big picture, this is like one-half of one percent—this was his walking-around money. And since it's all Bitcoin, I'll bet the IRS doesn't know a thing about it."

"I'm counting on that," Kate replied. "And that's why I called."

"Right—you can't exactly deposit this in your checking account," he said, chuckling. "Leave it to me—it will take some time to stay under the radar, but this is one of my specialties."

"I hoped you'd say that," Kate said. "Let's just split this—fifty-fifty."

"No way," Nomad protested. "I'd be dead if it wasn't for you—I'm not taking your money."

"It's not my money."

"It is now, Kate," he said, leaving no room for debate.

"Fine," Kate agreed, knowing it was pointless to argue. "Just move it for now, and we'll work out the details later."

Kate opened a covert communications channel, granting Nomad access to her laptop. And with a series of voice commands, Nomad took control of the vault.

Kate sat back while Nomad worked on moving the Bitcoin private keys.

"Just the keys," Kate cautioned. "This isn't a fishing expedition."

***

TUESDAY, APRIL 21st
5:00 AM EDT

KATE ALWAYS WOKE EARLY. Boo used to love that, but if she wasn't stirring by five, he would help. First came the nudge—his cold nose against her elbow. If that didn't work, his tongue would find an exposed toe.

But Boo was gone now, and mornings felt emptier without him. The familiar ritual had been replaced by silence. Her only companion was the memory of his wagging tail and soulful eyes. "Hey Boo," she whispered as if he could still hear her.

She rolled out of bed and sat on the edge, her hands brushing the cool fabric of her sleepwear. "Good morning, my love," she murmured, blowing Jake a kiss. "It's coffee time."

The suite's espresso machine hummed to life, the aroma of rich, dark coffee filling the air. Over her first double espresso, Kate mapped out her day. *I can work for a couple of hours, skip breakfast, and meet with the stylist at nine—I need something for the funeral.*

Kate tried not to think about Jake's funeral, but it was impossible to push aside.

Three days from now, on what would have been their fifth wedding anniversary, Senior Chief Jake Church, a retired Navy SEAL, would be laid to rest in Arlington National Cemetery.

As Kate thought about Friday, she preferred to focus on their marriage, life, and anniversary. *Five incredible years*, she thought. *Filled with adventure, love, and laughter—and nowhere near long enough.*

With the first espresso gone, Kate prepared another—she knew it would be a long day.

The meeting with the stylist was pleasant and brief—the master closet now held everything she might need for the next few days, along with a collection of all-black clothing.

"For Friday, I've curated a few options: trousers or skirts paired with tailored blouses and matching blazers, as well as a couple of classic dresses with wraps. There's also a longer coat in case the weather turns."

It was kind of her not to say the word, Kate thought. *Friday was quite enough.* And there was no pressure to decide. But with the weight of the funeral pressing down, the sheer number of choices felt overwhelming. *Not today. I'll try them tomorrow.*

The day vanished in a blur of identifying the corrupt files and then reviewing and organizing the readable ones by date, location, and event—it was slow, tedious work. *Maybe I could delegate some of this to Nomad,* she thought. *Keisha would probably be willing to help, too.*

But she shook her head, dismissing the idea. It wasn't hard work, and she trusted them—but she couldn't take the risk. "I don't know what's important, not yet," she murmured, leaning back in her chair. "The key to making sense of all this could be anything."

It was nearly midnight before Kate noticed the time. Frustration simmered as exhaustion crept in. Finally, she shut the laptop, pushed away from the desk, and headed for bed.

***

WEDNESDAY, APRIL 22nd
9:38 AM EDT

THE MORNING PASSED IN a barrage of files and disappointment. Jake's notes were meticulous but fragmented, like pieces of a puzzle scattered across a table with no edges to guide her.

Two ominous folders stood out: *The Final Roll Call* and *The Silent Watch*.

Everyone on *The Final Roll Call* was dead. Jake's annotations detailed their causes of death, ranging from suspicious accidents to outright assassination. Car crashes, sudden illnesses, staged suicides—all with an unsettling frequency and precision that defied coincidence.

Among the names were a handful of high-profile figures whose deaths had made international headlines.

Alejandro Suarez, CEO of EnergíaViva, a renewable energy giant in Spain—killed in a Barcelona carjacking.

Dr. Lila Kashyap, Senior Fellow and Director of the AI Research Lab at the Mumbai Institute of Technology—killed in an apartment complex fire.

U.S. Senator Henry Topping—drowned in a boating accident off Martha's Vineyard.

But many others were virtual unknowns—ordinary people whose deaths barely registered beyond local obituaries. *Jake put them on the list*, she thought. *There must be a reason.*

The Silent Watch was no less chilling. These individuals were missing, some for years, their disappearances cloaked in mystery. Most were now presumed dead, but Jake hadn't been so quick to accept that conclusion.

Dr. Jürgen Mayer, an epidemiologist specializing in viral outbreak modeling, vanished during a conference in Berlin.

Sophia Chen, a game theorist and AI ethicist, last seen boarding a flight to Geneva, never arrived.

Antonio Castaldi, a physicist working on modular nuclear power systems, disappeared from his home in Florence.

The more she read, the more doubt crept in. Jake had a sharp mind and unparalleled instincts, but the sheer volume of data he collected was overwhelming. She pictured Jake's "wall of crazy," what they called these boards at Langley—random bits of data pinned to a board searching for a pattern.

Jake's wall, hidden in the cabin's armory and guarded by anti-personnel mines, was a chaotic collage of newspaper clippings, photographs, and scribbled notes—all intricately linked by a colorful web of threads. Scarlet strands converged at the center, connecting to a stark black-and-white illustration.

The image hit her like a gut punch: red string crisscrossing a board, clippings, and photos pinned in random clusters. It wasn't just a memory of Jake's wall—she pictured the scene from *A Beautiful Mind*. She could see Russell Crowe's John Nash standing before a similar wall, piecing together an elaborate conspiracy that didn't exist.

Kate's chest tightened. *What if Jake was doing the same?* The thought terrified her. *He hid this work from me for over a year—why?* Kate wondered. *To protect me, or hide the truth? Was he seeing patterns or chasing ghosts?*

"No," Kate said out loud, silencing the inner voice. "At the center of Jake's wall was the sketch—a masked samurai wielding a sword and a single word: *RONIN*."

Ronin was real—she'd seen the video, watched him kill Francois, a harmless old man—and she knew the killer's identity.

After days of working in near total silence, hearing her own voice was startling, but the facts were reassuring. "Jake wasn't some tourist at the wrong cafe. The note in Jake's Paris hotel room said exactly when and where to meet. He was set up."

Kate's doubts crumbled. *Jake found something*, she thought. *Or someone believed he did—and that was enough to kill him. But I need to shift my focus—get a broader perspective.*

She closed the folders of the dead and missing and returned to scanning through the NanoVault's directory structure. She'd already concluded many of the files had no immediate value—hotel bills, miscellaneous receipts, and the team's expense reports. There were mission notes—and after-action reports, but none stood out. *If there were any major mission issues or failures—Jake would have briefed me long before now.*

In a *Building Plans* folder, she found a collection of architectural drawings, construction plans, and CAD files—sprawling, complex, and meticulous. *That's odd*, she thought. *No identifying marks—no project name or logos, not even an architect's signature.*

She frowned and ran a quick reverse image search. *Nothing.*

"I'll come back to you," she murmured, cataloging the folder for later.

A folder full of MP4 videos grabbed her attention. *Probably surveillance video,* she thought, but the first video she played took her breath away.

"Jake Church! You are so busted," she said, but couldn't stop smiling. "*Oh Kate—do you really have to record everything,*" she said, mocking his objections to recording their video chats.

And here they were—his own private collection of their videos.

"You sneaky, sentimental liar," she whispered, smiling through the sting of tears. "You have them all."

She grabbed another video at random—Jake was saying goodnight, his voice warm and steady as he blew her a kiss. Kate closed the file and shut the tablet, cradling it against her chest.

She blew him a kiss in return and, for the first time in a week, drifted into a deep, peaceful sleep.

***

THURSDAY, APRIL 23rd
6:38 AM EDT

ALMOST BY ACCIDENT, SHE spotted a single file buried in a cache folder—the kind of temporary folder created during updates or after a system crash.

Her heart pounded. The file was created two minutes before the attack. She hovered over the mouse, hesitated—then clicked.

The file contained a single word: *Albatross.*

But the file's metadata told the real story. This was a text message captured via a cloned cell phone—precisely the type of file she'd analyzed hundreds of times at the Agency.

In Paris, Deputy Director Boucher demanded to know why Jake's backpack had illegal cell phone jamming and cloning gear. Now she had an answer—Jake was tracking someone in close physical proximity, someone at the cafe.

The cafe's street cam video, she thought. *I need to see it again.* Kate hoped she'd never have to see it again, but this was different.

The video began as always: Jake at the café, his phone propped up for their chat. Marcus appeared, walking into frame. He glanced at the phone, greeted Kate, and teased Jake about being at the wrong cafe.

He was trying to pull Jake away, she realized. *I suspected a pretty waitress—Marcus never missed a chance to flirt with a beautiful woman.*

She fast-forwarded to the critical moment and froze the frame. Marcus stood on the street corner, eyes glued to a phone—but not the team's secure Blackphone. The phone in his hand was a Samsung.

"You son of a bitch," Kate whispered. *You sent the text. Albatross was a mission abort code—but it was too late.*

The video resumed: Marcus glanced back at Jake, his eyes wide as the screech of tires ripped through the audio. Jake's voice followed, sharp and urgent: "The kids," he shouted to Marcus. "Get the kids!"

Kate slammed the laptop shut. She couldn't watch anymore. She couldn't watch Jake die—not again.

The suite felt like a prison, the air too thick to breathe, the walls closing in. Kate grabbed her jacket and darted outside, letting her feet carry her away. It didn't matter where—she just needed to move, to think.

Her mind raced. The Paris attack, Marcus's role, the Albatross text—it all swirled in her head. *Jake loved Marcus like a brother*, Kate knew. *But he must have figured it out—or at least suspected—Marcus was Ronin.*

Kate wrestled with the image of Jake watching Marcus on the street corner, burner phone in hand—the panic in Marcus's eyes. *That explains Jake's last words*, Kate realized. *The warning. Jake knew I'd find out—and he knew what I would do.*

She bolted back to the suite. Jake was right—she wanted to kill him. *But Marcus didn't pull the trigger. He wasn't driving the van.*

Closing the door behind her. *This is bigger than Marcus, much bigger*, she concluded. *But he knows something.*

Whatever he knows, Kate was certain of one thing: Marcus wasn't going to tell her—not willingly.

Would Ryder help, she wondered, pacing the suite. As the CIA's Deputy Director, Margot Ryder could snatch Marcus off the street with a single phone call. *But Ryder would also cut me out of the loop—I'd never know the truth.*

Her gaze drifted to the black dress laid out on the bed. Her throat tightened, but she choked back the tears. *Not now,* she thought. *Tomorrow will come soon enough. Right now, I need to think. I need a plan.*

And that plan wasn't Ryder—that much she knew.

There was another way—a man with the resources and the ruthlessness to make it happen. Trusting him was dangerous—she knew that. But what choice did she have?

Vitali knows I killed Moore, Kate thought. *He probably knows about the others, too. That could be a problem. But right now, I need answers more than I need to be safe.*

She pictured the man she'd only met a few days ago but knew by reputation—his rise to wealth and power shrouded in mystery and innuendo. How much of it was true was anyone's guess, but one thing was certain: he had what she needed. *Would he do this for me,* she wondered. *Well, there's one way to find out.*

With a steadying breath, Kate grabbed her phone and dialed Vitali.

A cold determination settled over her, cutting through the haze of grief and confusion. For the first time, the path forward was clear.

Marcus Jones was as tough and disciplined as they came. Getting the answers she wanted wasn't going to be easy. For anyone.

Kate exhaled slowly, her grip tightening around the phone.

She pressed the call button. The line connected.

Then, just above a whisper, she admitted.

"Everyone breaks. Eventually."

Chapter 1

FRIDAY, APRIL 24th
4:15 PM EDT

JOINT BASE MYER-HENDERSON HALL, ARLINGTON, VA

KATE PREACHER SLIPPED AWAY the moment the wave of hugs and tears subsided. She sank into the Town Car's back seat, clutching Jake's folded flag like a lifeline.

"I'm sorry, ma'am," the driver said, turning off the radio. "I didn't see you coming."

"Don't worry," Kate murmured. "I'm surprised myself." She exhaled, gaze fixed ahead. "But it's time to go. Time to go home."

"Yes, ma'am."

Time to go home, she thought. She hadn't been back since the day she left for work—the day Jake was killed.

The exhaustion of the Arlington ceremony and the intensity of the memorial caught up with her. She slipped off her flats, tucked her feet up on the seat, and leaned into the corner.

The memory of Jake's last FaceTime call hit like shrapnel. *Love me?* She asked. But he didn't answer. *Couldn't* answer. And now, she would never feel him sweep her up in his arms, press his lips to her ear, and whisper, *Always... I will always love you.*

Four thousand miles away, her husband was alone in the fight of his life. She swallowed hard, struggling with the helplessness and the guilt. *There was nothing you could do.* That's what Jake would say, but she couldn't help wondering.

What if I was there?

We'd both be dead, Jake said, his laughter warm, effortless—like the answer was obvious.

Kate flinched. Not because he was wrong. But because, for a moment, he felt close enough to touch.

It's not funny, she whispered, her throat tight. You promised me. You said you would always be there. What am I supposed to do now?

Jake's voice softened. You know what to do.

The driver jammed on the brakes, and Kate jerked forward. She woke in time to see a white squirrel dash across the road.

"Sorry, ma'am."

"It's fine," Kate said. "I'm glad you could stop."

Jake always said white squirrels were good luck. She smiled.

They'd been driving for over an hour and were close to home. She loved this part of Richmond. Close enough to walk to work or to the river but far enough away that tourists never ventured. You didn't drive in Kate's neighborhood unless you lived there, and everyone who did knew they had found a slice of history and heaven.

Jake and Kate would take Boo on long evening walks along elm-lined streets. The canopy of hundred-year-old trees formed natural tunnels of greenery. They walked and talked and listened to the whisper of leaves flicking in the breeze. This was home.

The car glided past the historic mix of homes that reflected Richmond's rich Southern heritage and European influences. Cobblestone paths led to storybook gardens of magnolias and azaleas, but looking beyond the trimmed hedges and manicured lawns, every house had an American flag rippling in the breeze.

When the driver stopped, Kate was stunned. The red brick path to her door was lined with small flags, and the porch was awash in bouquets of flowers and notes. The entire neighborhood seemed to share in her grief, their gestures of sympathy palpable in the early evening light.

The driver opened Kate's door and offered his hand. She slid out, pressing Jake's neatly folded flag against her heart, and with the CIA briefing folder clutched under her arm.

Kate strode up the walkway, the driver following with her suitcase. The sea of flowers and flags blurred as tears threatened to spill over, but she forced herself to remain composed. Kate climbed the steps and stood in front of the door. The driver set the case down and disappeared back down the path.

That was thoughtful. She needed a moment and couldn't bear another *sorry for your loss,* another tribute to Jake's heroism. Every word was offered in love and support, but none could change the fact that she was alone—standing on the doorstep of the house they had restored and made their home.

She wiped away the tear that slipped down her cheek, turned the key in the lock, and stepped inside.

The entryway was bathed in the soft light of the setting sun, casting a golden hue over the photos lining the walls. Kate paused, her eyes drifting over snapshots of her life with Jake. There were wedding photos bursting with smiles, Jake in his dress uniform, handsome, proud. Even Boo, the gray-faced and scarred old black lab, dressed for the occasion in a black bow tie and starched white collar. There were casual snapshots of the three of them at the cabin. Each image a reminder of the life they built—and the life now gone.

Her gaze shifted to the family room, where a single light was still on—the lamp next to Jake's recliner. *I'll leave the light on for you,* Kate would say whenever Jake was traveling. It was their code, one of the dozens of little things that shaped their life and their love. She set the flag on Jake's chair, turned off the light, and stood for a moment in the darkness and shadow.

Moving into the kitchen, Kate opened the fridge out of habit. She knew there wouldn't be anything edible and wasn't hungry, anyway. Her movements were automatic, a way to occupy her hands and distract her mind.

Everything about the day blurred like a dream fading after waking, but the sounds lingered. The rhythmic clatter of the horse's hooves as she followed the caisson carrying Jake's flag-draped coffin. Rifle shots shattering the silence, and the bugler's haunting notes echoing across the cemetery. And the sharp, metallic sound of metal striking wood as Jake's brothers-in-arms drove their Tridents into his coffin. Each blow reverberating in Kate's chest.

She reached for a bottle of Pinot Noir, opened and filled two-thirds of a stemless wine glass. She paused, a fleeting smile tugging at the corner of her mouth. *Now that's a girl pour,* she thought.

The smile was one of the few she'd managed that day.

Taking a sip, she turned her attention to finding her popcorn air-popper and a bowl to catch the fresh kernels. She placed a dish of butter in the microwave and listened to the rhythmic popping of the kernels.

The glass slipped from her grip, shattering on the floor. The crash echoed in the empty house, sharp and hollow. Kate sank to the floor, sobbing, and buried her face in her hands.

Then she felt a presence—familiar, comforting. She imagined Boo laying alongside her, resting his head in her lap. She could almost feel his fur, a mix of coarse patches and thick raised scars. For a moment, there was a profound sense of connection and comfort.

"Did Jake send you?" she whispered, her voice breaking.

The house was quiet, except for the last few pops of corn. Kate took a couple of slow, deep breaths, trying to pull herself together. She imagined Boo sitting beside her, anticipating his share of the popcorn.

She sat there on the cold tile floor, knowing that if the neighbors could see, they'd think she'd lost her mind. But the kitchen had once been the heart of their home, their family, and she drew strength from the memory of her husband and Boo.

Kate rose to her feet, feeling a small but steady resolve. She wiped her tears, cleaned up the shattered glass, and grabbed another glass. She carried her wine and the bowl of popcorn to the living room. The golden flame of gas street lamps peeked through the windows.

She sat cross-legged on the couch, the bowl of popcorn cradled in her lap, the wine glass balanced on the arm, but when the bowl was empty and the wine gone, she moved to Jake's recliner. *How many times had she crawled into his lap,* she wondered. She would dangle her legs over the side, and he'd wrap those enormous arms around her. In those moments, she felt small, safe, loved. Tonight, there was only the flag for company, but she held it close, curled up with a throw blanket, and fell asleep.

***

10:30 PM EDT

Grant Collins approached the white utility van parked next to the curb. From a distance and illuminated by the soft amber haze of streetlights, the van appeared to be a typical utility vehicle. The service crew was hard at work on some emergency maintenance. Orange safety cones placed at the corners of the van alerted residents to stay clear.

Two men stood near the rear, clad in high-visibility vests, hard hats, and work gloves. One knelt beside an open manhole cover and appeared deeply engrossed in some intricate task below. A flashlight beam flickered intermittently, casting brief glints of light on the surrounding area. The other figure stood nearby, checking a piece of equipment and speaking into a hand-held radio. Both moved with the smooth efficiency of professionals, their ID badges catching the light as they turned and walked.

Grant noted the concealed weapons, nodded, and approached the rear of the van. He knocked once, then opened the door just wide enough to slip inside. At first, the red light of the interior appeared darker than the street and outlined the surveillance tech sitting in front of a monitor.

"Give it a minute," the tech said, his gaze never veering from the monitors.

Grant's eyes adjusted to the red glow. He took a seat, noting the van's compact efficiency. The hum of electronics filled the air. *This guy's dressed like the others but not armed. They're the muscle. He's the brains.*

"What's the status?" Grant asked.

"The target's been home for several hours. No visitors. Appears to be sleeping. There's been no significant movement for the last hour."

"Bedroom?"

"No. Front room. That's her heat signature on the monitor," the tech replied, pointing at one of the monitors. "She looks like an easy target if you wanted to go in tonight."

Grant let out a short, humorless laugh. "And exactly how many people have you killed?"

The tech shifted uncomfortably, his voice barely above a whisper. "None, sir."

Grant shook his head and gestured toward the wall of monitors. "Right. Thought so. Look, kid, I'm sure you're good at all... this," he said, his tone flat as his hand swept across the equipment. "But this is what I do, and the contract calls for an accident, not a home invasion. We stick with the plan. Got that?"

"Yes, sir."

"Everything in place for the intercept?"

The tech nodded, tapping a few keys. "Locked in. Richmond Pinnacle building, zero eight hundred. She heads for the airport right after."

"Good. Alert me immediately if anything changes."

Grant was struck by the irony of the contract. *The target was returning to Paris, hoping to find the sniper who killed her husband.* He smirked. *What would she do if she knew that man was watching her sleep?*

Grant stood and was about to leave when the van's electronics lit up.

"What's happening?"

"She's getting a call," the tech said. "Here, grab a headset."

***

10:42 PM EDT

Kate tumbled out of the recliner and crawled over to the couch. She could barely see and answered by reflex.

"Preacher," she said, her voice still thick with exhaustion.

"Kate. It's Margot. I'm sorry to be calling you so late."

"Margot? What time is it?"

"Almost eleven," Margot replied.

"What is it? What's wrong?"

"It's Marcus." Margot hesitated. "He's dead."

"There must be some mistake," Kate said, adrenaline now surging. "He's with Moshenski's men."

"They're dead."

"What the hell happened?"

"We're working the scene unofficially, of course," Margot said. "A friend at the bureau looped me in when UVA seismic sensors picked up what they thought was a minor earthquake."

"A bomb?"

"Well, not exactly."

"Margot, I'm too tired for guessing games," Kate said. "Just spit it out."

"The evidence suggests a drone strike."

"Christ," Kate exclaimed. "One of ours?"

"Whoa. Slow down," Margot begged. "Remember, this is an open line, and we don't know anything yet. Besides, it doesn't take a genius to strap a bomb on a drone."

"The last thing Marcus said to me was they'd kill him."

"Who would kill him?"

"That's what I wanted to find out."

"And you went to Moshenski instead of trusting me?"

"You play by the rules," Kate said. "Well, most of the time, and I needed answers."

Kate was quiet for a moment and paced the room. *Marcus was right,* she thought. *I did sentence him to death.* Part of her accepted his fate. As Ronin, he was a brutal killer. But Marcus was a friend, once—and Jake's best friend. She watched him fight to save Jake's life and cry when he failed. *Maybe it was a mistake to involve Moshenski,* Kate thought. *Whatever Marcus knew, whatever role he played in the Paris attack, now I'll never know.*

"Kate?" Margo asked. "Are you still there?"

"Yeah. Sorry. Just thinking," Kate replied. "You're sure it was Marcus? Absolutely sure?"

"I wouldn't be calling if we weren't operating from a high degree of certainty," Margot said. "The SUV was registered to the Ukrainian embassy in DC. Forensics collected fragments of clothing and service ribbons that match Marcus's Army Service uniform and record. And his hands were cuffed. The vehicle was transporting a prisoner. It all fits."

"Was he cuffed in front or behind the back?"

"What difference does that make?" Margot spat.

"You're right," Kate stammered. "Sorry—I'm still half asleep and trying to wrap my head around the news."

"Believe me, I understand," Margot replied, her tone softening. "But before this leaks out, I wanted you to hear it from me."

"I appreciate that—but something tells me that's not the only reason you're calling."

"No," Margot said. "It's not."

"You think I'm in danger."

"Whatever Marcus knew, whatever you were trying to learn, someone took extreme measures to ensure his silence."

Kate's eyes narrowed, her voice low but certain. "You think someone wants to stop my investigation before it even begins? And they'll kill me, too, if that's what it takes."

Margot's sigh crackled through the line. "The smart move would be to walk away. Right now."

Kate shook her head. "Not yet. I can't."

"You can. But I know you won't," Margot said. "I've been where you are now. Lost everything. Your heart shattered. You're thinking you've got nothing to lose, so why not? But there are people who care about you and who don't want you to die chasing Jake's ghosts."

"The people who care about me know whatever the price, I need answers," Kate said. "I leave for Paris on Monday."

"Fine. But you're on your own," Margot said. "After Moore's *accident*, there are eyes on every move I make."

"I understand."

"Do you?" Margot asked. "You're not a field officer."

"What's that supposed to mean?"

"It means there's more to staying alive than analyzing data," Margot replied.

"I'm not the girl you took to Syria," Kate snapped. "You told Jake to teach me to shoot. But he taught me more than you know, and I've been training with the operators ever since."

"Fair enough," Margot said. "Just keep your eyes open. If this was our operation, you'd never reach the airport."

"Noted," Kate said. "But there is one thing."

"What?"

"When the FBI wraps up their investigation," Kate began. "Can you get me a copy of the medical examiner's report?"

"No. This is an FBI case," Margo said, her tone leaving no room for discussion. "The last thing we want is them looking in our direction—questioning our interest."

Kate drew in a steadying breath, forcing an even tone. "I appreciate the call." Her voice was calm, confident—almost.

Margot's right, Kate thought. *With Marcus dead, I could be next*. Kate remained composed, almost serene, but there was a subtle shift. Her eyes sharp and calculating, with the hint of something hidden just beneath the surface.

I have no idea who or what I'm up against, she thought, and the corners of her mouth lifted ever so slightly. *But neither do they.*

***

GRANT HAD THE HEADSET cup pressed to his right ear during Kate's call. When the call ended, he turned to the technician. "You got all that?"

"Yes, sir."

"Who was that?"

With a few keystrokes, the tech had the answer. "Voice ID confirmed the caller was Margot Ryder, CIA Deputy Director, National Clandestine Services." With a mouse click, he continued reading, "And the call originated from her home in Langley Forest, McLean, Virginia."

"Preacher has friends in high places," Grant noted. "Whose Marcus?"

The tech kept typing. "Here's one possibility. Sergeant First Class Marcus Jones, U.S. Army, Retired. 75th Ranger Regiment. This dude is one bad-ass mother..."

"Or was," Grant interrupted. "Someone took him out. What else?"

"Multiple combat tours in Iraq, Afghanistan and Syria. Purple Heart, Silver Star, and Bronze Star with..."

"That's enough," Grant interrupted again. "I get why the Trident team would want him, and that explains the connection to Preacher, but not with Moshenski or the CIA," Grant said, just thinking out loud. "And did you catch the bit about Moore? Preacher knows something the CIA wants to keep quiet."

"What about her training? Does that change anything?"

"Nope. Just makes it interesting," Grant said. "But Margot was right—Preacher won't make it to Paris."

Chapter 2

MONDAY, APRIL 27th
2:32 PM CEST

UKRAINIAN EMBASSY, PARIS, FRANCE

Vitali Moshenski was an imposing figure—mid-70s, silver-haired, his amber-flecked hazel eyes sharp with quiet calculation. Sophistication draped over him as neatly as his tailored suits. He moved with the poise of a man who commanded power, his angular features set in permanent scrutiny. Hidden beneath the polished veneer was a man who clawed his way up from humble beginnings to the rarefied world of the ultra-wealthy.

The Ukrainian Embassy in Paris was one of Vitali's sanctuaries, a front for diplomacy and clandestine operations alike. Officially, his authority ranked just below the Ambassador's. Unofficially, many suspected the roles were reversed.

The grand building, its elegant façade adorned with wrought-iron balconies and tall, arched windows, exuded the timeless charm of Parisian architecture. The embassy's location in this historic edifice added an air of prestige and gravitas. Vitali's office did the same. It was stately and well-appointed, a reflection of his position.

Sunlight streamed through a large window, its curtains drawn back to reveal the tranquil Parisian street below. The soft afternoon light spilled across the room, catching the gleam of polished wood and gilded frames. Shadows stretched long and delicate over the artifacts and decorations lining the walls—subtle testaments to wealth, power, and a carefully curated image.

A heavy oak desk dominated the center of the room, its surface covered with neatly arranged stacks of papers, but Vitali's attention focused solely on the encrypted correspondence displayed on his computer screen. His brow furrowed as he scanned the contents, his mind working to extract the critical information obscured within the diplomatic language.

The sharp, insistent chime of an incoming text message on Vitali's KATIM phone shattered the tranquil atmosphere of the office. The phone's sleek, matte-black exterior hinted at the device's advanced capabilities, with military-grade encryption designed for the utmost secrecy and discretion. It was the kind of phone used by those who navigated the murky waters of power and influence.

As a man accustomed to handling sensitive information, Vitali reached for the phone, his movements deliberate and measured. The phone's screen lit up, casting a faint glow on his stern features. The message was marked with the highest level of priority encryption, but the sender was blank.

That's not possible, he thought. Vitali's heartbeat quickened, his instincts warning that this was no ordinary communication. With a swift tap of his finger, he opened the message — a video file.

Vitali braced himself for what was to come, and the video sprang to life, the image crystal clear but silent.

Aerial drone footage filled the screen. The camera locked onto a black, four-door SUV moving along a gravel road in a heavily wooded area. Vitali's breath caught in his throat. He recognized the vehicle and knew the three occupants. The overlay of a targeting system appeared on the screen, the digital crosshairs centering on the vehicle's roof, tracking its every movement with cold, mechanical precision.

The SUV drove deeper into the woods. The camera followed, the drone maintaining its relentless pursuit until the vehicle stopped. Adrenaline surged, and Vitali's heartbeat pounded in his ears. He knew what would happen next.

The projectile struck the SUV's roof dead center, penetrating the metal with sickening ease. In the next instant, a brilliant white flash filled the screen as the explosive detonated. The blast wave caught the hovering drone, and the camera shook.

Vitali watched, frozen, as the SUV's windows blew out, white-hot flames devouring everything inside. Molten metal dripped onto the gravel, the vehicle collapsing into itself—a funeral pyre of liquefied steel and bone.

No one could have survived, he thought, and the video ended. Vitali imagined the SUV reduced to a smoldering wreck in a matter of minutes. *That was the idea,* he thought. *Obliterate any hope of identifying the occupants.*

Shock and disbelief warred on Vitali's face as he struggled to process what he had just witnessed. The implications of the video were staggering, the ruthless efficiency of the attack suggesting a level of planning and resources that few possessed. His mind raced with questions, his analytical nature already working to dissect the footage, extract every clue, and plan his next move.

Two men dead. A prisoner gone. Kate's prisoner. This wasn't just an execution—it was a message. A warning. But for whom? Kate? Him? The video was anonymous. The sender unknown. Enemy or ally?

Vitali knew answers wouldn't come easy. Whoever sent the video hacked an encrypted communications channel on tamper-proof hardware and sent an anonymous message. *Who could accomplish such a thing,* he wondered. *There can't be more than a handful of hackers on the planet capable of such a feat.*

Nomad. The brilliant hacker in the motorized wheelchair. His location, his latest digital crusade—secrets Vitali would guard to the grave. *But Kate could reach him. And when Nomad learned she was in danger, he wouldn't hesitate.*

Reaching for a personal cell phone, Vitali dialed a number he knew by heart. When the call connected, he kept his voice steady. No identification was necessary or desired.

"We need to meet. Now. Privately," Vitali said and waited.

The line crackled with a faint pause. "Yes, the park."

His jaw tightened. "Fifteen minutes."

He ended the call with a sharp tap, slid the phone back into his pocket, his mind already shifting to the impending meeting—what he would say and what he wouldn't.

***

2:57 PM CEST

Vitali strolled into Square René-Viviani, the tranquil ambiance of the park contrasting with the urgency of his mission. He walked along the winding paths. The sound of children playing on the swings and the occasional bark of a dog provided a comforting, natural cover. The park, with its tall trees and dense foliage, offered many secluded spots perfect for a private conversation.

He settled on a bench partially hidden by a cluster of shrubs, the laughter of children and a distant melody from a street musician masking any sound that might carry beyond their immediate vicinity. Here, in this quiet corner of Paris, with fewer security cameras than the bustling boulevards and grander parks, Vitali felt a rare sense of security. It was the perfect place for an undisturbed meeting, away from prying eyes and electronic surveillance.

He waited, glanced around, and cataloged the park's occupants. *All clear,* he thought. *As usual.* In-person meetings were rare and discouraged, but circumstances rendered this one unavoidable.

Vitali watched from his secluded bench as the sleek, black Mercedes-Benz S-Class glided to a stop at the park's entrance. The car's tinted windows shielded its occupant from prying eyes, yet beneath the opulence and secrecy, the purr of a high-performance engine hinted at the vehicle's ability to escape and evade.

The driver, impeccably dressed, stepped out and swiftly moved to open the rear door. To the casual observer, he was just a chauffeur. Vitali knew better.

Left-handed, Vitali thought, confirming the carefully concealed handgun tucked inside his waistband. *Backup on his right ankle. God only knows what else he's carrying.*

Klaus Mueller emerged. The founder and Executive Chairman of the Global Economic Council moved with deliberate and dignified steps, betraying none of his 85 years. The cool, air-conditioned interior of the S-Class had shielded him from the Parisian afternoon heat, and as he straightened his jacket. Klaus surveyed the surroundings with a keen eye and signaled for the driver to remain.

Vitali noticed Mueller adjusting the cufflinks on his bespoke Cifonelli suit and suspected he drew Mueller away from important business. The spring heat and the casual atmosphere of the park contrasted sharply with the formal attire, making both men appear slightly out of place, but no one seemed to notice or care.

Vitali leaned forward, elbows on his knees. "Thank you for coming."

Klaus smiled thinly. "Your tone suggested I had no choice."

"This *is* a matter of some urgency," Vitali said. "And not something that can wait for the next meeting."

Klaus gestured with a casual wave of his hand. "Go on."

"As you know, Katherine Preacher will soon return to Paris."

"I understand that's her intention," Mueller said.

"It is imperative that she return," Vitali said. "She is coming at my invitation."

"As you informed us at the Moore briefing," Mueller noted. "I'm still not clear why you've involved her."

"With or without me, she's coming."

Klaus tilted his head, his tone taking on a sharp edge. "Do you still believe you were the target? How many times must I apologize? The Coalition was not involved—your attendance at the cafe was an unfortunate coincidence."

Vitali shook his head, his voice low and deliberate. "No, it is not that."

"Then what, my friend?" Mueller asked and smiled. "What is so urgent?"

"Preacher has her husband's NanoVault."

"Impossible," Mueller insisted. "I was assured his vault was destroyed."

"All I can tell you is that she is in possession of her husband's files."

"What files?"

"Exactly," Vitali said. "What files, indeed? More to the point, what do they contain? For the last two years, Jake Church traveled in many, perhaps most, of the areas where you have been pulling political and financial levers. And in some cases, leaving a trail of bodies and missing persons."

"You think us compromised?"

"It is a possibility," Vitali said. "One we cannot afford to ignore. Not when we are so close."

"And what do you propose?"

"Do nothing. Let her come. Investigate. And let us see where it leads—and to whom. She will come to me with whatever she finds."

Klaus studied Vitali for a long moment, the weight of his scrutiny palpable. "You trust her?"

Vitali met his gaze without flinching. "The point is, she trusts me."

"Very well," Mueller said. "Is there nothing else?"

"Is that not enough?"

"Quite."

The two men stood, shook hands, and walked in opposite directions. Vitali wanted to look back. He was curious if Mueller might reach for a phone, but he also knew the old German was too shrewd to take any action that might reveal his intentions.

Did Mueller know about the video? Perhaps. The answer would come in time. For now, Kate was safe. For now.

Chapter 3

KATE'S WEEKEND BLURRED INTO exhaustion. She spent it wrapped in soft socks, leggings, and one of Jake's old t-shirts—olive green, threadbare, COFFEE, OR DIE. She'd nearly tossed it a dozen times. Now, it was priceless.

A collection of frozen food, most of it Jake's and some of it long out of date, eased what little appetite she had. She didn't dare go shopping. The last thing Kate wanted was to do anything normal, like going places she and Jake would go or seeing any of the people they saw every week. She just wanted to be left alone and was grateful the neighbors seemed to understand.

Kate gathered the notes and flowers from the porch and sat on the couch with a few of the cards in her lap. Dorothy's note lay on top, her elegant handwriting a relic of another time. *Nobody writes anymore. And Jake never could.*

Dorothy was the first to welcome Kate and Jake to the neighborhood with an unforgettable fresh-baked apple pie. When Dorothy's husband passed and with her sons living hours away, Jake would pop over to see if there was anything she needed. Jake's quiet kindness was one of the things she loved most. *There was always something to fix. And somehow, he always came back with pie.*

Kate pulled Dorothy's card from the envelope and read, *My Dearest Kate*. Her hands trembled. The words seemed to swim on the page, blurring together as tears welled up. *I can't do this,* she thought. *Not yet. Maybe when I get back. But not now.*

She slipped Dorothy's card back into the envelope, collected the notes, and set them on Jake's chair. The old leather recliner, the one piece of furniture Jake brought into the marriage, was now something of a shrine. Jake's flag surrounded by the love and admiration captured in the many dozens of cards and letters. Kate smiled, and the tears gave way to pride. *You were loved by many,* she thought. *But none more than me.*

Her collection of classic black and white movies kept her company all weekend and helped occupy her mind. Jake didn't understand her fondness for these films and refused to watch them at first. The breakthrough moment was Christmas Eve, their first in the new house. She convinced him to watch *The Bishop's Wife* by offering to watch *Die Hard.* Both became annual favorites. But it was the handsome and charming Cary Grant and gorgeous Loretta Young that cracked open the door to exploring more of these classics.

The knockout punch came one quiet evening. After pretending to object, Jake agreed to watch one of Kate's top-ten. The 1943 pairing of Humphrey Bogart and Ingrid Bergman. Jake was drawn to *Casablanca* in a way that she couldn't explain, and he never tried. But this one always found its way back home. The year never passed without a big bowl of popcorn, Jake and Kate, and Boo curled up on the couch.

The empty bowl of popcorn slipped off the edge of the couch and wobbled on the floor. Kate stirred from a deep sleep and stretched out, eyes closed, senses stirring. From the TV, a deep, raspy voice caught Kate's attention. She sat up and watched.

Onscreen, Casablanca's airport lay shrouded in fog. Propellers hummed, a plane waiting. Urgency. Finality. Words left unsaid.

"Where I'm going, you can't follow. What I've got to do, you can't be any part of."

I get it, but you can't protect me, she thought. *Not anymore. This is my war now. Time to pack.*

***

8:15 AM EDT
RICHMOND PINNACLE BUILDING, RICHMOND, VA

Kate Preacher guided Jake's Jeep into the parking lot of the Richmond Pinnacle building. She backed into a visitor's spot directly opposite the main doors. *Always back in*, she thought. It was one of Jake's many protocols, some more annoying than others, but this one might have saved her life.

Nine days ago, from this very spot, Kate shoved the Jeep into reverse and floored it. The rear end jumped over the parking lot berm and plowed backward through the flowers and bushes that lined the parking lot. She skidded to a stop on the sidewalk and escaped. Now, in the rear-view mirror, she saw the shrubs and flowers she obliterated had been replanted, erasing any sign of the chaos that unfolded that night.

Kate took a deep breath, bracing herself for the task ahead, and did a quick mirror check. Her auburn hair pulled back into a practical ponytail, a few wispy strands framing her face. She dressed for a long day of flying and chose her outfit with care, selecting pieces that were both practical and stylish. With Paris as her final destination, she was determined to look more like a returning Parisian than an American tourist.

Dark J Brand skinny jeans, a cream silk Chloé blouse, and a charcoal McQueen blazer—sharp, understated. A Hermès scarf draped at her throat, more than just fashion, a trick to soften her scars. The Prada combat boots? Style with function. If she needed to run, she could.

She reached for the messenger bag on the passenger seat. The weathered leather strap had softened with age. She sometimes wondered if the bag was a kind of security blanket but didn't care. Nestled inside, among a pair of tablets and miscellaneous digital forensic tools, were the two items that prompted her meeting with Leslie. Kate slipped the strap over her head, keeping the bag in close, and climbed out of the Jeep.

***

Grant Collins sat in the back of the mock utility van across from the Richmond Pinnacle building. Orange cones diverted pedestrians. Two workers in high-vis vests played their part. Inside, the tech hacked into the traffic control system while Grant monitored the surveillance feeds.

Katherine Preacher's Rubicon swept into the parking lot and backed into a visitor's spot. "Nice rig," Grant said, admiring the jeep's thirty-five-inch tires, and expedition gear. "And right on schedule," he announced, checking his watch. "Do we have control?"

"Any minute now…," the tech began. "I'm in. Let me have your phone."

The tech installed his custom traffic-control app on Grant's phone and handed it back.

"How does it work?"

"Look here," the tech said and pointed at the phone's screen. "This is the status of the North-South light, and that's the East-West. Just select the one you want to change, and then tap Green, Yellow, or Red. It's that easy."

"I see that," Grant said. "What I meant was, how is this possible?"

"Oh, that. I hacked into the system the city uses for traffic flow management and emergency vehicle override. To the system, your phone looks like a firetruck."

"And you're sure it works?" Grant asked. "Everything is riding on this working exactly as you said it would."

"Try it," the tech said. "Go see for yourself."

***

KATE WALKED TOWARD THE Pinnacle Building's towering glass doors, her steps measured and purposeful. A grim smile tugged at her lips when she spotted the freshly patched asphalt and scorched curb, a reminder of the SUV she torched. *Thermite grenades make one hell of a mess,* she thought. *And leave it to Jake to keep a few toys in the Jeep's truck vault armory.*

The building's glass doors became a gauntlet Kate hadn't expected, and she froze on the sidewalk while others passed by. The glass spanning from floor to ceiling created an expansive, transparent barrier between the building's interior and the outside world. It was pristine, perfect, like nothing happened. But Kate heard bursts of automatic gunfire. She saw shattered glass and the two men who strode into the lobby. And Pete, the night security guard and friend, lying in a pool of blood, his eyes pleading for mercy.

Kate's stomach clenched with guilt. *If I hadn't come to the office,* she thought. *Pete would still be alive. Linda would still be pestering him to lose weight. Instead, she's a widow.* Kate owed her a visit, an explanation, anything to ease her suffering. But the words stuck like glass shards in her throat. *How can I explain the men that killed her husband were here to kill me?*

A young man, with his eyes locked on his cell phone, didn't see Kate standing there and bumped into her. He was sorry, but Kate was grateful. She locked away the dark thoughts for the moment and passed through the doors. As expected, the cool blast of the AC wrapped around her, and she was thankful for the blazer.

She passed by the turn-style entry kiosks and approached the security desk. *My badge is probably still active,* she thought. *But let's not find out. Coming back is complicated enough already.*

The cavernous lobby absorbed the rhythmic tapping of heels and muffled conversations. The soft ding of the elevators punctuated cheerful greetings and hurried phone calls as the building's occupants and guests stepped in, and the elevators disappeared.

The security desk was staffed by someone Kate didn't recognize. The fifty-something guard was busy scrolling through his phone.

"Excuse me," Kate said, but the guard didn't flinch. Infusing her voice with a politeness she didn't feel. "I'm here to see Leslie Dodd."

The guard glanced up, "Name?"

"Katherine Preacher."

The guard's head snapped up, his eyes widening as he took in the woman before him. "Mrs. Preacher! Yes, of course, I'm so sorry. Ms. Dodd is expecting you."

He scrambled out from behind the desk, practically falling over himself to escort her through the turnstiles. With a swipe of his keycard, the way was clear, and Kate followed him to the elevators. When the doors opened, another wave of his keycard lit the button for the 18th floor, and Kate stepped inside.

As the elevator doors closed, the guard's expression softened. "We're all very sorry for your loss, Mrs. Preacher."

Kate managed a tight smile and nod as the doors shut. As soon as she was alone, she let out a shaky breath, leaning against the wall for support.

Her chest tightened, an unfamiliar panic rising in her throat. She gripped the handrail, knuckles turning white. The walls seemed to close in around her. The air thick and heavy. Kate forced herself to take a deep breath, counting silently in her head as she practiced her combat breathing—the pattern Jake said he and the team used to steady nerves and focus on the mission. *That's it, she heard Jake coaching. You got this.* The breathing helped, but thinking about Jake and recalling his voice was all she needed.

***

GRANT CHECKED THE VAN'S surveillance cameras. The surrounding area was clear, so he cracked the rear door and slipped out. He crossed the road and took up his street corner position. From that location, he could monitor the Pinnacle parking lot and Kate's Jeep. He assessed the rest of the setup. The chartered tour bus was strategically placed to block the view of cross traffic. Down the block, a fully loaded, thirty-ton cement mixer waited to make its run. Grant could see the truck's cement drum rotating and hear the diesel motor idling.

"Let's give this a try," he thought and looked for a target. The low, throaty rumble of a high-performance engine caught his attention. The owner of a sleek, black Porsche 911 Carrera S revving the twin-turbo engine again and again. *Jeez. Give it a rest,* Grant thought. *You wanted my attention. You got it.*

The Porsche headed for the parking lot exit. Grant's thumb hovered over the Red button. The minute the 911 hit the street, the driver punched it, racing toward the green light.

Grant tapped the button. The light flashed red. The Porsche screeched to a halt. The driver pounded the steering wheel, stared up at the light, and mouthed a single four-letter word.

"That'll work," Grant mumbled. He set the traffic light back to normal. "Now we wait."

***

THE ELEVATOR DINGED. KATE straightened up, squared her shoulders, and waited for the doors to slide open. She stepped out into the lobby of Frank, Burman and Dodd, her boots sinking into the plush carpet. And waiting for her, with a gentle, welcoming smile, was Leslie Dodd.

Leslie looked as polished and put-together as ever, her blonde hair swept back into a sleek chignon, her suit crisp and tailored. But there was a softness in her eyes, a warmth that Kate had only seen twice before. Kate understood. Leslie's persona was a carefully constructed necessity. She carved out a position of power and respect in a world dominated by men, earning a partnership in a major international law firm. It was Leslie who taught Kate that the men who underestimate you will regret that mistake.

"Kate," Leslie said, stepping forward and capturing Kate's left arm. "Let's go straight to my office."

The two women walked down the mahogany-paneled hallway toward the executive wing.

"Thanks for seeing me on such short notice," Kate said.

Leslie waved off her concern. "For you, always." She gestured towards her office. "Come on in. I had them set up coffee and pastries. Just in case."

When they were both inside, and the door closed behind them, Leslie wrapped her arms around Kate.

Kate returned the hug, both of them blinking back the tears that threatened to fall. Neither said a word and when they separated, Leslie directed Kate to the couch. The adjacent coffee table had two steaming mugs of coffee and an assortment of pastries.

"I'm glad you're here," Leslie said. "How are you holding up?"

Kate wrapped her hands around the warm mug, struggling to find the words. "Honestly? It's the hardest thing I've ever done," she admitted. "Some days, it feels like I'm sleepwalking through a nightmare. I got home early Friday evening and have no idea what happened to the weekend. But that's not why I'm here."

"Heading back to Paris?" Leslie asked.

"I am," Kate said. "Officially, what happened was a senseless act of terrorism."

"But you believe it was something else."

"I know it was," Kate said. "Jake wasn't killed by terrorists, and I can prove it, but that raises questions no one wants to ask."

"No one but Kate Preacher," Leslie said. "How can I help?"

"My flight leaves at noon, but before I leave the country, there are a couple of personal and legal matters that need attention. And there's no one on the planet I trust or respect more than you. I'd like to retain you as my personal attorney."

Leslie raised an eyebrow. "I'm flattered. But the firm has—"

"I don't want to hire the firm." Kate's tone was sharp, surprising even herself. "I want *you*. And I've recently come into a substantial sum of money, so I can afford the best."

Kate removed a Golden Quantum NanoVault from the messenger bag.

"I know that vault," Leslie said. "That's Devin Moore's. That thing never left his neck, and trust me, I mean never."

"You and Devin?" Kate asked.

"Yes, Devin and I," Leslie remarked with a smirk. "Purely recreational."

"You naughty girl," Kate said, returning Leslie's smirk. "I thought clients were off the menu."

"Well, he wasn't *my* client," she said and laughed. "We crossed paths at some fundraiser. Boring as hell, but the champagne was excellent. We'll save that conversation for another day. What I want to know, is how did you get Devin's vault?"

"That too, is a conversation for another day," Kate began. "One that needs attorney-client privilege, but the short version is that he gave it to me. And that includes everything that's on it."

"The Bitcoin bounty?"

"Yes, and more."

"Then why are you flying commercial? Charter a jet. Better yet, buy one," Leslie said, and they both laughed.

"It feels good to laugh," Kate said. "Thanks."

"Anytime. Now that you're my client. What's on the agenda?"

"Trident Security and the team are now my responsibility," Kate said. "These are friends. Family. And given the significant change in my financial situation, I need to be sure that all of them are secure, no matter what happens. I need a complete set of estate planning documents. The full meal deal."

Leslie stepped over to her desk and grabbed a pad of paper. On the way back to the couch, she started on the list.

"OK. Living Will, POA, Advance Healthcare Directives..."

"Exactly," Kate said, and she handed Leslie a folder. "I've collected everything you'll need to prepare the paperwork, but I need a favor."

"Just name it."

"No, I want you to think about it," Kate said. "And you don't have to answer right away."

"Please, just get to the point, or you'll never make your flight."

"I'd like you to be my representative in these documents. Executor, Power of Attorney, Medical Directives. Everything. You're the one person I know I can trust with my life and my wishes."

"I'd be honored," Leslie said without a moment's hesitation, but with glassy eyes and a tremor in her voice, she continued. "But Kate, I have to confess. You're scaring me. What aren't you telling me?"

Kate reached out and took Leslie's hand, "I'm sorry. I didn't mean to scare you.

If I could say more, I would. And there's one more thing." Kate retrieved the other item from her messenger bag, cloaked in a dark blue fabric. "I'd like you to keep this in your office safe."

Leslie raised an eyebrow. "Looks mysterious. What is it?"

Kate unwound the layers of fabric. Each fold peeling back more than cloth—it unraveled memories she had buried deep. The morning sunlight struck the blade, sending flashes of light dancing across the room.

"Is that the..." Leslie's words trailed off, sensing the weight of the moment.

"Yes," Kate said, her voice flat, her gaze locked on the weapon.

Both women were drawn to the hypnotic beauty of the blade's wavy patterns, reminiscent of flowing water or the delicate, marbled grains of ancient wood. The Damascus steel bore a slightly darkened hue, a testament to the carbon-rich alloy. The unique patterns, forged from layers of folded steel, made the blade both distinctive and highly valued—a historical treasure in any other context.

In Suliaman's hands, it had been an instrument of terror—one he proudly proclaimed *tasted the blood of enemies and infidels for centuries.*

Kate's hand pressed against her chest, brushing the raised scar tissue beneath her fingers. Her heart raced. The memories she fought to suppress surged forward. The dim light of the interrogation room reflecting off the blade, the calloused hand pressing the knife to her chest, the razor-sharp edge piercing her flesh. She closed her eyes hard, forcing herself back into the present.

Leslie placed a hand on Kate's arm. She opened her eyes, exhaled, and watched as Leslie wrapped the knife and swept it away.

"It'll be safe here," she said softly, slipping the bundle into her wall safe. "And I'll have the papers drawn for your estate. Where are you staying?"

"Hotel de Portales."

"Excellent," Leslie said, her smile and tone suggesting she was happy to change the subject. "I've been there. It's lovely and very exclusive. I'll arrange for our French partner to deliver the estate plan for your review and signature. Now, you better get going. You've got a long day ahead of you."

***

KATE'S EXIT FROM THE building triggered an alert on Grant's phone, and he focused his attention on her Jeep. Kate tossed a bag onto the passenger seat and climbed in. Moments later, she headed for the exit and merged into the mid-morning traffic.

It's show time, Grant thought, and he was ready. Thumb poised over the Red-Light button, his breathing slow, controlled, like a sniper waiting, ready to press the trigger.

The cement mixer was ready too, the diesel engine revving. With full traffic management control, the tech ensured the block was clear, and the cement truck had a straight shot at the intersection. The truck pulled away from the curb.

Accidents have more moving parts and rely on patterns of behavior. Grant counted on Kate being sensible, even cautious, and not one to run a red light. His timing was perfect. Kate stopped just a few feet from his location and waited for the light to change.

The engineering of the trap was all Grant's. Precision sniper training is more math than most realize, and hitting a moving target is an essential skill. In this scenario, Grant calculated where the truck needed to be when he sent Kate into the intersection. Unlike a bullet, the driver could change course if Kate wasn't directly in front of him. There was no chance she could escape being hit. *Katherine Preacher's not flying to Paris today*, Grant thought. *Maybe never.*

The MACK truck accelerated, its gears shifting, speed building, and obscured from Kate's view. Grant monitored the truck's progress. *Wait for it,* he thought. *Forty miles per hour. When the nose reaches the streetlamp. Now!*

Grant pressed the button. The light flicked green. Kate barely hesitated—one glance, then forward.

His cell phone shrieked—a sound reserved for one message.

ALBATROSS

"What the...," he began, but there wasn't time to think or speak. Kate's jeep passed the first line on the crosswalk and was crossing the second when Grant sprinted off the curb. The Jeep's tires screeched and skidded on the asphalt.

Grant's hand slammed onto the hood—a crack like a deer strike. He vaulted, rolling onto the windshield, momentum pinning him there. The Jeep screeched to a stop. He slid off, landing hard on his back.

Kate jumped out of the Jeep, her expression a mix of shock and concern. "Are you OK?" she asked.

Grant got up, wincing slightly but pushing through the pain. He heard the cement mixer roar through the intersection just feet from where he was standing.

"Did you see that?" Kate said. "That guy almost hit you. And he would have hit me."

Grant feigned ignorance, shaking his head. "No. Sorry, I missed it," Grant lied. "Still a bit rattled, I guess. Are you OK?"

"Me?" Kate asked. "Yeah, I guess so. Better than I deserve. If I hadn't hit you, we might not be having this conversation. I guess that makes you my guardian angel, but I think we should call an ambulance and get you to the hospital. Just to be safe."

Grant brushed off his clothes and offered Kate a reassuring smile. "I've had worse on the rugby pitch," he said with a slight chuckle. "I'm such an idiot. This was entirely my fault." Grant's hand stroked the back of his head and landed on a fresh bump. "Ouch."

"Seriously, that could be a concussion."

"No, I'm fine. Really," Grant insisted.

"At least tell me your name," Kate said. "And let me pay to have your jacket cleaned."

Grant hesitated for a moment. He didn't want this to get personal, but his back story was rock solid. "Grant. Grant Collins," he replied, pulling a business card from his jacket pocket.

Kate glanced at the card, "You're a wildlife photographer."

"I am," Grant confirmed. "I just wasn't expecting an elephant charge on the streets of Richmond."

They both laughed, but honking horns and impatient drivers shut that down.

"You should go," Grant said. "We're blocking traffic."

"Well, as long as you're OK?"

"I am," Grant said. "Truly."

Kate opened the driver's door and climbed up on the Jeep's rock rails. "I know that accent," she said. "What part of England are you from?"

"Manchester."

"Well, Manchester," Kate said. "I'm Katherine. Thanks for saving my life."

He took a deep breath, relief flooding through him. *What the hell just happened?* He limped away, vanishing into the crowd as the Jeep sped off. *Why abort? He could have ended this. Right here. Right now.*

Grant's phone buzzed again. The message was another single word.

PARIS

This one needed no explanation.
Whatever happens next happens in Paris.

Chapter 4

ATLANTA AIRPORT, ATLANTA, GA

Kate's flight to Atlanta was uneventful. The four-hour layover wasn't a hassle—it was strategy. An experienced traveler knew how to work the system. The overnight flight, the DeltaOne lay-flat bed, all of it designed to land in Paris at 8:30 a.m. with some sleep behind her.

The Delta lounge was spacious, quiet, and comfortable. Limited Pinot Noir options aside, it had one advantage—proximity to the least-crowded Starbucks and Ecco, the best restaurant in the terminal. No time for a real dinner, but enough for Ecco's charcuterie board and a glass of wine before heading to the gate.

Kate searched the lounge for a spot to settle in. She found a comfortable chair in an area that, for the moment, was free of exhausted children or loud, obnoxious businessmen on cell phones. She set her messenger bag on the adjoining chair as a personal space buffer and removed the classified folder.

Margot Ryder's invitation to Jake's Arlington burial came with strings. Kate knew that Margot's guilt over what happened in Syria was a powerful lever, and the CIA's AAR (After Action Report) on the Syrian mission was a down payment on Margot's debt.

Seeing Margot again was hard—but necessary. Kate closed her eyes, the classified folder heavy in her lap, and was back in Arlington.

"Did you bring it?"

"I did," Margot said. "But I have to admit I'm torn."

"I still have clearance."

"It's not that."

"Then what?"

"You put Syria behind you years ago," Margot said. "Why open old wounds?"

"They're already open," Kate said. "Now I need closure. I haven't played chess since before Syria, but I had no choice recently, and there was a fleeting image from my captivity. Something I can't quite recall."

"And you think photos of being beaten and tortured will help?"

"I know how it sounds," Kate said, "But I realized something this week."

"What's that?"

"I'm stronger now than I have ever been."

Margot was right about one thing. I don't need the hospital photos. The forensic images were carved into her memory—deep as the scars they documented. Her bruised and swollen face and split lips, the raw, raised welts that crisscrossed her back, legs, and feet. And that shirt—stiff with dried blood and agony—had to be peeled away from the knife-point etching carved into her chest.

She could still see the base nurse, the first woman to witness her injuries. The nurse's wide eyes filled with horror she couldn't mask, and the gasp—sharper and louder than the pounding in Kate's ears. The doctor hustled her out of the exam room, but it was too late. *I can still see her,* Kate thought. *I'll never forget that face, that look.*

The rigid scars tracing her chest, breasts and abdomen were daily whispers of what she endured—and what she survived. Long after the physical pain faded, the nurse's reaction lingered. Kate expected everyone to respond the same way, and many did. But not Jake. *You've got your scars, I've got mine,* he'd say. *Some you can see, some you can't. Don't give them power—don't let them define who you are.*

With the folder open less than an inch, she flashed through the stack of eight-by-ten images, looking for one she knew, at least she hoped, would be there. Kate found the photo she wanted, pulled it from the file, and slipped the file back in her bag.

The photo on her lap was a chessboard, and the game was in progress. *It is white's move.* That's what Zhukov said. *White's move.* The photo, the chessboard, and Zhukov's voice echoing in her head put her right back in Syria—in captivity.

The beatings had stopped. Kate didn't understand why, but she was glad for the reprieve, whatever the reason. In the suffocating darkness of the cell, she'd lost all sense of time. Days, weeks—she couldn't tell. The questions, the beatings, even the meager offerings of food and water came sporadically, at random, or not at all. She understood the tactic. *Everyone breaks. Eventually.*

Major Mikhail Zhukov was once a hero of Russia's Spetsnaz—until Beslan. His team was slaughtered. His wife and daughter were among the hundreds killed. His world erased.

It was Putin's first term, and for three agonizing days, with over 1,100 hostages trapped inside that school, the world held its breath. When the siege finally ended, the toll was unimaginable: 334 dead, including 186 children. The violent, chaotic assault was a disaster. Putin needed a scapegoat. Who better than an officer lying in a coma?

Branded *The Butcher of Beslan* by Russian media, Zhukov's conviction was a foregone conclusion. His death in prison had seemed inevitable—until he crossed paths with Vitali Moshenski. A Ukrainian political prisoner, Moshenski helped Zhukov survive. When Zhukov regained his strength, he returned the favor. Bonded by shared loss, the two men became brothers in all but blood. Two years later, when Moshenski bought his freedom, he negotiated for Zhukov's as well.

From that day forward, Moshenski consolidated his power with Zhukov at his side. In the shadows, Zhukov thrived—mercenary, loyal enforcer, self-proclaimed merchant of death.

Kate winced, brushing her hand across her ribs. The blow echoed through her memory—the massive punch that cracked her ribs and left her gasping for air. *He wanted to know how I found him*, she thought. *But I never told him. I couldn't.*

Zhukov never pressed again. Something in him shifted after that. Something Kate hadn't understood until Vitali Moshenski gave her the missing piece.

Zhukov realized I was a Beslan orphan.

But how? The question haunted her as she let the memory return, dragging her back to the dark, airless room. The tubular steel chair. Wrists bound to the chair's cold, unyielding arms, ankles strapped tight to its legs.

She could see Zhukov's face towering over her, his black, penetrating eyes boring into hers, searching for weakness. Then the punch. The explosion of searing pain that knocked the breath from her lungs. His face was inches away, his vice-like hands clamped around her bare forearms, pinning her in place.

For an instant, his eyes changed. Recognition. Hesitation. Then, just as fast, he stepped back and left.

From that moment forward, nothing else mattered. There were no more questions. He ordered the Syrians to clean my wounds, find new clothes, and feed me. And gave strict instructions that no one was to lay a hand on me.

The next day, at least I think it was a day, I was taken back to the interrogation room. This time, I wasn't bound to the chair, and there were no guards, just Zhukov and I and a chessboard. But the game was already in progress, and black was in trouble.

"It is white's move," he said.

I swung a leg up and sent the board flying. He laughed and set it up again, only out of reach this time. When I refused to play he took the board away, but returned the next day and the next. He never spoke except to say, "It is white's move."

Kate studied the chessboard photo. *White's move. Looks like an easy win. So why did it feel like a trap?*

"Excuse me," someone said, jarring Kate's attention. She looked up at a well-dressed gentleman in his thirties, horn-rim glasses, graying at the temples. *Accountant*, she thought.

He held up a charging cable, a sheepish smile on his face. "Would you mind? Mine doesn't seem to work."

Kate forced a polite smile. "Of course. No problem."

"Thank you so much," he said, plugging in his phone charger. "I'm Elliot, by the way. Elliot Cunningham."

"Kate," she replied, shaking his outstretched hand. *Oh great,* she thought. *A talker.*

Elliot nodded at the photo. "You play?"

"Not since college," Kate said, lying.

He smiled. "Me either. Princeton."

"MIT."

Elliot chuckled. "Ouch."

Kate arched a brow, mock offense lacing her voice. "Excuse me?"

"Oh, sorry," he said, holding up his hands apologetically. "Just recalling how badly we lost to MIT my senior year." Elliot leaned closer, gesturing to the photo. "That's interesting. May I?"

Kate hesitated, then handed it over. "Does this look familiar?"

He studied the image, and after a moment, he nodded. "I'm not positive, but I have an idea. If I'm right, it's white's move—but black set a trap."

"You're right. It is white's move," Kate said, her tone cautious. "But I don't see a trap—looks like game over in five moves."

"That's the Lasker Trap," Elliot said. "Rare. Aggressive. Hard to spot, harder to pull off."

Kate raised an eyebrow. "As in Emanuel Lasker?"

"Exactly. It's a Queen's Gambit response. Bold. Risky. But if Black pulls it off..."

"Black is definitely in serious trouble," Kate said. "I can't imagine someone intentionally playing into this position."

"And that's the trap. If we can find a board, I'll show you."

"I can bring one up on my tablet," Kate offered.

Elliot glanced at his watch and frowned. "Oh, sorry, I didn't see the time. My flight will board soon, and I should get to the gate." He stood up, gathered his belongings, and checked the charge on his phone. "That will have to do. Thanks for the charge, and good luck with the game."

Kate smiled, watching as he disappeared into the terminal crowd. The Lasker Trap. A rare move, hard to spot—almost impossible to escape once set. *Why would Zhukov think I'd recognize it?*

She slipped the photo into her bag, but the thought wouldn't let go. *Was this a message? A warning? Or was I already in play?*

A glance at her watch. *Wine o'clock. Time to eat. Time to think.*

Her flight would board in a few hours.

Returning to Paris was her decision. *White's move.*

Was it the right one?

Or was she stepping into a trap?

Chapter 5

CHARLES DE GAULLE AIRPORT, PARIS, FRANCE

KATE STIRRED AS THE first-class cabin came to life. Attendants whisked away breakfast trays. Groggy passengers stretched, rolling up bedding, returning seats to upright positions. Kate didn't mind skipping breakfast—she wasn't hungry—but a double espresso would do nicely if there was still time. She adjusted her seat, pulled out the service table, and waited. A flight attendant arrived moments later with a minuscule espresso cup. *That's a double*, she thought. *Oh well. I'll grab another later. Need to stay awake today.*

She sipped the espresso, chasing a dream that dissolved on waking. *I was just a girl. Five, maybe six.* Only the sensation remained—of being young. Between the loss of her father and a year later, both her mother and brother, she'd locked away most of her childhood. For this Russian orphan, a new life in America, this life, began when she was adopted.

Kate hoped the chess photo would yield something. Learning the picture depicted a classic trap from another era was interesting, but without context, it was still meaningless. It didn't answer the key question. *Why did Zhukov want me to see it, to play it,* she wondered. She loved the notion of the subconscious mind operating like a computer's "background process." She would formulate a question, set her mind to the task, and wait for the answer. Kate expected the answer would come, but not this morning.

As a first-class traveler, she was among the first to head for immigration, but with several other flights arriving simultaneously, it looked like she was in for a long wait. *That's easily an hour,* she thought. *Maybe two.*

Vitali's text message was a surprise.

> **Proceed to the Flight Crew immigration line. Your VIP escort will meet you there.**

Brief. To the point. Proper. *We're not texting buddies,* Kate thought. But something felt off. *He needs to tell me something. Ah, Marcus. They would have informed Vitali immediately after identifying the embassy vehicle.* But she couldn't shake the feeling there was more.

Kate's instincts unnerved Jake—until experience proved them right. She didn't question how she knew things, only that she did. The analyst in her called it subconscious data processing. The operator in her trusted it. So did Jake. So did the team.

Just beyond the much shorter crew immigration line, Kate spotted a short, balding man in a dark gray suit. His insistent waving got her attention, and when their eyes met, his face lit up. Kate concluded this was her VIP escort. He approached one of the immigration officers, pointed at Kate, and smiled again. The officer passed through the checkpoint, brushing past an Air France flight crew, and took Kate's elbow.

"Mrs. Preacher," he said in a formal, monotone voice. "Come with me."

Kate's pulse kicked up. This wasn't an escort. It was a detention. They bypassed her VIP contact. One glance at his baffled face confirmed it—he wasn't part of this. So, before she was out of earshot, she called out, "Call Moshenski." She hoped the name alone might have some impact on the officer, but if it did, he didn't let it show. He was all business and led Kate into a small examination room.

Not Syria, Kate thought, smirking. *But I know an interrogation room when I see one.*

Kate's gift for languages was something she tried to keep out of official records and reports when possible. Pretending she didn't speak fluent French, she spoke only in English and played the confused and irritated tourist.

Kate folded her arms, her voice edged with irritation. "Was I in the wrong line?"

The officer remained silent, his gaze fixed ahead. *Not the one in charge,* she thought. She shifted her focus to the mirror. "Can we move this along? It's been a long day. I'm tired, hungry, and I just want to check into my hotel."

Kate hadn't noticed the officer's earpiece, but when his right hand pressed on the device, she knew he was getting instructions.

"Mrs. Preacher," he said. "We need to examine your passport and any electronics you have on your person or in your handbag. We have already collected your luggage for review."

Kate removed her smartwatch and began pulling items out of the messenger bag. She paused, her fingers brushing over the pile of items. "I have a better idea." She tossed her passport, wallet, and lip balm onto the table, shoving everything else back into the bag. "Here." Her voice was firm as she handed it over. "Run the whole bag through the scanner—let's keep this moving."

***

BEN SHEPARD WATCHED THROUGH the two-way mirror, his steel-blue eyes unreadable. Weathered. Graying. But sharp.

A former CIA Station Chief who thrived in murky waters. Civilian life had been good to him.

Expensive suit.

Same cold instincts.

She looked about the same, only different. *Polished. Professional. Controlled.*

How long had it been? Seven? Eight years?

Something in her eyes. *Harder. Calculating.*

Not the timid girl who stepped off the plane in Syria.

But dangerous?

Unlikely.

Ben didn't take his eyes off Kate. "What do you think?"

Vivek adjusted his magnifying headset, his tone matter-of-fact. "It's locked down tight. No surprise, considering her line of work. But I can crack it."

"I'm sensing a but."

"It'll take longer than usual. And..."

Ben turned to him. "And what?"

"She might notice," Vivek said, hesitating. "And if she does...?"

"I'll take that chance," Ben said. "We're flying blind. I need to see where she goes, who she talks to, and what she knows. So, just get it done."

Vivek—dressed in a lab coat, a lighted, magnifying headset, and a wristband that linked him to an anti-static mat—looked part surgeon, and part mechanic.

Every precaution was taken to perform surgery on Kate's equipment while minimizing the possibility of permanent damage or discovery. Minutes passed, but one by one, Kate's equipment was disassembled, laid out on the mat, and reassembled with GPS trackers and listening devices.

Ben checked his watch and stared through the mirror at Kate. *The longer this takes,* he thought. *The more suspicious she'll become. She might not even use this equipment if she suspects.*

"How much longer?" Ben asked, his tone clipped, eyes flicking to his watch.

Vivek straightened, pulling off his headset with a satisfied grin. "Done."

Ben slid Kate's gear back into her bag and handed it to the immigration officer, who was waiting just outside the door. "Everything's fine," he said. "False alarm. She's free to go."

***

When the immigration officer didn't return right away, Kate assessed how long she'd been in the room. *No clock, watch, or phone. Interesting,* she thought. *An explosive scan takes minutes. It's been way too long. They're looking for something.*

Kate's sense of time was extraordinary, and when the officer returned, she guessed, "Twenty-two minutes." He glanced at his watch and scowled. "Did you find what you were looking for?" she asked.

"No, Madame." And realizing his mistake, attempted to correct. "The scanner was busy, but you're free to go. Your escort and luggage are this way."

The officer guided Kate back out the same way she came. She was hoping for a glimpse behind the mirror at whoever was pulling the strings, but they remained out of sight. *Probably Boucher. It had to be.* Deputy Director Laurent Boucher, DGSI. The man leading the café bombing investigation. Officially, it was still terrorism. Unofficially? She had questions.

Kate tangled with Boucher just weeks ago when she claimed Jake's body and personal effects. *I definitely bruised his ego,* she thought, recalling the intensity of their last meeting, the accusations, and the slap that sent his glasses flying.

And Lord knows, having his authority usurped by an American and a woman left a mark. But as the head of the investigation, she needed Boucher. *I hope he arranged this little interlude—maybe that will make us even and tomorrow's meeting a little less stressful.*

The meeting with Boucher was first thing in the morning, and with the time change, Kate was relieved to learn the French business day started at a civilized nine in the morning. *Plenty of time to caffeinate and prepare for a round of verbal jousting.*

But she had to admit, Boucher surprised her, responding personally to the request and readily agreeing to meet. She was ready to play the Moshenski card, but Boucher folded first. Still, she wasn't naïve. If he ordered the baggage search, he thought she was hiding something. *Hoping to catch her off guard, dig through her electronics.* Kate smirked. *Not a chance in hell.*

As promised, Kate's VIP escort was waiting. The smile was gone, and perspiration glowed on his bald head, but he had Kate's bag and led her toward the car.

Something's changed.

"Were you able to reach Mr. Moshenski?" she asked as they walked.

"Yes. He was most unhappy, and I am to bring you straight to the embassy."

Kate frowned. *That wasn't the plan.*

"I expected to meet with him tomorrow and have a chance to check in and freshen up."

"I'm sorry, Madame," he said with finality. "We must go straight to the embassy. But I will wait and take you to the Hôtel de Pourtalès at the conclusion of your meeting."

Kate exhaled slowly. *No point arguing. I knew my arrangement with Vitali came with strings.*

I didn't think the leash would be this short.

She slid into the back seat.

The doors locked.

The car pulled away.

Chapter 6

CHARLES DE GAULLE AIRPORT, PARIS, FRANCE

TALYA AVIRAM WAITED IN the shadows of Charles de Gaulle's VIP parking zone. Black leathers, black helmet—just another rider, invisible to security cameras. The crisp morning air kept her comfortable, but the wait troubling.

The last time Kate arrived in Paris, there was a target on her back and an attempt on her life. Talya could only hope this time would be different, and Forest's instructions were explicit—*deploy whatever resources you need, but don't let Kate out of your sight.* Everyone on the Trident Security team knew that was easier said than done, and tension was building.

Kate's flight landed an hour ago. Talya's observer confirmed she entered the expedited Flight Crew clearance line—VIP escort in place, fast-track guaranteed. But Kate wasn't through. Something was wrong.

Talya's voice cut through the comms. "Report."

"Mockingbird's still in immigration."

"Visual?"

"Negative."

She's been detained, Talya thought, but couldn't imagine why. *Of all the people, why would you hold Kate Preacher?*

Talya stood next to the Yamaha MT-09, a gloved hand resting on the handlebar, but waiting never meant relaxing. With heightened senses, she scanned for even the smallest detail out of place. The VIP area buzzed with cars, and passengers, and luggage. *The area directly above would be complete chaos,* she thought. *Tourists, taxis, and buses all vying for space and attention.* At this level, the passengers moved with seamless efficiency, sliding into the back seats of polished limousines while drivers loaded way too much luggage. *Kate will travel light. A single suitcase. And that ancient shoulder bag.*

The matte-black motorcycle was Talya's silent shadow. The scent of gasoline and motor oil grounded her—a machine as much a part of her as the gun on her hip or the knife in her boot.

Talya's helmet comm system crackled to life with the message she waited to hear.

"Mockingbird is on the move. ETA loading zone, 5 minutes."

Talya exhaled, her tone steady. "Copy."

With a fluid motion, Talya swung her leg over the bike and settled onto the seat. The supple leather of her suit creaked softly as she shifted, finding the perfect balance point. Her gloved hands gripped the handlebars, the textured surface providing a reassuring sense of control. She reached forward, her fingers on the ignition key. With a quick twist, the MT-09 roared to life and then hummed into a steady idle. Talya checked her watch. *Any second now.*

"I have eyes on," Talya reported, her voice low and steady. Even from a distance, Talya caught the shift—Kate scanning, assessing, just as she had for the last hour. *Situational awareness sharp as ever.* The area was clear. The approach was clean, and Kate glided from the terminal's exit doors and into the vehicle. Talya smiled. *One suitcase and shoulder bag. Nailed it.*

Kate's limo pulled away, and Talya revved the engine. A deep growl echoed off the concrete walls, and she eased into the flow of traffic, heading for the city. The morning air whipped past Talya as she followed the limo, weaving through traffic on the A1 and thirty minutes later merging into the Peripherique. The Paris "ring road" could take you east or west around the city, and this is where Talya's advance work paid off.

There were two likely destinations. The first was straight to Kate's hotel—the Hôtel de Pourtalès, the small luxury residences known for exclusivity and frequented by wealthy patrons and celebrities seeking a quiet place to rest, work, or rendezvous without the paparazzi. The second was Kate's benefactor, Vitali Moshenski, at the Ukrainian Embassy—while this seemed less likely, especially after a long flight, plans were made to monitor the embassy as well.

Talya broadcast an update to the surveillance team, "Mockingbird is flying west. Repeat. West."

"Copy that. Moving to secondary."

Talya tightened her grip on the handlebars, keeping the bike shadowed behind a delivery van. When the limo veered right, she didn't follow. Instead, accelerating past the intersection—heading for the embassy.

"Mockingbird is flying solo," Talya said. "East on Rue de Grenelle. Copy?"

Whether Kate spotted the surveillance or the driver was a close protection professional intentionally using the longer route, the team had the route covered.

"Visual," echoed in Talya's helmet as another member of the team confirmed they had eyes on Kate's limo. "Eight minutes out."

Talya's thumb tapped the press-to-talk (PTT) button on the handlebars. The double-mic click acknowledged the message, and she sped on to the embassy. *I'll be there in three—and tucked into the alley long before she arrives.* Talya was in position when Kate's limo approached. The fortified gates opened, the ram barriers dropped, and the limo disappeared into the embassy's underground garage.

She pressed the PTT button again and reported. "Mockingbird is in the cage."

No sign that anyone knows she's here—yet. But as Talya maintained her vigil on the parking entrance, she thought back to the attack just weeks ago and the boy she killed.

When Talya stepped out of the Hôtel de Crillon that morning, the world thought she was Katherine Preacher—the widow of *l'Américain*, the American hero.

And so did the young man who offered her flowers.

He smiled. *Young and innocent*, she thought. But then he dropped the flowers. Eyes glaring. Screaming.

"Allahu Akbar."

What happened next was pure reflex. Years of training and combat colliding in milliseconds.

I didn't plan to sever his carotid. That's not something you plan. But when a knife is hurtling toward your throat, you do whatever it takes to stay alive.

When Talya joined Trident, she knew protecting high-profile clients, their family, and their friends meant high risk. And Jake's training put it in perspective.

Jake's voice was clear in her mind:

"If there's a knife, you'll get cut. A gun, you might take a hit. But you fight. You protect the client. That's the job."

Talya had survived. The ruse worked. Kate made it to the morgue. The mission intact.

But that boy—too young. Her youngest kill.

Would she do it again? She knew the answer.

Hopefully, not today.

She checked her mirrors. Then the entrance.

Still clear. For now.

Her grip tightened on the throttle.

Watching. Waiting.

Talya exhaled.

So far, so good.

But that could change—fast.

Chapter 7

TUESDAY, APRIL 28th
10:10 AM CEST

CHARLES DE GAULLE AIRPORT, PARIS, FRANCE

BEN SHEPARD LEANED AGAINST a pillar outside baggage claim, eyes scanning the flood of arriving passengers. His gaze settled on a familiar figure. Grant Collins. Purposeful stride, built like a soldier, his sharp features set in stone. The two men locked eyes, exchanged a nod, and fell into step—silent, wary.

Grant didn't break stride. "Touching reunion."

Ben shrugged, his eyes scanning the terminal. "I was here anyway. Preacher came through about an hour ago."

Grant halted, shoulders squaring. "What the hell happened?" His voice turned lethal. "I was seconds from finishing it when the Abort came in."

Ben exhaled slow. "Told Mueller it might be too late."

"Mueller's call?" Grant asked, his tone edged with suspicion.

Ben scoffed. "Mueller's call? Everything is Mueller's call. And the coalition's."

Grant guided Ben toward a quiet corner of the arrival terminal, "Do you know why?"

Ben shook his head, his jaw clenched. "Only that she has something with her that could be important, maybe even a threat."

"What's the plan?"

"That's why I'm here," Ben replied. "I had her detained long enough for my guy to inspect her equipment."

"And?" Grant asked, a hint of impatience creeping into his voice. "Did you find what you wanted?"

"No. Couldn't clone her devices. Encryption's airtight—way beyond our reach in the time we had."

"So, you don't have a plan," Grant said. "You should have let me finish what I started, and whatever she has would have died with her."

Ben raised a hand to cut him off. "Hang on. It wasn't a total loss. We planted trackers and bugs. We'll know where she goes, what she does."

Grant's brow arched. "She'll find them."

Ben smirked, his tone confident. "Everything's dormant. No signal minimal power. If she checks, there's nothing to find. Not yet. We'll let her run, let her think she's making progress, then collect everything."

As they exited the terminal, the warm Parisian air hit their faces, a stark contrast to the air-conditioned atmosphere inside. Grant's shoulders tensed, his words laced with a quiet intensity. "In the meantime, it's my neck on the line. I'm the one she's hunting."

"Afraid of her?"

"Should I be?"

Ben scoffed, shaking his head. "Not a chance. She's an analyst, a geek. You'll see—we've got this under control."

Grant's expression remained unconvinced, his instincts honed by years of covert operations. "We'll try your way, for now," he said. "But if she gets close, I'll do it my way. I'm not throwing away years of work building this identity."

Ben's hand shot out, gripping Grant's arm with surprising strength. His voice dropped to a dangerous whisper. "Don't do anything without clearing it with me first. If Mueller thinks either of us has gone rogue, there's nowhere on the planet we can hide."

"Mueller doesn't scare me," Grant said flatly. "And neither do you."

Ben's eyes narrowed. "Don't be stupid. Be grateful you're on the inside."

CHAPTER 8

UKRAINIAN EMBASSY, PARIS, FRANCE

KATE'S LIMO SLID INTO the shadowed depths of the Ukrainian Embassy's underground garage. As it eased to a stop, a familiar figure waited—Vitali Moshenski, hands clasped, unreadable, behind a polite smile. Trim, distinguished. As always. But Kate knew better. *He wouldn't be here unless something was wrong.*

An embassy garage attendant opened Kate's door, and she stepped out, nodding at the driver, who she knew would wait for her return.

"Mr. Moshenski, I didn't expect you to greet me personally."

"Please, call me Vitali," he reminded her. "May I call you Kate, or do you prefer Katherine?"

"Kate's fine," she said. "I'm just surprised to see you here in the garage."

"Ah, yes." Vitali gestured toward the hallway. "Embassy protocol would have us meet in the grand hall. But I've never been one for diplomatic theatrics. Besides, our first stop is the medical center."

"Zhukov?" Kate asked. "He's here?"

"Yes."

"And his condition?"

"Mikhail is stable," Vitali said. "I prefer to keep him close—he is well cared for here. Perhaps you will visit? He might respond to a familiar voice.

"You think he might respond to my presence, my voice?" Kate asked, entering the medical center.

"One can always hope."

Kate paused outside Zhukov's room. "Whatever my connection with Zhukov," Kate said. "It's still a mystery to me, but I do have questions."

"Then I encourage you to ask them," Vitali said. "I will pray that he wakes and answers."

Vitali stood alongside Mikhail's bed and placed a hand on his chest as if to stir a napping friend. "Mikhail, you have a visitor."

Kate observed the man in the hospital bed with a clinical detachment at first. Skin color, breathing, and the bandage around his head wound. The monitors clicking nearby tracked heart rate, oxygen and blood pressure. He had compression balloons on both legs that inflated and deflated to assist with his circulation. *He looks comfortable,* Kate thought. *Better than I expected under the circumstances. Like he might open his eyes any second.*

"He looks good," Kate said, glancing across the bed at Vitali and then directly into Zhukov's face.

Kate leaned in, voice soft but firm. "Enough of this, old man. We have work to do." No response. Just the steady beep of the monitors. She exhaled, straightened, and shrugged. "It was worth a shot."

Vitali smiled and turned to leave, but Kate leaned in and whispered in Mikhail's ear. "Don't you die on me," she said. "We have unfinished business." Kate kissed his cheek. It was an impulse she couldn't explain. But she was grateful. The man she hunted in Syria, even despised, had saved her life. And she had no idea why.

"Can you arrange for a chessboard?" Kate asked.

"Yes, of course."

"Just leave it nearby," Kate added. "I'll set it when I return."

"I am glad to hear you will return," he said. "The chess set will be waiting."

They stepped out of Zhukov's room and across the hall. Kate's gaze drifted to another unconscious patient, head and face fully bandaged. Only his nose and eyes were visible. IV drip in his arm and monitors, like Zhukov's, tracking vitals.

"Another café victim?"

Vitali's expression darkened. "Not exactly."

Kate turned to him, sensing the shift. "What does that mean?"

Vitali stepped closer, his voice low. "You knew him as Red."

"I don't understand," Kate said. "Are you telling me that's…"

Vitali interrupted, "We do not say his name, and none here know it. The man you knew is dead. His dying wish and your promises were fulfilled. The insurance payment to his ex-wife and trust fund for his daughter were quite clever. They were grateful, and both are now safe, thanks to you."

Kate's breath caught. "But how..." Then it clicked. "Zhukov. He was there. He saw everything."

Vitali nodded. "And asked for my help. A man willing to die for his daughter, he said, deserves a chance to live."

"And the bandages?"

"Insurance," Vitali replied. "The days of new identities, even planting deep backgrounds, are not enough. With his daughter's life on the line, he insisted on being certain she remained safe. That required a new face. One that would fool facial recognition. More surgery is to come, and his recovery will be long and painful."

"And what's in it for you?"

"Direct as always—one of the things I appreciate about you."

"Then answer the question."

"He had a choice," Vitali said. "Die quietly, peacefully, as the man he once was, and no one would ever know he survived the encounter at your cabin."

"Or what?" Kate insisted.

"Or suffer the pain and agony of rebirth and join me."

"Join you?" Kate asked. "Join you in what, exactly?"

"Let me show you," Vitali said, his voice now somber, his face grew sullen.

This is the darkness I sensed, Kate thought. *There's something I need to see.* They took the elevator to the third floor and marched down the hall. The looming cloud of what Vitali wanted Kate to see hovered over them, and neither said a word until they were secure in Vitali's grand office.

Vitali directed Kate to the chair opposite his desk, and he took the one next to her. He pulled the KATIM phone from his suit pocket, unlocked the phone, and handed it to Kate.

As a digital forensic expert, Kate recognized the device and was well aware of their use in government and diplomatic circles. She noted Monday's date on the last message, and last Friday's timestamp on the attached video file. She pressed play. Drone aerial footage began, and Kate attempted to increase the volume and realized the audio track was scrubbed. She thought the audio might provide some context, and its absence raised questions.

"Is that your vehicle?" she asked, but never took her eyes off the video.

"Yes."

"So this is rural Virginia, out past Arlington," she said. "Then the occupants are..."

"My men," Vitali confirmed. "And Marcus."

This is it, Kate thought. *This is how Marcus died.* Not that she didn't believe Margot. She did. But some part of her hoped it was a mistake or even a lie. When the targeting array appeared on the screen, Kate held her breath. Like Vitali, she knew what that meant. She'd examined enough battlefield footage—recognized a drone ready to fire.

The blast hit like a sledgehammer. Kate jerked back. "Christ. What the hell was that?"

"An incinerator charge," Vitali replied. "Probably Russian."

"You think Russians killed Marcus?"

"The explosive was likely Russian," Vitali said and raised an eyebrow. "You are not surprised?"

"No, I was contacted by...," Kate began. "By an associate and told there was an explosion involving a Ukrainian Embassy vehicle. As you might imagine, I have mixed emotions about Marcus, but I'm sorry about your men. I didn't mean to drag you into...whatever this is."

"You wondered why I would ask the man downstairs to join me. This is why. This is the new face of war. Automated. Anonymous. Without borders and accountable to no one."

"Like the BountyHunters."

"Yes. The BountyHunters are one weapon in this new war," Vitali said. "But there are others. Mikhail and I have sought them out for over a decade."

"A decade?" Kate asked. "Before Syria?"

"Yes. There is more to Mikhail's presence in Syria than you know, but..."

"Let me guess," Kate interrupted. "I need to ask Zhukov. You know this is getting old."

"I understand," Vitali said. "But I ask you to accept that I am bound to an oath that I can not and will not break. All may judge my life and actions as they see fit, but my word is my honor."

"Fine," Kate snapped, knowing it was pointless to press. "But where does Ro...the man downstairs fit in the grand scheme?"

"We need honorable men, like the man downstairs, to walk the warrior's path, even knowing where it ends. There are powerful forces determined to reshape our world."

"Like Devin Moore?"

"Yes. And no," Vitali said. "Moore was a visionary, a dreamer who believed his NanoVaults were the ticket to real power. Admittedly, they *were* a serious threat. We all have secrets and weaknesses—and Moore was adept at collecting and exploiting them to his advantage. But underestimating you was literally a fatal mistake."

The bastard tried to kill me. Four times. Left a trail of bodies in his wake—lives shattered all to fuel his ambition. She could still hear him gasping—her throat strike crushed his trachea. Kate had reached for a knife—knew how to save him.

And stopped.

After everything—the blood, the wreckage, the certainty it would continue if he lived—she let him die.

"With Moore out of the game," Kate began. "Who are you fighting?"

"I'm hoping you will help me answer that question," Vitali replied. "Starting with who sent this video. I thought perhaps our secretive young friend might be of assistance once again."

"Perhaps," Kate said. "I'll need to take the phone. And I can't make any promises."

"I understand," Vitali said smoothly. "All I ask is your word—anything you or your associate uncover comes to me first. No one else."

Kate hesitated. She wasn't sure which part felt heavier—the demand or the cost.

But she nodded. "You have my word. Now, if there's nothing else."

"Of course. It has been a long day," Vitali said, and with a finger on the embassy's intercom, he directed his assistant to alert Kate's driver and escort her back to the garage. He handed Kate a business card that was blank except for a phone number. "This is my private cell. I am at your disposal. Anytime. Day or night."

"Is this my *get-out-of-jail-free card*?" Kate asked and smiled, but she could see that Vitali didn't understand the reference.

"Let us hope it does not come to that—but I have secured the items you requested."

In the corner of Vitali's opulent office, there was an antique Louis XVI armoire. The intricate woodwork and gilded details of the armoire perfectly complemented the room's historical decor. He crossed the room and opened its doors with a gentle tug. The interior had been gutted and inside was a distinctly modern safe.

Kate resisted her natural inclination to watch him open the safe, but his reflection in the window confirmed her suspicion. *Two-factor locking mechanism,* Kate thought. *A six-digit code and a biometric thumb scan.* Kate had never seen one like it. *I guess when you're rich enough, you can order whatever you want and destroy an antique to hide it.*

With a knowing smile, Vitali retrieved the case from the armoire and set it on his desk, the worn, textured leather offering a stark contrast to the smooth, polished wood beneath it.

"As requested," Vitali said, his voice low and conspiratorial. "I trust you will find everything meets your specifications."

Kate approached the desk and opened the case. Nestled in the padded foam interior were two Glock handguns, a 43 and 43X, both configured with Shield Red Dot optics. Tucked alongside were a pair of Zev Technologies threaded barrels, JK 105 CCX suppressors, and four fully loaded magazines for each weapon.

She had no way to know what she might face, but she was on her own, and the last time she was in Paris, someone tried to kill her. This combination of equipment let Kate balance concealment with suppression for whatever mission and clothing constraints.

Kate looked up at Vitali, a smile playing at the corners of her lips. "Perfect," she said, her tone filled with appreciation. "Thank you. This is exactly what I need."

Vitali's gaze lingered on the open case. "Let us hope you will not need them," he said softly. "But if you do—do not get caught. Even I can only do so much. These could put you beyond my reach. Beyond anyone's reach."

Chapter 9

TUESDAY, APRIL 28th
11:34 AM CEST

HÔTEL DE POURTALÈS, PARIS, FRANCE

Talya's team was in position, eyes on every entry and exit, with special focus on the garage. A woman in sunglasses adjusted a stroller canopy, the pastel blankets hiding a lifelike doll. A casual tilt, a quick glance—just enough to confirm the limo's occupants as it pulled away.

"Mockingbird is mobile," Talya said quietly into her comms. "Eastbound on Rue de l'Ambassade."

Two blocks ahead, a man in a faded delivery uniform lounged against a motorcycle, phone pressed to his ear. His mirrored helmet caught the limo's reflection—perfect line of sight, zero suspicion.

"Visual confirmed," he said. "Maintaining position."

Talya's double-mic click acknowledged receipt. Others along the route to the hotel would track Kate's progress while she sped directly to the destination. The bike allowed Talya to weave through traffic and down alleys. And she arrived ten minutes ahead of Kate and met with the team monitoring the hotel's entry and exit points.

The hotel team had nothing unusual to report, and Talya concluded that Kate's arrival in the city was successful—under the radar of any imminent threat. She and rotating members of the team would monitor Kate throughout her stay in France, but she breathed easier that Kate's arrival was going smoothly.

Just need to get her inside now, she thought. *And phase one will be complete.*

The arriving stretch limo wasn't Kate's. All eyes were on the unexpected arrival.

A rooftop operative zoomed in, his camera tracking the limo's occupants. The driver stayed put, but the front passenger door swung open. A man stepped out—dark blue suit, comms wire trailing from his ear. Head on a swivel, scanning the perimeter.

Private security—probably some celeb. The hotel secured a reputation for its discretion and high-profile clientele.

Talya's voice cut through comms. "Eyes up. We need an ID on the package."

A high-profile guest could be trouble. Leaks happened—especially when celebrities craved attention more than security. If this one had a publicist with loose lips, Kate's anonymity was already in jeopardy.

When the close protection operator concluded the location was safe, he opened the limo's rear passenger door. The first person to step out caught Talya by surprise.

Whoa, Sebastian Vargas, Talya thought, recognizing the head of Vargas Security. *This package must be filthy rich.* When Talya left Mossad, she interviewed with Vargas. He had a stellar reputation, took only the crème de la crème as clients, and had the highest pay rate in the business. But there was something about the man that made her skin crawl. She met Jake and several of the guys on the Trident team and never looked back.

This should be interesting, she thought while waiting to see who would emerge. Vargas scanned the area and then offered his hand to the client. *It's a woman.*

Talya didn't need an ID. The oversized Dior sunglasses couldn't mask the style, beauty, and effortless grace. *Isabella Marquez.*

The American actress, entrepreneur, and philanthropist was an international icon. While she rose to fame in her early twenties, first as a model, then as an Oscar-winning actress, her Bella Beauty cosmetic line catapulted her into billionaire status.

Vargas checked his watch, said something to Isabella, pecked her cheek, and then walked away.

That's odd, Talya thought. *What's so important you don't even escort the client into the hotel. And why only one operator?*

The lone member of the security detail led the way and held the door for Ms. Marquez as the limo drove away. *No bellman. No luggage,* Talya thought. *She's already checked in and just returning.*

Talya's team reported Kate was two minutes out, and she watched Kate arrive.

Her driver popped out of the car and held Kate's door as she stepped onto the sidewalk.

She picked up a little something from her Ukrainian friend, Talya thought, and smiled. *Knowing Kate, it's a Glock 43, maybe a 48. Red dots and probably suppressed. It won't come as a surprise, but Forest won't be happy.*

Talya's voice carried quiet satisfaction over the line. "Mockingbird is in the nest. Phase one is complete."

Given the hotel's penchant for privacy, room assignments were carefully guarded secrets. Talya suspected the fifth floor, the top and most exclusive level, but the specific apartment would take a little time to nail down.

Time to brief Forest. She checked her watch. 5:30 a.m. South Carolina. *Perfect—he's up.*

***

TUESDAY, APRIL 28th
5:40 AM EDT

THE SAWMILL TRAINING COMPLEX, LAURENS, SOUTH CAROLINA

FOREST HICKMAN, RETIRED NAVY SEAL and interim head of Trident Security, had his hands wrapped around a steaming cup of Black Rifle coffee. The dimly lit dining room of the Sawmill training center was just waking for the day's training.

The catering team was bringing in breakfast trays filled with scrambled eggs, bacon, and sausage, along with baskets filled with freshly baked pastry and biscuits. Forest's room was just down the hall, and the moment he could smell the coffee brewing, he was up and out. The others would be along soon enough, but for the moment, he enjoyed having the table to himself. *The last calm before chaos.*

Forest scanned the day's training schedule—plenty of surprises lined up. The Trident Security team was in high demand, both for their executive protection services and their training expertise. The decades of continuous, leading-edge military training combined with mission-proven experience meant that training with this team was the fast track to insights most law enforcement and SWAT teams could never accumulate on their own.

The Phoenix SWAT team they've been training for the last two days were halfway through the program. With the core program behind them, it was time to kick things up a notch, and Forest was determined to turn up the heat.

The Sawmill Training Center is the brainchild of Steve Brown, a U.S. Army Special Operations senior officer with over 30 years of SOF experience. With two-hundred-fifty acres equipped with various tactical environments, if you can imagine it, you can train for it at the Sawmill. With sniper scenarios, entry breaching, CQB coordination, hostage rescue, and more, the Arizona team was about to take their capabilities to new heights.

Forest had a devilish, almost boyish smile. *They'll be tired tonight,* he thought. *But our job is to get them ready for whatever the cartels throw at them.* Forest understood that the Phoenix SWAT team faced powerful and deadly forces, and unique challenges. Drug smugglers, human traffickers, political and financial kidnapping and ransom, and a growing number of criminally insane and unpredictable. He planned to equip this team with as much as he could in the days they had left.

Mike was the next to arrive, another of the SEALs and former team members Jake recruited. At six-two, two hundred fifteen pounds, Mike was an imposing figure that could deescalate an executive protection situation with sheer presence. He was also the team's lead sniper and ran Trident's long-range precision rifle training. Mike glanced at breakfast, which wasn't quite ready, and settled for coffee before joining Forest.

"Morning, Arkansas," Mike greeted, sliding into a seat with his coffee.

Arkansas Dave, from Young Guns 2, was a call sign Forest wore with pride as a Razorback fan from Little Rock. Virginia Beach was home now, but there was still a slight Arkansas accent, which was more pronounced when he was angry. You didn't want to see Forest angry, but that didn't stop Mike from pushing his buttons.

"Maybe we should drop Arkansas and go with Thor."

Forest didn't look up from his notes. "What are you on about now?"

Mike smirked. "Your new look. Long flowing brown hair, almost shoulder-length—like Thor's. Except Thor's six-three, and you're...well..."

Forest finally glanced up, a grin tugging at his lips. "Talk about coming up short," he said with a laugh. "And you owe me twenty bucks."

"Kate went straight to the embassy?"

"Yep. I called it."

"I figured it was a fifty-fifty bet hotel or embassy," Mike said and fished out his wallet. "Can you believe Deon bet on shopping?" Mike tossed Forest a twenty, "How's she holding up?" Mike asked, leaning back in his chair.

Forest took a sip of coffee. "Immigration was the only hiccup, but everything's been by the book. Talya should check in soon—I've been following the chatter."

"We should be there," Mike said, his tone firm.

Forest nodded, his expression tightening. "Agreed. I tried, but she shut me down hard. Kate's the boss."

"You know we all love Kate," Mike said. "But putting you in charge shows a serious lack of judgment."

Forest was about to throw his coffee mug at Mike's head when Talya called. "Saved by the bell," Forest said and stepped away to take the call. "Everything OK?"

"Yes, we're good," Talya reported. "Kate's checking in now."

"Good. That should be it for tonight," Forest said. "Kate's a room-service, work-in-the-room business traveler. And she'll want to be ready for the Boucher meeting tomorrow."

"Let's hope she doesn't slap him this time," Talya added. "Or worse. And that reminds me. She left the embassy with a briefcase."

"That figures," Forest said. "I'm sure Moshenski can get his hands on anything he wants, but that complicates things. She's not licensed in Europe. We'll need to work on that. In the meantime..."

"I know," Talya interrupted. "No police."

"Was there anything else?" Forest asked.

"One more thing," Talya added. "Vargas is here—and Isabella Marquez is his package."

Forest straightened in his chair. "Wait. You're telling me Isabella Marquez is staying at Kate's hotel?"

"Is that a problem?"

"Might be," Forest replied. "It was a few years ago—before you came on board..."

"She's the actress from that film festival, right?"

Forest nodded. "So you've heard the story?"

"Bits and pieces," Talya said. "Actress-client, Cannes red carpet. Marquez was the client?"

"That's the one," Forest said, leaning back. "Big red carpet moment, cameras everywhere—and she's practically naked."

"I'm sure it wasn't *that* bad."

"Don't believe me? Look it up…it's all online," Forest said. "You'll see… there's nothing left to the imagination."

"So, what happened?"

"You know, Jake. He's close. Focused. Eyes on the crowd," Forest said. "Next thing you know, Marquez has both arms around his neck, plants a big wet kiss on the lips, and wraps a leg around him. The cameras went crazy. Outside of a war zone, I've never heard anything like it. And for the next few days, it's huge tabloid news. She's married. Jake's married. She's gorgeous. He's handsome. It got blown way out of proportion."

"Oh, poor Kate."

"Exactly," Forest said. "Kate knew it was a setup. A stupid PR stunt, but that didn't stop the press from hounding her."

"It's a small hotel," Talya added. "They're bound to cross paths."

"I know what you're thinking," Forest said. "But you can't warn Kate. You're not supposed to be there. Besides, it was years ago, water under the bridge. I doubt Kate would even care."

Talya chuckled, her tone laced with amusement. "Wow. For a married guy, you really don't understand women."

Chapter 10

HÔTEL DE POURTALÈS, PARIS, FRANCE

KATE FOLLOWED HER DRIVER to the entrance, suppressing a smile. *Vitali had called it discreet—this was practically invisible.* No signage. No grand awning. Just a dark-brown door set into the stone, blending into the historic facade like a secret waiting to be found.

Among a select clientele, the Hôtel de Pourtalès was considered a luxury apartment building that operates somewhat like a hotel, offering high-end apartments for short-term stays. The apartments, often rented by celebrities and socialites among other wealthy individuals, suited those seeking privacy and luxury and who could afford both.

The driver held the door and followed behind with Kate's bag. The foyer was small but elegant. Nothing like the grand lobby of the Hotel de Crillon and none of the bustling crowd of guests, bellman, or reception staff. Here, a single staff member stood behind a marble desk, and he welcomed Kate to the hotel with a simple "Bonjour Madame."

The driver deposited Kate's bag and disappeared without a word. *Vitali must keep his staff well paid and under strict instructions not to solicit tips,* she thought. *And between the delay at the airport and the embassy stop, I suspect my driver is happy to be on his way.*

The young man at the reception desk indicated where Kate could leave her bag, and he would have it delivered to her suite. Kate noted the perfect English. *He's probably fluent in several languages,* she thought. *Given the hotel's international clients.* He offered Kate a sealed envelope that simply said, Opera Suite. *No names. No initials. They take this privacy thing seriously.*

The handwritten note welcomed her to the hotel, provided some general guidance, and included the key to her fifth-floor apartment.

At the end of the narrow hallway, Kate heard an elevator motor and noticed a well-dressed man and woman waiting for its arrival. *Must be pretty slow,* she thought, given the sound, and she had the sense they'd been waiting awhile. She took a chance on being able to reach them before it departed.

The elevator dinged softly, the weathered brass doors hesitating before parting with a slow, deliberate hum. The mechanism moved like it had all the time in the world, revealing the interior inch by inch. Marble tile floor, French oak paneling, and a broad-shouldered man in an ill-fitting suit.

The man in the elevator didn't move. He remained pressed against the back railing as the woman and her escort stepped inside. By the time Kate arrived, the elevator doors were closing in the same laborious journey they took to open. Kate hoped the gentleman at the front would see her approach and hold the door. *I guess chivalry is dead,* she thought, when he didn't move a muscle.

The woman stood back from the doors and tucked off to the right. She clearly hoped the large, dark sunglasses would obscure her identity, but her Prada leather bag and Jimmy Choo Stilettos screamed celebrity. *Isabella Marquez,* Kate knew. *Unmistakable.* And looking at the man, standing like an offensive tackle. *Private security. I'll wait.*

When the gap between the doors was less than a foot, something changed. The woman shrank into the corner, her body folding in on itself. Kate felt it before she saw it—this wasn't hiding. *This was terror.*

The woman's head lifted just enough—panicked eyes locking on Kate's. Then her fingers curled, tucking her thumb into her palm.

The universal silent plea for help.

The elevator doors slid shut.

Kate flew to the front desk, grabbed the clerk with both hands and demanded, "What room is she in? Isabella Marquez. What room?"

"I can't...," he began.

Kate seized his wrist, twisted sharply—bone grinding against cartilage. He hit the floor with a gasp. "You need to call the police, but first, give me her room number and the fastest way to get there." A little more pressure on the wrist, he relented.

"Fifth floor," he gasped. "Same as you. The Concorde Suite at the end of the hall. Take the stairs."

Kate shoved her belongings under the desk, fixing the clerk with a sharp glare. "Don't touch those," she snapped. Shrugging off her jacket and scarf, she barked her next command. "Call the police. Tell them there's a robbery assault in progress. Do it. Now!"

She hoped the elevator was as old and slow as it appeared and launched herself up the stairs, taking two at a time. *If I push, I can beat them*, she thought. Rounding the second-floor landing, her breath came faster but controlled, a steady rhythm drilled into her by years of intense training with Jake and the Trident team.

Should have kept the case, the voice in her head admonished. *There wasn't time,* she pushed back, arguing with herself. *You saw that guy—he's huge, and you're unarmed.*

Kate pushed past the third floor, her body a machine—lean, strong, trained for moments like this. Most people would falter, muscles screaming, lungs burning. But Kate wasn't most people. Her legs drove upward, her mind focused on the terror in the woman's eyes.

I should have geared up before I left the embassy, she thought. *But you'd think I could at least make it to the hotel. Focus, Kate. Focus.*

The fourth floor landing blurred past, but there was no relief, no letting up. Jake's training echoing in her ears—*be relentless, unstoppable.* She felt the familiar burn deep in her thighs, the strain in her lungs, but none of it mattered. The woman's life depended on her getting there first.

Kate reached the fifth floor, the handrail slick under her palm, but her grip only tightened. With a last surge of energy, she catapulted herself onto the fifth-floor landing, her momentum nearly carrying her into the wall.

For a moment, Kate allowed herself to double over, then drop to one knee. *You are the weapon,* she thought, preparing for what came next. She stood, opened the stairwell door, and heard the elevator's feeble ding at the far end of the hall. *They're here,* she thought, sprinting down the hall. *I need to get in close. Whatever his plan, I need to break the loop—force him to reorient.*

Break the loop was Jake's shorthand for Colonel Boyd's famous four-point OODA Loop. *Observe. Orient. Decide. Act.* The brain's decision-making cycle. His weapon doesn't matter. The brain is the key, and to gain an edge she needed a distraction, something to make his brain reboot.

The elevator motors hummed, the doors parted. Just inches at first. Kate's boots smacked the polished marble floor, each step echoing sharply through the hallway as she raced closer. She searched the hall for a weapon, anything that might even the odds against the towering, two-hundred-and-fifty-pound brute looming in the elevator. Then—salvation. A room service cart. Kate snatched the champagne bottle mid-stride, grip tightening around the neck.

Isabella appeared first, pushed out by the attacker, who had a massive hand wrapped around the celebrity's upper arm.

"Bella!" Kate's voice rang out, playful and slurred. "Come on, join me! You know I hate drinking alone."

The man with Isabella snarled at Kate. "Go away, you drunken bitch," he barked, gripping tighter and driving Isabella toward the Concorde Suite's apartment door.

Armenian, Kate thought, recognizing the hard, clipped cadence. She was close enough now to see the blood smeared across the elevator floor as the doors closed behind them. *Just a little closer. I'll press, and he'll come shut me up. What's one more body?*

"Bella, don't go," Kate said, her voice growing louder as she slurred her words. "I must show you what I bought today. The necklace is stunning and a bargain at thirty-thousand Euros."

Kate stumbled forward, bumping into the wall, sliding along the fabric panels, and grabbing at a hanging tapestry while inching closer. Her eyes locked on to the Armenian's white-knuckled grip, crushing Isabella's arm.

At the Concorde Suite's door, the Armenian released Isabella's arm, and his hand disappeared behind his back. He turned and lunged at Kate, his bloody eight-inch blade racing toward Kate's stomach.

She twisted away from the attack—the blade slicing air instead of flesh. With both hands gripping the bottle, Kate swung with everything she had. The impact cracked against his skull—dull, brutal. Bone met glass, and blood spattered the marble.

He staggered, letting out a guttural grunt as the impact sent him reeling. Blood ran from the gash near his temple as he dropped to his hands and knees, shaking his head like a dazed bull.

"Get inside," Kate shouted, her eyes locked on the towering man as Isabella's trembling hands struggled with the key.

She tightened her grip on the bottle and swung again, aiming for the base of his skull. The second strike landed with a dull crack, the blow driving him face-first onto the marble floor. His head hit hard, the sound echoing down the hallway, the knife sliding beyond his reach.

Kate risked a glance over shoulder and saw Isabella stepping inside the apartment. It was only a second, but it was a mistake. *You don't get to say when the fight's over. How many times had Jake stressed that point?*

The Armenian roared. Charging like a wounded elephant, crashing into Kate. His massive arms locked around her torso, driving her through the half-open door and slamming her onto the floor with bone-cracking force.

Pain exploded in her back as the wind rushed from her lungs. She struggled to breathe, to fight—her strikes sharp and deliberate. Her right thumb shot toward his eye but glanced off his cheekbone. A blade-hand strike to his throat met muscle as unyielding as braided steel cables. She twisted her hips, driving an elbow into his ribs, but his massive frame absorbed the blow like stone. His vice-like grip on her throat crushed her resistance, cutting off her air, squeezing the life out of her.

Isabella screamed and leapt onto the Armenian's back, her nails digging into his face, clawing at his eyes. Blood welled under her talons as the man groaned and shook his head to break free. With a single brutal motion, he grabbed her hair and hurled her forward. She was airborne, slamming face-first into an end table, sending a ceramic vase crashing to the marble floor.

Kate gasped for air, her vision blurring. Isabella's desperate act bought her a moment, and she seized it. The sound of the vase shattering rang in her ears like Jake's voice. *Look around*, he would say. *There are force multipliers everywhere.* Her right hand searched the floor, blindly groping for anything—a weapon, a shard of glass. Her fingers closed around Isabella's shoe.

The stiletto heel fit Kate's hand like a dagger. Adrenaline surging, she drove the five-inch heel into the Armenian's left eye. His primal scream erupted as his hands flew toward the searing wound.

Kate summoned her strength, her hoarse cry ringing out as she struck again, driving the heel deeper—an ice pick piercing the orbital cavity. The steel tip punctured the pons, that vital walnut of tissue where the brain stem meets consciousness. His massive frame shuddered and froze in place. His hands dropped limp at his sides, and for a moment, he knelt like a puppet with its strings severed. Then, with one final groan, he collapsed onto the floor.

Kate wriggled free from the Armenian's dead weight and crawled to the sobbing Isabella. She wrapped the woman in her arms. "It's over," Kate rasped, her voice raw from the assault. "And you're OK. Just breathe. That's it. Slow, deep breaths."

***

12:11 PM CEST

Sebastian Vargas strode down Rue Tronchet on his way back to the Hôtel de Pourtalès. At 45, the Colombian-American's executive protection business was one of the best in the business, with a stable of Hollywood actors and executives topping his client list. Sebastian's athletic build reflected his dedication to his craft as a top-tier security professional, and his handsome, chiseled features and tailored suits exuded an air of unwavering confidence.

He entered the understated lobby of the hotel and checked the time, but the moment he arrived, the junior clerk rushed out from behind the reception desk.

"Mr. Vargas," he said, his voice a mix of confusion and urgency. "The police are on their way."

"The police? Why? What's going on?"

"Honestly, sir. I don't know," he said. "A crazy American woman nearly broke my arm, insisted I tell her where Ms. Marquez was staying, and then told me to call the police."

"And where's this crazy woman now?" Vargas demanded, his voice sharp.

The clerk hesitated. "She...ran up the stairs."

"And Isabella?"

"She went up to her suite with Mr. Ramirez."

Sebastian glanced at the clerk's name tag. "It's alright, Mark," he said. "You stay here, and I'll go check on Isabella. When the police arrive, call the room. Oh, and don't mention the crazy American. This whole thing might be a simple misunderstanding, and we won't bother the police if it's nothing."

He headed for the elevator but couldn't shake the sense that something was horribly wrong. Still, it was part of the job to keep the police and the press at bay, and until he knew what had happened, he'd play it safe.

The elevator's arrival confirmed his fears, and he glanced over his shoulder to be sure Mark couldn't see. In the corner, he saw Carlos Ramirez, the close protection operator he assigned to stay with Isabella. His body crumpled, blood pooling beneath him, his eyes fixed on the ceiling.

Sebastian was careful not to step in the blood as he entered. He thought for a moment about whether he should press the button, but they arrived days ago, so his prints and every other hotel guest would already be present. He cursed the time it took for the elevator doors to close, praying no one would approach, and finally, the lift started rising. *Nobody was supposed to get hurt.*

He tapped his foot impatiently, willing the elevator to move faster and praying it didn't stop on any other floors. Every second counted now. When he passed the fourth floor, he drew his primary weapon. Holding the SIG P320 in tight and high-ready, he stepped back from the door. The elevator's arrival was the starting gun. The doors peeled open. He scanned over the top of his front sight, peering left, then right as the gap widened. On the ground was a blood-streaked knife and a champagne bottle. Convinced the hallway was clear, he exited in one swift move and approached Isabella's room.

The Concorde Suite's door was ajar, the lock splintered. Isabella sobbed on the floor, Kate crouched beside her. At the sound of his approach, she turned.

"Preacher?" he asked and lowered his weapon.

"It's clear," Kate replied. "All clear."

Sebastian holstered his weapon, crossing the room in two quick strides. Kate released Isabella, stepping back as Vargas took a knee next to his client.

"It was horrible," Isabella began. "I've never been so scared in my life. He had a huge knife. I told him he could have whatever he wanted, just don't hurt us." Isabella started crying again, and Kate located some tissue. "Thank you," she said. "And those eyes. I'll never forget his eyes. He laughed and killed Carlos. Insane. Just insane."

Kate rounded up a glass of water, handed it to Vargas, and he offered it to Isabella. "Here," he said, offering her the water. "You should hydrate. Your body's flooded with adrenaline, and this will help."

"Your man is in the elevator," Kate said, half whispering.

"I know," he said. "I've locked it out, so he won't be going anywhere."

"I'm sorry I couldn't help him."

"You ran up five floors and saved Isabella," he said. "I think you did everything humanly possible."

"It was a team effort," Kate said and looked over at Isabella. She was shaking and sobbing. "If the kid called the police, they should be here soon."

"He did," Vargas said. "And you should go."

"Are you asking me to leave a crime scene?"

"I am," he said. "I know what you've been through. And I can guess why you're back in Paris. The last thing you need is more publicity."

"You're right," Kate said. "This hotel was supposed to help me stay out of the headlines. But stepping away could make things worse."

"Trust me. This will be a much cleaner robbery-homicide investigation if you're not involved. He killed my man and targeted Isabella. Clearly self-defense. We've got this handled."

"Please," Isabella said between tears. "You saved my life. The least we can do is try to keep you out of it. Let Sebastian handle this. Please."

"What about the desk clerk?" Kate asked. "And my things—I left them under the front desk."

Sebastian waved it off. "Mark knows his job. He'll follow instructions. I'll have him use the service elevator to bring everything to your room."

"Alright," Kate finally agreed.

"Where's your room?"

"Other end of the hall."

"Go. Stay there. Don't open the door for anyone except for Mark with your luggage. If the police knock, ignore them."

Chapter II

TUESDAY, APRIL 28th
12:25 PM CEST

HÔTEL DE POURTALÈS, PARIS, FRANCE

TALYA LEANED BACK ON her motorcycle, eyes fixed on the hotel's entrance but relaxed for the first time all morning. The surveillance had gone smoothly. Talya ensured Kate's safe arrival, brought Forest up to date, and was about to leave when her helmet radio crackled.

The surveillance team was monitoring police and emergency radio chatter when they caught the broadcast.

10-24, Hôtel de Pourtalès, 7 Rue Tronchet

Talya's heart raced as she processed the intercept. *Kate's Hotel. Assault in Progress. I need to get in there.*

She revved her motorcycle, bolted out of the alley, and sped towards the hotel. From the opposite direction, a pair of police cars, sirens blaring, flew around the corner. They screeched to a stop in front of the hotel, silenced the sirens, and leapt from the cars. The four *gardiens de la paix* raced towards the entrance.

A third police car arrived as Talya was jumping from the bike. One officer joined the others inside, but one remained at the entrance. She pulled off the helmet, chestnut hair tumbling free. *Confidence is the key—just walk in like you own the place.* She stepped forward, but the officer blocked her path."

"Excuse me, officer." Talya's voice was calm but firm. "I have urgent business with a special guest at this hotel."

The officer's brow furrowed. "Who?"

Talya hesitated, leaning in. "I can't say. If word gets out, it'll cost me my job."

He crossed his arms. "No name, no entry."

Talya leaned in, whispering, "Isabella Marquez."

The officer's eyes widened. "She's here?"

"Trying to avoid the press. You understand."

"Yes, of course, but I'm under strict orders not to let anyone enter the building."

She placed a hand lightly on his shoulder, her voice softening. "Please. I really need this job."

The officer sighed, glancing toward the entrance. "Fine. But if anyone asks, you've been inside all morning."

A small smile flickered across her face—her relief masked by a playful wink. "All morning," she repeated and slipped inside.

Talya entered the lobby, and another transmission crackled through her earpiece.

Two confirmed fatalities. Both male.

Relief mixed with apprehension as she processed the update. *She's alive*, Talya thought. *Now, I need to see if she's injured.* Her eyes swept across the lobby, stopping at a familiar sight: Kate's messenger bag and the briefcase abandoned beneath the reception desk.

Approaching the young man in the hotel uniform, she glanced at his name tag. "Mark," she said, her voice low and urgent. "Those items—the messenger bag and briefcase—belong to my client. I need to deliver them to her immediately."

Mark hesitated, his eyes darting between Talya and the guest's abandoned items. "I... I'm not sure I can allow that, ma'am. With the police investigation ongoing..."

Talya fixed him with a piercing stare, "Listen to me carefully. Every second counts. You're going to tell me what room she is in, and I'm going to collect and deliver those items. She may be in danger, and it's my job to protect her."

"Like Mr. Vargas?"

"Yes, Mark," Talya said. "Exactly like Mr. Vargas. Now, what room is she in?"

The front desk clerk, surprised by Talya's intensity and massaging his sore wrist, simply nodded. "Alright. She's in the Opera Suite on the fifth floor. The police have secured the elevator, so I'm afraid you'll have to take the stairs."

Talya slipped Kate's messenger bag over her head and grabbed the briefcase and clothing. She spotted the police at the end of the hall, examining the elevator and taking notes. *No urgency*, she thought. *Whatever happened is over, but I still need to see her. And can't leave these things lying around.*

Floor by floor, Talya debated knocking. *Forest will be furious when he finds out I broke protocol. If he finds out—under the circumstances—will Kate cover for me?*

On reaching the fifth-floor stairwell landing, Talya took a moment to collect her thoughts, but whatever came next, there was no turning back now. She knocked on the Opera Suite door, heard footsteps, and a moment later, the door opened.

Kate opened the door, smirking. "Took you long enough." She pulled Talya into a quick hug. "Set that stuff anywhere."

"You knew?"

"Yeah, I knew. But don't take it personally. You and your team did a fantastic job."

"Then how?"

Kate smirked. "Forest is a terrible liar. There's no way he was OK with me coming back alone. But don't worry. For now, it's our secret. We'll deal with Forest later."

Talya dropped into a chair. "Thanks. Now, let's get down to business," she said, her tone shifting to professional concern. "You sound hoarse, and those bruises on your neck look nasty. Let me see if I can find some ice."

She wandered to the suite's bar, discovering a fully equipped kitchen, and returned a moment later with ice wrapped in a towel. "Try this."

Kate reclined on the couch, setting the towel against her neck with a sigh. "Feels good," she murmured. "I've got Arnica in my med kit—and concealer, of course—but this helps."

Talya gestured at Kate's neck. "From those bruises, I'm guessing he was a big guy. Where is he now?"

Kate's tone was dry. "End of the hall—or on the way to the morgue."

"Let me guess—Isabella Marquez?"

Kate raised an eyebrow. "How'd you know?"

"We saw her arrive with Vargas," Talya said. "Forest thought it might be a problem."

"It was," Kate admitted. "Awkward for a moment when I realized who she was, but when she signaled for help, none of that mattered."

"And the man with her?"

"Dead. Nothing I could do about that," Kate said and closed her eyes. "He got stuck in the elevator with the Armenian."

"Armenian?"

"I recognized the accent. What's their situation here in Paris?"

"Like elsewhere in Europe. Weapons. Prostitution. Robbery. For starters," Talya said. "So, a target like Marquez makes sense."

"He was in the elevator when the doors opened."

"And her security let her enter?"

"I know. Huge mistake, and maybe Isabella insisted, but he knew she'd be there."

"Set up?"

"No question—the timing's too perfect," Kate said. "But they didn't know I'd be there."

"Right person. Wrong place." Talya said. "You really should work on that."

They both laughed, and Kate coughed. "Ouch."

"Bruised ribs?"

"Yep," Kate said. "But for the record, I was in my apartment, sound asleep after a long flight. Heard nothing. Did nothing."

"And you expect the police to buy that Isabella Marquez killed someone? Something her protection detail couldn't do?"

"Yeah, I know how it sounds," Kate agreed. "But that's how Vargas wants to play it. Keeps me out of the press, which helps, and the evidence sort of works in her favor."

"What evidence?"

"The dead man has her Jimmy Choo stiletto heel in his brain."

Talya blinked. "You killed someone with a shoe?"

Kate's lips quirked into a smirk. "No. Isabella Marquez did."

"Copy that," Talya said, standing. "I should go. The team will want an update." She glanced back, a faint smile tugging at her lips. "Don't worry—I'll keep our little meeting off the record—for both our sakes."

Talya headed for the door and spotted the briefcase. "Forest said to remind you—you're not licensed..."

"I know," said Kate, cutting her off. "Don't get caught."

Chapter 12

HÔTEL DE POURTALÈS, PARIS, FRANCE

With Talya gone, Kate exhaled, taking in the suite. More apartment than hotel room—Parisian elegance fused with modern ease. High ceilings, open space. Room to breathe after the chaos.

Kate stepped onto the balcony, letting the city unfold. The Seine shimmered below, winding through Paris like a silver ribbon. In the distance, Notre-Dame, wrapped in scaffolding, still reached for the heavens.

Battered and scarred, Notre Dame endured, with restoration work gradually piecing the cathedral back together. Kate and Jake knew a thing or two about scars and loss and restoration. The videos of Notre Dame burning filled Kate with a profound sorrow, and most predicted she could never rise again. Looking at her now was inspiring. Each time tragedy struck, the French people responded with resilience and dedication.

Kate stepped back into the living room, adorned with a plush, cream-colored sofa, a sleek glass coffee table, and an intricately patterned area rug that added color to the warmth and comfort of the space. But what she wanted most was a long, hot bath.

She shed her travel-worn clothes, leaving them in a heap on the living room floor. *A pile of Kate.* The image of Jake teasing her or tripping over her clothes made her smile.

The lavish bathroom, a sanctuary of marble and gleaming chrome was larger than her first apartment. An oversized soaking tub dominated the room, an invitation to let go. She ran her fingers along the cool, smooth edge of the tub as she circled it, admiring the way the soft, recessed lighting played across the swirls of gray and white stone.

Kate twisted the polished taps, and a cascade of steaming water gushed forth, filling the basin. The hotel's custom blend of bath salts promised *relaxation and rejuvenation, a soothing balm for both body and spirit. Worth a shot,* she thought and added the salts to the water.

While the tub filled, Kate explored the rest of the bathroom's amenities. A huge, glass-enclosed shower dominated one wall, its rainfall shower head and multiple body jets offering a tantalizing alternative to the bath. Plush towels hung from heated racks, ready to enfold her in their warm embrace.

The vanity stretched along another wall, a vast expanse of veined marble topped with double sinks and a generous array of luxurious toiletries. Kate recognized some brands. *What? No Bella Beauty products,* Kate thought and smiled. *Isabella is going to have to work on that.*

Kate settled into the tub, wincing as the movement pulled her bruised ribs and the water struck the other minor cuts and scrapes, but the heart of the fragrance bloomed. Soft notes of lavender wove through the steam, mingling with the clean, slightly medicinal scent of eucalyptus. The combination was comforting and began working its subtle magic.

She let her head fall back against the edge of the tub, the aroma of the bath salts wrapping around her like an invisible, fragrant cocoon. The bright, uplifting citrus and soothing lavender calmed her racing thoughts, while eucalyptus and frankincense eased the day's physical trials.

The tears came without warning. Kate wiped them away, hearing Major Carter's voice: *Tears cleanse the soul.* The Major, the Casualty Assistance Officer at Dover and a widow, understood Kate's loss better than most and the journey of grief and bone-deep loneliness.

"This is how it will be," the Major whispered in Kate's ear. *"It springs from deep inside, and often when you least expect it, but my husband always said tears cleanse the soul."*

The tears retreated, and in the warm, scented embrace of the bath, Kate's burdens seemed to recede, if only for a moment. She drew a deep breath, filling her lungs with the bath's layered fragrance—citrus bright, lavender soft, eucalyptus sharp—and felt some small part of herself begin to uncoil and prepare to face whatever lay ahead.

Wrapped in a plush hotel robe, her hair turbaned in a soft towel, Kate tilted her head, examining the bruises in the mirror. "Not too bad," she murmured. A wry smile tugged at her lips. "If I can hide my scars, I can hide anything."

Padding back into the bedroom, she tossed her suitcase onto the bed. She pulled on leggings, cozy socks, and one of Jake's old Chick's Oyster Bar t-shirts—an XL that swallowed her. When he was away, she wore his shirts to wrap herself in his scent, his warmth. Now, they were hers—and wearing them helped keep him close.

She placed a lunch order with room service, opting for a Caesar salad and a club sandwich with fries, and hoped the meal would arrive sooner than the hour they estimated. *I should have ordered then bathed,* she thought. *Too late now, but I can use the time.*

Kate unlatched the briefcase and went to work. The Glock 43X—threaded barrel, suppressor, red dot sight. A smooth cycle check. Locked slide. Satisfied, she set it aside.

"No Glocks on the table," Kate said with a wistful smile. It was a running joke she shared with Jake and a familiar sight in their home.

She turned her attention to the smaller Glock 43, deciding to leave the stock barrel in place for now. While the suppressor likely wouldn't be necessary, Kate wanted to have the option. She ran through the same function test as before, locking the slide back when finished.

With the weapons check and setup complete, she headed for the bedroom to unpack. *First things first,* she thought and retrieved the packing cube with her lingerie. Her lingerie bag had the essentials for the trip—comfortable sports bras and boy shorts, a full suite of La Perla pieces in shades that matched the fashion choices she packed, and a collection of Glock holsters.

Knowing that Vitali would secure everything she requested, Kate brought the holsters she knew would work with the outfits she planned. Packing them with her underwear was a calculated choice, and considering the surprise immigration inspection, it was also effective.

Back in the living room, with a pair of holsters, Kate began loading and securing the weapons. She started with the Glock 43, her preferred carry gun. Retrieving a six-round magazine from the briefcase, she pressed her thumb against the top round, confirming the magazine's condition. She inserted the magazine into the gun and released the slide. With a round chambered, she topped off the magazine. "Six plus one," she said, satisfied with the weapon's condition.

Kate chose the Kydex Fabriclip holster and slid the 43 into place, the distinctive click of the Kydex signaling a secure fit. She positioned the holster inside the waistband of her leggings, appendix carry style, and locked the fabric clip in place. With a slow, partial draw, she confirmed she could easily lift her shirt, grip the gun, and have the holster remain securely in place. A final check in the mirror and a tug on Jake's shirt verified the weapon was well-concealed for the evening.

Happy now, she thought, imaging Jake smiling and nodding. The concealed carry life was a carefully considered choice, and it was her choice. *There are no safe places, Jake would say.* And she learned he was right. Self-reliance became a way of life. When Kate was dressed, she was armed, but she also understood the limitations. *If it's not in your hand, it's not your primary weapon.* Their training time pushed well beyond firearms. Kate loved every minute she spent with Jake—grappling, punching, kicking, even the bruises and blood, both hers and his, were badges of honor.

Her tummy rumbled, and she glanced at the wall clock. *It's only been thirty minutes,* she thought. *I don't think I can survive another thirty. I better see what I can find in the kitchen.* But the knock on the door was the answer to a prayer. *Oh, thank God. I'm starving.* She welcomed the service trolley and could smell the French fries.

The young woman who brought the food offered to set the dining room table, but Kate declined. "Just leave the cart," she said. "And I'll serve myself. Do I need to sign something?"

"No, Madame. It is all arranged."

"Merci beaucoup," Kate replied, and the server departed.

The moment Kate was alone, she plowed into the food. She popped a fry into her mouth, savoring the salty crunch. "These are fantastic," she said, reaching for another. "I guess I needed the carbs."

With the food problem solved, Kate thought about priorities. *I need Nomad,* she thought and calculated the time in New York. *Seven-thirty? Way too early for that boy. I'll just let him know we need to talk and to ping me when he's up.*

***

4:57 PM CEST

KATE REVIEWED HER NOTES for the meeting with Deputy Director Boucher. She expected a battle and developed a plan of attack. There were things she knew about the Le Cafe Pierre attack and about Jake's death—things Boucher didn't know and could change the course of his investigation. And there's likely to be evidence, some collected at the scene, more collected through street cameras, Kate wanted to examine—if she could convince Boucher that it was in his best interest to collaborate.

The knock on the door was soft but shocking. Kate set aside her tablet and approached the door. Her right hand firmly gripping the Glock tucked in her waist. She stayed clear of the door and peephole, opting for cover near the door's hinges. "Qui est-ce?" Kate asked in French to find out who was at her door.

"It's Bella," came the English reply. "May I come in?"

"This isn't a good time," Kate said. "I was just doing some work for an important meeting tomorrow, and I'm not exactly dressed for company."

"Please," Isabella said, her voice trembling slightly. "I promise I won't stay long."

Kate's fingers relaxed on the grip of the gun as she leaned against the wall, debating. Then Isabella added, almost sheepishly, "I brought wine." Kate couldn't help but smile and noted the time, *Well, it's almost wine-o'clock,* she thought. *Why not?*

She opened the door, surprised to find Isabella Marquez looked nothing like the glamorous celebrity she'd seen in the elevator or in countless magazines and red-carpet events.

Gone were the designer clothing, sky-high heels, and even the impeccably styled hair synonymous with Isabella's public persona.

Instead, the woman standing at Kate's door dressed for comfort, her long, dark hair pulled back in a simple, loose ponytail that cascaded down her back. She wore a pair of soft, heather-gray sweatpants that hung comfortably on her hips and a simple, white cotton t-shirt, loose and relaxed.

Relief at Bella's casual appearance prompted a warm and understanding smile. Kate stepped aside, inviting Isabella into the suite. *She's just a person,* Kate thought. *Who's been through hell and wants to be comfortable and safe. I get it.*

Isabella headed straight for the bar, obviously familiar with the apartment's layout. *She's been in this suite before,* Kate thought. *Over the years of dodging fans and the press, she's probably stayed in most of these suites.*

"What's on the menu?" Kate asked, joining Isabella at the bar.

Isabella held up the bottle, inspecting the label. "2015 Domaine de la Romanée-Conti La Tâche. Ever had it?"

Kate shook her head, a small smile playing on her lips. "Not this one, but it's hard to go wrong with a French Burgundy."

With two glasses poured, Isabella raised her glass and offered a toast, "To better days."

Kate tapped her glass against Isabella's. "To better days," she echoed. "And the greatest good. Let's sit down."

As they moved toward the couch, Kate spotted the pile of clothes on the floor and hurried to gather them.

"Oh, please," Isabella said, waving a dismissive hand. "You should see my apartment. I couldn't get out of my clothes fast enough and into a bath. It took me an hour—and a Xanax—to stop shaking."

Carrying the bottle, Isabella followed Kate into the living room. They sank into opposite corners of the couch, each tucking a foot beneath them. To a stranger, they might have looked like old friends savoring a moment together.

After a sip of wine, Isabella tilted her head, curiosity bright in her eyes. "What's the 'Greatest Good'?"

Kate paused, her fingers tracing the rim of her glass. *The elephant in the room,* she thought. *Better to face it head-on.*

"It's something Jake and I used to say," Kate began. Her voice softened, each word measured. "I don't remember when or where it started, but it became part of every toast." She hesitated, her voice catching. "And we sealed it with a kiss."

Isabella's smile faded. "I'm sorry," she said.

"It's OK. I enjoy remembering and celebrating our life together. The Greatest Good is an acknowledgment that we never know what lies ahead, so we wish for whatever is the greatest goodness for those we toast."

"That's so sweet," she said, topping off both glasses, but just beneath the surface, Kate could see the emotion building.

Isabella cleared her throat and wiped away the tear slipping down her cheek. Her voice softened. "I'm sorry about Jake. And for the pain I caused you both."

Kate met her gaze, her voice steady. "It's alright. Truly."

"I've regretted my stupidity ever since that day, and when I saw the news...when I saw what Jake did in Paris, I realized I would never have the chance to say I'm sorry or thank him."

"Thank him?" Kate asked, curious if there was more to the incident than she knew.

"My third, and I might add, last marriage was in trouble," Isabella said. "In the still moments between press briefings and photo shoots, Jake and I would talk—a thoughtful listener—and a perfect gentleman." She closed her eyes for a moment. "I still remember how his face lit up when he talked about you. I'd never seen a man love like that. The way I wanted to be loved."

Kate's tone was measured but curious. "Then why the kiss? Publicity stunt? Or were you hoping for something else?"

Isabella nearly choked on her wine, shaking her head emphatically. "More? With Jake? Not a chance. His heart was all yours. But I did hope my husband might step up. Instead, he stepped out."

"Good riddance," Kate said, raising her glass in a mock toast.

Isabella matched the gesture. "Agreed," she said, a faint smile softening her expression. "Your husband gave me an incredible gift. An insight into what love should be—what it could be—and I've never looked back."

Kate hesitated—her voice soft but sure. "Jake had a way of touching lives. I don't think he ever really understood just how much." She paused, her gaze dropping to her glass. "He changed my life...and in some ways, he still is."

For a moment, silence filled the space between them, heavy with unspoken understanding.

"Are you hungry?" Isabella asked, breaking the quiet. "The food's quite good."

"The fries are fantastic," Kate noted and smiled. She sensed Isabella didn't want to be alone. Not yet. "Let me grab the menu. We'll get something ordered and have them bring up another bottle."

"I'd like that."

Over dinner and a second bottle of wine, Kate got a crash course in celebrity life—feeding the social media beast, the games, the illusion. She discovered Bella, as her friends called her, was much more than stardom and accolades. As an entrepreneur, her Bella Beauty products were a phenomenon and funded her foundation's global charitable efforts.

"What's life like in Hollywood?" Kate asked.

Isabella laughed. "Hollywood? I left those fruitcakes years ago."

Kate nearly spit out her wine. "That was not the answer I was expecting. All of your products, and yes, I use your moisturizer, list the headquarters as

Hollywood, CA."

"Marketing, my dear. Who wants to buy beauty products from Montana?"

"You live in Montana?"

"It gets worse," she said and smiled. "I live on a ranch, and I have a second home in Tennessee. Of course, I travel more than I'd like. That's partly why I wanted to come see you—I'd like you to come with me."

"Come where?"

Bella offered an apologetic smile. "Sorry. My brain's running ahead of my mouth. I'm in Paris for a few days handling promotion and distribution deals, then I'm off to Motapa."

Kate nodded, her expression thoughtful. "Beautiful country. Once." Memories from her CIA days flickered through her mind—rebel factions, military coups, despots. "Decades of unrest tore it apart. Poverty, corruption, crime—it's been a long road back."

"That's the point of the trip," Bella noted. "The new President is a good man, elected fairly by a burgeoning democracy. Now, he's trying to rebuild after decades of decline, and my foundation is helping with new schools and teacher training."

"That's fantastic," Kate said. "I hope he can survive the inevitable political turmoil and global pressure." *And assassination attempts,* Kate thought but kept that to herself.

"I pray he can survive," Bella said. "That's why I'm going. I hope to put a spotlight on him, his country, people, and mission—especially the children. But I'd be lying if I said wasn't concerned, and after today, I'm terrified."

Kate leaned forward, her tone serious. "I won't sugarcoat it—a trip like that is risky. But Vargas is solid, and his team knows what they're doing."

Bella hesitated, then asked, "Can I tell you something in confidence?"

"Yes, of course."

"I think Sebastian is having financial difficulty," Bella said. "I know he recently sold his home. And this trip was the first, in all the years we've worked together, where he asked if I could pay him in advance. He explained it away, but he was clearly anxious that I agree. I didn't mind. Every business has its challenges, and I was happy to help."

"That is unusual," Kate agreed. "But a trip of this magnitude would have extraordinary expenses and staffing requirements."

"He thinks I should cancel."

"I'm not surprised," Kate said. "You're a high-profile target, and the publicity around your visit will alert every rebel and criminal in the country. Honestly, that's an executive protection nightmare."

"And exactly why I'd love to have you by my side," Bella said. "I've seen what you can do."

"I'm sorry," Kate began. "I have pressing commitments here in Paris, and even if I could go, I doubt Vargas would approve."

Bella laughed, her tone light but insistent. "Forget Vargas. I'm the boss, and you'd be coming as my guest."

Kate opened her mouth to refuse, but Isabella cut her off, her eyes pleading. "Don't say no. Not yet. We leave Saturday. Just...think about it."

Kate forced a small smile. "I'll think about it."

It was a lie.

She walked Bella to the door. The close protection operator was waiting, scanning the hallway with professional vigilance.

Then, as Bella stepped into the hall, she turned back.

She wrapped her arms around Kate and, in the embrace, whispered, "Jake was right. You are a remarkable woman."

Bella pulled away, her hands on Kate's shoulders, her eyes locking on hers. "And I owe you my life."

Kate watched her disappear down the hall, but the words lingered.

"Jake was right."

Her fingers tightened around the doorframe.

Jake had been right about a lot of things.

And this time, it got him killed.

Chapter 13

NOMAD'S FORTRESS, MANHATTAN, NY

Nomad maneuvered his chair around the spacious, adapted bathroom and directly under the sink. The hum of the electric toothbrush echoed off the concrete walls, and with a subtle flick of his wrist, he guided the brush to the sink, the minty foam swirling down the drain. The sounds of Nomad starting his day prompted Keisha to announce that she was available to assist.

"Need the razor?" Keisha called from the kitchen, her voice carrying over the hum of his chair.

Nomad glanced at his reflection, noting the shadow of stubble on his jaw. *Yeah, pretty ragged,* he thought. *Not today.*

"No time," he responded, and his exit from the bathroom tripped the motion sensor. The lights dimmed, and the bedroom lights went off as he rolled into the kitchen. "I've got work to do."

His smart chair, a marvel of his own design, glided across the floor, its oversized, all-terrain wheels effortlessly navigating the rugs Keisha insisted on adding. The rugs, along with a handful of carefully chosen comfort items, softened the otherwise cold and sterile former parking garage.

Keisha stood near his workstation, her arms crossed, an eyebrow raised. "You missed breakfast. And lunch. What kept you up so late?"

"Work."

"And what's so important that you're not eating or sleeping?" she asked.

"It's a surprise."

"If it's for Kate, tread lightly," Keisha said. "That girl's been through enough and heading back to Paris is going to be hard."

"I know, but I can help."

"And the last time you helped, you nearly got her killed."

"This is different," Nomad said. "I've been digging through Jake's files..."

"Hang on. How did you get a copy of Jake's files?"

"Kate asked for help with a little Bitcoin banking—the files were sitting right there—after everything she went through to get them..."

Keisha's eyes narrowed. "You made a backup? And now you're digging into the most precious and private thing she owns?"

"You're making me sound like a creep."

"Because you are!"

"It's not like that," Nomad said. "Moore's files are encrypted and some of Jake's files are corrupt. She can't see them or read them, anyway, not yet. What if I can? They might be important."

"Are those the only files you've touched?" she asked, but before Nomad could answer, he spotted Kate's message.

"I don't have time for this," Nomad said. "Looks like Kate needs to talk. And she wouldn't reach out if it wasn't important."

***

8:25 PM CEST

KATE WAS SLIPPING INTO bed when Nomad's encrypted video chat popped up on her tablet. She accepted the call, "Are you just now getting up?" she asked. "Another all-nighter?"

"Something like that. What's up?"

"This is big," Kate said, leaning closer to the screen. "Time-sensitive. Someone sent drone footage—anonymously—to a KATIM phone."

Nomad blinked. "That's...not possible."

"But someone did," Kate said. "I saw it, and I have the phone."

"Wow. This is uncharted territory," Nomad said. "So, you need to know who sent it, and I'd like to figure out how they did it."

"There's more," Kate added, her voice tightening. "The drone's weaponized. It obliterates the vehicle it's tracking."

Nomad's voice dropped. "And the people inside?"

"Never had a chance."

"I'm guessing you knew someone in the vehicle."

"Yes," Kate said. "Someone I used to trust. And now they're dead."

"I'm sorry," Nomad said. "I'll do whatever I can, and as fast as I can, but this one won't be trivial."

Kate nodded, her tone softening. "I know the drill—no promises. Just do what you can."

"What are you thinking?"

"The soundtrack's gone, and that might not be the only manipulation."

"OK. I'll need you to dedicate your Linux tablet to the connection," he said. "I'll walk you through the setup. Hopefully, I can collect what I need remotely, but there's only one way to find out."

***

3:14 PM EDT

Nomad linked to Kate's tablet and pulled up the drone footage.

Kate was right—someone had edited it. Not just the soundtrack.

He fed it into his servers, looping it frame by frame.

"Is that real?" Keisha asked, watching the SUV explode into a ball of bright white light.

"Yes," he said. "Kate would like me..."

"Lord, not again," Keisha muttered. Her voice sharpened. "Kate's okay, right?"

"She's fine and wasn't anywhere near the explosion."

"Thank God," Keisha said. "But asking you to have a look means she's involved somehow, isn't she?"

"Someone she knew was in the car," Nomad said quietly. "I think she feels responsible."

"Did you tell her about Jake's files?"

"Not the right time," Nomad muttered.

Keisha folded her arms. "Make time. Or I will."

***

9:00 PM CEST

KATE SET A BEDTIME target and was glad it finally arrived. The challenge with significant time zone travel is to stay awake the first day, but it's the fastest way to reset the body clock. Today was uniquely challenging, given the sprint up the stairs and the adrenaline surge of fighting for her life. Even after the bath and the wine, there was still a faint electric buzz she couldn't quite shake.

Kate curled onto her side, propping her iPad on the pillow.

I need to see him.

She was grateful she'd recorded their calls—despite Jake's complaints.

"Recording again?" Jake teased.

"Yes, smart ass. Some of us miss our spouses."

Jake smirked. "You're right. I'm sorry."

Kate grinned. "Nice. That's my new ringtone."

For all his mock protests, Kate was shocked to find Jake's NanoVault had copies of *her* recordings. *That little liar*, she thought. *He loved to watch them as much as I do.* Scrolling through his list, she landed on the one she knew was his favorite—because it was hers, too. Jake had been on assignment with the Trident Security team, escorting a Texas oil executive across the Middle East. By the time they arrived in Dubai, he was ready to say goodnight.

The FaceTime call had found Kate working in the backyard. She was wearing a simple cotton tank and shorts, hair pulled back in a ponytail, tucked through the back of a ball cap to keep it off her neck. She had sprinted to grab the phone, still sweaty from the heat, a dirt smudge across her cheek.

Kate smiled every time she played this video—both because of how disheveled she looked and because of the way Jake looked at her.

"Hey, Gorgeous," Jake said, his grin lighting up the screen as his head sank into the hotel pillow.

Kate laughed, brushing her hand across her forehead. "Gorgeous? You sure? I look like something the cat dragged in."

Jake's eyes lit up, studying Kate's face. "Trust me. You're beautiful. That smile lights up your face, and in the sunlight, I can see the gold flecks in your eyes. That face is the first thing I want to see every day and the last every night."

Kate rolled her eyes playfully. "You've got to be kidding. I've seen the women in Dubai. Lounging on beach chairs, strutting through those glitzy nightclubs. And then there's me—the ragamuffin." She pointed to her disheveled hair and rumpled T-shirt.

Jake chuckled, shaking his head. "My ragamuffin," he laughed. "If only you could see what I see. You'd know just how beautiful you really are."

Kate's teasing smile softened. "It's OK," she said quietly. "I see the way you look at me—that's all I need."

Jake's mischievous eyes twinkled. "Hey you, my eyes are up here," he teased.

"Busted," Kate laughed, her tone lightening again. "But what did you expect? Bare-chested, bedroom eyes—you look like the cover of a Spicy Romance novel."

"When I get back," Jake said, his grin widening, "I'll show you how the story ends."

"Alright," Kate teased, her eyes sparkling. "But I'm expecting plot twists—and a surprise ending." They laughed together, the warmth of the moment filling the space between them.

For a few minutes, they talked about the mission, how things were going, and her life at the law firm. Kate could have talked for hours—and sometimes they did—but she knew Jake needed sleep.

"Love me?" she asked.

"I adore you," Jake replied.

"I know. I can feel it," Kate said with a smile. "But you know what I want to hear."

"I will always love you."

"There we go," she said, smirking. "Funny how you know just what to say—once I tell you."

"Sweet dreams, my love," Jake murmured, blowing her a kiss through the screen. Kate smiled softly. "Sweet dreams."

Kate lingered on the last frame—Jake's smile frozen in time.

Her hand hovered, then closed the screen.

A single tear slipped onto the pillow.

She closed her eyes, holding on to him until sleep took her.

Chapter 14

WEDNESDAY, APRIL 29th
1:00 AM CEST

HÔTEL DE POURTALÈS, PARIS, FRANCE

Sebastian Vargas slipped out the rear entrance of the Hôtel de Pourtalès. The metal door slamming behind him as the cool night air struck his face. A nervous pat to his jacket pocket—Isabella's bracelet was still there.

Vargas scanned the deserted street, hands unsteady as he lit a cigarette. The first drag didn't help. The smoke burned, mixing with the bitter taste of fear.

I'm so screwed, he thought. *These Armenians aren't known for their forgiving nature. Hopefully, the bracelet will be enough to keep his fingers.*

Exhaling, a plume of smoke rising above his head, Vargas scanned his surroundings. *No curious onlookers,* he thought. *No sign of a tail.* Satisfied that he was alone, he slunk into the alleyway and disappeared into the shadows.

A single yellow bulb flickered at the far end, barely cutting the gloom. Stone walls loomed, streaked with faded graffiti. The air stank of piss and rotting garbage.

Vargas swallowed hard, fighting the urge to vomit.

Halfway down the alley, they stepped from the shadows. Two hulking figures.

Vargas's heart lurched. His hand twitched toward his gun.

"Easy, Vargas," a gravelly voice rumbled from the shadows. "Don't do anything you'll regret."

Vargas forced his hand to relax, letting it fall to his side. "Narek." Vargas forced the name out, his tone wavering despite his effort to sound calm. "Didn't expect you to show up in person."

Narek stepped forward, his craggy face carved from shadow and light—skeletal, unreadable.

"Mr. Sarkesian is displeased," Narek said flatly. "Extremely."

Vargas forced himself to stand straighter. "No one was supposed to get hurt."

"Your man put up a fight," Narek said, his voice sharp with accusation. "That was a mistake. Your mistake. And now we're down a man—and the boss wants answers."

"There were...complications," Vargas muttered, swallowing hard. "But I've got something to make things right. It's valuable." He reached into his pocket, his fingers closing around the cool metal of the bracelet.

A fist slammed into Vargas's gut. Air vanished. He doubled over, wheezing—then was yanked up and smashed into the wall.

"Complications?" Narek snarled, his face inches from Vargas's, his features contorted with rage. "You promised us an easy score. Instead, we've got a dead man and a world of trouble."

"The bracelet," Vargas wheezed, fumbling for his pocket. "It's worth ten thousand, easy. Take it, and I swear I'll make this right."

Narek plucked the glittering bauble from Vargas's pocket, the gems glinting even in the meager light. He examined it for a moment, then pocketed it with a grunt. "Pretty," he admitted. "But hardly worth the mess you've made."

The second Armenian loomed closer, a massive silhouette in the dim light. Vargas felt a cold sweat break out along his spine. "Please," Vargas blurted, desperation cracking his voice. "I can fix this. Just give me a chance. I swear I won't let you down."

Narek considered him for a long, agonizing moment. Then, with a curt nod to his companion, he released his grip on Vargas's shirt.

"One more chance, Vargas." Narek's voice dropped, each word deliberate. "But if you screw this up, we'll take you to the catacombs. Deep into the cold, dark tunnels where the rats are always hungry. First, we'll take your fingers. One by one. Then, your toes. And let the rats feast on your bleeding stumps." He leaned in, his breath hot against Vargas's ear. "By the time we're done, there won't be enough left to identify."

He stepped back, his eyes glinting with malice. "So, what's it going to be, Vargas?" Narek asked, his voice low and venomous. "A bullet here and now—or one last chance? Fail again, and you'll be just another set of bones in the Paris underground."

"I...I can fix this," Vargas stammered, his voice barely above a whisper.

The Armenians melted back into the shadows.

Vargas slid down the wall, legs useless, ribs screaming. His pulse hammered.

A gust of wind funneled through the alley, carrying the stench of rot and urine. He coughed, spitting bile onto the pavement.

The weight of the warning settled in. The cold, the darkness, the rats.

Somewhere in the distance, a siren wailed.

Vargas wiped his mouth with a shaking hand and forced himself to stand.

He needed to move—and fast.

Chapter 15

WEDNESDAY, APRIL 29th
8:00 AM CEST

DGSI HEADQUARTERS, PARIS, FRANCE

KATE PREPARED FOR HER meeting with the Deputy Director Boucher by thinking through what to wear and what to bring. Like Langley, she knew the DGSI's (Direction Générale de la Sécurité Intérieure) building security would be tight and classified. But simple precautions were easy to anticipate.

Kate swapped her messenger bag for a sleek Kate Spade cross-body—perfect for high-security meetings. Essentials only: phone, wallet, passport. Lipstick, compact, hairbrush—harmless. Notepad and pen? Risky, but she'd take the chance.

Kate suspected they'd have a modern body scanner and wanted to ensure she didn't trigger any alarms. A simple leather band watch replaced her smartwatch, and pearl studs were the only jewelry. Her leather flats were attractive shoes and matched the tailored slacks and blazer but with no extraneous metal. A quick look in the mirror revealed the missing item. The cream-colored silk blouse sitting atop the La Perla camisole was lovely, but a light silk scarf added the finishing touch.

She stepped out of the sedan in front of the DGSI's unmarked headquarters. No signage. Cameras discreetly placed. Bollards. Reinforced entry.

Yeah, this is the place.

She entered the main door and approached the security desk. A single security officer sat behind a wall of thick bullet-proof glass. Two more men, in full tactical gear and armament, held the corners of the small room. As requested, Kate slid her passport through the slot to the man behind the glass. He ran the passport through a scanner while confirming her appointment with the Deputy Director.

Having passed the first gauntlet, the security officer pressed a button. Kate heard the distinct buzz of a magnetic lock and entered the screening area. The minute she was inside, the lock reengaged. *Trapped between two layers of hardened security,* she thought. *If my body was some kind of chemical explosive, they'd just have to wipe me off the walls.* Then she spotted the floor drain and smiled. *Or just hose them off.*

Kate set her bag on the scanner belt and stepped into the L3 ProVision body scanner.

Arms raised. Low hum. Two seconds.

Green light flashed—cleared.

She retrieved her bag and a claim check for her phone and pen.

They're not taking any chances.

An unarmed security officer led Kate through the corridors. Jake's voice echoed in her head: *If they're not armed, they're not security.* She smirked and kept walking.

They walked through wide, well-lit corridors, passing various secured doors and checkpoints. The hallway's minimalist decor focused on functionality over aesthetics. As they walked, Kate noticed the subtle presence of plainclothes agents, a reminder of the building's purpose.

When they reached an elevator, the escort used an access card to select the top floor. The ride up was swift and silent, the officer maintaining a professional stance and demeanor. When the elevator doors opened, Kate was met by a gentleman in a dark gray suit. In French, the young man thanked the guard and then turned to Kate, "This way, ma'am," he said in perfect English.

Kate thought it best not to shatter his illusion that she only spoke English. "Thank you."

He directed Kate to a seat in the beautifully decorated outer office area, and he returned to the desk just outside the Deputy Director's office door. *Ah, he's the executive assistant,* Kate realized. *I'm surprised Boucher didn't tell him I speak French.* Kate noted the time. As planned, she was five minutes early, but she expected to wait no matter how early she arrived. The showmanship of office politics and authority was similar the world over, and there was no reason to assume it would be any different at the DGSI.

***

9:00 AM CEST
LA DÉFENSE BUSINESS DISTRICT

BEN SHEPARD'S CORNER OFFICE, on the 35th floor of Coeur Défense complex, had breathtaking views of the city skyline and the iconic Arc de Triomphe. The office reflected his value to the Global Economic Council and served a purpose. Officially, the GEC leveraged Ben's decades in clandestine services to provide intelligence and guidance in their many international endeavors, but whispers in the hallways suggested he was something more. No one quite knew what Ben's position entailed, but he had a reputation for solving problems quickly and quietly.

He checked his watch. *She's inside by now*, he thought. *And her electronics are secure.* With a satisfied nod, he made his way down the hallway to Vivek's office.

In contrast to Ben's sleek, light-filled workspace, Vivek's was a windowless, tech-driven world. An array of computers, monitors, and diagnostic equipment cast an eerie glow across the space. He was wearing his signature lab coat and headlamp—the same outfit he wore at the airport—and hunched over his workstation.

When Ben entered, Vivek glanced up. "Is it time?"

Ben gave a curt nod. "Alright. Show-time." One by one, Vivek connected to the micro-miniature tracking and monitoring devices idling inside Kate's devices. Her phone was the first to connect. One of the monitors in his office displayed a city map and a slow, strobing, green light identifying Kate's location at the DGSI building.

"Can you pull up recent history?"

"Sure," Vivek replied, and with a few swift keystrokes, the monitor painted a sequence of starts and stops and connected lines. "Here's the airport and the drive into the city. That's the Ukrainian Embassy. And then the hotel. That brings us to this morning's trip to the DGSI."

Another monitor lit up as the tracking devices in Kate's pair of tablets came online. The iPad was inactive and charging, but the Linux tablet was active and connected to the Internet.

Ben's voice sharpened. "Why is it gibberish? A broken sensor?"

Vivek shook his head. "No. Tracker's fine. Tablet's online—encrypted connection."

"So we can't see who she's talking to?"

"Not yet. Let me try—"

Ben scoffed. "Don't bother. We can count on Preacher using military-grade encryption."

"That appears to be the case."

"She's up to something," Ben muttered, his tone dark. "And she's not working alone."

Vivek hesitated. "What does that mean for us?"

Ben's jaw tightened. "It means if I can't rein her in, Grant will shut her down—his way."

***

9:10 AM CEST
DGSI HEADQUARTERS

"The Deputy Director will see you now," the young man said, standing to open the door for Kate.

"Good morning, Mrs. Preacher," the Deputy Director began. "I am Deputy Director Adrien Gaillard."

Kate fought to hide her surprise. A tall, distinguished gentleman with salt-and-pepper hair and a neatly trimmed beard rose from his chair and stepped out from behind an impressive dark walnut desk. As the man approached Kate, she noticed he moved with the effortless grace and confidence of someone accustomed to authority. He extended his hand, a warm smile on his face.

"I know you were expecting Mr. Boucher, but he is currently on leave," Adrien said. "Only temporary, I'm sure. But as you have come all this way, I didn't want to cancel the meeting."

Kate shook Adrien's hand, noting his expensive, well-tailored suit and the glint of a gold watch peeking out from beneath his cuff. Everything about Adrien Gaillard exuded an air of refinement, wealth, and power, from his impeccable appearance to his commanding presence. *Boucher was a serious investigator,* Kate thought. *This guy is window-dressing. Someone they brought in to distract me.*

As they exchanged pleasantries, Kate couldn't help but wonder about the reason for the sudden staff change. She made a mental note to have Vitali press his contacts for information on Boucher's absence as she assessed Adrien Gaillard and the role he might play in her mission.

The surrounding office reflects its occupant: elegant, understated, and filled with an unmistakable sense of purpose. Walls lined with bookshelves filled with weighty tomes on history, politics, and international relations, interspersed with a few carefully chosen works of art. *This is Boucher's office,* she thought. *Whatever happened was so fast, this guy hasn't yet redecorated.*

Kate took a seat in one of the plush, leather-upholstered chairs in front of the desk with a mix of anticipation and uncertainty. The plan for Boucher included trading facts and evidence she had for access to whatever he had collected. But everything just changed. *As they say in battle,* Kate thought. *No plan survives first contact.* And the little voice in her head was screaming. *You can't trust him. Don't reveal anything.*

"Mrs. Preacher," Adrien said, his tone smooth and polite. "How may I assist you?"

"Please, call me Kate," she replied, her tone warm but deliberate. "May I call you Adrien?"

"Yes, of course," he said. "Now, Kate, you've come all this way. And returning could not have been easy. What were you hoping to learn from Monsieur Boucher?"

"Honestly, at our first meeting, things were, shall we say, a bit tense."

"So, I understand."

"Maybe we can start fresh," Kate suggested, her voice calm but probing.

Adrien's lips curved into a polished smile. "Of course."

"I believe people still consider the tragedy at Le Cafe Pierre a terrorist attack."

"Yes, that's true," Adrien said. "No one imagines it could be anything else."

"Has anyone credible claimed responsibility?" Kate asked, watching him closely.

Adrien's smile didn't falter. "Too many to count, unfortunately."

Liar, Kate thought. *No serious player would touch this.*

"We continue to investigate, naturally," Adrien continued. "But we may never know who was responsible."

"Adrien, as your predecessor knew, I'm a nationally known digital forensic expert."

"Yes, I am aware of your capabilities and expertise."

"I was hoping..." Kate began. "That is...I was thinking you might want..."

"Mrs. Preacher," Adrien interrupted, dropping the pretense of familiarity. "We have our best people examining a veritable mountain of digital evidence. They do not require assistance."

"Of course," Kate said. "I didn't mean to suggest that they did or to step on anyone's toes. I was just offering..."

"Allowing the spouse of a victim to join an active investigation," Adrien said smoothly, "would be entirely inappropriate. I assure you, Deputy Director Boucher would agree. Our hands are tied." Adrien stood and asked, "Now, if there's nothing further?"

The meeting was over.

Kate was no closer to the truth than when she was on the street.

She rose to leave, keeping her movements unhurried. Controlled. But every nerve in her body was on edge.

As she stepped into the hallway, the young assistant smiled politely. Kate returned the expression, but inside, her mind raced.

Boucher had agreed to this meeting. Now he was gone.

Coincidence?

Or a warning?

Kate moved toward the exit, resisting the urge to look over her shoulder. She needed answers. And she wasn't leaving Paris without them.

Chapter 16

WEDNESDAY, APRIL 29th
10:15 AM CEST

LE CAFE PIERRE, PARIS, FRANCE

KATE LEFT THE DGSI headquarters, her frustration simmering just beneath the surface, angry she allowed herself to hope. *Petty bureaucrats*, she thought. *That was stupid, Kate. You know better. Why did I imagine this might be different? Boucher!* She realized it was Boucher's enthusiastic acceptance of her meeting request that gave her hope. *Was that a ploy*, she wondered. *If so, why the sudden departure?*

She wandered and walked the streets of Paris, her mind churning, her feet carrying her almost unconsciously towards the one place she planned to avoid—until she was ready.

From a distance, the café looked so normal, inviting. The cheerful red awning fluttered in the breeze. Round tables and wicker chairs stretched out to the sidewalk. If not for the makeshift memorial, the sea of flowers, cards, and photos, you would never guess this had been the scene of unimaginable horror and death just two weeks ago.

Kate took a deep breath, steeling herself, and crossed the street. The clatter of dishes and the hum of conversation washed over her as she approached. She chose a table at the edge of the seating area, as far from the memorial as possible, and sank into a chair.

A young waitress appeared at her elbow. "Bonjour, madame. Que puis-je vous servir aujourd'hui?" *What can I serve you today?*

Her voice was gentle, her smile warm, but Kate recognized the sadness lingering in her eyes. Kate saw it every time she looked in the mirror. *Was she working that day,* Kate wondered. *Perhaps she's grieving for friends or questioning why she's alive.* Surviving is a burden that few understand, but Kate did.

"Un double espresso, s'il vous plaît," *A double espresso, please,* Kate replied.

The waitress turned to go, and Kate glimpsed the name tag pinned to her apron. *Janine.*

Could she be, Kate wondered. *Is that Jean-Paul's wife?* Two weeks earlier, when Kate arrived in Paris, she needed a way into the L'institut médico-légal, the Paris morgue. Given the magnitude of the attack and the number of dead, the main entrance was total chaos. Just as it had been following the Bataclan attack.

After Bataclan, for many families, it took days—agonizing, endless days—to see and identify their loved ones. But Marcus had cut through the chaos with single-minded determination. He found a way into the morgue, bypassing the media frenzy that descended like vultures on l'Américain—*the American hero*—and the death threats circling her. Swiftly, discreetly, with the kind of precision Kate now recognized as the hallmark of his double life, Marcus delivered her to Jake.

Even now, she couldn't reconcile the man who fought to save Jake's life with Ronin, the shadowy figure who profited from death. Had Marcus's futile attempt to abort the Paris café attack been born of loyalty to Jake or guilt? Had he been trying to protect her, too? Or was it something darker, a collision of conflicting identities she would never untangle?

The guilt rose again, sharp and unrelenting. Marcus's death was a wound she carried, a debt she could never repay. His plan shielded her from the media frenzy and the glare of public grief—and may even have saved her life.

She closed her eyes, the memory of the warehouse pressing in. His voice had been calm but urgent. Arranging her transportation was a final act of protection—one she hadn't asked for but couldn't forget. And it left her with questions she would never answer about a man she had never truly known.

"So, this is the plan?" Kate asked. "We drive into the morgue in an ambulance?"

"Not quite," Marcus said. He reached inside and pulled out a pair of black body bags. "We're going in these."

"You've got to be kidding me?" Kate asked. "Can you even breath in those things?"

Before Marcus could answer, the ambulance driver approached.

"Madame, I assure you that you are safe in my hands," he said. "My name is Jean-Paul. Jean-Paul Marsat and I would drive you safely through the gates of hell

and back if you so desired."

"Let's hope it doesn't come to that," Kate said. "But I'm a little confused and, frankly, concerned. When they discover our little ruse—and they will—you'll be out of a job."

"That is of no concern," Jean-Paul said. "Over the last eighteen hours, I've made five trips to the L'institut médico-légal. I carried many directly from the cafe and a few that died at the hospital."

"I'm sure that was very difficult."

"Indeed. Very hard, but I am also most grateful my wife was not among them."

Marcus interrupted, "Jean-Paul's wife worked at the cafe."

"Qui, Madame. Janine, mon amour, was inside the cafe when the shooting began. She faced the door, saw a gunman approach, and made the sign of the cross," Jean-Paul said, and he did the same as he spoke. "Janine knew she would never see our children again, but the man didn't shoot."

"That's on Jake," Marcus said. "The crazy bastard drew that asshole away from the cafe and back into the street. God only knows how many more would be lying in the morgue."

"So," Jean-Paul said. "My job means nothing. Your husband was the answer to my wife's prayer."

The waitress returned with Kate's espresso, setting it down on the table with a gentle clink. Kate murmured her thanks and wrapped her hands around the warm ceramic, letting the heat seep into her skin and sipping the thin layer of crema.

She was just setting the cup back down when a voice startled her.

"Excusez-moi, madame. Êtes-vous... Katherine Preacher?"

Kate looked up sharply. The waitress stood beside her, clutching the small gold cross around her neck, her expression hesitant but earnest. "I'm sorry," Janine said quickly, her voice wavering. "I didn't mean to startle you, but... I recognize you. You're l'Américain's wife, Monsieur Church's widow, aren't you?"

At the sound of Jake's last name, Kate felt her throat tighten. She glanced around, worried that the other patrons might have overheard, but no one seemed to pay them any attention.

"Jean-Paul's wife?" Kate asked, her voice softening.

"Qui, madame," Janine replied, sinking into the chair beside her. "I can hold my children, kiss my husband, because..." Janine's voice cracked, tears spilling over.

"I know," Kate murmured, reaching out to clasp Janine's trembling hand. "Jean-Paul explained Jake was the answer to your prayer."

"I'm so sorry..." Janine began but couldn't continue as the tears streamed.

"Thank you," Kate said, her voice steady despite the tears in her eyes. "For reminding me of l'Américain—my husband, the hero."

Janine squeezed Kate's hand, then took a deep, shuddering breath. "I'm sorry if I upset you. It's just... when I saw you sitting here, I knew I had to say something."

Kate shook her head. "No, don't apologize. I'm glad you spoke up and sat down." Kate said. "My heart aches, but it's comforting to think of the lives he saved—your life."

"Jean-Paul will be thrilled to know we've met," Janine said, a faint smile breaking through her tears. "We have a modest home, but I make an excellent Boeuf Bourguignon. I'd love for you to visit and meet our children."

Kate nodded, her lips curving into a small smile. "That's so kind. I can't this trip, but next time I'm in Paris, I promise. But tell me, how is Jean-Paul? Were there consequences for helping me? Did he lose his job?"

Janine laughed softly and shook her head. "No, madame. This is France. It's not so easy to fire someone here. And besides, I think his superiors understood. These were extraordinary circumstances."

Kate nodded, a small smile tugging at her lips despite the gravity of the moment. "Please thank him for me," Kate said. "What he did...I'll never forget."

Janine returned the smile, squeezing Kate's hand one last time before letting go. "I will. And thank you, madame. For your husband's bravery. For your own strength. I will never forget."

With that, Janine turned and walked away, leaving Kate alone with her thoughts and her cooling espresso.

Kate watched her go, a mix of emotions swirling in her chest—grief and a wound that she knew would never fully heal.

And a connection to this place, to these people that she couldn't explain.

Jake gave his life to save as many as he could, and their gratitude was moving.

The morning hadn't gone as she hoped, and the last place she expected to go was the cafe, but she was glad she did. Kate set down her empty cup, taking one last look around the café. The memorial wrapped around the base of the streetlamp was a riot of colors. Bouquets of flowers, candles, and heartfelt notes lay carefully placed, their colors stark against the dark metal. *Jake was there*, she thought. *In every flower, every note, every life he touched.*

Kate recognized the black cast iron lamppost and the intricate scrollwork, from the Paris street-cam videos she borrowed from Boucher's laptop. She'd watched the videos dozens of times, trying to nail down Jake's last words as he struggled repeatedly to say something to Marcus. She turned to a friend, a linguistic expert at the CIA, who confirmed her fears. Jake was angry, and the last thing he said was *Kate's relentless. She will kill you.*

The thought of Jake's last words and the prophecy of Marcus's death shocked Kate back into the moment. *That's where it happened,* Kate thought. *Jake was standing right there.* Kate's analyst brain began searching the scene, and for a moment, she boxed up the grief and focused on capturing every detail. *This is why I'm here.*

She walked over to the lamp, recreating the video in her mind. *Jake would have been standing about here,* she thought. *He sees Vitali's grandson, Stephan, cradling his fiancée. He steps towards them. Three rapid shots. Handgun. 9mm. Jake's next to the lamp when the sniper fires.*

Kate recalled the distinct sound she heard on the recording of Jake's last call and the CIA's audio analysis, identifying the .338 Lapua Magnum—effective range: 1,500 meters.

With that round and a precision rifle, a skilled sniper could engage even beyond that.

I believe a British sniper used that round in Afghanistan—a confirmed kill at a record 2,500 meters.

She began scanning rooftops.

Where were you?

A plan was forming in Kate's mind. If she could find the sniper's location, there might be evidence. *The odds aren't good,* she knew. *Not for a pro, but the DGSI didn't even know there was a sniper. They wouldn't have looked.* That's when Kate spotted it. A thin, brightly colored orange streamer tied high on the lamppost, fluttering in the breeze. It was out of place amid the solemnity of the memorial. Kate looked for Janine and spotted her floating among the tables and patrons.

She waved Janine over. "Do you know what that is?" Kate asked, gesturing toward the streamer.

Janine shook her head. "Non, madame. It's not part of the memorial."

"So, it was there before..." Kate hesitated. "Before the attack?"

"Yes, but not long."

"Why do you say that?"

"It is still vibrant," Janine said. "And the owner does not allow postings of any kind. If he had seen it, he would have asked one of us to remove it."

Kate's breath caught.

A wind flag.

A sniper's tool—placed in advance to gauge wind corrections for a long-range shot.

Her pulse pounded. *If it was there before the attack, the sniper hadn't just taken the shot—he'd known exactly where Jake would be.*

Her chair scraped against the pavement as she shot to her feet.

Kate turned back to Janine, grabbing her in a quick embrace, pressing a kiss to each cheek. "I can't wait to meet your children," she said, her voice warm but rushed. "And I adore Boeuf Bourguignon."

Then she spun toward the street.

The taxi slowed, and Kate lunged, yanking open the door. "Hôtel de Pourtalès."

She settled into the seat, exhaling sharply, but her mind was already ahead of her.

She needed to get back to her laptop. Now.

Chapter 17

WEDNESDAY, APRIL 29th
10:40 AM CEST

HÔTEL DE POURTALÈS, PARIS, FRANCE

KATE BURST INTO HER suite, slamming the door behind her, adrenaline surging. She stripped off her business attire and pulled on black Lululemon pants, a cashmere sweater loose enough to conceal her Glock, and sneakers. *Ready.*

Focus, Kate. One step at a time.

She settled at the ornate desk, unlocked the iPad, and opened the video she liberated from Boucher. With the images burned into her memory, she knew exactly how far to jump into the recording. Stopping moments before the sniper's bullet struck, she zoomed in.

Janine was right, she thought. *It was already there.*

The lamp post streamer, looking like an orange scrap from some recent promotion, was barely noticeable to an untrained eye. But it was there, on the day, at the moment the bullet struck. Kate leaned in closer, her breath catching as she watched the footage frame by frame. The streamer was still, then fluttered.

He didn't hold for the wind, she thought, a chill running down her spine. *There was no wind when he pressed the trigger, but not while the bullet was in flight.*

Kate's analytical mind kicked in, running through the myriad calculations of a long-range precision rifle shot. The curve of the earth, temperature, distance, angle of fire, and more, but it was a gust of wind that changed everything. For a brief, sacred moment, she allowed herself to believe the breeze was the breath of God—something more than coincidence.

The realization hit her like a physical blow. This tiny, unpredictable gust of wind altered the course of the bullet. It couldn't save Jake's life—the bullet's impact was still devastating, the damage ultimately fatal—but it bought him a few critical minutes, and Jake used that time to save one more life, to save Stephan. Vitali's grandson was alive because Jake stayed in the fight.

She let the video play on for what she hoped would be the last time, but she wanted to see it. Jake survived long enough to get a hand on the AK beneath him, prop it against his body, and pull the trigger. Frame by frame, she watched Jake struggle to grab and aim the rifle, but there was something else—something she hadn't seen in her single-minded focus on Jake.

Kate rolled the video forward, back and forward again until she was sure. *He said something*, she realized. *The gunman. He said something to Stephan—then he pointed the gun, and Jake sent him to hell. What did he say*, Kate wondered, but looking at Stephan, rocking and cradling the body of his fiancée, she doubted he even heard, or cared, what the man said. She made a note to ask Vitali how his grandson was doing.

Turning her focus back to the task at hand, one thing was certain. *I need more video.* If she was right, the shooter, or someone close to him, placed the streamer well before the attack. *At least a day or two*, she thought. *In a city known for its video surveillance, the shooter would not want to be seen anywhere near the area the day of the attack.*

If Boucher's laptop was still active, she might still have access. *Only one way to find out.*

Kate masked her identity and launched a locator scan.

The device was online—but hidden.

She took a breath. *Time to roll the dice.*

Kate connected directly to the laptop. Her reward was the mirror image of the laptop's screen. "My code's still working," she said and smiled. "I'm in." But her smile vanished when she watched the mouse move on the screen. *I'll have to wait,* she thought. *I can't reveal my control while someone is using the laptop.* So she waited and watched.

The notepad opened.

> **Kate?**

"What the hell?" Kate muttered.

> **I need your help.**

> **Who is this?**

> I placed your husband's silver cross in your hand.

Boucher. Or a trap.

> We need to meet, but you're being watched.

> **I know.**

> No. Not your team. Others. Can you get out without being seen?

> **Yes. Thirty Minutes**

> Place du Tertre. No electronics. None. Visual bona fides?

He knows I'll need a disguise to leave unseen, Kate thought and pictured exactly what she needed.

> **Black motorcycle leathers. Helmet on my left elbow.**

Boucher knows a thing or two about digital forensics, Kate thought, but she continued monitoring to ensure he covered his tracks. With their entire conversation in a single unsaved note, there would be no trace evidence, but there was one last step.

Kate observed in silence as Boucher erased their shared note line by line, leaving the screen blank. *Not a trace. Perfect*, she thought. *Now, I just need to get Talya on board.*

***

11:10 AM CEST

COUER DÉFENSE BUILDING

Ben Shepard charged into Vivek's office. "This better be good," he demanded and hovered over his chair.

"It's not good," Vivek said, fear gripping his throat. "Preacher somehow connected directly to Boucher's laptop."

"The bastard reported that stolen."

"It might not be him. Could be whoever stole it."

"No, it's him," Ben said, thinking out loud. "Someone must have tipped him off. We cleared out his office and seized his work computer, but no laptop. Claimed he was about to report the theft."

"Preacher's clearly more than a digital forensics expert."

"You're saying she's a hacker?"

"Yeah, the laptop must have her C2 code."

"In English."

"Command and control software," Vivek explained. "She can connect, see everything he sees and does, capture his keystrokes..."

"Passwords?"

"Absolutely."

"Ah! She grabbed the street-cam video using his account," Ben said. "Now, it makes sense."

"We closed Boucher's account," Vivek assured Ben.

"And all of the surveillance video?"

"Gone," Vivek said and smiled. "If she hacks back into the DGSI servers, it won't matter. There's nothing left."

***

11:15 AM CEST

HÔTEL DE POURTALÈS

Kate grabbed her phone, wondering about Boucher's concerns. *Better safe than sorry*, she thought. *We have protocols for a reason.*

She crafted a text message to Talya's open channel number so that anyone monitoring would view the conversation as innocuous and unimportant.

Hey T, are you close?

Yes. What's up?

I forgot to pack my vitamins.

No problem. What do you need?

I'd love some B6 and D2.

Be there in five.

The knock on Kate's door was Talya, with her motorcycle helmet tucked under her arm and a messenger bag slung over her shoulder.

"Nice touch," Kate remarked, gesturing to the messenger bag with a small nod. She gave Talya a quick hug as she stepped inside and then closed the door behind her. Talya was about to speak, but Kate put a finger to her mouth, and the two of them headed for the kitchen.

Kate opened the kitchen faucet and started the microwave, "Now we can talk," Kate said. "Just a precaution."

"I was going to say that a bag like yours was hard to find," Talya began. "But now I'm just glad I have it."

"You're the best," Kate said, flashing a grateful smile.

"Make sure to remind the boys on the team," Talya shot back with a grin.

"I will," Kate said, and they laughed.

"Here's your B6," Talya quipped, handing over the burner phone. "My numbers are in there—open line, GhostChat, and the team's emergency channel."

"GPS?"

"Disabled."

"Now, about the D2," Talya said, her tone shifting to concern. "What's going on? Why do you need me to double for you?"

"I've been in contact with Boucher."

"I know. Wasn't that the whole point of the meeting this morning?"

"Right. You don't know."

"Know what?"

"He was suspended," Kate said. "I met with his replacement. Adrien Gaillard."

"Never heard of him."

"I'm not surprised. He was clearly not DGSI. Expensive suit, watch, shoes. He was placed in Boucher's office to take the meeting and shut down any hope of cooperation."

"What about Moshenski? I thought his connections were going to open doors."

"Oh, the door was open, alright, but someone rearranged the chairs. I was going to have Vitali do some digging, see what he could find out..."

"But Boucher came looking for you."

"In a manner of speaking," Kate said. "He wants to meet. No electronics. And he says I'm being followed."

"Well, you are," Talya said. "But I'm disappointed he spotted us."

"Don't feel bad, he's a pro, but he wasn't talking about you," Kate said. "He specifically said there are others."

"What's the plan?"

"We change clothes," Kate said. "And I'll take the bike."

"And I wait here until you get back?"

"No, I can't take the chance that the surveillance team follows me," Kate added. "Bring up one of the follow cars, like you called for an Uber, and drive around until you hear from me."

"Just drive around while you're loose in the city."

"Yep. Go buy something — something Kate would like."

"That's not funny," Talya replied. "Do you want Forest to kill me?"

"Fine," Kate relented. "Have someone at Place du Tertre, but they'd better be invisible. If Boucher senses them, he'll bolt."

Kate put her finger to her mouth to signal Talya not to say anything and then pulled her phone out of a small, black, Faraday bag, and then slipped it back in and sealed.

"You think it's compromised?" Talya asked.

"Until I know for sure. And that reminds me..."

"Grab a scanner on my way back?"

"Smart girl," Kate said and smiled. "We need to know exactly what we're dealing with. Boucher could just be paranoid."

"How do you want me to use the bag?"

"Pull the phone out when you leave, and leave it out as much as you can. If you or the team need to talk, drop it back in the bag."

"Won't that look suspicious?"

"Yes, so try to leave it out, but if it goes dark, like now, they'll just think the signal's blocked, the bug is flaky, or there's interference from something."

"Like the microwave."

"Exactly."

"Alright. Let's do this," Talya said, and she stepped out of the motorcycle boots and unzipped the snug-fitting leather jacket. Beneath was a moisture-wicking compression shirt and sports bra. Kate left to put on comparable items and retrieve the Glock 43. She returned with clothes for Talya, including the oversize, dark-tinted sunglasses and large floppy sun hat.

Within minutes, the transformation was complete. Talya tucked her hair up to mask the slight difference in color. Kate clipped the Glock to the leather pants, zipped the bottom half of the jacket, and checked the mirror.

"How does it look?" Kate asked, twisting in the mirror to check for any telltale bulges.

"You're good," Talya said with a smirk. "A pro might spot the Glock. Not that they'll be looking at your gun."

Looking back in the mirror, Kate blushed. Talya's snug-fitting leathers were more provocative than she expected and accentuated her figure. She zipped the jacket up higher and tried on the helmet.

Talya was the first to leave, taking Kate's phone with her. If Boucher was right, Talya could draw attention away from the hotel, and her team could get eyes on whoever was following Kate.

Kate left a few minutes later, smiling at the woman she saw walking past the lobby mirror.

She was no longer Kate Preacher.

She was Talya Aviram—a woman who moved with cool, feline grace, a ghost who could vanish like smoke.

Kate adjusted her grip on the helmet. *I like pretending to be someone else. Maybe too much.*

She stepped into the street and swung her leg over the bike. The engine rumbled beneath her as she slipped on the helmet and lowered the visor.

Then Talya Aviram pulled into traffic—and Kate Preacher disappeared.

Chapter 18

PLACE DU TERTRE, PARIS, FRANCE

Kate guided Talya's motorcycle through Montmartre's tight streets, parking just outside the Place du Tertre. The square was alive with artists, tourists, and café-goers—perfect cover.

She swung off the bike, tugged off her helmet, and let her hair fall loose. Somewhere in the crowd, Boucher was watching.

A man in his early 50s was tucked into the shadows, observing the entrance while hiding his face. Despite his efforts to blend in, there was an undeniable air of authority about him. His sharp, observant eyes scanned the crowd, searching for any signs of a tail or potential threat. When his gaze locked onto Kate, she saw a flicker of recognition cross his face, followed by a slight nod of approval at her disguise. He waited a moment longer, ensuring that no one seemed to follow her, before making his way towards her.

"Madame Preacher," Laurent greeted softly, his voice barely audible above the square's bustling din. "You followed my instructions?"

Kate nodded, patting her jacket. "No electronics. As requested."

"Your watch?"

Kate rolled back her leather sleeve, revealing the minimalist Tissot on its plain band.

"Excellent," he said, a hint of apology in his tone. "But one can never be too careful, especially in light of recent events."

"Recent events?" Kate asked, her tone sharp.

"Your detention at the airport," Laurent said. "And the search of your luggage."

Kate narrowed her eyes. "I assumed that was your doing."

"I understand, but no. I was suspended the morning you arrived in Paris."

"Then how did you know?"

"I may not be at work, but I still have contacts and friends. I came up through the ranks and like to think that my work, my reputation, meant something to many at the DGSI."

"Unlike the posh posers, who belong to the right clubs and were handed titles," Kate said. "Like the twit sitting in your office right now."

Laurent laughed out loud. "Yes, I see you understand. Let's find somewhere quieter," Laurent said, his tone measured. "Hungry? Or just a coffee?"

Kate considered for a moment. "A double espresso would be perfect. I could use a little liquid courage."

Laurent nodded, a ghost of a smile on his lips. "Of course. Come, I know just the place."

Boucher led Kate through the crowded square, weaving past artists and café tables.

Good choice, she thought. *Too much noise for eavesdropping. Too many eyes for an ambush.*

When they reached a quiet café corner, Boucher ordered coffee. Kate got straight to the point.

"Tell me about the airport detention," she said.

"I don't know who arranged it except, they are well connected."

"Like Vitali Moshenski?"

"Yes, exactly, and perhaps it was," Laurent said. "But given his help when you were here last, I think it is unlikely."

"What help?"

"It is my understanding that after the attempt on your life, Mr. Moshenski had phones ringing all over the Palais Bourbon and the National Assembly. His connections run deep, and if my suspicions are correct, we may need them again."

"What do you suspect?"

A waiter arrived with a pair of ceramic cups, espresso for Kate, coffee for Laurent. When the waiter was beyond earshot, Laurent looked around and leaned in. "I suspect the café attack was staged," Laurent said, his voice low. "A cover for an assassination."

Kate leaned forward, her brow furrowing. "You think someone would stage a terrorist attack—kill dozens—just to cover one target?"

"I would like to be wrong," he said. "But I've seen too much to ignore the possibility."

Kate sensed the lingering pain written on Laurent's face. She knew he lost his wife and son at the Bataclan concert massacre. *This is a man who has seen the darkness,* she thought. *Jake had the same look.*

"If the attack was staged, who do you believe was the target?"

"Moshenski's an obvious target," Laurent said. "Power attracts enemies. During the attack, two men chased him down an alley. Or perhaps his grandson, Stephan—killing him would send a message to keep Moshenski in line. Were it not for Jake, Stephan wouldn't have survived." Laurent's voice dropped. "And then there's your husband."

"I know you have questions about Jake."

"And they remain unanswered," Laurent said and sipped his coffee. "Why was he in possession of surveillance equipment? What did he hope to learn, and did his efforts make him the sniper's target?"

Kate choked on her espresso at the mention of a sniper, the cup trembling slightly as she set it down. "You know about the sniper?"

Laurent's smile was grim. "I do now. You used my credentials to access the street cam footage, didn't you?" he asked. "I know what you downloaded—saw what you saw. Heard what you heard. The audio evidence and physical impact were compelling but not conclusive. And yet, I've been sidelined while my suspicions remain ignored."

"You're right," Kate admitted. "And I planned to share what I know in the spirit of cooperation and hoped to gain access to the evidence you've collected. To start, I need to see the street cam video covering the cafe in the days prior to the attack."

"Then you agree," Laurent said. "This was a well-planned and coordinated attack with one variable they could not foresee."

She sipped her espresso to mask the catch in her throat. "If Jake was their target," Kate said, her voice firm, "they didn't know who they were dealing with—or what they were about to unleash."

"I wish I could help you..." Laurent began.

"Hold on," Kate interrupted. "I know your suspension complicates things, but there must be someone in the DGSI that can help me, someone you trust."

"Yes, of course. It's not that."

"Then what?"

"The DGSI's surveillance footage is gone. An accident." Boucher's voice dripped with sarcasm.

Kate exhaled sharply. "Convenient."

"It means someone inside DGSI wanted it buried."

Kate scanned the street, pulse ticking up. "Are you suggesting someone in the DGSI is behind the attack?"

Laurent scanned the surrounding area, and Kate did the same. She realized an accusation of that magnitude could get them both killed.

"My suspension," Laurent began. "A massive destruction of evidence and closing down the investigation. These things don't happen in a vacuum. It could be the DGSI or even higher. Much higher."

The gentle clatter of dishes and murmur of conversations provided a subtle backdrop and distraction. Kate finished her espresso and considered the gamble she was about to take. She leaned in, her voice low and serious.

"Laurent, what do you know about the Coalition?" she asked, her eyes searching his face for any flicker of recognition.

"The Coalition? I've heard whispers and rumors—never anything concrete. It's said that, like a coalition of male lions, there's a group of powerful men operating in the shadows, pulling strings on a global scale. But as far as the DGSI is concerned, it's more myth than reality."

Kate nodded, her expression grim. "Yeah, just another conspiracy theory and that makes it easy to ignore, block, and discredit any serious investigation."

"Is that what Jake was pursuing?"

"Not intentionally," Kate said. "At first. But in the world of global executive protection, you track the international hot spots, threat vectors, and key players. That's how you keep your clients alive. From his notes and files, I've learned that Jake spotted a pattern. Apparently, random kidnappings, disappearances, and murders with global implications. I think he was collecting evidence the Coalition is not only real but on the cusp of a major event."

"Like the cafe attack."

"No, I believe that was only an opening move," Kate said. "Right now, they're moving pieces around the board, setting a trap."

"Killing dozens was just the beginning?"

"I'm afraid so," Kate said. "I hoped that tracking down the shooter might lead to his employer."

"And the Coalition?"

"If the Coalition is real, we need to break through their wall of secrecy," Kate said. "I thought the sniper might be a lead, but without evidence…"

"There might be a way," Laurent interjected. "Your… particular set of skills could help."

"Go on," Kate said and listened as Laurent worked the problem.

"The DGSI video is gone—all of it—and I suspect beyond recovery. It's likely they knew you would try to salvage whatever you could and turn to me for help."

"You think that's why you were suspended?"

"It makes sense," Laurent said. "My credentials were in the logs, they assumed I was working with you, and the meeting we scheduled confirmed it."

"Alright, that's how we got here, but what does that have to do with my 'unique skills'?"

"The city-wide video surveillance system is managed by the Préfecture de Police. No one in the DGSI has access to that system, so the original video should still be intact."

"Unless their influence extends into the Préfecture."

"But it's a chance," Laurent said. "Perhaps the only one we have."

"I'll take it from here," Kate said. "The less you know, the better. But your note said you needed my help."

"My reputation is all I have," he began. "This job is my life, and the safety of Parisians my mission. I will help you wherever I can and with whomever I can persuade to join our cause, and you will help me reclaim what was stolen from me."

Kate stood and pulled Laurent into a brief, firm hug, guilt flickering at the edges of her thoughts. *I dragged him into this fight,* she thought. *But at least I'm not alone.*

She gave Laurent the number of her burner phone and wasn't surprised he had one as well. "Perfect," she said. "We'll use these for now, and I'll let you know the minute I have a plan.

"Should I destroy the laptop?

"No," Kate began. "Let them believe we're unaware. Take it back to wherever you've been hiding, leave it there, and disappear. They'll have that location, so it's not safe."

"But as long as the laptop is still there…"

"Exactly," Kate said. "If you're right about my electronics, I'll keep them entertained and away from us."

***

1:00 PM CEST

KATE CLIMBED BACK ONTO Talya's motorcycle and wove through Paris's streets, taking unnecessary turns and doubling back. By the time she reached a small park, she was sure—no tail.

She killed the engine, set her helmet down, and exhaled. Time to plan her next move.

With the burner phone in hand, she reached out to Talya to coordinate her return to the hotel.

> Hey T, meeting complete.

> > Copy. What's your ETA?

> Thirty.

> > Be there in twenty.

That'll work, Kate thought. *I want to be sure they see her return before I get there. But first, one quick stop.* She passed several independent phone repair shops while confirming she wasn't being shadowed and circled back to the closest one. With her electronics off limits, except for their strategic value, she needed new equipment.

Kate slipped into a narrow electronics shop, its window cluttered with second-hand phones and tablets. The bell chimed as she entered.

A middle-aged man behind the counter straightened. 'Bonjour, madame. How can I assist you?'

Kate seized the opportunity to reply in French to disarm the shopkeeper's hope of fleecing an American tourist. "Bonjour, monsieur. Quels modèles d'iPad avez-vous en stock?" *What iPads do you have in stock?*

She knew exactly what she was hoping to find, but avoiding specificity at this point gave her room to negotiate. In the end, Kate had the iPad she wanted and a used Dell laptop she could wipe and configure as a replacement for her Librem PureOS tablet. And she pressured the owner to throw in a small black backpack to get the equipment back to the hotel. The proprietor collected far less than he wanted but still more than the equipment's value. Kate knew he would be happy to have the cash, and now she could work undetected.

Chapter 19

WEDNESDAY, APRIL 29th
1:30 PM CEST

HÔTEL DE POURTALÈS, PARIS, FRANCE

Talya strode into the hotel lobby, the shopping bag completing the illusion of Kate's errand. A quick wave to the desk clerk ensured no questions.

She exhaled. The tail had been competent but predictable—one car, no rotation. They had no idea who they were dealing with. Kate would've lost them in ten minutes just for the sport of it.

Jake always said she had a gift for it—like she could feel it.

Talya clenched her jaw. *Jake is why I'm here*, she reminded herself, pressing the elevator button. *For Kate.* Talya owed Jake everything. He'd hired her when she thought her career was over, taking a chance on someone whose ghosts had driven others away. Trident Security wasn't just a job. Jake gave her a family when she'd given up on the idea of belonging anywhere.

She saw her reflection in the elevator's weathered brass doors. *He would've understood the decoy mission, wouldn't he?* Jake always believed in the team making judgment calls and trusting them to adapt. *Forest, though—Forest would see this as reckless. And maybe it was.* But the idea of being pulled from Kate's protection detail scared her more than Forest's temper.

The elevator chimed, and the doors slowly parted, Talya squared her shoulders. *Time to get back to work*, and she stepped into the elevator.

"Kate!" Isabella's voice rang out, sharp and urgent. Talya glanced up, spotting Isabella Marquez rushing toward the elevator with her bodyguard in tow.

Talya's heart raced, but she kept her expression calm. Isabella, mistaking her for

Kate, slipped into the elevator just as the doors closed. Realization dawned on her face, and she was about to speak, but Talya shook her head, pressing a finger to her lips.

"Sorry, Bella," Talya began. "I was lost in thought. Come—let me show you what I bought."

Isabella didn't miss a beat, stepping into the improv role with ease. "Lovely. I can't wait."

They entered Kate's suite while the bodyguard waited just outside the door. As soon as the door clicked shut, Talya whirled around, placing her hand gently but firmly over Bella's mouth. She leaned in close, her voice a barely audible whisper, "Don't speak. Not yet."

Bella's eyes widened, a mix of confusion and fear flickering across her face. Talya held a finger to her lips again, a silent plea for trust, before making her way into the kitchen. She turned on the faucet, the sound of running water filling the room, providing a veil of white noise.

Returning to Bella's side, Talya murmured, "Kate will be here soon, but first, I need to sweep the room for listening devices. Just play along until I'm finished, OK?"

Bella nodded, her posture tense as she watched Talya retrieve a small rectangular device from the shopping bag. Talya unfolded the antennas, her movements swift and precise. She placed an earwig in her right ear, ensuring that no one else could hear the device's audio output, and switched on the bug detector.

"Bella?" Talya asked. "Can I get you something to drink?"

A soft hum emanated from the device as it came to life, its screen illuminating with a complex array of frequencies and signals. Talya began her methodical sweep of the room, her steps measured and deliberate. The bug detector worked by emitting a signal that would bounce off any hidden devices, picking up on the unique frequencies that listening bugs used to transmit information.

"Thanks. I'd love some water."

As she approached potential hiding spots—the intricate chandelier, the air vents, the gilded picture frames—the device emitted a series of beeps, indicating it was scanning the area. Talya's brow furrowed in concentration, her eyes locked on the screen as she moved from one corner of the room to another.

"Sparkling or still?"

Near the desk, the beeping grew more insistent, and Talya pressed on the earwig to secure the fit. Kate's tablets, both the iPad and the Librem, rested on the polished wood surface. Talya leaned over the desk, and the detector's display spiked. *They're both transmitting,* she thought. *But only the Librem is running.*

"A bottle of Evian sounds good," Bella said. "But I know my way around the kitchen. I'll help myself. Can I bring you one?"

"Yes, please."

Talya's eyes narrowed as she focused on the screen. With a deft twist of a dial on the side of the detector, she tuned the device to isolate the signal more precisely.

"So, you've been busy?" Bella asked, keeping the conversation rolling.

"Well, it's Paris," Talya said. "I can't resist at least a little shopping."

Talya made her way to the bedroom, where she found Kate's watch on the nightstand charging pad. The steady beep of the detector confirmed her suspicions. *Even her watch,* she thought, and that reminded her. *The phone.* She headed back to the living room, retrieved the Faraday bag and removed Kate's phone. With a wave of the detector, she had the answer. *Boucher was right.*

"Mind if I have a look?"

"Yes, of course. I'm eager to hear what you think."

"Ah, Versace. I love silk," Bella said. "And what a glorious scarf!"

Talya shut off the faucet, the silence amplifying her discovery.

She turned to Bella, her voice low and urgent. "We need to go. Now."

Bella's eyes widened, and she gave a quick nod. Without missing a beat, she slid seamlessly into character.

"You know," Bella said, voice airy but pointed, "I have a Brunello Cucinelli silk blouse that would be perfect for you. The champagne hue would be lovely with your skin tone."

Talya followed her lead. "I'd love to see it."

"No time like the present."

They stepped into the hallway, leaving behind whatever ears might be listening.

"Follow me," Bella said and headed down the hall. "My regular apartment is still a crime scene."

"I heard," Talya said. "I'm so sorry."

"It gets worse," Bella said. "That's what I wanted to discuss with...I mean, that's what I wanted to discuss."

Talya nodded her appreciation. With Bella's bodyguard within earshot, she was still Kate, and until Kate was back in the hotel, she was still at risk.

***

2:00 PM CEST

HÔTEL DE POURTALÈS

KATE NAVIGATED THROUGH THE bustling Parisian streets, expertly weaving through the traffic until she reached the front of the Hotel de Portales. She dismounted, keeping the helmet and backpack in place until she reached the door. She strode through the entrance with the quiet confidence and demeanor of a returning guest and headed for the elevator. A glance at the uniformed attendant loitering behind the counter revealed a young man glued to his phone. He didn't even glance up as Kate passed by. *The hotel may be known for its anonymity,* she thought. *But its security needs work.*

While she waited for the elevator to arrive, Kate retrieved the burner phone from her pocket and alerted Talya to her return.

> T, I'm back

> Third Floor, Suite Tronchet

> Copy

A flicker of curiosity crossed Kate's mind at the unexpected location, but the text was clean. If there was trouble, Talya would have signaled for Kate to arrive armed and ready to engage.

When Kate stepped off the elevator, she saw Bella's security standing outside the suite. *Interesting,* Kate thought. *This is Bella's new suite.* A slight nod to the man guarding the door was the only introduction she needed. Kate knew he would recognize her, but discretion was part of the job. She knocked on the door, Bella answered and ushered Kate into the room. With the door closed behind her, Bella took on the role of host and headed for the Kitchen.

"What can I get you?" Bella asked. "We have everything. Water, juice, soda. Of course, we have oodles of wine and a full bar," and laughed at the suggestion they might all need a drink.

Kate slipped off the backpack and plopped down into one of the over-stuffed chairs. "Just water, please. Thanks," Kate said and looked over at Talya. "So, tell me. How did you two meet?"

Talya smirked. "Isabella caught me at the elevator—thought I was you. It didn't take her long to figure it out, but she played it perfectly for her security. Once we got to your suite, she kept the conversation flowing while I swept for bugs."

Bella handed Kate a glass of water. "Well, darling, I am an actress, after all," she said, her flamboyant gestures and tone a caricature of a self-indulgent performer, "Improvisation is my forte."

The women laughed, Bella bowed and then took a seat on the couch.

Kate couldn't help but smile at Bella's quip, appreciating her quick wit and adaptability in the face of an unusual situation. *Stress, surprise, and resilience under pressure reveal true character*, Kate thought. *This is one smart, tough woman. I like her.*

"I guess the bottom line is that we're all here because my room isn't safe," Kate noted. "What did you find?"

"You were right," Talya said. "The room's clean, but they tagged all of your devices, even your watch. No video, but complete GPS and audio coverage."

"You got all that by walking around the room?" Bella asked.

"The scanner's capable of locating the frequencies, identifying the source, and then capturing and analyzing the data."

"Can we backtrace," Kate wondered.

"It's a long shot," Talya said. "Whoever did the work knew what they were doing and covered all the bases. This has to be intelligence agency tech. It's as good, or better than anything I've used. What's in there?" she asked, gesturing towards the backpack.

"I did a little shopping on the way home," Kate said, a hint of pride in her voice, and she pulled out the new iPad and laptop.

"You knew about the bugs?" Talya questioned and raised an eyebrow.

"I had reason to be suspicious and prepared...just in case," Kate replied. "There's work I need to do and can't stop now. I can't risk anyone finding out or trying to stop me."

"From what I've seen," Bella began. "You'd be a hard woman to stop, but would you mind if I changed the subject? There's something I need to discuss."

"Of course," Kate said. "What's on your mind?"

"Talya, I don't mean to be rude..."

"Say no more," Talya said and stood. "You better hang on to this," she added and tucked the scanner into the backpack. "Now, if you're done playing with my bike, I need my clothes back."

"I don't know," Kate said. "That was fun. The power. The freedom. I might need one of those."

"The bedroom is that way," Bella added, nodding down the hall. Kate and Talya left to exchange outfits.

***

When Kate and Isabella were finally alone on the couch, Kate sensed the angst Bella had hidden this entire time. *She is a talented actress*, Kate thought. *This is serious.*

Kate leaned forward, her voice soft. "What's wrong? What happened?"

Bella's tears spilled over. "I was robbed. Damn it—I didn't want to cry. Sorry."

Kate handed her a tissue. "Don't apologize. Between yesterday's assault and now this? You've earned it. And someone told me recently: tears cleanse the soul."

Bella smiled and regained her composure. "I'm not sure when, exactly, or even how. My jewelry box was in my suite, with a crime scene seal since...you know."

"When did you realize the box was gone?"

"This morning. I have an event this evening and wanted to retrieve a few things that I would need, including a very expensive necklace."

"Did you call the police?"

"No, I called Sebastian," Bella said. "The call went straight to voice mail, and I haven't seen or heard from him all morning."

"After yesterday, I understand keeping this quiet," Kate said. "I don't like that Vargas has gone dark. Did he mention anything unusual before he disappeared?"

Bella hesitated. "Just a quick phone call—something about handling an issue personally."

Kate's fingers drummed against her water glass. That wasn't like Vargas. A man of his reputation didn't vanish without reason.

"What kind of issue?"

"He didn't say. Just hung up."

A muscle tightened in Kate's jaw. Someone had his full attention, but why? She had a thought and didn't like where it led.

"I have to admit, given his reputation, I'm disappointed. His job is to be here with you," Kate said. "And you never leave a client without some way to reach you. What would you estimate the value of the missing items?"

Bella thought for a moment and closed her eyes. Kate imagined Bella picturing the items in the box, recalling their purchase price or estimating what they might cost to replace. "I'd say three hundred," she began. "No, more like four hundred thousand, in round numbers."

"Seriously?" Kate asked, her eyes wide, her tone revealing her surprise. "You travel with jewelry worth hundreds of thousands of dollars?"

"It's the image," Bella said. "I don't exactly wear them at the ranch, but this is Paris, with paparazzi staged at every venue and event. And admirers expecting to see Isabella Marquez in catwalk gowns, couture shoes, chic handbags and glittering with gems."

"Insured?"

"Yes, of course," she said. "And I wouldn't even concern you with the matter if it was just about the money."

"Then what?"

Bella's voice dropped. "There's one piece I can't lose. A gold pocket watch. It hasn't worked in years, but it was my father's."

She exhaled a quiet laugh, more to herself than to Kate. "I know how it must sound—fretting over a worthless trinket."

Bella's fingers brushed over the stem of her wine glass, but she wasn't really holding it. Just touching, remembering. "He was a railroad engineer, gone for days at a time. But when he was home, I'd curl up in his lap and play with that watch. He told me it was magic—that it would always bring him back to me."

Kate stayed silent, letting Bella sit in the memory.

"He was right," Bella whispered. "He's been gone for years, but when I hold that watch, it's like he's still with me."

Kate's chest tightened. She didn't remember her father—not really. She was five when he died, seven when she lost her mother and brother. Memories of her adoptive family and their kindness were sweet and warm, but she had nothing like Bella's memories—and nothing tangible to connect her to a past she locked away.

She couldn't help envying the father's love written on Bella's face.

"I can't make any promises," Kate began and cleared her throat. "But there is someone. A man here in Paris that might help. I'll see what I can find out."

Chapter 20

WEDNESDAY, APRIL 29th
2:30 PM CEST

HÔTEL DE POURTALÈS, PARIS, FRANCE

KATE STEPPED INTO HER suite, wrestling with Bella's robbery and the stolen watch. The soothing strains of classical music filled the suite. *Clever girl*, Kate thought, appreciating Talya's ingenuity. *She gave them something to listen to that might just put them to sleep.*

With purposeful strides, Kate collected the tablets and Vitali's KATEM phone and carried them into the bedroom. *Better to have these in one place,* she thought and stacked them on the dresser. *Now let's see what we can find on the TV.* Kate picked up the remote and began flipping through the channels, searching for something that would provide a suitable distraction for her unseen audience. Her eyes lit up when she stumbled on a marathon of "Des Racines et des Ailes," a series that delved into the rich tapestry of French history, culture, and breathtaking landscapes. *If that doesn't bore them to death, nothing will,* Kate mused, a wry grin playing on her lips. She returned to the living room, closing the bedroom door behind her.

Kate settled at the desk and retrieved the new equipment. She set to work, her fingers flying as she configured both devices. Cloud-based backups and encrypted folders from her library of open-source and proprietary tools helped speed the process. Jake used to say, *don't fall in love with your weapons — be effective with whatever you can get your hands on.* That's how Kate approached her devices. Hardware dies, often at the least convenient moment, but access to the cloud meant she was prepared to use whatever she could get her hands on.

With the rebuild process underway, Kate wrestled with the offer to help Bella. The attempted robbery yesterday and subsequent success could mean only one thing—planned and executed by a team. And the death of a gang member didn't even slow them down—they came right back for more. Kate considered what she knew. *Armenian. Organized. Ruthless.* One name came to mind. *Aram Sarkesian.*

The CIA tracked the major Crime Syndicates, especially those with links to arms trafficking. In Paris, that was Stvener, an Armenian syndicate. Loosely translated, Stvener is *The Shadows,* and that's where Sarkesian preferred to operate. He loathed the flamboyant, nightclubbing Russian Lamborghini thugs. Sarkesian was reserved, even sophisticated, but Kate knew he was just as deadly.

If this was an Armenian operation, Sarkesian's fingerprints would be all over it. Kate thought. *He might even have approved.* That realization made what she was considering even more ludicrous.

Kate paced the room, shaking her head. "This is insane. It's just a watch." She exhaled sharply. "This has nothing to do with why I'm in Paris."

Saying it out loud. Talking to the empty room. Acknowledging the insanity of even trying to pierce the veil of secrecy around a criminal syndicate sparked a memory, a sensation. This wasn't the first time she'd gone down the rabbit hole following her instincts. *Nothing to do with why I'm in Paris,* she thought. *Or does it?* That thought was still hanging in the air when she decided what to do.

Kate grabbed the burner phone, launched the GhostChat app, and texted Vitali's private number. *He won't recognize my phone,* she thought. *But that won't matter. I suspect the universe of people with his private number is minuscule.*

> This is K. I need a favor.

> Go on.

> Can you arrange a meeting with Sarkesian?

> It is too dangerous.

> That's why I'm asking for your help. I need this meeting—and your protection.

There was no response for several minutes. *Maybe I should send another text,* Kate thought. *Try to plead my case.* The longer she waited, the greater the temptation, but some part of her knew better. *Just wait. He's making it happen.* And she was right.

10:00 pm. Out front. No hardware.

Unarmed was par for the course, and she wouldn't have risked it. *Can't afford to send the wrong message,* she thought. *This was a business meeting.* Kate was a little surprised Vitali didn't ask about a text message from a new phone or why the meeting was important. But she appreciated the trust and faith that Vitali placed in her and the freedom to do things her way. In the back of her mind, she could hear Margot say, *You're not a field agent.* And Kate had to admit, this was unfamiliar territory. *Let's just pray this works.*

Kate checked the time. *Still way too early for Nomad, but I don't need more video to map what I already know.*

With the iPad propped up on a stand and the Linux laptop open beside it, she launched the 3D modeling software. The goal now was simple. Take what she knew, combined with what was publicly available on the Paris attack, and find the building where the sniper took the shot. Identifying and eliminating potential locations was likely to be a fairly tedious process, but such was the life of a CIA analyst, and Kate's focus and attention to detail made her one of the best.

Google Earth gave her the raw data she needed with a virtual view of the streets of Paris and remarkably detailed satellite imagery. Then she turned to the street cam video she borrowed via Boucher's laptop. She needed to place Jake precisely where he was standing and the direction he was facing when the sniper round struck him in the back.

Kate collected her emotions, and as Jake would say, she tried to put them in a shoebox and set them on the shelf. To complete the 3D model, she needed to place a six-foot, two-hundred-pound mannequin on the screen and model the bullet striking the lung.

She found herself in the kitchen, aimlessly opening drawers and cabinets with no idea what she might find or even why she was looking. All she knew was that she couldn't finish the model, not yet.

It's late, she thought. *And I haven't eaten. No wonder I'm losing it.* She placed a room service order for a late lunch and found a small bag of potato chips. Kate raced through the chips, realizing how hungry she was—held the bag up high and tapped the last few crumbs into her mouth. She crumpled the empty chip bag and took a deep breath. "You've got this. You've done this before—dozens of times. Just focus."

Kate engaged the analytical brain and locked in. Anything within 270 degrees in front of Jake—low probability. She focused on the ninety-degree arc behind him. Three buildings remained.

All three buildings were tall, offered clear views of the lamppost streamer, and fell within the calculated range. One was a residential apartment with windows and balconies facing the cafe. The office building didn't have operational windows but offered rooftop access with a line of sight. And a historic building with a chaotic blend of ornate architectural elements and modern ventilation equipment on the roof.

Kate rotated the model, examining each building from every angle, from street level to rooftop, and added lines tracking possible bullet trajectories and distances. She considered the sniper taking up a position inside the residential building. *He could set up well back from the window to avoid detection,* she thought. *But what about the tenants? No. This guy can't risk being seen.* The office building posed a similar risk of unintended contact. *Even a minimal security presence posed a risk,* she thought. *With an event this big, he needed to be a ghost.*

She found herself drawn to the satellite view of the remaining building. *What is this,* she wondered. *The rooftop is complete chaos.* Ornate sculptures and decorative elements from the original construction intermingle with modern air handling units, ducts, and satellite dishes. *Fantastic view of the cafe.*

Kate clicked on the image and explored the building's history, ownership, and current function.

Le Palais de l'Éclipse was constructed in the late 19th century and named for the solar eclipse visible during its completion. Originally, the grand residential palace of Comte Jean-Baptiste de Montclair, but the palace fell into disrepair, losing its luster as maintenance costs soared and the aristocratic lineage declined. By the mid-20th century, it was designated a cultural landmark, preserving its historical significance amidst urban development.

In recent years, Le Palais was purchased privately and meticulously restored, transforming it into an exclusive event venue. It now hosts high-profile galas, art exhibitions, and private functions, preserving its historical charm while serving a contemporary purpose.

A quick check on the venue's website confirmed there were no events scheduled on the day of the attack or the day before. *Lots of time to set up,* she thought. *But how did the sniper access the roof?*

Kate studied the model like she might a chessboard. *I know what I would do.* But to prove her theory, she needed access, and to gain access, she needed Boucher. *He'll still have his credentials, and they won't know he's suspended.* She liked the idea, and that wry smile crept back onto her face. *Boucher's not going to like it, but I'll cross that bridge tomorrow.*

***

WEDNESDAY, APRIL 29th
12:30 PM EDT

NOMAD'S FORTRESS, MANHATTAN, NY

Nomad eased the joystick forward and docked his chair at the workstation. *Back again and ready to do battle,* he thought. *Feels like I just left.* A glance at the time confirmed he got a solid six hours of sleep. That was the magic number. Anything less, and he wasn't quite himself. Much longer, and he was grumpy all day. But with so many projects underway, he was eager to get back to work. He lived for the challenge, and embraced the Holmesian attitude that the "game was afoot," but pursuing tasks for Kate took on an even grander purpose and joy.

He checked the progress on recovering Jake's damaged files and smiled. *That's promising,* he thought. *The data fragments are coalescing into words. It's taking longer than I wanted, but at least there's hope.*

Another system was analyzing the video sent to Moshenski's KATEM phone. *The video edits were sophisticated. Nearly flawless,* Nomad observed. *But nothing's perfect. That may change, but not yet.* Nomad wondered how long before AI made it impossible for him to discern authentic from manipulated. But for the moment, one minor flaw was enough for him to confirm there was a significant piece of the video missing and to launch a search for the drone's original, unedited transmission.

Nomad's connection to Kate's Librem tablet was still secure and probing the phone for any sign of intrusion or vulnerability. *It doesn't look good,* he thought. *That thing is every bit as secure as they claim.* But he had a hunch and spent half the night tracking down another KATEM on the Darknet. He overpaid, but nabbing the stolen device was worth it to test his theory. Still, this wasn't exactly Amazon Prime. He'd have to wait, but with a third-party courier service and an anonymous drop box, he hoped Keisha might pick it up over the weekend.

"Oh crap," he said and ordered his system to open up a video chat session.

"What's the matter?" Keisha asked and came out of the kitchen.

"It's Kate."

"Is she OK?"

"Yeah. Yeah. I got caught up in my work and didn't see her comm request."

Keisha folded her arms. "And you better tell her."

"I will," Nomad muttered, pivoting his chair as Kate's face appeared on the screen.

"Tell me what?" Kate asked, her tone sharp.

"We'll come back to that," Nomad said, and he pictured Keisha rolling her eyes. "If you're hoping for an update, there's not much to report. Not yet, anyway."

"Hoping, sure, but not expecting. I know the drill. This work can be a test of one's patience."

"Then what's up?"

"As if I haven't given you enough... this is big, and the clock's ticking."

"Alright. What do you need?"

"I need you to hack into the video surveillance system of the Paris Préfecture de Police."

"Oh, I thought you were going to ask me for something challenging."

"Are you kidding?"

"Yes, but you started it."

"Funny," Kate said. "I know it's a lot to ask, but here's the situation. Someone got to my contact at the DGSI."

"Boucher?"

"Yeah, he's out, and it gets worse. All the street-cam video related to the attack is gone—accidentally deleted."

"Of course," Nomad mocked. "That happens all the time with counter-terrorism agencies."

"Anyway," Kate said, trying to focus Nomad's attention. "I need to see the video. There's a chance the camera near the cafe caught the sniper hanging a streamer."

"A what?"

"A strip of bright orange nylon he might have used as a wind gauge."

"So you don't need the real-time feed."

"No, definitely archive," Kate said. "Assuming someone hasn't gotten to it. One more reason we need to move fast."

"In theory, archive storage will be easier than real-time if I can get into the system," Nomad said, thinking out loud. "The encrypted camera feeds would have been a real...Well, I'll know soon enough."

"Hi, Keisha," Kate said, spotting Keisha on the video feed. "Is Julian behaving himself?"

"Hardly," Keisha began. "And one look at you tells me you haven't eaten. I swear you two are peas in a pod."

"I just ordered, mom. I promise," Kate said and smiled. "Julian...I mean, Nomad...what was it you wanted to tell me?"

Nomad squirmed. "Tell her, or I will," Keisha muttered.

"We had a deal," Kate said. "No more secrets."

"Tell her right now or I swear I will," Keisha whispered in Nomad's ear.

"I wanted it to be a surprise..."

"It's a surprise, alright," Keisha interrupted.

"Come on. Let's have it."

"I've been working on...And I've had some success...but it's too early to know..."

"Oh, for Christ's sake," Keisha jumped in. "He's working on a copy of Jake's files."

"You're doing what?" Kate asked, and her tone sent chills down his spine.

"Please, Kate," Julian begged. "Just hear me out..."

Kate's voice cracked, her words trembling with anger. "Julian, how could you? Those files...They hold some of our most personal moments."

"I haven't watched or read any of that," Nomad interrupted. "I swear on my mother's grave."

"Why should I believe a word you say? You spied on me for years."

Nomad's voice cracked, and he struggled to speak. "I know what I did was wrong. I know I nearly got you killed. But I swear—I'm still trying to make it right. That's why I took the files."

"Run that one by me again? You stole from me to say you're sorry?"

"I know how it sounds when you say it like that."

"And how you would you say it?"

"Jake might have been killed for something in those files."

"I've been through them a dozen times, maybe more."

"But Jake told you to solve the puzzle."

"You did watch the video!"

"No, you told me. You said Jake wanted you to do your thing, see what he and everyone missed, and solve the puzzle."

"I tried," Kate said and choked back the tears. "Now, I'm doing it my way."

"But what if you can't solve the puzzle because you don't have all the pieces?" Nomad asked. "That's all I'm trying to do. And, so far, I have little to show for it, but there's still a chance. I'll stop if you ask me to, but I can do it. Just give me a chance. Please."

Kate disappeared from view and returned a moment later, tissue in hand, dabbing her eyes. She exhaled slowly, her voice steadier now. "Alright. Recover what you can and send me everything—no matter how disjointed or fragmented it might seem. But Julian, my heart is in your hands now. Please, don't break it."

The video chat ended, and Keisha helped wipe Nomad's eyes and nose. "I know that was hard," Keisha said. "But she needed the truth—and you needed her blessing."

Chapter 21

WEDNESDAY, APRIL 29th
10:00 PM CEST

HÔTEL DE POURTALÈS, PARIS, FRANCE

At exactly 10:00 PM, a midnight blue Mercedes-Benz S-Class glided to the curb. Understated. Luxurious. Just like Sarkesian.

A well-dressed man stepped out, nodding as he opened the rear door. "Mrs. Preacher. Please get in."

Kate slid into the leather interior, pulling a Faraday pouch from her purse. "I'm being followed," she said, slipping her phone into the bag. "They're tracking my phone."

A faint smile played on the driver's lips as he smoothly pulled away. "As expected, ma'am. Arrangements have been made."

Barely a block away, Kate heard the screech of tires behind them. In the side mirror, she saw a large delivery van blocking the street.

Her driver glanced into the rear-view mirror, smiled, and then looked back at Kate. "Your shadow won't be going anywhere for a while."

In the distance, Kate could hear someone yelling and horns blasting, but that faded as the Mercedes accelerated. After a few sharp turns, the driver spoke again. "We're clear, but you'll need to put this on." He handed her a black hood. "For your safety as much as ours."

Kate didn't argue. If the wrong people thought she knew Sarkesian's location, it would be Syria all over again. She pulled the hood over her head, plunging into darkness.

***

10:07 PM CEST

LA DÉFENSE BUSINESS DISTRICT

Vivek was monitoring Kate's electronics, recording every sound and GPS location. It was boring work, made even more tedious by Kate's choice of entertainment. The classical music was terrible, but the French television documentary was even worse. He programmed an audio track filter to monitor the input and alert him if it detected live conversation.

Shepard insisted Vivek text him with updates every hour until Kate retired for the evening, but there was little to report. The morning updates noted Kate's trip to the DGSI and her walk to Cafe Pierre, but most of the updates were the same message every hour.

Location: Hotel. Communication: None. Visitors: None. Activity: None.

The team tasked with following Kate coordinated with Vivek, and he provided location data. This allowed them to keep a safe distance and even pretend to turn and stop to avoid detection. Then Vivek would direct them to Kate's location. The model worked beautifully during Kate's shopping expedition, and everyone anticipated a quiet night.

Vivek didn't notice that Kate turned off the TV, but when her location changed, he tuned in. *I'll bet she's going to bed,* he thought. *Maybe a snack first.* The location data mapped to her suite's floor plan, and within a few feet, it was fairly accurate. He smiled when he saw Kate walking through walls, but he could distinguish between bedroom, living room, and kitchen. When he saw the hallway and elevator, he alerted the follow team.

Stay Alert! Target is on the move.

Moving didn't mean she was leaving, but they needed to be ready. Before the team could even reply, Vivek knew Kate had exited the hotel and cranked up the volume to capture anything she might say.

Dark Blue Mercedes pulled up to the curb. Driver is

exiting. Target is approaching.

Vivek recorded a barely audible man's voice, *Mrs. Preacher,* followed by *Please get in.* He was typing the alert to Shepard when Kate's GPS data and audio input went dark. "Oh shit," he said and texted the shadow team.

Lost tracking data. Do not lose target!

Target in sight. Plate FR-562-XN, Region 75

Armed with the license plate and the Paris regional identifier, Vivek began typing, but before he could complete the search, another message arrived.

Target lost.

Vivek's stomach dropped. His hands slammed the desk, sending papers flying. *I had one job. One. And I blew it...*

Vivek thought maybe he should get Shepard on the phone. *What if he's with someone, or he answers, and I freeze?* He chose the coward's path, sent Shepard a text, and two seconds later, his phone rang. With the first ring, he already knew who it was, but he glanced at the caller ID just to be sure. By the second ring, he couldn't breathe, but his brain was screaming, *Answer the damn phone.* He put the phone on speaker to keep his hand free to work.

"Yes, sir," he stammered.

"What the hell just happened?" Shepard demanded.

Vivek swallowed hard. "She stayed in her suite most of the day—."

"I know that, you idiot! What I don't know is how you lost her."

"I alerted the shadow team that she was in the elevator and on the move. Then they reported a car pulled up to the curb, and she got in."

"Then everything went dark?" Shepard asked. "No signal whatsoever?"

"Yes, sir," Vivek confirmed. "I immediately told the shadow team to stick with her."

"How did they screw up?"

"I don't yet have that information."

"You better have it by the time Grant and I arrive," Shepard said. "You've got thirty minutes."

Vivek's hands were trembling as he ended the call. *He's bringing Grant? That can't be good.*

***

UNDISCLOSED LOCATION, PARIS

KATE SAT IN THE back seat of the Mercedes, contemplating the wisdom of the meeting she requested. She was in Paris for a reason, and this wasn't it. *What the hell am I doing,* she wondered. *This could ruin everything.* If it was just about the money, the thought of intervening would never have crossed her mind, but this was something else, and she knew to trust her instincts. *All I know is this is exactly where I need to be and where I need to go. I'm sure of it.*

She didn't map the route in her head. There was no reason to recall the stops and turns. The road conditions didn't matter, neither did the background noise or the vehicle's approximate speed. She wasn't being kidnapped, and she genuinely did not want to know where she was going.

When the vehicle stopped, this time longer than usual, Kate listened out of habit. She recognized the whine of an electric motor, a ratcheting chain, and the metallic groans of a heavy steel door rolling up. *That sounds familiar,* Kate thought. *Reminds me of the warehouse where they staged the ambulance. Let's hope this isn't another body bag trip.* The vehicle drove on, and she felt the tires climb over the door's entrance frame.

"We've arrived." The driver's voice was calm. "You may remove the hood now."

Kate tugged the hood free, grateful for the fresh air and relief from the oppressive fabric. The stale air inside was hot and suffocating, and she tried not to think about how long it had been since anyone washed it or how things went for the hood's previous occupants.

She set the hood on the back seat and felt the Faraday bag alongside. *Assuming Vitali could ensure my safety, I'll be wearing it again on the way back,* she thought. *Or it won't matter.*

Blinking and rubbing her eyes, she cleared her vision and focused on the vehicle's interior. Kate estimated the ride at thirty-two minutes, and when she could focus on her watch, she realized it was about thirty. *Not bad,* she thought. Tracking the passage of time was a skill that surfaced when she was in captivity, where disorientation and confusion were the goal, and she searched for ways to remain focused and sane.

She popped open the passenger door, slid out, and let her eyes adjust to the warehouse fluorescent lighting. She took a deep breath. The cool night air was a welcome contrast to the stuffy interior of the hood. The man waiting for Kate's arrival gestured for her to follow. He was an imposing figure with a muscular build, around 6 feet, 2 inches tall. *Looks like Big Mike,* Kate thought, picturing Mike Graham, one of Trident's core team. *Mike's taller and with a warm smile. Just as deadly,* she thought. *And the last thing you'd see was that smile.*

This man's no-nonsense demeanor and dark, piercing eyes said he took his job seriously, but it was the weathered face and a few visible scars that painted a picture of a man accustomed to violence. The AK-47 in his hands hung from a worn leather strap, and the scratches on the rifle's finish were a sign of heavy use. Kate took in her surroundings, noting the heavy security presence. Guards with the same air of alertness and propensity for violence were stationed around the perimeter or patrolled the interior. Most carried AK-47s, but a few had M4s, and their sidearms were Glock 17s. *Nobody's getting in here uninvited,* Kate thought. *And you don't leave without permission.*

Kate followed her guide past rows of Renault and Mercedes-Benz lorries. Forklifts buzzed like worker bees—every movement precise. *Whatever they're loading—it's going out tonight.*

***

10:37 PM CEST

LA DÉFENSE BUSINESS DISTRICT

The door to Vivek's office swung open with a force that sent a ripple through the room. He turned away from the labyrinth of monitors, computers, and diagnostic equipment and looked into the glaring eyes of Ben Shepard. Just behind Shepard was Grant Collins, and his thinly veiled frustration sent a chill down Vivek's back.

Before anyone could speak, Vivek launched the dashcam video and began narrating Kate's escape.

"Moments after getting into the car, we lost all digital contact."

"She figured it out," Grant said. "I told you she would."

"Hang on," Shepard said. "What's the status of her other equipment?"

"Still tracking," Vivek replied. "Her iPad is idle, but the Linux tablet has maintained a continuous encrypted connection this entire time."

"Then explain to me what happened to her phone," Grant demanded.

"Probably a Faraday bag," Vivek added. "The bag blocks electromagnetic signals. Nothing gets in or out."

"I know what it is," Grant snapped.

"Just keep going," Shepard insisted.

"I warned the team that I lost contact and told them to stay close," Vivek continued. "The Mercedes pulled away from the curb, passed the alley, and the follow car pursued."

They all watched as the shadow car jammed on its brakes to avoid ramming into a delivery van.

"So, it was a setup?"

"Yes," Vivek replied and continued. "The delivery van darted out of the alley, completely blocking the road."

"Smart," Shepard added. "The narrow road made a natural choke point. One way in, one way out, no way around."

The video continued, they heard horns blaring and drivers yelling, and then a second van pulled up behind.

"Completely trapped," Grant noted. "They're lucky it wasn't a hit. They'd be dead."

"Carefully planned," Shepard said. "And executed with precision."

"I warned you," Grant said. "There's more going on with this woman than we know."

"You're giving her too much credit," Shepard said. "She didn't set this up. She just went for a ride. Vivek, what do we know about the vehicles?"

"All three vehicles are registered to legitimate businesses and different holding companies," he replied. "But they all link back to Arem Sarkesian."

"That explains how we lost her," Shepard said. "Sarkesian guards his operations like his life depends on it."

"Sarkesian? How could she even make contact?"

"That's easy," Shepard said. "Had to be Moshenski. The question is, why?"

"Seriously?" Grant asked. "You know why."

"Let's continue this in my office," Shepard said and turned to Vivek. "Alert me the minute she returns to the hotel, and I want confirmation that we still have full digital tracking."

Grant followed Shepard into his office and closed the door behind him.

"I'm not waiting around while you play telephone tag with Preacher," Grant announced. "And I'm not risking years of work over some grieving widow."

"Calm down," Shepard urged. "Have a seat. Take a breath. She's not going to learn anything from Sarkesian. His business relies on secrecy, and he's not going to throw that away. He'd lose everything."

"Then why did she meet with him?"

"I'll find out. I've got people on the inside," Shepard said and leaned back in his chair. "I'll know more in a day, two at most."

"You do that," Grant said. "But I've got a plan of my own."

"And what's that?"

"We let her play detective," Grant began. "If she's as good as you say, it won't take her long to figure out where I took the shot—hell, she probably already knows."

"Hang on," Shepard said. "Preacher's good. One of the best. But she had the full resources of the CIA at her fingertips."

"She doesn't need them," Grant said. "Think about it. We know she had access to Boucher's laptop and grabbed the street cam video."

"So she knows exactly where her husband was standing and the direction he was facing," Shepard said. "Add Google's satellite view…"

"Now, you're getting it," Grant interrupted. "Frankly, pretty trivial from that alone to eliminate most of the buildings around the cafe. Off the top of my head…there's two, maybe three, possibilities. Trust me, if she's everything you say, she'll figure it out. You just need to be in position."

"We'll know if she goes anywhere near the cafe."

"No!" Grant snapped. "Do not rely on your trackers. You need to sit on l'Éclipse until she shows—it's time to give her what she wants."

"And what's that?"

"The man who shot her husband," Grant smirked, rising to his feet. "But you know what they say, be careful what you wish for. Now, this is where you come in…"

***

UNDISCLOSED LOCATION, PARIS

THE FRENZY OF SARKESIAN'S warehouse activity faded, replaced by the echoing sounds of their footsteps on the concrete floor. They reached a freight elevator, and her escort pressed the button. *Only one way to go from here*, Kate thought, as they waited for the elevator's arrival. The descent was smooth but seemed to last an eternity. *At least eight, maybe nine, or even ten floors.* When the doors finally opened, Kate found herself in a different world entirely.

The Paris catacombs stretched out before her, an eerie labyrinth of ancient stone corridors. Makeshift strings of lights illuminated the path, casting long shadows and revealing glimpses of the centuries-old remains. The skulls and bones that lined the walls witnessed Kate's arrival and followed her as they navigated the twisting passageways. Kate recognized the sound of distant gunfire, growing louder as they approached a well-lit chamber. Her escort handed her a Peltor ComTac headset and a pair of Wiley X safety glasses. *This is top-of-the-line gear*, Kate realized. *These guys know their stuff.* And Kate suspected Afghanistan was where they got it.

The path opened to an enormous chamber, and Kate's eyes fell on the man she'd come to see. Aram Sarkesian was examining a crate of weapons and randomly selected an M4 from the middle of the case. In his late 50s, Sarkesian's face bore the subtle marks of a life lived in the shadows of power and danger. The deep lines on his forehead and those framing his eyes spoke to years of high-stakes decision-making and stress, still, he rose within the ranks without scars. *None that are visible*, Kate thought.

Sarkesian handled the M4 with ease, revealing both his weapons competence and the slightly calloused hands of a man accustomed to hard work despite his elevated status. A simple gold wedding band was the only reminder that beneath the hardened exterior of a criminal leader was a family man. Kate knew he had two sons, eight and ten, and a daughter who was only five. In one continuous move, he inserted a 30-round magazine, slapped the bolt release, slid the fire control into full auto, and aimed.

The target hovering at fifteen meters was a standard paper target of a human torso, with defined zones for center mass and headshot scores. Even with ear protection, the burst of a dozen rounds was intense. Kate's eyes widened when she saw the result. The heart of the target was completely obliterated, with a remarkably tight grouping of 8-10 inches. *That's impressive,* she thought. *It's challenging to hold that tight in full auto.*

As the echo of the gunshots faded, Sarkesian turned to face her. He laid the weapon down on the bench next to a collection of other firearms, and Kate assumed they were all for purchase or sale and being inspected and tested.

Kate stepped forward, extending her hand. "Mr. Sarkesian, thank you for agreeing to meet."

Sarkesian offered a faint smile. "Vitali and I are old friends. And it never hurts to have a man like Vitali owe you a favor."

"I must admit, that was an impressive string of fire."

"A merchant should know his products," he said. "Would you like to try?"

"May I?" Kate asked, pointing at the array of weapons on the table.

"Of course, be my guest," he said. "Whatever you like."

Kate picked up the Glock 17, an enormous gun in her small hands, but she brought the gun up, squeezed off three rounds, and set it down. Sarkesian nodded to one of his men, who pressed the target retrieval switch. The overhead cable spun, and the target came flying in and then stopped.

"Nicely done," Sarkesian said, noting Kate's rounds were all head shots. Left eye, right eye, and nose.

Then she picked up the M110 Semi-Automatic Sniper rifle and examined the weapon's configuration. *Harris bipod. Nightforce scope,* she noted. *This configuration showed someone knew exactly what they wanted.*

The rifle was known for its accuracy and rapid follow-up shots. Chambered for 7.62×51mm NATO rounds, the rifle balanced stopping power and range. It was a trusted companion among Special Forces in Afghanistan because of the varied and often challenging terrains of the Afghan mountains and deserts, and the desert tan finish supported Kate's suspicion regarding the origin of the weapons.

"How long is your range?"

"Two hundred meters."

"Would you mind?" Kate asked and took a seat at the gun bench before Sarkesian could even answer.

Sarkesian just nodded, and the target track motors spun up as the target hurtled to the end of the track.

Kate tucked in behind the rifle and pulled it into her shoulder. With a solid cheek weld, she peered through the optic and pressed forward slightly, driving the bipod into the surface of the table. It was a safe bet the gun was zeroed at one hundred meters, so she held her point of aim about one-half mil above the point of impact. *Now, breathe,* she thought. Exhaling slowly, she followed the crosshairs to the point of aim, held, and pressed the trigger to the rear.

The rifle pushed against her shoulder, but with a solid hold, she was coming right back on target when she heard the supersonic snap of the bullet breaking the sound barrier and then the thunderous report of the rifle. With her sights back on the target, she was ready for a second shot but just smiled. Kate flipped the safety on before letting go of the pistol grip. Eying the brass cartridge on the table, she swept it into her pocket and stood up.

"Let's have a look," she said, pretending she didn't already know the result. The retrieval cable spun, and the target came flying back. The total silence gave way to hushed whispers when Sarkesian's men saw Kate's hit, dead center, bridge of the nose.

With the range testing complete, Kate removed her eye and ear protection and approached the chair near Sarkesian.

"May I sit?" Kate asked, gesturing to the chair opposite him.

Sarkesian nodded, reaching for a glass. "Please, make yourself comfortable. Water?"

Kate shook her head. "No, thank you."

Sarkesian sipped his water, studying her. "Vitali told me you were exceptional—a woman of, shall we say, unique capabilities. I'm pleased he was not exaggerating. Now, how may I be of assistance?"

"A friend of mine, Isabella Marquez, was the victim of an attempted robbery."

"Yes, I saw this in the news. Very tragic, two men died. But why come to me?"

"One of the dead men, the one who attacked her, was Armenian."

"How do you know this?"

"I was there," Kate said. She removed her scarf, revealing the bruises on her neck.

Sarkesian's gaze sharpened. "It was you—you killed him."

Kate met his eyes as she wrapped the scarf around her neck. "Yes."

Murmurs rippled through the room, anger simmering in the corners. Sarkesian raised a hand, silencing them instantly.

"Was he one of your men?" Kate asked.

"He was known to me," Sarkesian admitted.

"A second robbery," Kate began. "One not reported to the police took something that I'm hoping to recover."

"Something valuable?" Sarkesian asked and raised an eyebrow.

"Something personal," Kate said. "A gold pocket watch that belonged to Isabella's father."

"A noble endeavor," Sarkesian began. "But I can not help you." He stood to signal the meeting was over, but Kate didn't move.

"How much does he owe you?" Kate asked. "Vargas. How much?"

"So you know about Vargas?" Sarkesian asked.

"I do now," Kate replied, noting the smirk on Sarkesian's face.

He sat back down, his hands clasped under his chin. "More than he can pay."

"Is he still alive?"

"For the moment," Sarkesian said. "You wish to buy his freedom?"

"I only want the watch."

Sarkesian laughed. "I like you. And the jewels?"

"Keep them. They're insured," Kate said. "And I'm told they're worth at least four hundred thousand."

"Ms. Marquez is fortunate to have such a good friend," Sarkesian said. "If it means that much to her, she can have the watch... for one hundred thousand, and Vargas goes free."

"Fifty, and you can keep Vargas," Kate countered, suspecting it would be risky to just accept.

"Perhaps you should speak with your client before rejecting my very generous offer."

"She doesn't know that I'm here," Kate began. "And I'd like to keep it that way."

"And the payment?"

"Would come from my personal account," Kate said. "Do we have a deal?"

Sarkesian's silence was unnerving. He appeared deep in thought but never took his eyes off Kate's face. *Now I'm spooked. No doubt exactly how he wants me to feel,* Kate thought. *But you know the rule, Kate: whoever says money first, loses.*

"No," he said, finally breaking the silence. "I won't take your money. But tell me, why did you come here? What did you hope to gain?"

"Honestly, I'm not sure," Kate replied. "Coming here, meeting you, for a worthless watch didn't make sense, and still doesn't. Yet, here I am."

"You should go," Sarkesian said and stood.

"Wait. Please. I was only five when I lost my father, no older than your daughter is now," Kate said. "I have so few memories of those early years and nothing so precious as Bella's memory of curling up in her father's lap and playing with his watch. Perhaps you and your daughter are creating memories like that now—memories she will carry with her for the rest of her life. I will never know that joy, but Bella does, and I hoped you might help her hold on to them."

"You think me a sentimental fool," Sarkesian laughed.

"You are clearly no one's fool," Kate said and looked into his eyes. "But I've known many strong and dangerous men. Men like you, with a warrior's spirit and the heart of a lion, who still made room in their hearts for the ones they loved and for the innocent."

"Men like your husband?"

"Yes," Kate said, her voice firm, determined. "Men like my husband."

"I am truly sorry for your loss," Sarkesian said and added something in Armenian Kate didn't understand.

The silence that followed could not have been more than a minute, but Kate could feel her heart racing. *What have I done,* she wondered. *What is he waiting for?* His man returned carrying a sleek, matte-black case and held it in front of Sarkesian. He lifted the lid, and bright white light illuminated the interior. From several feet away, Kate could see the rainbow radiance of the light striking a diamond necklace and flying around the room.

Sarkesian reached inside the box, and from the top shelf, he withdrew a gold pocket watch. "I knew it was special the minute I saw it," he began. "A scratched and broken old watch, sitting alongside this stunning necklace and earrings. Do you know what it says?"

"No, I don't," Kate admitted. "Bella never mentioned an inscription."

"It says, *A father's love is timeless.*" Sarkesian thrust the pocket watch into her hand. "Take it. A worthless trinket."

Kate suspected the public assertion was for the benefit of the surrounding men. She couldn't be certain, but for a moment it looked like his eyes were glassy, but then he blinked, and it was gone.

"And Vargas?" Kate asked.

"Ah, yes," Sarkesian said, clearly contemplating his options. "Do you have any idea why he came to me for a loan?"

"No, I don't," Kate admitted. "My guess would be a poor investment or gambling debts."

"Yes, in a way that's true," he said. "And remarkable, given the reason you're here. You see, Vargas placed a five million dollar bet on the love of a father, and he lost."

"I don't understand," Kate said. "How do you place a bet on love?"

"You'll have to ask him, but perhaps I am a sentimental fool," Sarkesian said, laughing as they walked back through the catacombs. "His debt is paid, and I will set him free, mostly unharmed, but if he crosses my path again, I will kill him."

"Thank you," Kate said, cradling the watch in her hand. "I hope you know what this means."

"Oh, I do," Sarkesian said with a sly smile. "A favor for a favor and a woman of your skill may come in handy one day."

The elevator motors hummed as the freight carriage worked its way back down, but Kate's instincts were screaming. *Don't go. There's something more. Something he wants to say but can't.*

The elevator arrived, the doors opened, and she looked back at Sarkesian. *What is it? What does he know?* She stepped inside, and images of his world flashed in her mind. Arms dealer. Gun Range. Cases of rifles and ammunition. The M110. A sniper rifle. *He procures specialty equipment for discerning clients.*

"Do you know who shot Jake?" Kate's voice echoed against the grated elevator doors.

Sarkesian's hesitation was brief, but his eyes locked onto hers. "I know only this...he is a dead man ."

Whatever he knows, he'll never say, Kate thought. *It would be bad for business. But he's right about one thing. When I find him, I will kill him.*

CHAPTER 22

THURSDAY, APRIL 30th
1:07 AM CEST

HÔTEL DE POURTALÈS, PARIS, FRANCE

KATE SLIPPED INTO HER hotel room, her mind still reeling from the encounter with Sarkesian. The weight of Bella's watch in her pocket was a comforting presence, but the Armenian crime lord's parting words echoed in her head: "I know only this...he is a dead man."

Kate set up her encrypted tablet and launched a video chat.

"Everything okay?" Nomad asked.

"Why do you ask?"

"It's 1 AM in Paris, and you connected with an unknown device."

"Couldn't sleep," Kate said. "New gear. It's secure."

"Well, good timing. I've been reviewing the street-cam video."

"You got it?" Kate's voice carried a mix of surprise and anticipation.

"Seriously? Are you trying to hurt my feelings?" Nomad teased.

"You said it'd be tough," she shot back.

"I did," he admitted, chuckling. "But I was just being modest."

"Well, stop. It doesn't suit you."

"OK. Fine, down to business. I not only downloaded all the archive videos for the full week, plus the day of the attack. It's all sitting in your folder, but I think I figured out what you were looking for."

"Enlighten me." Kate leaned forward.

"Even better. Let me show you."

Kate's heart was racing. *Did he really know what I was hoping to find,* Kate thought. *Could he have video of the sniper?* Kate leaned forward and stared at the screen. She heard Nomad's voice commanding his system to select and play the video.

The rain-drenched street next to Café Le Pierre was nearly empty. Timestamp: two days before the attack. Almost midnight.

A man approached the lamppost, face shadowed by a wide-brimmed hat. White. Tall. Scarf pulled up, collar turned high, leather gloves concealing his hands.

He lit a cigarette, scanned the area, then scaled the pole with eerie precision. In seconds, he secured the orange streamer. The descent was just as smooth. One last glance, then he vanished down an alley.

"That's him," Kate murmured, her voice barely above a whisper. "But I was hoping..."

"For a face," Nomad finished for her. "I get it. I'm still hunting for footage—maybe something shows him coming or going."

"You won't find it," Kate said, her tone resigned. "He hung it himself—that much is clear. This guy's a pro. Doesn't trust anyone and probably works alone."

"Moves like an acrobat," Nomad observed.

Kate nodded slowly. "Definitely athletic, but there's something else—something about the way he moves...it'll come to me."

"In the meantime, we don't have much to go on," Nomad admitted. "Nothing I could run through facial-rec—from visible skin and the lamppost dimensions, we have a white male about six-one."

"Have you hunted for reflections? Maybe a car window or storefront?"

"So far, no luck," Nomad said. "And the rain's not helping."

"The rain..." Kate mused. "That's probably why he chose that night. The streets are empty..."

"Yeah, the rain," Nomad mumbled. "But maybe..."

Kate knew Nomad was just thinking out loud, and it was best not to push or probe, so she changed the subject. "What about the KATEM phone? Any luck?"

"Luck? No," Nomad said, frustration creeping into his tone. "As predicted, it's impenetrable. Whoever cracked it—pulled off the impossible. There is one possibility, but it'll take a couple of days to test."

"And the drone video?"

"They didn't just strip the audio. The edit was seamless—but not perfect. I found a fragment. Might be enough."

Kate's pulse quickened. "You think the drone's original feed is still out there?"

Nomad grinned. "Long shot—but worth a try."

"Brilliant," Kate said, her mind racing. "We know where the SUV was hit. Given the remote area, the drone's signal had a limited number of paths back to the operator."

"That's the idea," Nomad replied. "Here's hoping it works."

"If you find anything, alert me immediately. I don't care what time it is," Kate instructed. "Understood?"

"Yes, ma'am," Nomad teased like he was following orders. "Oh, I almost forgot. The autopsy report you wanted. It's gruesome, so I would advise against flipping through the photos. Is there something specific you wanted to know?"

"What does it say about handcuffs?"

"Handcuffs?" Nomad asked. "Let me see...condition of remains, charred and fragmented...body position, seated upright...Here it is...Remains exhibited evidence of restraint...handcuffs were found positioned in front of the body, indicating..."

"That's enough," Kate interrupted. "And you're right, probably best I don't see the report."

Kate ended the call and wrestled with the autopsy news. *I wanted to know,* she thought. *Margot's convinced Marcus is dead. That's enough. No distractions. Front sight focus.*

She opened the encrypted folder on the Darknet server and went right back to the video Nomad played. Kate studied the black-clad figure, head down, walking toward the lamp. She paused right before he scaled the post and advanced frame by frame.

His ascent was swift and graceful, each motion precise and economical. He didn't so much climb as flow up the lamppost, using minimal contact points and leveraging his body weight with expert control. His legs wrapped around the pole in a smooth, spiral motion while his arms worked in perfect coordination to pull himself upward.

His movements were fluid, effortless, Kate thought. *Not just strength—familiarity. Not an acrobat—a climber.*

Kate watched again and again. The way he walked. Moved. Something about it... familiar. A memory tugged at the edges of her mind. *Do I know him?*

She shook the thought away. *No. Just tired.*

CHAPTER 23

THURSDAY, APRIL 30th
6:45 AM CEST

HÔTEL DE POURTALÈS, PARIS, FRANCE

KATE'S NIGHT WAS A blur of fragmented dreams—Marcus fighting to save Jake, Moshenski's men dragging him away, an SUV erupting in a blinding flash. She groaned, shoving off the tangled sheets. "I give up."

Coffee. Shower. Focus.

She carried the double espresso into the bathroom, downed the last drop, and stepped into the shower. Kate emerged twenty minutes later, almost ready to face the day. She searched for something suitable, believable, on the TV and settled on euronews. With the news to occupy her eavesdropping fans, she closed the bedroom door and headed for the desk.

Caffeine and adrenaline worked their magic as Kate war-gamed ways she could leave the hotel without being seen. *The rooftop?* A satellite analysis shut that down. *No way—I'm good, but I can't fly.*

A sharp knock pulled Kate from her thoughts. 7:45 AM. She checked the peephole—Sebastian Vargas, stiff, uncomfortable.

She opened the door, her gaze flicking to his bandaged hand.

Sebastian forced a half-smile. "Kate, I know it's early, but can we talk?" He lifted his injured finger. "Damn car door. Lucky I didn't lose it entirely."

Kate's eyes narrowed. "You better come in." She stepped aside, closing the door behind him. "Sebastian, I know what happened. You're lucky Sarkesian didn't keep the finger as a souvenir."

Relief flickered briefly in his eyes before shame overtook him. "So... it's true. I have you to thank for my freedom."

"No." Kate's voice was sharp. "You have me to thank for your life."

Sebastian's gaze fell to the floor, his head bowing under the weight of her words. "You're right. I owe you my life."

Kate paced. "Isabella could've been killed. Your man was butchered." She stopped, leveling him with a glare. "What the hell were you thinking?"

"No one was supposed to get hurt." Vargas's voice was hoarse. "In and out before we returned. I sent Bella in with Ramirez, expecting her to call me—report the robbery. When the call didn't come, I went back. You know the rest."

"That was your deal? No one gets hurt?" Kate's anger simmered beneath her words. "And you thought dealing with *The Shadows*—one of Europe's most notorious crime syndicates—would go smoothly? God, Vargas, I don't know whether to laugh or cry."

"Please, I beg of you, don't tell Isabella."

"Isabella? You should beg me not to call the police."

"You're right," Sebastian said. "And I would understand if you did."

"Explain it to me," Kate said. "No bullshit. No spin. Why did you go to Sarkesian?"

Sebastian swallowed hard, his hand shaking as he reached into his jacket pocket and pulled out his phone. He hesitated but then tapped the screen a few times before holding it out toward Kate.

His voice dropped to a whisper. "Her name was Sofia—she had just turned eight."

Kate took the phone, glancing at the screen. A photo of a smiling young girl beamed at the camera, sitting on her mother's lap in what looked like a suburban backyard. Vargas swiped, showing the next image: the same girl, but this time bound and gagged. Her eyes were wide, red, terrified. Seated behind her were a dozen half-naked girls, some older, a few younger, all with the unmistakable half-dead eyes of heroin addicts.

Images of abused and sex-trafficked young girls were something Kate had seen before and analyzed for the DEA. Images of the innocent and helpless that still haunted her nightmares. She was quick to shove the phone away, her anger still lurking but tempered now with a flicker of understanding.

"They killed her mother," Sebastian's voice cracked. "Then sent the photo. Forty-eight hours. Five million. Or she joins the others."

Kate's expression darkened. "Oh, God. I know this. Javier Cortez—the

Congressman from Arizona."

"Yes. He matched our profile," Sebastian replied. "Wealthy, successful businessman turned politician. He'd just secured a second term and was meeting land development partners in Nicaragua. When we took the escort contract, I suggested he leave his wife and daughter at home, but he insisted—a birthday present for his daughter, so we configured two teams."

"Why the split?"

"My team took Cortez downtown for a meeting," Sebastian explained. "His family went directly to the house, and the convoy was ambushed entering the compound. Automatic weapons shredded the lead car—that team never had a chance. The family's driver had some room to maneuver but not enough to escape, and he was shot point blank."

"Jake had the team review the incident reports—he flagged the wife's murder," Kate said. "Thought it was strange they didn't take both."

"It wasn't an accident," Sebastian said. "They executed her."

Kate's pulse ticked up. "You think Cortez was working with the Cartel?

Sebastian hesitated. "We'll never know. But when I got the team alert, the Congressman was already in a meeting—with the wrong kind of people—he looked frightened. My job was to get him out of there, so I don't know what was said or who was there, but they were angry."

"When did you realize what happened?"

"We had just secured Cortez in a backup location when a few photos and the ransom text arrived," Sebastian said. "Between photos of his dead wife and terrified little girl, Cortez lost it."

"I can imagine," Kate said.

"No, it wasn't grief," Sebastian said. "He's yelling and screaming that it's all my fault. And then it was all about the money."

"What do you mean?"

"He said he couldn't put his hands on that much money, that fast...not without losing everything, and begged me to help," Sebastian said. "He figured in my line of work I had connections—knew people."

"And you did," Kate realized. "You knew someone with a pipeline to Sarkesian."

"Intellectually, I knew it wasn't my fault, but in my heart...," Sebastian said. "I asked Cortez to leave his family home, and it was his decision, but you saw the photo. We both know these animals. They prey on innocence. I had to try, and

Cortez swore on his daughter's life he could get me the money, he just needed time—thirty days, tops."

"We both know how that turned out," Kate said. "When the feds filed corruption charges and froze his assets, Cortez blew his brains out rather than face prison."

"I sold everything. Investments, bank accounts, house, cars, jewelry, guns—anything worth something to someone. I cut the team to a bare minimum—just enough to meet contracts."

"Like Bella's," Kate said. "That's why you asked her to pay in advance."

"Exactly," Sebastian said. "I didn't have the cash flow to cover expenses or the time to wait for her office to process my invoices. And that's when Sarkesian offered me a way out."

"The robbery was his idea?"

"Yes. It's no secret Isabella is one of the world's wealthiest women," Sebastian said. "And the tabloids fill pages with photos of her couture outfits, dripping in jewels."

"Tell me about the girl, Sophia," Kate said. "Where is she now?"

"She's on a small farm in Vermont with her aunt and uncle on her mother's side," Sebastian said, showing Kate another photo. Sophia's smiling, her arms wrapped around the neck of a Golden Retriever.

Sebastian gave her a chance, Kate thought. *Something her father never did.* Kate tried not to think about the alternative, but images of Senator Cahill and revelations of his debauchery only reinforced the gut-wrenching reality of the true evil found in some men's hearts. *Sebastian may be a fool, but he's not evil.*

Kate handed back the phone. "You gambled with your client's life."

Sebastian stared at the floor. "I know. Whatever happens next—I owe you my life."

Kate's tone was ice. "And Isabella? Can your team even cover Africa?"

"We can," Sebastian insisted. "We've done all the groundwork. Plus, she's staying in the Presidential Palace, and President Bongani's providing full military escort and transportation. This one's clean."

"And then?"

Sebastian straightened up, pain and regret clear in his eyes. "Let me keep her safe one last time. After this trip, I'll tell her the truth and walk away."

"If Trident had assets available, I'd tell you to walk away right now," Kate said. "I'll try to arrange backup, and if I can, you'll take it—no questions. And when this is over, you'll tell her the truth. The whole story. If you don't, I will."

"Of course," Sebastian said. "Your offer to help is very generous. More than I deserve."

"We agree on that," Kate said, and reaching into her pocket, retrieved the old pocket watch. "Here, give this to Bella."

"What is it?" Sebastian asked.

"Only the most precious thing she owns," Kate replied, a hint of frustration creeping into her tone. "I persuaded Sarkesian to return it. He threw you in for free."

"That doesn't sound like the man who took a meat cleaver to my hand," Sebastian said. "He wants something."

"Yes, he made that very clear—a favor for a favor," Kate said. "He'll collect someday. But not today."

Kate opened the door—then shut it again. "How did Sarkesian's men get in and out unseen?"

Sebastian exhaled. "There's a service elevator to the kitchens."

Kate crossed her arms. "Show me."

Sebastian drew a quick map on the hotel notepad. "From the kitchen, a back alley leads to the delivery bays. Time it right, and you can slip in and out without anyone noticing."

Kate took the note and closed the door behind him. Armed with an exit strategy, she could finally search for answers.

But she needed Boucher.

And this time, she wouldn't take no for an answer.

Chapter 24

THURSDAY, APRIL 30th
7:00 AM CEST

HÔTEL DE POURTALÈS, PARIS, FRANCE

KATE STOOD AT THE window, watching Paris wake—morning traffic growing on the streets below, her fingers drumming the burner phone. *Was Vargas a mistake? Should I have forced him out?* She exhaled and dialed Talya.

Talya answered on the first ring, her voice crisp. "Everything okay?"

Kate broke protocol, so Talya's concern wasn't surprising. "I'm fine," Kate blurted. "Sorry to call, but I need you to make some discreet inquiries."

Talya's tone shifted. "Sounds like something's wrong."

"No—well, maybe." Kate hesitated, then pressed on. "Bella's heading to Motapa in a couple of days, and she might need backup."

"Bella?" Talya teased. "Nickname terms now?"

Kate smirked. "She's... not what I expected. But that's not why I'm calling."

"Isn't Vargas handling her security?"

"He is," Kate replied but paused. "I'm not sure it's enough."

"Spidey-sense or something concrete?"

"Both," Kate admitted. "Motapa's a powder keg. China wants back in, Wagner mercs may still be lurking, and the GEC..." Kate hesitated. "They're circling, too."

"The GEC? I thought they were the good guys."

"So did I. So does everyone, but Jake's files suggest otherwise." Kate's free hand clenched into a fist. "I can't shake the feeling that Isabella's walking into a storm, and Vargas—he may not be equipped to handle it."

There was a moment of silence on the line. "Alright. What do you need?"

"Can you check if we have any resources near Motapa? Quietly," Kate said. "I don't want to spook Forest—it's one in the morning in South Carolina—but reach out to him later. Meanwhile, see if any of your Mossad contacts or contractors might be an option."

"You know, calling Forest blows my cover," Talya warned. "He'll know we've been working together."

"It's Forest," Kate said and laughed. "He already knows. Don't ask me how. But he knows."

"Copy that," Talya agreed. "When I'm looking to see who's available, can I assume budget is not an issue?"

"Whatever it takes." Kate paused, then added softly, "I know it might seem odd, given everything else that's going on, but I won't sleep if I think she's going in without cover."

"There's nothing odd about it, Kate. It's who you are." Talya's voice was warm with understanding. "Okay, I'm on it. Now, do I need to worry about your plans today?"

"I'm glad you asked," Kate said, her voice low and determined. "Here's the plan..."

***

KATE TOOK A DEEP breath, steeling herself for the next call. *Talya was easy,* she thought. *Boucher's another matter entirely.* She dialed Boucher's burner phone, hoping he hadn't already discarded it for another.

The phone rang several times before a cautious voice answered. "Oui?"

"Laurent, it's Kate."

A pause. "Kate? This isn't safe—"

"I know. But I found the sniper's location."

"Mon Dieu," Boucher breathed. "But Kate, I can't—"

"Listen to me, Laurent. Please," Kate pleaded. "I need to get into Le Palais de l'Éclipse, and onto the roof. There may be trace evidence. I can't do it on my own but with your credentials..."

"You forget. I am suspended."

"They won't know," Kate said. "It's a privately owned event center, with nothing scheduled for today. If you flash a badge, insist the visit is official police business, we'll walk right in."

"Impossible," Boucher said firmly. "It's too dangerous. They're watching me. Watching you. Just waiting for an excuse—"

Kate's voice sharpened. "What's your plan? Hide forever? You think they'll give you your job back? They want puppets, not truth-seekers. Is that you now?"

Silence hung heavy on the line, and Kate pressed on. "No, I didn't think so. The day we met, I saw it—you care. You're not a bureaucrat, not a politician. You want the truth as much as I do—for your wife, for your son, for the lives you can still save."

"Alright," Laurent said. "But how can we meet without being discovered?"

"There's a connection between the hotel and the next building," Kate explained. "It leads to a service alley. From there, I can slip between buildings and reach Impasse des Deux Anges. Do you know it?"

"I do," Laurent said reluctantly. "It's a narrow alley, good cover."

Kate checked the time. "Thirty minutes?"

"Thirty," Laurent agreed, his voice resigned before the line went dead.

One more call. Kate dialed the front desk from the room phone, putting it on speaker.

"Bonjour, Madame," the young man answered. "How may I be of service?"

"Yes, good morning," Kate began. "I'm not feeling well today and will be resting. Please hold all calls and let housekeeping know."

"Of course," he said. "I will ensure that you are not disturbed. I hope you feel better soon."

"Merci," Kate said and quietly closed the bedroom door as she left.

Kate checked herself in the mirror. Glock 43 at her waist, spare mag left pocket, knife right. *Don't get caught.*

Kate examined the reflection in the hallway mirror, adjusting the Sandro tee as she turned sideways. Her fingers traced the subtle embroidery along the side—a designer touch that separated the shirt from classic tourist. The soft, dark fabric draped perfectly over the high-waisted trousers and masked both the pistol and extra magazine.

She slipped on the Alexander McQueen blazer, slid the messenger bag over her shoulder, and smiled. The woman in the mirror was every bit the casual city dweller, not an armed forensic investigator.

Chapter 25

THURSDAY, APRIL 30th
7:30 AM CEST

LE PALAIS DE L'ÉCLIPSE, PARIS, FRANCE

Talya settled into a seat at Le Café Pierre. The aroma of fresh croissants and rich espresso wafting through the air, a stark contrast to the somber atmosphere that still clung to the area.

Despite her resolve, Talya's gaze drifted to the makeshift memorial—photos, wilted flowers, scrawled notes. A faded newspaper lay among them, its front page frozen in time: Jake, AK-47 in hand, moments before his death. The headline: "Que Dieu bénisse l'Américain." *God Bless the American.*

She swallowed hard, the lump in her throat threatening to overwhelm her. Not now, she told herself, pushing the ache aside. Jake wouldn't want that. She had a job to do. Still, Jake's absence felt like a physical ache. He was more than a boss—he pulled her from the depths of her own personal hell. He was a mentor and a friend. And now it was her job to safeguard the one thing in this life Jake held most dear.

***

8:00 AM CEST

Shepard parked the nondescript Renault Megane, its gray body blending into the morning traffic. Just another forgettable car, just another face in the crowd.

The early morning light cast long shadows on the historical building's ornate façade. From his vantage point, Ben could see the ornate details of the palace's architecture, the intricate carvings, and the imposing entrance, and more importantly, he could scan the roof line for any sign of movement.

If Grant's right, Shepard mused, eyes fixed on the rooftop edge overlooking Le Café Pierre, *she'll show. That's where it happened. That's where he took the shot.*

With binoculars within reach, he sipped his coffee, trying to shake off the fatigue from the restless night spent planning.

***

As the city stirred to life around her, Talya's keen eyes scanned the street. A gray Renault sedan crawled past, ignoring prime parking spots before settling into a space with a clear view of Le Palais de l'Éclipse.

Talya smirked. "Gotcha." Kate nailed it—they knew she'd find the building, and she knew they'd be watching.

Talya adjusted the book on her table, angling its spine towards the car. To any casual observer, she was just another Parisian engrossed in her phone. In reality, her fingers danced across the screen, controlling the high-resolution camera hidden within the book's pages.

Talya's hidden camera snapped crisp shots—jawline, a glint of Breitling, the shoulder-holster bulge. *Old-school. The suit? Brioni, maybe Zegna. And that is definitely not your car. Now, how about a profile shot?*

***

8:15 AM CEST

Ben's phone buzzed, jolting him from his thoughts. The caller ID was Grant Collins, and Ben answered on the first ring.

"Everything set?" Grant asked, his voice echoing on the speakerphone.

"I'm in position," Ben said, voice low and tense. He glanced up again at the roof line.

"Where is she now?"

Ben checked the GPS signal from Kate's phone. "Hasn't moved from the hotel," Ben answered. "What if she doesn't show?"

Grant chuckled, a low, calculated sound. "She'll come. Preacher can't resist the scent of evidence. It's like a lion with a tethered goat. Just make sure you're ready—there won't be a second chance."

"And if she's not alone?" Ben asked. "What if she has help?"

Grant's tone turned almost giddy. "Even better," he said. "We need collateral damage to sell the story, and taking out someone she knows is better than random tourists."

The line went dead, leaving Shepard alone with his thoughts. He admired Kate, her tenacity and intelligence, qualities that made her both a formidable opponent and a valuable pawn in their game. And he knew Grant was right. *She'll come. She always does. And that's her weakness.*

***

THURSDAY, APRIL 30th
9:00 AM CEST

LE PALAIS DE L'ÉCLIPSE, PARIS, FRANCE

SHEPARD KEPT HIS EYES fixed on the entrance, fingers tapping nervously on the binoculars in his lap, mind racing with anticipation. The first sign of movement was at precisely 9:00 AM. He brought the optics up and watched a figure on the inside unlock the front doors. Ben's pulse quickened. "Any time now," he muttered to himself, and trained his eyes on the steps leading up the building's grand entrance.

The streets were already bustling with locals, merchants and businessman, schoolchildren, and university students. The echo of chaotic conversations mixed with the sounds of the morning commute traffic. He knew Preacher could be hard to spot amid that activity, but the minute she climbed the stairs, she'd be exposed. As if on cue, two figures caught his attention, crossing the street in front of the building.

A man and a woman, with their backs turned to his position, walked toward the entrance. Ben raised the binoculars, focusing on the pair. From behind, he studied the woman first - tall, slender, with auburn hair cascading over her coat. Her movements were fluid yet alert, head swiveling subtly as she scanned her surroundings. *That's her,* Ben concluded. *But who's that with her?*

Ben's attention shifted to her companion. The man stood around six feet, his posture exuding quiet authority. His gait matched Kate's - purposeful but unhurried. Ben noted the charcoal suit jacket and neatly trimmed salt-and-pepper hair. *Professional. Not extravagant.* "Who are you?" Ben wondered aloud.

As the pair ascended the steps, Ben held his breath, waiting for a clear view of the man's face. *Come on,* he thought. *Let's have a look.* At the landing, the man reached for the door handle, turning slightly to hold the door for Kate. At that moment, his profile came into view. "Laurent Boucher," Ben said out loud, the name heavy with implication. *That was a mistake, old friend. You should have stayed in hiding.*

Grant Collins answered Ben's call with a simple question. "Is she there?"

"Yes," Ben replied. "You were right."

"And I'll bet her phone is still at the hotel."

Ben realized he was so focused on the entrance he wasn't monitoring Kate's GPS, but Collins was right. The phone was still at the hotel. The moment of silence was all Collins needed.

"I knew it," Collins said with smug confidence. "Underestimating her was a mistake. Is she alone?"

"Boucher is with her."

"Even better," Collins said. "Call me when it's done."

***

When Mr. Brioni turned, glancing over his shoulder, Talya's patience paid off. She snapped a near-perfect three-quarter profile shot, her fingers flying over the screen to adjust the resolution. *That should be enough for facial rec,* she thought, and studied the image on her phone. *Angular features, grayish-blue eyes. Tan and weathered, but not old. Fifties, I'd guess from the gray in his hair, a faint scar on his left cheek.*

She glanced at her watch. *This should be about right,* she thought. *And here they come.* As Kate and Boucher climbed the steps, she noted how Mr. Brioni's posture stiffened, his surveillance becoming less discreet. He brought the binoculars up and kept them on target. *He's trying to identify who's with Kate.* Mr. Brioni put down the optics and picked up the phone. *Ah, he just recognized Boucher, and someone needs to know.*

Talya watched the front doors. *If the ruse works,* she thought. *Kate will be in there for a while. Let's see if Mr. Brioni has a social media profile.* She cropped the photo, did a quick image search, and was disappointed by the number of hits—politicians, actors, businessmen. *I guess he's got one of those faces. Average man in his fifties. No distinguishing marks or scars—at least none that I can see. Well, since I'm not going anywhere.*

***

KATE STRODE INTO THE lobby of l'Éclipse and into a breathtaking testament to the opulence and grandeur of a bygone era. Soaring ceilings adorned with intricate frescoes depicting scenes from classical mythology. Crystal chandeliers, their facets catching the morning light streaming through tall windows, casting prismatic patterns across the room. Everywhere Kate looked, she knew no expense was spared in the restoration, from the marble floor to the gilt-edged wood paneling. *This was a labor of love,* she thought. *From a very wealthy patron.*

Boucher flashed his badge at the young woman behind the reception desk, his authority silencing any awkward questions. Kate noticed the subtle widening of the employee's eyes and the way she straightened her posture. Kate was guilty by association and granted the same authority. The young woman handed Boucher the rooftop door key, directing them toward the elevator, one of the modern conveniences required to serve the public.

From the top floor, they took the service stairs to access the roof. They stepped into the morning light, and the rooftop door clicked shut. Kate wasted no time, pulling on gloves, booties, and kneepads. She offered a pair to Boucher, who scoffed.

"This is absurd," Boucher muttered, crossing his arms.

Kate's steely gaze didn't waver. "Then stay out of my way," she shot back.

"Until proven otherwise, this is a crime scene."

Boucher opened his mouth, but Kate's expression must have changed his mind. He raised his hands in surrender and stepped back.

Kate prowled the perimeter of the building first, determined not to miss anything and contemplating how the sniper came and went. The lobby security cameras and state-of-the-art alarm system suggested that roof access from the interior was far less likely than the exterior. The exterior cameras were adequate quality but directed toward ground floor doors. *They're just capturing anyone who enters and exits normally,* she thought. *And might not even be recording.* She made a note to ask on the way out.

She paused at the railing—faint scuffs on the metal. She peered over. *Sheer brick wall. Narrow alley below. No cars. Maybe a motorcycle—easy rappel and a clean escape.*

"Here," she murmured, more to herself than Boucher. "This is where he escaped."

Kate saw where the rope polished a small section of the railing, and she pictured how an experienced climber could use a double-rope rappel and a figure-eight descender to reach the ground. *From this height*, she knew. *Maybe two seconds to the alley. Retrieve the rope and vanish seconds later.* Scattered grains of rooftop gravel on the ledge added credence to her theory, and she'd already surmised the sniper was a climber, but nothing brought her any closer to a name.

Her focus shifted from the sniper's rooftop access and escape to where he set the overwatch position. With the range finder in hand, Kate moved to the edge of the building facing Café Le Pierre. From the sound analysis of Jake's FaceTime call, she knew the shooter's approximate distance from Jake's phone. The range finder helped her eliminate the extreme corners of the building, narrowing the search area, and she edged toward the center. *This is the area*, she confirmed, spotting the orange wind flag fluttering on the lamppost and verifying the distance. *This is where he monitored the attack and shot Jake.*

***

TALYA SCROLLED THROUGH THE image results, her focus shifting between Mr. Brioni's photo and social media profiles. Each mismatched face brought a fresh wave of frustration. Then she froze. *Hang on. Who's this? Benjamin Shepard,*

Founder Sentinel Intelligence Solutions. She glanced at the image search result and back at the man in the car. *That's him! Now, who the hell are you, and why are you following Kate?*

The Sentinel Intelligence company profile and mission statement were meaningless corporate nonsense—clearly, no one ever reads this fluff. But among the who's who collection of client logos, one stood out. *The Global Economic Council. Maybe that's who's tracking Kate's every move, but isn't this way below your paygrade,* Talya wondered. *Whoa! He was CIA.*

The intentionally brief BIO on the Sentinel website noted Benjamin Shepard's Georgetown University Master's Degree in International Relations and a decade of service as the Middle East Regional COS. *Christ...he was the CIA's Chief of Station when Kate was in Syria. Kate needs to know,* and Talya started typing.

> Your stalker is Benjamin Shepard.

When there was no reply, Talya asked for confirmation.

> Copy Last?

It took a moment for Kate to reply. *She must be considering the implications,* Talya suspected. *And maybe what action I should take.*

> Good Copy. Do Not Engage.

***

KATE SLIPPED THE PHONE into her back pocket.

"Was that important?" Boucher asked.

"No," Kate lied. "Just my people checking to see if I needed anything."

She fished the small Garrett Pro-Point metal detector out of the messenger bag and slipped the headset over her ears. The device hummed to life with a low, slow buzz in her ears and a slight vibration in her hands. This device was the key to locating the sniper's spent shell casing. *If, by some miracle, he didn't police his brass.* Kate knew it was a long shot—a professional never leaves brass behind, but in a moment of chaos, it was a possibility she couldn't ignore.

While she walked through a methodical pattern, waving the device, her thoughts were on Talya's news. *Ben Shepard. He and Margot butted heads from the minute we landed in Syria*, Kate thought. *There's no way she asked him to keep an eye on me. Whatever he's up to, it's not CIA.*

The first hour of scanning was nothing but false positives pinging endlessly in Kate's ears—ventilation, wiring, discarded cans from rooftop trysts. Boucher grew impatient, abandoning Kate in search of what little shade the rooftop offered.

The sun and fatigue were taking a toll on Kate, too. She was about to conclude the search was wasted effort when the detector sang a new tune and jumped in her hands. Her heart raced as she homed in on the source. There, wedged beneath a sheet of black roof flashing, gleamed an unexpected prize.

"Laurent!" she called out, her excitement barely contained.

Boucher was at her side in an instant, watching Kate extract the shell casing with her forceps. It was more difficult to remove than she imagined. "Must have rolled under here," Kate began. "And I'll bet the shooter stepped on it."

Kate recovered the brass shell, but a quick look at the caliber sent a chill down her arm, raising the hair on the back of her neck. She fought to remain calm. *Trust no one,* she thought. That was Jake's warning. *Let's see where this goes.*

"What do you think?" Kate asked, holding the casing for Boucher to examine.

"7.62×54," he said, recognizing the round immediately.

Kate nodded in agreement, pretending she didn't already know.

She stood, pulled an evidence bag from her pocket, and dropped the round inside.

"Dragunov?"

"Probably. Right caliber," Boucher replied. "The Russian sniper rifle is easy to acquire and deadly—I mean, highly accurate at this range."

"In the hands of a trained marksman," Kate added.

"That's true. There's no shortage of Dragunov's on the black market," Boucher noted. "But training is another matter."

"That doesn't narrow it down much, maybe former military." But it wasn't the shot that required skill. She could make the shot and countless others. It was the entry and exit, the climb and the escape, that set this shooter apart from others.

Kate sealed the casing in an evidence bag and wondered if she was being watched. She took her time with the bag and scanned the surrounding buildings, anything with a view of the l'Éclipse rooftop. *Is Boucher compromised,* she wondered. *Did he accept my request for a reason?*

"We need to get this analyzed," she said, testing Boucher's attitude and resolve.

"Do you know someone who could? Someone willing to overlook your... current situation?"

Boucher's expression darkened momentarily. "You can't be serious," he said. "The chances of getting a usable print—"

"Are about as good as finding anything up here in the first place," she finished, a hint of a smirk playing at her lips. "But here we are."

"I'll make a few calls," he said. "But I make no promises."

"I understand. In the meantime, hang on to it," Kate offered as another test. "In case you find someone."

"No, too risky," he said. "If I'm caught, the evidence will disappear, and this time, I might disappear with it. I'll contact you when I have news."

Kate pushed the evidence bag deep into a pants pocket and began packing up her gear. *Boucher's either very clever, or he's clean,* Kate thought. *My gut tells me he's clean, and whatever happens next, he's in as much danger as I am. Maybe more.*

***

Talya sat patiently while Kate explored the building's rooftop for over an hour, and Shepard never moved. She spotted Kate using the range finder along the edge of the roof, and when she disappeared below the edge, Talya pictured Kate on her hands and knees, examining every square inch of the area where the sniper took the shot.

The time crawled by, marked only by the ebb and flow of café patrons and the gradual shift of shadows across the square.

A buzz on her phone shattered the monotony. Kate's message sent a jolt of adrenaline through Talya's body.

Moving. Yellow.

In one fluid motion, she pocketed her phone, scooped up the book, and tossed some Euros onto the table.

All Talya knew for sure was that Kate was coming out and to stay sharp. *Kate doesn't scare easily,* Talya knew. *But something raised the threat level.* She climbed on the back of the Yamaha slipped on the helmet, her eyes darting between the stairs and Benjamin Shepard—tracking his focus, looking for any overt movement.

Kate and Boucher emerged from l'Éclipse, heading down the stairs toward the sidewalk's bustling lunchtime crowd and the sea of shopping bags and briefcases. Boucher's car was near, but Talya knew the pedestrian density would slow their progress.

Shepard started his car but didn't move. *What's he waiting for,* she wondered. Kate reached the bottom of the grand stairway, and she and Boucher entered the sidewalk fray. Talya sat on the back of her idling bike, ready to merge into traffic.

When his cell phone appeared, Talya's gut clenched. *Car bomb?* But when he pressed the phone to his ear, she relaxed. *Thank God,* she thought and took a deep breath. *Just making a call—someone needs to know Kate's on the move.*

***

KATE'S INSTINCTS SCREAMED—THEN SHE saw him. A man in a dark suit, moving too smoothly, too focused. Sunglasses hid his eyes, but a tattoo peeked above his collar. Her pulse jumped. His hand slipped into his jacket.

She slipped the fingers of her left hand under the front edge of her shirt, right wrist pressing against the Glock in her waistband. *Rip and grip,* she thought, ready to yank up the shirt while her right hand gripped and drew the pistol.

When his hand emerged, wrapped around a phone, Kate took a breath. He answered the call, but his head and focus never wavered. Neither did Kate's. He slipped the phone back into his jacket pocket and pulled a pistol.

"Gun!" Kate yelled, fighting to rise above the midday chatter. With her shoulder, she shoved Boucher hard, sending him stumbling as the first muffled pop of a suppressed weapon cut through the air.

Kate's Glock cleared her holster, and rocking the gun toward her target, her training took over. *Close the distance.* She lunged forward, her body a coiled spring. Her left arm up, she pushed the assassin's gun away from her and Boucher, and his second shot rang out, shattering the windshield of a parked car.

Kate jammed the Glock against his ribs. Two rounds. No effect. BODY ARMOR. She drove the muzzle under his chin and fired.

Screams erupted as the pedestrians woke to what was happening and scattered like startled birds, but in a heartbeat, it was over. The gunman lay motionless. Kate's point-blank shots left an acrid smell of burning fabric and flesh and a pool of blood spreading beneath his head. Kate's eyes darted, searching for others, her weapon in tight to her chest, out of sight but ready. Convinced he was alone, she holstered her gun and turned to check on Boucher.

Her heart sank when she saw him propped against a car, blood seeping between the fingers that clutched his side, each ragged breath a battle for oxygen.

"Go," he wheezed, flecks of red staining his lips. "You can't be here."

Before Kate could protest, tires screeched. A car skidded to a stop beside them. Kate's hand flew to her weapon, but a familiar voice cut through the chaos.

"Kate put the gun away!" Shepard's voice cut through the chaos. "Help me. We've got to get him in the car—now!"

The driver's door flew open. He jumped out and wrapped his arms around Boucher's chest, dragging him towards the vehicle.

"Get the door!" he ordered. "And get inside."

Kate's mind raced, but her body moved on autopilot. She yanked open the passenger door, scrambling inside as the man maneuvered Boucher into the back. Kate grabbed Boucher's shoulders, pulling him fully into the car as warm blood soaked into her clothes.

The driver leapt back behind the wheel, horn blaring as he scattered onlookers and peeled away from the curb.

"Shepard," Kate's voice was thick with disbelief. "What are you doing here?"

"Saving your life," he growled, eyes locked on the road ahead. "Keep pressure on that wound."

Kate pressed down on Boucher's side, feeling his life slip away beneath her fingers. The city blurred past the windows, sirens wailing in the distance. With adrenaline surging, Kate's brain flooded with questions, but only one erupted.

"Where are we going?"

Kate saw him look back at her in the rear-view mirror.

"Are you injured?"

"No."

"Are you sure?"

"It's not my blood," Kate shouted over the roar of the engine and squealing tires. "Where are we going?"

"Closest hospital," he said. "That won't ask questions."

***

Talya was trapped. Gunfire shattered the air, triggering chaos—women screaming, people running, brakes screeching. Shepard's Renault sped from the curb, horn blaring as it carved a path toward Kate. Traffic froze, pedestrians darting over and between cars. Talya gunned the Yamaha, maneuvering between the vehicles to escape the gridlock.

Kate climbed into the Renault's back seat, her hands slick with blood as she hauled Boucher inside. Talya's heart slammed against her ribs as she jumped the curb, weaving onto the sidewalk—the wail of approaching sirens adding to the cacophony. She flew past the fallen gunman, his blood-soaked face lifeless, dodging frantic pedestrians and running traffic signals as the car sped away.

Her focus locked on the Renault disappearing into the chaos. She couldn't lose them. *Kate knows Shepard. But does she trust him?* Talya's jaw tightened. *She must. It's the only explanation. And I know where they're going.*

Hôpital des Armées Percy wasn't the closest hospital, but it was the most discreet. Like Walter Reed in Maryland, Percy handled high-profile government and military figures with absolute secrecy.

He knows Boucher, Talya thought. *And he knows Boucher's credentials will get them through the gates.*

CHAPTER 26

THURSDAY, APRIL 30th
12:33 PM CEST

HÔPITAL D'INSTRUCTION DES ARMÉES PERCY, PARIS

BOUCHER'S BLOOD SEEPED THROUGH Kate's fingers as she fought to keep pressure on the wound. The car swerved violently, horns blaring. "Come on, people, move!" she muttered, her grip tightening as Boucher gasped. *Trying to save a man's a life.* She rolled him onto his side, one hand steadying him, the other shoving her Glock beneath Shepard's seat. The ID in Boucher's jacket pressed against her palm. *I might need that.*

Shepard's continuous horn tapping alerted both the military guards and hospital staff of an incoming emergency. Kate peered out the window. Past the manicured hedges, she saw the discrete but unmistakable presence of armed military personnel stationed at strategic points. The Renault screeched to a halt beneath the emergency entrance canopy. Armed guards materialized on either side of the car, their hands twitching toward their sidearms until they registered the scene.

Kate burst out of the car, blood staining her clothes in jagged streaks. She held up Boucher's credentials to the guards, her voice urgent and steady despite the chaos. "Le directeur adjoint de la DGSI a été blessé par balle dans une tentative d'assassinat. Il a besoin de soins médicaux immédiats." *The Deputy Director of the DGSI was shot in an assassination attempt and needs immediate medical attention.*

The guards stood aside, waving in the waiting medical team, who rushed out to the car. An emergency triage team of nurses and doctors transferred Boucher to a gurney, and Kate dumped as much detail as she could. Gun-shot wound, time of the injury, her attempt to pack the wound, and observations on Boucher's breathing.

Kate followed the gurney through the large, automatic glass doors and toward the interior hall and another guard. She presented Boucher's credentials again and insisted that she was required to stay with him until instructed otherwise by her superiors. Between the perfection of her French, the blood on her clothing, and the look in Kate's eyes, the guard relented and let her pass. Beyond the entrance doors, she saw Boucher's gurney, surrounded by medical staff, disappear into an exam room. *He's so pale, she thought. He lost a lot of blood.* As the exam room door closed, Kate said a silent prayer and took a seat in the surgical waiting room.

A small TV in one section of the room distracted a couple of young children while their mother waited nearby, her crossed leg bouncing while she flipped through the pages of a magazine she wasn't reading. Kate guessed that her husband, the children's father, was probably military. *Whatever happened,* she thought. *Was unexpected and serious. Maybe a training accident.*

Shepard's arrival cut through Kate's spiraling thoughts. "How did you get in?"

He shrugged. "Friends in French intelligence," he said, taking the seat next to her. "And I made sure you were cleared, too. Boucher's credentials helped."

"They haven't said anything yet," Kate added. "But he didn't look good."

"No, he didn't. And neither do you," Shepard said, nodding at the blood-soaked shirt. "Want me to see if I can find something for you to put on?"

"That can wait," Kate said. "What I want to know is why you were following me?"

"You're welcome," Shepard replied smoothly.

Kate's eyes narrowed. "Fair enough. If Boucher lives, he owes you his life. Now answer my question."

Shepard held her gaze, weighing his response. "A mutual friend wanted me to keep tabs on you," he said, his tone unreadable. "After Jake's death...and the attack on you...I get it now." He paused, just long enough to feel intentional. "I'm sorry about Jake. We didn't always see eye to eye, especially after Syria. But his skill? His resolve? I never doubted that."

Jake didn't suffer fools, Kate thought, studying his response—the words sounded genuine, but Shepard was trained to sound genuine.

"Margot told me I was on my own," Kate said. "And last I checked, she wasn't a fan of yours either."

Shepard smirked. "Neither were you, last I checked."

Kate let that hang in the air for a beat. "So why are you here?"

"You don't trust easily," Shepard observed. "I get it—that's smart." He exhaled through his nose, like a man indulging a question he didn't have to answer. "Let's just say my current employers see value in knowing where you stand. If you're looking into something sensitive, that's a risk—for a lot of people. Some of them might want to help you. Some might want to stop you."

Kate studied him. Shepard was playing it just close enough to the truth to be believable, just vague enough to be dangerous.

"From the suit, I gather the private sector is treating you well," she said. "And the Renault is not your car."

Shepard chuckled. "Same old Kate. You don't miss much." He leaned back, studying her. "We could use an analyst of your caliber."

Kate's lips curled slightly. "Who's 'we'?"

"Mostly former intelligence folks, like yourself," he said. "We're paid as International Security Consultants and do what we've always done—track the players, assess the risks. Only now, we advise global corporations and foundations."

"Sounds expensive."

"Yes, very," Shepard agreed. "But they can afford it."

Kate held his gaze. "Like the GEC?"

A flicker. Just a flicker of something—a calculation behind his eyes. Then, gone.

"Yes," Shepard said. "Among others." He glanced at his bloodstained suit with mild distaste. "And for the record, my personal car is a gorgeous Black Sapphire BMW, which I'm thrilled isn't drenched in your Boucher's blood. Though my assistant will not be happy when I return his Renault."

Kate barely heard the last part. Her mind was already turning.

The GEC. It wasn't just a passing name-drop. Shepard expected the question. Kate filed that away for later.

The emergency room's triage doctor entered the waiting room. He glanced over at the young woman and the kids and then over at Kate and Shepard. He approached Kate, pulling up a chair, his French spoken in hushed tones. "Deputy Director Boucher is in surgery," he said. "The bullet damaged his liver and punctured his lung. There was significant blood loss. Did you pack the wound?"

"Yes," Kate replied. "I hoped it would help."

"You probably saved his life," the doctor said. "He'll be in surgery for hours, so it will be some time before we know if he's out of the woods, but you gave him a chance."

When the doctor left, Shepard turned back to Kate. "I know why you're here," he said. "Margot warned me. You don't think the cafe attack was terrorism, and you're looking for proof. Am I right?"

"I have proof," Kate said, pulling the evidence bag from her pocket. "I recovered this from the roof of l'Éclipse."

"May I?" Shepard asked, holding out a hand. Kate passed him the evidence bag, watching his reaction.

"Dragunov?" he murmured.

"Looks that way," Kate said. "Boucher was going to check for prints."

Shepard's brow lifted. "That's a waste of time."

"And a pro wouldn't leave brass behind," Kate countered. "Yet here we are."

"It's not admissible," Shepard began. "No court—ah, that doesn't matter, does it? This isn't about justice."

"No," Kate said. "Nothing can bring Jake back, but there's something else going on."

"What do you mean?"

"Jake had been collecting information, trying to piece together something," Kate said. "Something big. Important. And the last thing he did was ask me to figure it out."

Shepard leaned forward. "Do you know what he found?"

"No," Kate said and struggled to get the words out. "His files were hopelessly damaged. I have a few recordings of our calls, and those are precious, but nothing more."

Shepard reached out, his hands gently covering Kate's. "I'm sorry. I can see how much this means to you." He picked up the evidence bag, turning it over in his hands like a rare artifact, his expression thoughtful. "Let me take this," he said, his voice soft but firm. "I'll see what I can find—no promises."

"You're serious?" Kate asked, wiping her eyes. "You'll have someone look?"

"But no promises," he said. "Understood?"

"I understand. But I have to try," Kate said. She stood and hugged him.

"I'm guessing you're staying until Boucher is out of surgery."

"I can't leave. Not yet," Kate agreed. "He wouldn't be here if it wasn't for me, but you should go."

Kate tore the corner of a waiting room magazine and scribbled her phone number. "Call me if you find something, anything."

***

BEN SHEPARD LEFT THE hospital and sauntered toward the borrowed Renault. *I will have to do something about all that blood,* he thought. *But even if I have to buy the kid a new car, it was worth it.*

He called Grant, finding it difficult not to smile as he dialed. "You were right," he said. "Collateral damage was the key. She bought it and I'm in."

"She handed it over?" Grant asked his tone somewhere between impressed and amused.

"Sealed up in a pristine little evidence bag," Shepard replied, his smirk audible over the phone.

"I knew she wouldn't stop until she found something," Grant said. "Is Boucher dead?"

"Not yet. But he won't make it through the night," Shepard replied. "Sorry about your man. I didn't expect Preacher to be armed."

"She saved me the trouble," Grant said. "No loose ends." His tone sharpened. "What about the files? Are we exposed?"

Shepard hesitated—a fraction too long. "Not a chance," he said, leaning against the Renault. "She swore they're corrupted. It's personal, not intel."

Grant's tone sharpened. "You're sure? Enough to bet our lives? If Mueller finds out you're wrong—"

Shepard exhaled. "I'm not wrong."

"That's good timing," Grant said. "I leave town on Saturday."

"Motapa?"

"Yes, back to Africa," Grant said. "If Mueller's negotiations don't go as planned, I'll be there to light the fuse."

"Understood," Shepard said. "Don't worry. I've got this. Preacher's investigation ends tomorrow. One way or another."

"Just stick to the script," Grant said. "She'll do the rest."

Chapter 27

THURSDAY, APRIL 30th
12:33 PM CEST

HÔPITAL D'INSTRUCTION DES ARMÉES PERCY, PARIS

KATE SAT LOST IN thought, the rhythmic beeping of distant medical equipment and hushed conversations creating a somber backdrop. She fought the confusion of emotion and adrenaline. *Boucher might die,* she thought. *And for what? So, I could retrieve planted evidence?* A figure in crisp surgical scrubs approached, and Kate looked up. The woman's face obscured by a surgical mask, and hair tucked neatly beneath a pale blue cap. Latex-gloved hands gripped a clipboard with an air of authority.

Her instincts flared. The nurse's stride, the tension in her shoulders—off, but not threatening. As the woman approached, Kate honed in on the faint crinkle at the corners of her eyes. The nurse stopped and raised a clipboard, her voice a low whisper.

"Madame, veuillez me suivre s'il vous plaît." *Ma'am, please follow me.*

Recognition flashed across Kate's face. Relief tinged with concern. "Talya," she murmured, her voice barely audible. "How did you..."

Talya's gaze swept the room. "Not here." Her tone left no room for argument.

Kate followed, marveling at Talya's ingenuity and commitment. They stepped into a private consultation room, locking the door behind them. "This is a heavily guarded military hospital. How did you even get in here?"

Talya smirked, her voice light with humor. "Relax. I didn't kill anyone."

Kate's expression softened just slightly. "Boucher's still in surgery. Collapsed lung, liver damage, massive blood loss. But he has a chance."

"And the guy in the car?" Talya pressed, her smirk fading. "I spent my morning photographing him, but clearly, you know him."

Kate's jaw tightened, her voice clipped. "When I knew him, he was CIA. Chief of Station in Syria."

Talya raised an eyebrow. "Syria—that explains a lot. Is his company a front for the Agency?"

"Not likely—not after Syria," Kate said. "He got the blame, Margot got the glory, and...well, you know what I got."

"What I can tell you is he arrived early and selected a spot where he could monitor the building entrance and the roofline," Talya said. "When he saw you weren't alone, he called someone."

"He wanted someone to know Boucher was helping me," Kate noted. "What else did you see?"

"I got your text that something was wrong and was ready to move," Talya said. "Mr. Brioni, that's what I called him, started his car, but didn't move. Not at first. I expected him to pull away from the curb once you and Boucher reached the sidewalk, but he just made another call."

Kate's lips pressed into a thin line. "That bastard set us up." Her mind replayed the moments on the sidewalk. She and Boucher, side by side. A man in a dark suit moving through the crowd, deliberate, focused. His dark glasses hid his eyes, but his posture and tension screamed threat. When his hand dipped into his jacket, Kate's fingers twitched toward her weapon—until he pulled out a phone.

Her stomach turned to stone. The moment snapped into focus. The phone. The calm way he spoke. *Shepard wasn't just tracking her—he was pulling the trigger.*

"What's the plan, boss?"

"Let me think," Kate said, talking out loud. "I may not know who I'm playing, but I'm beginning to see the board." Kate pictured the moves and counters, her mind racing through recent events like moves on a chessboard.

Kate exhaled, the words slipping out before she even realized it. "Bait. Block. Threaten. Capture. Trap."

Talya's gaze sharpened. "You're thinking like a chess player?"

Kate met her eyes. "No—I'm thinking like the prey. The trap's been set—the question now is how to turn it to our advantage. That's where you come in."

"Whatever you need," Talya said.

"The first priority is protecting Boucher," Kate said, her tone firm. "If he survives surgery, they'll try to finish the job."

Talya frowned, her disbelief clear. "Why him? He's no threat to anyone."

Kate's voice dropped, her expression dark. "It's the endgame. Jake was tracking something—terrorist attacks, mysterious deaths, disappearances. It looked random.

"But it's not?" Talya asked, leaning forward slightly.

"Jake didn't think so," Kate said. "Neither do I. Not now. And that means…"

"They still want Boucher gone," Talya interrupted, her expression hardening.

"He's a good man. Honest. And in a pivotal position. That's a risk they won't take," Kate replied, her gaze unwavering. "Can you get someone in here to monitor him? If I'm right, it will be tonight."

Talya squared her shoulders, her voice resolute. "I can stay."

"No, you're with me."

"Copy. I'll make a call. We'll have guardian angels in place within the hour."

"As soon as I know Boucher's out of surgery, I'll get a car back to the hotel," Kate said. "And there's some equipment I want you to locate."

"And tomorrow?"

"My room first thing," Kate replied. "Shepard's next move is obvious, but we have to wait for it—then it's my turn."

Kate returned to the waiting room while Talya slipped out of the hospital to arrange for help. Hours passed as Kate waited for news. She stepped back through the pivotal moments of the last few days—Marcus being handcuffed and led away with Moshenski's men, his fiery death, her narrow escape from the speeding cement truck, detention at the airport, compromised electronics, and Boucher bleeding out in the car.

Images swirled in Kate's mind—fragments of timing, place, and circumstance coalescing into something just out of reach. *Where is this leading me?*

Then her breath caught.

Oh, God. My gun. It's in Shepard's car.

Kate's heart hammered against her ribs. Her gun. Her prints. If Boucher died, Shepard didn't need to kill her—all he had to do was drop the weapon at the scene.

She could already see the report.

Deputy Director of DGSI murdered. Unregistered firearm recovered. Prints match Katherine Preacher, former CIA.

A wave of nausea rolled through her with an unsettling realization. *Her opponent was always two steps ahead.*

Before Kate could even contemplate the risks, the surgeon came in to speak with her.

"The bullet punctured his lung, but that was a straightforward repair," the surgeon began, his tone measured. "The liver was more complicated. We had to remove the damaged tissue, but the liver regenerates—it'll heal with time. For now, he's in the ICU. There's significant risk of complications, but the surgery went as well as we could have hoped."

She knew what the doctor didn't say. The next 24 to 48 hours were critical. It was also one reason Kate knew if someone was coming for Boucher, it would be tonight.

Chapter 28

HÔTEL DE POURTALÈS, PARIS, FRANCE

KATE STEPPED INTO THE lobby, leaving behind the chaos of the day for the hushed opulence of marble and soft lighting. She exhaled, savoring the solitude. *All I want is to strip off these clothes, pour a glass of wine, and sink into a hot bath.*

The elevator chimed, and Isabella Marquez stepped out, a vision of effortless glamor. Her entourage of assistants and security flanked her, but Kate barely noticed them. *She is stunning*, Kate thought. *A big event, no doubt.* The emerald green silk clung to Bella's frame. Elie Saab couture, if Kate had to guess, the intricate beadwork catching the light with each step.

Kate instinctively stepped back, slipping toward an alcove. Too late. Bella's gaze locked onto hers. She gasped, her gaze fixed on the bloodstains. Ignoring the couture gown and abandoning her entourage, Bella rushed forward and enveloped Kate in a warm, unexpected embrace.

"My God," Bella whispered, stepping back just enough to scan Kate's face. "Are you hurt?" Her voice was barely above a breath. "Tell me you're alright." Before Kate could answer, Bella pulled her in again, clutching her as if she might disappear.

The genuine concern etched across Bella's face and her total disregard for the role of Isabella Marquez she played only moments before caught Kate off guard. The wave of emotion was unexpected.

"I'm fine," Kate murmured, steadying her voice. "Not my blood."

Bella's eyes filled with tears, and she nodded.

"Stop," Kate said, forcing a smile. "You'll ruin your makeup."

Bella pulled a tissue from her clutch and dabbed at her eyes and nose. "Nothing that can't be fixed," she said. "And that's their problem," she added, nodding over her shoulder at the crew waiting behind.

"You look amazing," Kate said, happy to change the subject. "Simply stunning."

Bella dabbed at her eyes with a tissue, trying to compose herself. Then, with a subtle smile, she opened her clutch to reveal the pocket watch nestled inside. "I know you recovered it—Sebastian told me."

"I had a hunch," Kate said, brushing off the effort. "And it paid off."

Bella shook her head, her smile tinged with disbelief. "Don't think for a minute I believe that," Bella scolded. "But thank you. For everything."

"Ms. Marquez," someone interrupted. "The car is here, and we really should be going."

Bella leaned in, kissed Kate's cheek, and smiled. "Duty calls," she said with a small shrug before gliding back toward her waiting entourage.

Kate watched her go, the emerald gown sweeping across the floor. *I didn't expect Vargas to say anything,* she thought, surprised. *Maybe there's hope for him after all.*

Chapter 29

HÔTEL DE POURTALÈS, PARIS, FRANCE

KATE JOLTED AWAKE, HEART pounding. The dream lingered, hazy but insistent. She blinked at the bedside clock—sleep was a luxury she couldn't afford. With a sigh, she swung her legs over the edge, bare feet meeting cool hardwood.

She moved through her routine, mind racing ahead of her first espresso. Dressed in dark jeans and a fitted black top, she started the Jura machine. The rich aroma filled the suite. Double shot in hand, she sank into the armchair by the window and opened her laptop.

The encrypted video channel chimed softly as Nomad's avatar appeared on the screen. "You're up early, even for you. Everything all right?"

Kate paused, took a slow sip of her espresso, and stared out the window. "Depends on what you mean by 'all right,'" she said with a wry smile. "I woke from the strangest dream. A lion roared at the foot of my bed."

"Sounds more like a nightmare."

"No, it wasn't scary," she said, her voice thoughtful. "It was like we understood each other. He just looked at me—old, regal, like some ancient king. Three scars, one under his eye and two across his cheek. It felt...significant."

"That's cool," Nomad said. "To recall it so vividly, he must have left quite an impression."

"I still find it a little haunting, but that's not the weird part," Kate said. "I slid out of bed, and was standing, staring at him. Then he lowered his head and bowed."

"I don't think lions bow," Nomad teased. "Pounce, yes. Bow, not so much. So what did you do?"

"I bowed, of course," Kate said and laughed. "It seemed like the proper thing to do, and when I looked up, he was gone."

"I rarely remember my dreams," Nomad said. "Except when…"

Nomad's voice suddenly trailed off, like he was deep in thought. "Except what?"

"Except when I can walk," Nomad finished quietly.

Kate's heart clenched, but before she could respond, Nomad changed the subject. "I have good news, sort of, on the KATEM phone."

"That's great. Let's have it."

"I don't know who sent the drone video, but I know how," Nomad said. "They piggybacked on a KATEM phone from Moshenski's contact list."

Kate leaned forward. "They used the authentication cache to bypass identity protocols. That's…brilliant."

"Wish I'd thought of it," Nomad admitted.

"But you did," Kate countered.

"I found it," he corrected. "Not the same thing, but still useful."

"It is—this is huge," Kate mused, her mind already racing. "Moshenski's secure list can't be that long. Someone on that list is compromised or complicit."

"There's more," Nomad continued. "My work on the street cam video is paying off."

Kate's pulse quickened. "Did you get an image?"

"Not yet. But believe it or not, the rain is actually helping. There's no single reflective surface with a clear image, no shop windows, cars, not even an ATM camera. But there are thousands of tiny fragments, fractals really, in the rain."

"You've got to be kidding me?"

"Believe me, I know how crazy it sounds," Nomad said. "But I've got an AI flattening all the drops and assembling the pieces, and it's actually working. I'm getting a face."

"That could be the break I need," Kate said. "Long story, but except for spotting the streamer and the street cam video, Paris has been a bust. Just a trip down the rabbit hole and about to hit a dead end. A face could change everything—if we can match it to a name."

"Glad you brought that up," Nomad said. "Still have any back doors into the CIA's system."

"Maybe," Kate replied. "Why?"

"I'm thinking that CIA's facial recognition software will be much faster and tap data sources I can't access."

"Like military and intelligence sources."

"Precisely. Can you get me in?"

Kate hesitated. *Margot said I was on my own, that she was under a microscope,* Kate thought. *If I let Nomad into the system, it's only a matter of time before Margot's notified. Will she cover for me again or serve me up to save her career? If I can find Jake's killer, I don't give a damn.*

"I'll get you in," Kate said, her tone defiant. "Be ready. When they find the connection, and they will, we'll never get back in."

"Got it. One shot. I can do this."

"Alright, I'll send you the protocol via GhostChat. Just remember facial recognition only. This is not a shopping trip, so keep your eye on the prize."

As the call ended, Kate stood, moving to the window. The first rays of dawn were just beginning to paint the Parisian skyline. A beautiful day was on the horizon, but her thoughts remained dark. *Did Boucher survive the night? Would she survive the day?*

***

A soft knock at the door pulled Kate from her thoughts. She moved swiftly to the door, her hand instinctively gripping her backup weapon. She peered through the peephole, relaxing as she confirmed it was Talya.

Kate opened the door, ushering Talya inside while scanning the hallway and locking the door behind them. Talya, looking fresh despite the early hour, carried a small, hardened equipment case. Her eyes sparkled with a mix of excitement and urgency.

"You were right about Boucher," Talya said, her voice low and intense. "He's fine," she added, a hint of a smile playing at her lips. "But the morgue has a new John Doe."

"It's not over," Kate muttered. "And we can't risk moving him."

"Already handled," Talya assured her, setting the case down. "The hospital thinks Mossad is protecting a high-value operative."

Kate raised an eyebrow. "How?"

Talya shrugged. "Called in favors. Best you don't know, in case this goes international."

"Right," Kate nodded, her gaze falling on the case Talya brought. "I see you found one."

"Yes," Talya confirmed. "Think we'll need it?"

"No idea," Kate replied. "But at some point, in the next twenty-four hours, I'll be walking into a trap, and I'll take all the intel I can get."

Talya opened the drone case, and Kate leaned in, marveling at the miniature device nestled within. "Just remarkable," she breathed. "What's the flight time?"

"Twenty to thirty minutes, max," Talya replied. "Obstacle avoidance, infrared, and night vision can all chew up the battery, so best not to push it."

"And the signal range?"

"Somewhere between 100-200 meters, depending on building materials and transmission obstacles," Talya explained.

Kate nodded, her mind already planning. "Let's hope that's enough."

"Nothing yet from Shepard?"

"No, not yet," Kate sighed. "He needs to chew up some time to help create the illusion, but it will be today." Kate gestured toward the suite's living area. "In the meantime, make yourself comfortable."

"Coffee?" Talya asked a hopeful note in her voice.

"What would you like? The Jura in the bar makes like thirty different drinks."

"Espresso works," Talya said. "Double, please."

Kate smiled. "Another thing we have in common."

***

7:15 AM CEST

WHILE KATE AND TALYA waited for Shepard's next move, Kate updated Moshenski. *I can't risk telling him everything I know. But if things go south, there are things he should know.*

She dialed his private line, and he answered immediately. "Good morning, Kate," he began. "I hoped I would hear from you today. I trust your meeting was satisfactory?"

"Yes. Very," Kate replied. "Vitali, thank you again for making the connection and ensuring my safety."

"I made the connection against my better judgment," Vitali said. "Your safety was entirely in Sarkesian's hands, so I am relieved to know you are unharmed."

Kate was a little unnerved to learn that she was walking the tightrope without a net, but there was no looking back now.

"I spoke with Nomad this morning, and he made an interesting discovery."

"He knows who sent the drone video?"

"No, but you might," Kate said. "Nomad discovered how the message was sent," Kate explained. "It had to piggyback on another KATEM phone—one on your authorized contact list."

"My contact list is the list of suspects?"

"That's the starting point. It's possible the video was sent without their knowledge or consent," Kate replied. "In that case, someone you know and trust could be compromised."

"Or involved," Vitali said.

"Yes. We can't ignore that possibility. And in that case, they're working with someone with extraordinary technical skills. To discover and exploit this vulnerability, on a phone that Nomad concedes is impenetrable, was a remarkable achievement."

"What would you advise?"

"I'll return your phone," Kate began. "There's nothing more we need from it, and Nomad's confident your direct communications remain secure."

"But somewhere among the recipients, an enemy lies in wait," Vitali said. "I debated whether the anonymous sender was an ally or enemy; the latter now seems the more likely, and the video *was* both a demonstration and a threat."

"And a mistake."

"How so?"

"Whoever did this is close," Kate said, her voice measured. "They're in your inner circle and banking on your trust and ignorance—we can work with that."

"And what of your progress?" Vitali asked. "Are you any closer to an answer?"

"There have been several setbacks, I'm afraid. Including the Deputy Director of the DGSI being suspended for no apparent reason and evidence being misplaced or even destroyed."

"Incompetence or conspiracy?"

"You know what I think, but we need proof. I crossed paths with someone I knew at the Agency—he might be of some help," Kate said and abruptly changed the subject. "And Zhukov, any change?"

"None worth noting," Vitali said. "But Mikhail is still with us, and that is something. I am sure you have much to do, but let me know if I can be of any assistance."

"Of course," Kate said. "I appreciate the support."

The call ended, and Kate swallowed the guilt of holding back so many details. *Maybe I should have said more,* she wondered. *Given his connections, he might already know Boucher is in the Army hospital, and a woman matching my description killed a man.*

"But no police," Kate muttered. "Not yet. Either my gun is still hidden in the back of Shepard's car, a car he borrowed, or he has it—either way, that could still blow up in my face."

***

8:45 AM CEST

KATE'S CELL PHONE RINGING shattered the monotony of waiting. The distant ringing served as a reminder that Kate had relegated her phone to the bedroom to keep her work and conversations private. Giving Shepard that phone number was part of playing the game. *He has reason to suspect I know about the bug,* Kate thought. *But introducing a little doubt couldn't hurt.*

Kate answered the phone, and the first words out of Shepard's mouth were, "We need to meet."

"Did you find something?"

"Not over the phone."

"Alright. How about Place du Tertre?" Kate asked, recalling the busy little square in the heart of Montmartre.

"Perfect," Shepard replied. "Twenty minutes?"

"I'll be there."

"Do me a favor."

"If I can. What is it?"

"Leave everything electronic in the room," he said. "Even your watch."

Kate left the phone in the bedroom and sat across from Talya.

"That was Shepard. We're on."

"I know that face," Talya said. "What's wrong?"

"The call went exactly as I expected," Kate began. "He was distant, mysterious. Said we need to meet right away."

"What am I missing?"

"He told me to leave all electronics behind—even my watch." Kate frowned, her mind racing. "Why would he care about tracking or surveillance? It doesn't fit."

Talya tilted her head, considering. "Unless he's trying to go off script."

"What do you mean?"

"Could he be trying to break free of whoever has their claws in him?" Talya asked. "Maybe he's going to ask you for help and needs to be sure no one knows."

"I suppose that's possible. Anything's possible," Kate said. "But it feels like a poisoned pawn to me."

"And for those of us who don't play chess?"

"Sorry. Just thinking out loud. It's a gambit, a ploy, to go after something that appears unprotected and walk right into the trap."

"I get it," Talya said. "The 'no electronics' request is to make you think he's vulnerable and help sell the value of the intel he's acquired."

"Now, that sounds like the man who called in the hit on Boucher and I."

"What's our move?"

"We keep playing," Kate said, her expression firm. "If this is a trap, I need to see the whole board before we make our move. Drop me at Place du Tertre."

Talya gave a quick nod. "Consider it done."

Chapter 30

FRIDAY, MAY 1st
9:00 AM CEST

PLACE DU TERTRE, PARIS, FRANCE

THE ROAR OF TALYA'S motorcycle echoed off ancient stone facades. Kate, arms wrapped around Talya's waist, leaned into each turn, her mind racing faster than the bike beneath them. The cool morning air whipped past, carrying the mingled scents of fresh baked bread and coffee, the telltale signs of Paris waking.

Near Place du Tertre, Talya pulled into a shadowed alley. Kate swung off, removed her helmet, and let her hair fall loose. "Thanks for the lift." Her voice was calm but firm. "Just blend in. Coffee, nothing more. No contact."

Talya nodded, her eyes hidden behind the visor. "Watch yourself," Talya said, her tone a mix of concern and caution. "Field work is Shepard's domain."

Kate's lips pressed into a thin line as she swung the bag over her shoulder. "Why does everyone keep reminding me I'm not a field officer?" she muttered, her words swallowed by the low growl of Talya's bike pulling away.

The walk to Place du Tertre gave Kate time to settle into her role. By the time she reached the bustling square, she was the picture of a relaxed tourist, taking in the sights and sounds of the artists' haven.

Shepard sat with his back to the wall, scanning the square. A plain folder lay beside his untouched coffee. He gave Kate a slight nod.

Kate slid into the seat across from him, brushing her hair behind her ear. "Beautiful morning," she said, the words light, casual—like two old friends, while hiding the tension crackling between them.

"Let's get this out of the way first," Shepard said, sliding a small, unassuming package across the table. "These should be familiar."

She lifted the package, recognized the weight, and guessed at the contents. "My...equipment?"

"Exactly. Keep them close and out of view," Shepard advised, his voice steady. "But let's hope it doesn't come to that."

"Thank you," Kate said, genuine surprise in her voice as she tucked the package next to her on the seat. *That was an interesting opening move,* Kate thought. *Give up something valuable to gain my trust. Well played.*

A waiter arrived with coffee for Kate, which caught her by surprise, but Shepard explained. "Double espresso, as I recall?"

"Yes. Thanks," Kate replied, eying the folder on the table. "Is that for me?" she asked, reaching for it.

"Not exactly," Shepard said, his hand holding down the folder. "But that shell casing you found—we got a hit on a latent print."

Kate kept her expression neutral as he opened the folder. He removed a single photograph and placed it on the table. The hard-eyed man in the image seemed to glare up at her.

"Who is he?" Kate asked, eyes on the photo.

"Tariq al-Masri," Shepard said, tapping the image. "Egyptian. ISIS-trained. Iran, Iraq, Syria."

"And captured in Afghanistan," Kate said, her tone sharpening. She leaned closer, tracing the details in the image. "I recognize the coding on the photo. This is an intake photo from Bagram."

"Where he was in custody until—"

"We abandoned the base and the country," Kate interrupted, her voice low and tight, each syllable heavy with the weight of lives lost. "And now we can add Jake and thirty-two more souls to the price of betrayal."

"Until now, he's been a ghost."

"A deeply committed, highly trained ghost, with an even bigger reason to hate the West."

"I know what you're thinking," Shepard said. "And I need to stop you right there. This needs to go to the DGSI."

"And then what?" Kate snapped. "The bureaucrats sit on the intel until the next attack. The press reports *the suspect was known to authorities,* and no one did a damn thing. Christ, Shepard... how many more have to die?"

"I know it's hard to swallow," Shepard pleaded. "And I'll push it best I can.

They can set up surveillance—monitor communications. This could be much bigger than one man, and if it is, they need to know."

Kate cradled her head in her hands, rubbing her face and shaking her head. It was minutes later when she put her hands down. "You're right," she conceded. "We go cowboy on this guy, and we risk missing something big." She regained her composure and looked him in the eyes. "Do you have a location?"

"Yes."

"Good. Let's take a look."

"Are you listening? You're not going near him," Shepard snapped.

"Relax. Just surveillance," Kate countered. "If the DGSI drags its feet, we lose valuable time. Let me do my job."

"It's not your job anymore," Shepard said. "Remember, you left."

"That's not what I meant," Kate shot back. "And you know it. I owe to it Jake, and the innocent lives taken, to find whoever was responsible and stop it from happening again."

Shepard hesitated but relented. "Absolutely no contact," he said. "Zip. Nada. None. Got it?"

"Relax. I got it," Kate said. "But I need to see what we're dealing with and what equipment I might need."

"I can help with equipment."

"That won't be necessary," Kate said. "Between Trident Security assets in the area and local resources, I can have everything I might need by tomorrow. Nothing can happen tonight anyway."

"I just need a minute," he said. "Nature calls."

Shepard rose from the table, his chair scraping softly against the cobblestones. A brief glance at the waiter earned him a nod toward the rear of the café. Kate didn't need to see her to know Talya had slipped into the crowd, a shadow trailing Shepard's every move. *That's my girl*, she thought. *Stay close. We might get lucky.*

***

SHEPARD LOOKED FOR A quiet corner near the men's room. He confirmed that Kate's table wasn't visible and reached for his phone. The call to Grant Collins caught him boarding the flight to Nairobi, and Grant stepped out of line to talk privately.

"Good timing," Grant said. "Another ten minutes, and I would have been on board. Fill me in."

"It was textbook," Ben said. "You were right about the Afghanistan angle. She was seething. I think she'd kill this guy with her bare hands if she had the chance."

"And the location?"

"She can't wait to have a look but swore it's purely for surveillance," Ben said, and they both laughed.

"Predictable," Grant sneered, admiring his plan. "Tell someone they can't have something, and they want it all the more."

"Are you sure you weren't with British Intelligence?" Ben asked, chuckling. "I better get back, but I'm sure it will be tonight."

"Why so sure?"

"She wants to collect some surveillance equipment and made a point of saying *nothing can happen tonight.*"

"You're right," Grant said. "She's going in tonight. Maybe you should go take a nap. You're not getting any younger, and it could be a long night."

"Screw you," Ben said, and they both laughed. "Good luck in Motapa."

"Brother, luck has nothing to do with it. Text me when it's done."

***

9:48 AM CEST

KATE SPOTTED TALYA CROSSING the square, getting ready to leave. Talya's right hand swept her hair behind the ear, and her index finger tapped twice. *I knew he was making a call,* Kate thought. *And Talya caught something useful. So far, so good.*

"Ready when you are," Shepard said, approaching the table.

"Let's go."

Shepard dropped a few Euros on the table. "Remember," he said. "We're just looking."

Kate nodded, a hint of triumph in her eyes. The square was buzzing now with artists and easels and the first wave of eager tourists wandering among the colorful stalls. The pair made their way down the sloping streets of Montmartre, navigating against the flow of pedestrians heading up to the square.

They approached Shepard's sleek BMW M8. He unlocked the doors, and Kate eyed the luxury ride.

"Business must be good," she remarked.

"It is," Shepard smirked. "And she's brand new."

"Want me to take off my boots?"

"No. Just don't shoot anyone," he said, laughing.

"I'll try to restrain myself."

Shepard moved to the passenger side, opening the door for Kate.

"Well, look at that. I guess chivalry isn't dead."

"Not dead," Shepard sighed, walking around to the driver's side. "Just grievously wounded."

The BMW roared to life, slipping out of Paris's cobblestone embrace with a throaty purr. Inside, the cabin was a world apart—sleek leather, ambient lighting, and the faint, sterile scent of a new car. Kate sank into the plush leather seat and found herself wrapped in a cocoon of high-tech comfort and near-silent elegance. *Not exactly the Rubicon,* she thought. *And not really my style.*

The scenery gradually shifted from the charming and touristy to the gritty and industrial as they made their way towards the outskirts of the 18th arrondissement. Fifteen minutes later, they found themselves in a long-forgotten corner of Paris. Abandoned warehouses loomed on either side of pothole-riddled streets. Graffiti-covered walls told silent stories of urban decay, while makeshift shelters spoke of the area's current inhabitants. Here and there, a freshly painted facade or a construction sign hinted at attempts at revitalization, but they seemed to fight a losing battle against overwhelming neglect.

"Flashy car for this neighborhood, don't you think?" Kate observed as Shepard slowed the BMW, scanning for a discreet place to park.

"Hadn't planned on coming here when I left home this morning," Shepard retorted, pulling into a spot he deemed both relatively safe and discrete. "Besides, we're not staying long. And neither of us is getting out of the car, remember?"

"What do you expect me to do from here?" Kate asked, opening Shepard's package. "I need a closer look."

Kate pulled the Glock from the package.

"What do you think you're doing?"

"I'm not walking in this neighborhood unarmed."

"It's broad daylight."

"And that makes it safe?" Kate asked, knowing Shepard wouldn't answer. "I won't be long."

"No, I'm coming with you."

"Stay here," Kate said. "Your car's in more danger than I am. Seriously. I got this."

Kate stepped out, tugging her jacket snug to conceal the Glock. She scanned exits, sightlines, and blind spots. No electronics needed—just instincts. The distant rumble of Talya's motorcycle reassured her. *One street over*, Kate guessed, covering the back side of the building. *I should clear out so she can deploy the drone.*

She returned to the car, making sure Shepard watched her approach. *Don't want to surprise him,* Kate thought, smirking. *He might shoot himself and get blood all over his new car.*

Back in the passenger seat, Kate summarized her observations. "It's a two-story structure, but lower level looks like a burned-out shell. If Tariq's here, he's on the upper level. No sign of cameras or sensors. He may think the isolation is enough, and the location is secure."

Shepard's face darkened as he cautioned, "I'd be careful with that assumption. When captured, he was assembling suicide vests, and the file shows he's a skilled bomb maker."

"And still has all of his fingers?" Kate asked. "That's pretty rare for an ISIS explosives geek."

"Are we good to go?" Shepard asked. "Back to your hotel?"

"Yes. Thanks," Kate replied. "I can collect what I need for remote surveillance. In the meantime, you brief the DGSI, and let's hope they step up." She paused, the DGSI reminding her. "Any update on Boucher?"

Shepard's expression remained neutral. "Still critical. Touch and go."

That's Shepard's way of saying Boucher is still a target, she thought. *He's still hoping to kill him and blame the death on the severity of his injuries.*

Chapter 31

FRIDAY, MAY 1st
3:56 AM EST

PERSONAL RESIDENCE, CIA DEPUTY DIRECTOR, McLEAN, VA

Margot Ryder was used to early mornings, but when her encrypted phone buzzed, she woke instantly. She recognized the caller. *This will be about Kate. Either she's dead—or in trouble. Again.*

She sat up, tone clipped. "Bring me up to speed."

"I'm sorry to call so early," the young man said, voice tense. "We've had another breach."

Margot threw on her robe. "Preacher?"

"Yes, ma'am."

"Where is she this time?"

"Facial recognition," he replied. "She's running a system-wide scan across military and intelligence services—domestic and foreign."

Margot paused mid-step, the implications sinking in. She crossed the room, picking up her tablet as she walked into the hallway. "Hang on," she said. "I want to see it. Give me a minute to log in."

The app loaded painfully slow. Margot drummed her fingers, impatience mounting. "All right," she said as the image appeared. "What am I looking at?"

"The image was AI-extrapolated," the young man explained. "Based on some kind of rain refraction algorithm—never seen anything like it."

Margot squinted at the blurred yet unmistakably human face. "Is this enough for a match?"

"Yes, ma'am. The key features—eyes, cheekbones, nose—they're accurate. If this guy is in the system, the scan will find him."

"Let it run," she ordered. Margot leaned against the counter, her voice steady but tinged with urgency. "And if she finds a match, send it to me immediately. Full background detail. Last known location."

"Yes, ma'am."

"And remember—"

"I know," he interrupted. "This stays off the books. Your eyes only."

"Of course it does."

Margot closed the call and stared at the faint glow of the tablet in her hands. Kate wouldn't stop—she'd warned her to stay clear of the Agency's systems, but here they were. Again.

Exhaling slowly, her lips pressed together as she weighed the risks and considered the danger. *Just what are you chasing this time, Kate? And how far are you willing to go?*

Chapter 32

FRIDAY, MAY 1st
11:00 AM CEST

HÔTEL DE POURTALÈS, PARIS, FRANCE

A KNOCK AT THE door pulled Kate from restless waiting. *Too soon. Something's wrong.* Tension coiled as she approached the door.

Kate peered through the peephole. Bella—in jeans and a vintage tee. A stark contrast to last night's couture.

She opened the door wide, her voice softening. "Bella." The warmth in her tone mirrored her unexpected relief. "Come in." She stepped back, gesturing toward the sofa.

Bella's eyes crinkled as she returned the smile. "I hope I'm not interrupting?"

"Not at all," Kate said, grateful for the distraction. "Have a seat."

Bella perched on the sofa's edge. "I leave for Motapa tomorrow—and I wanted to ask, one last time, if you'd consider joining me."

Kate's eyebrows rose in surprise. "Bella, I—"

"You're obviously in Paris for a reason," Bella rushed on. "I imagine, Jake, and what happened here is that reason. And I have no right to ask, but it would only be for a few days, and we'd fly right back."

Bella raised a hand like she was brushing a stray hair off her cheek, but Kate saw her press just beneath her eye. *She's trying not to cry.*

"What's going on?" Kate asked.

"I'm sorry," Bella said. "I really don't want to cry. That's not who I am."

"You're one of the most capable women I've ever met," Kate said, leaning forward, her voice laced with sincerity. "And stunning, by the way—even without makeup, which is honestly annoying."

They both laughed, and Bella relaxed, exactly as Kate hoped. "Now, what's the problem?"

Bella fidgeted with her bag strap, her gaze distant. "Honestly, I wish I knew. This isn't like me—and don't ask me to explain it, but I can't shake the sense something bad is about to happen."

"That's not surprising," Kate began. "You were attacked, beaten, and watched me kill a man. Then robbed and nearly lost the most precious thing you own. I'd be surprised if you weren't wondering what's next."

"You really think so?"

"What you're feeling is completely normal, and trust me, I know what I'm talking about."

Understanding flickered across Bella's face. "That helps," Bella said and stood. "I think I just needed a little perspective. This might surprise you, but I don't have many friends. And none that know me, not really."

For a moment, Kate imagined escaping to Africa. But reality snapped back. Talya would return soon. She needed to focus.

"I'd like to think we're friends," Kate said. "And under other circumstances, I'd be on that flight tomorrow. I love Africa and look forward to returning someday. But even if I could break away, and I'm not saying I can, I'm traveling light and don't have much that would work in that climate."

"Oh, that's not even challenging," Bella said. "I could probably guess your sizes and have a dozen outfits on the plane in an hour, so don't tempt me."

"That's gracious and amazing, but I'm afraid the answer is still no," Kate said. "Now, if I don't see you before you leave, have a great trip. I hope Motapa realizes how fortunate they are to have your support."

Kate hugged Bella and said goodbye but with a palpable sense of regret. There was a draw to return to Africa she couldn't explain. *Not just for Bella's sake,* she thought. *I'd go back in a heartbeat.* She smiled, recalling the bizarre dream and the image of a lion roaring and bowing at the foot of her bed. *I have no idea where that came from,* she thought. *But that reminds me, I need to see if Talya or Forest made any progress on backup for Vargas.*

***

Kate took a deep breath, the faint scent of Bella's signature perfume lingering in the air. She rested her forehead against the door, eyes closing as the weight of her plan settled on her shoulders.

No time for second-guessing, Kate thought. *It's my move.*

Another knock announced Talya's arrival. The look on her face told Kate everything she needed to know—they had a lot to discuss.

Talya stepped in, the drone case tucked under her arm, her expression grim. "You weren't kidding when you said this was a trap. What did you call it?"

"The Poisoned Pawn."

Talya shook her head and handed Kate the memory card. "This is more like *Game Over*—you won't believe what they have waiting for you."

Kate slid the memory card into her laptop. "Did Shepard's call turn up anything useful?"

"Two things," Talya began. "First, he's confident you bought the entire story."

"Perfect. That's exactly what I wanted. What's the other?"

"He says you're going to the warehouse tonight," Talya said and hesitated. "Look, I know that was the plan, but before you decide, you need to watch the video."

Kate's world narrowed to the screen.

"The cell jammer blocked any surveillance on the warehouse, and I started with a high-altitude thermal scan," Talya began. "Just to confirm if anyone was inside. It was clear, so I searched for a way to get in. I wasn't having much luck and finally took a chance on a transom window."

Kate watched the drone hovering in front of a narrow window opening. The drone eased forward, then down, and slipped inside.

"That was some serious flying," Kate said.

"Believe me, I was sweating. But we got lucky. Virtually zero wind today. Otherwise..."

"Shattered drone and blown operation."

"But this is where it gets interesting."

Kate's breath caught as she saw a figure seated at a desk staring right at them. "Is that...?" she began.

Talya nodded grimly. "Tariq al-Masri. He didn't show up on the scan..."

"Because he's already dead," Kate concluded.

Talya pointed at the screen, her tone clipped and urgent. "There's more. I cycled through all the scan modes—thermal, infrared, even spectral."

Kate leaned closer, her eyes narrowing. "What's that?" She pointed at a flickering streak of green light just inches above the floor.

"A laser trip wire," Talya confirmed, her voice edged with grim certainty. "Waiting for you." She hesitated, her fingers hovering over the laptop. "But this...this is the part you need to see."

The drone footage shifted, the camera easing forward through the darkened interior, each move deliberate, cautious, avoiding unseen dangers. The screen stilled, focusing on the figure slumped in the chair.

"Tariq," Kate murmured. "Is he—?"

"Rigged to blow?" Talya cut in. "Oh yeah."

The drone hovered, revealing Tariq—strapped to a chair, eyes wide, a suicide vest wired tight.

Kate shot to her feet, pacing the room as adrenaline surged through her veins. "They didn't just want me dead," she said, her voice sharp with fury. "They wanted to make it a spectacle."

"The vest is packed," Talya said grimly. "Enough C4 and shrapnel to turn anyone inside that building into confetti."

Kate exhaled sharply. "Shepard sent the gunman for Boucher. But this? Next-level. You were right—this is *Game Over.*"

"There's one more thing you should see," Talya said, and Kate returned to the laptop. "The battery was running low, so I didn't get everything, but I did a quick pass over the desk and the wall behind Tariq."

Kate paused the video and examined the frame. A desk cluttered with photos, building plans, and handwritten notes. Kate zoomed in on a series of photos pinned to the wall—photos of Jake.

"Jake was being watched," Talya said. "I'm surprised he didn't know."

"He knew," Kate said. "But couldn't risk involving the team or me—too dangerous."

"Given the variations in clothing and locations," Talya observed. "They were watching him for days."

Kate recognized a photo of *Le Palais de l'Éclipse.* "We know this building," Kate said. "And that's the satellite view of the roof...the red circle was the sniper's location."

Talya gestured at the photos. "They're pinning it all on Tariq."

"Exactly. Framing him as the mastermind—and me as the final victim."

"I can hear it now," Talya said dryly. "Former CIA analyst Kate Preacher hunted down the Café Pierre terrorist, only to become the terrorist's last victim."

"Closing the book on the attack and Jake's murder and keeping you, the team, or anyone else from digging any deeper." Kate paused, a dangerous glint in her eye.

Talya folded her arms, narrowing her eyes. "I know that look. Forest is going to kill me, isn't he?"

"Only if we survive."

"Way to look on the bright side."

Chapter 33

FRIDAY, MAY 1st
10:00 PM CEST

HÔTEL DE POURTALÈS, PARIS, FRANCE

Kate and Talya analyzed the warehouse, debating Shepard's vantage point and entry options. Kate's encrypted phone buzzed—Nomad. "I need to take this," Kate said, stepping away from the table.

She answered, tension creeping into her voice. "Tell me you've got good news."

The crackle of Nomad's voice didn't inspire confidence. "I wish I did."

Kate's stomach dropped. "The facial rec?"

"Came up dry," he admitted, frustration bleeding into his tone. "I've run it through every system I could access. Nada."

Kate pinched the bridge of her nose. *Sarkesian knows. If only he could have said more—or I had a way to make him.* But she wasn't CIA anymore—no black sites, no extraction teams.

She recalled their meeting, the flicker of something almost human in his eyes when she pressed. *He despised the sniper. Maybe even feared him.* But instead of a name, he'd given her an epitaph. A cold certainty settled over her. He wasn't being evasive—he was telling her exactly where to look. Her eyes snapped open.

"Julian, are you still connected to the CIA's facial recognition system?"

"I've asked you not..."

"I know. I know. And I'm sorry," Kate interrupted. "Nomad, please, just answer the question."

"Yeah, surprisingly. I'm still in. Why?"

Thanks, Margot, Kate thought. *She must know about the breach by now, and she's giving me as much leeway as she can.*

"I need you to run one more search. But this time, I want to add a parameter," Kate said. "Let me know when you're ready."

Kate heard Nomad's voice commands queuing up another search, the same military and intelligence databases.

"Okay," Nomad said. "What's the parameter?"

"Subject: Deceased."

"Did you say deceased?"

"I know how it sounds," Kate replied. "But I'm playing a hunch. There's a chance someone gave me a clue."

Nomad keyed in the filter. "It's running—what clue?"

"I begged an arms dealer to give me a name—I think he wanted to tell me—and maybe he did. He said, *I know only this—he is a dead man.* I took it as a compliment, believing when I found the sniper, I'd kill him."

Nomad's gasp came through the line. "We got a hit."

Her pulse quickened. "Talk to me."

"Duncan Harris," he said, his voice tight with urgency. "British Army. SAS—22nd Regiment."

"Twenty-two SAS," she repeated. "Special Forces. Figures."

"Let's see..." Nomad scanned the dossier. "Iraq, Afghanistan, confirmed kill at 2,026 meters."

"He's a sniper," Kate said. "Apparently, one of the best."

"Was a sniper," Nomad said. "Says here he was killed in action during Operation Shadow Viper, and awarded the British Conspicuous Gallantry Cross. The citation notes that *Sergeant Harris continued to engage the enemy even as his position was targeted by rocket-propelled grenades, ultimately sacrificing his life to ensure the success of the mission and the safety of his comrades.*"

Kate's mind raced, piecing together the implications. "He fits the profile."

"Except he's dead," Nomad countered. "They gave him a medal and everything."

Kate stood, pacing the room. "Someone wants the world to think he's dead. Sarkesian knew—and you know a little something about being dead, so don't pretend you're surprised."

"Fair enough, but it's not a trivial task. Not at this level," Nomad added. "I was a kid with virtually no footprint. This guy's a war hero."

"You're right, and who do we know with the resources to pull this off?" Kate asked. "CIA? MI6? Hell, it could even be GRU. One thing's certain: the Agency will kill the connection when they realize we have a match. Grab everything you can, as fast as you can, and push it to my folder."

"I'm on it," Nomad said, mirroring Kate's urgency.

"When you have it, start checking Paris airport surveillance video," Kate said. "Is that going to be a problem?"

"Nope, those cameras run on the same city-wide surveillance system I already own," Nomad replied.

"Excellent," Kate said. "Let's see if you can spot a dead man walking. If he's still here, I want to know when he arrived and from where. If he left, we need to find out where he's headed."

"What are you working on?"

"I have plans to meet a former associate," Kate said. "From Syria."

"At this time of night? That can't be good," Nomad said. "Nothing good came out of Syria."

"Almost nothing," Kate said, picturing Jake's smile. "But you're right about this guy, and you'll appreciate the metaphor. I've been offered a poisoned pawn."

"Don't get greedy, Kate. Not now," Nomad begged. "For Christ's sake, we just caught a break. Why not wait to see where it leads?"

"I can't wait," Kate said. "My actions have already put one man in the hospital. If I don't make my move tonight, if I can't convince them they've won, I won't get out of Paris alive."

"What if they kill you tonight?" Nomad asked. "And I locate the sniper?"

"That's an easy one," Kate said, a grim smile forming. "Give his name and location to the team. They know what to do."

Nomad's voice dropped to a whisper. "Kate, don't...don't die on me, okay?"

Kate softened, the tension easing from her tone. "That's the plan," she said, her warmth slipping through. "I'm glad you're back in my life. I've missed you too."

***

10:45 PM CEST

KATE CHECKED THE TIME—FIVE minutes. The kitchen staff are heading out, leaving their best exit route undisturbed. She had to assume eyes were still on the hotel. If they didn't reach the warehouse unseen, none of this would matter.

She cast a glance toward Talya, who met her eyes with a slight nod.

One last pass through their communication protocols and gear checks—no room for mistakes. Kate adjusted the earpiece beneath her helmet, ensuring the secure line was active, while Talya did the same, fingers flicking over her rig with practiced ease. They moved like two synchronized elements, each knowing the other's rhythm, anticipating needs without speaking.

Talya led the way to the alley, where a matte-black Fiat 500e sat tucked into the shadows. The electric vehicle, acquired through methods Talya saw no need to disclose, would let them ghost through the city in near silence. Before getting in, Talya tapped the roof twice—*stay sharp*. Kate answered with a thumbs-up, sliding into the passenger seat.

Their approach was smooth, methodical. Talya parked two blocks from the target, cutting the engine and coasting the last few feet before easing to a stop. Kate scanned the street ahead, then tilted her head toward the exit. *Clear*. They slipped out, closing the doors with barely a whisper of sound.

The night swallowed them whole.

A clouded, moonless sky smothered what little ambient light Paris offered, leaving the streets in a deep, impenetrable black. Dressed head-to-toe in black, they weren't just moving through the shadows—they became the shadows.

They kept to the edges, passing the skeletal remains of abandoned buildings. Shattered windows and corroded steel beams loomed like forgotten sentinels. The industrial area's decay pressed in around them, but with AN/PVS-31A binocular night vision mounted to their helmets, they owned the night. The world around them burst into a vivid wash of green-lit detail—every crumbling scaffold, dented storage tank, and twisted piece of rebar stood out in sharp relief, clear as daylight.

Kate exhaled slowly, her mind sharpening with each breath. *Perfect conditions*, she thought. *Absolute darkness. Silent approach. The right gear.* All tilting the odds in their favor. *I just might get out of this alive.*

Talya gave a quick two-finger signal. *One minute.*

Kate responded in kind. *Acknowledged.*

Then, without a word, they pressed forward—two ghosts slipping deeper into the night.

At the warehouse, they spotted a single occupant in a nondescript vehicle—parked safely out of the blast radius but with a line of sight to the warehouse's front door. *Shepard bought a front-row seat,* Kate thought. *Well, sit back and enjoy the show.*

Kate and Talya synchronized watches and split up. Kate disappeared into the darkness. Her form was just a shadow as she approached a large trash bin—a benne—nestled below the stairs. *This is perfect,* she thought. *Secure. Concealed.*

She crouched behind the bin, listening for anything out of place. Silence. Satisfied, she removed her helmet, the night vision rig sliding off with it. She tucked them into the bag, then unzipped her hoodie, peeling it away in one smooth motion and revealing the cream-colored shirt beneath. The cool air hit her skin, stark against the heat trapped in the thick fabric. She stuffed the hoodie and gear into the bag and lowered it into the bin. Out of sight. Out of play.

Kate reached up and gently pulled the hair tie free, letting her hair fall around her shoulders. She checked the time, visualizing Talya's progress. The helmet and the hoodie were hot, but she still had a few minutes to cool down before Talya was in position. She ran her fingers through her hair, loosening any tangles, allowing her scalp to breathe, and waited.

✳✳✳

TALYA MOVED WITH DELIBERATE precision to the back side of the warehouse. Their analysis of the drone video and satellite imagery located a point of entry—a row of windows and a stack of wooden pallets that could give her the height she needed to unlatch a window and climb inside.

With a muted grunt, she shifted the pallets into place and climbed up. Teetering on top of the damaged pallets, she struggled to keep the stack from collapsing. *I see why these were abandoned,* Talya thought. From her waistpack, she retrieved a glass cutter and a rubber suction cup. She pressed the suction cup against the glass, anchoring it before tracing a circle with the cutter. The glass made a faint, crisp popping sound when she tapped the glass, and the circle piece broke free.

Talya set the glass aside and reached through the opening. Her fingers fumbling for the latch, she located and lifted the lever. But when she pulled against the window frame, it didn't budge. *I was afraid of that,* she thought. *Probably hasn't opened in years.*

She dipped back into the waist pack and retrieved a small can of lubricant. Extending her arm and the can in as far as she could reach, she sprayed the hinges.

Talya set the can on the windowsill and checked the time. *I'm behind schedule,* she thought. *Kate will move into position soon.* After giving the lubricant a moment to seep in, she tried again. The window creaked and groaned but moved. She cycled the window open and closed until it opened just wide enough.

Talya removed her helmet, setting it on the pallets, and with a deep breath, she gripped the window frame and pulled herself up. In one fluid motion, Talya twisted her body, leading with her right shoulder. Her head and upper body slipped through the opening, bending at the waist, arms reaching for the interior floor. As she pulled herself further in, her elbow brushed against the lubricant can. It wobbled.

Her heart leapt into her throat. *Go, go, go,* she thought. *You've got to catch it.* Tucking her legs and sliding through the narrow gap, Talya kept her body tight against the wall beneath the window, landing in a low crouch.

The moment her boots hit the floor, Talya froze. The soft clang of metal hit her ears—the can slipping, wobbling, then rolling. Time stretched, her pulse hammering as she tracked its path. She couldn't see the tripwire, but she didn't need to. The can was rolling straight for the invisible beam and gaining speed.

In that instant, Talya saw her death—and Kate's. The explosion. The fireball. The blast wave ripping them apart.

She lunged, fingertips grazing the can as it rolled forward—the fate of two lives hanging on a heartbeat, on whether gravity claimed its prize before she could snatch it back.

Don't move. Don't even breathe. Talya pressed down, stopping the can, but control still teetered on the edge. The smallest shift could set it loose again. She had no idea how close she'd come to being vaporized—only that she couldn't let it move—not one millimeter.

With excruciating patience, she clawed the can back—a quarter inch at first, then another. Now, she could slide her fingers over the top, keeping it steady. Only then did she exhale.

Talya pulled the can to her chest and pushed to her feet. With a deep breath, she set it aside safely out of the way, then grabbed her helmet and night vision gear. She resisted glancing at the tripwire—she didn't need to know. Didn't want to.

Move. Now.

She checked the time. *Three minutes.* Talya's eyes narrowed as she examined the intricate web of wires woven into the suicide vest. Mossad training and experience disarming such devices had honed her ability to read their deadly intentions. She quickly identified the leads connected to the laser trip wire's photoelectric sensor.

Reaching into her pack, she retrieved a compact digital timer, a pair of wires dangling from the side, and the display glowing softly. Talya confirmed her watch, and the timer matched to the second. *Two minutes, ten seconds.* She took a slow, deep breath to steady her hands and slow her heart rate. *If I read the wiring correctly,* she thought. *The timer will become an active part of the trigger circuit. If not...well, let's not go there.* With deft hands, she clipped the first wire. The second hovered for a moment, and then she attached and released the clip.

Sixty seconds, she thought. *Gotta go. I'll just grab what I can.* She ripped Jake's photos down off the wall and, in one giant, scooping motion, grabbed as many of the papers from the desk as she could. It wasn't everything she wanted, but better than nothing. Talya rolled up what she grabbed, stuffed them into her waistpack, and headed for the open window. *Thirty seconds.*

Talya landed on the pavement with a thud and ran for cover.

***

KATE WAS IN POSITION, standing on the landing at the top of the warehouse stairs. A single dim bulb illuminated the entrance, and in the light-colored shirt, she knew Shepard would have eyes on her—and that was the goal.

A sudden crash echoed from the side of the warehouse. Kate suspected Talya's makeshift pile of pallets toppled over. *That entry was risky*, she thought. *But at least now I know she's out, she's safe.* Kate checked her watch. *Twenty-three seconds. That's cutting it pretty close.*

She tried the warehouse door, just in case, but she expected it to be locked. The small leather lock pick set was already in her hand. The French Vachette deadbolt was a simple pin-tumbler mechanism and not much of a challenge. *I'm sure that was the idea,* Kate thought. *Nothing too obvious, like an unlocked door, but don't make it hard.* She slipped the tension wrench and pick into the lock. *Slow is smooth. Smooth is fast.* Kate had the five pins set and the lock picked in six seconds. *Not my best, but that will do.*

Kate slipped the burner phone from her pocket, her thumb hovering over Shepard's number. The text, prepped and ready, felt heavy in her hands. Timing was everything. It didn't matter that he wouldn't recognize Kate's number—the magic was in the message.

> Ben, I'm sorry. I know you were only trying to help, but I'm going in. If Tariq's in there, he's a dead man.

She couldn't help but smirk at the irony of the message and watched the seconds click off on her watch. *About now, Shepard's focusing on my hands*, she thought. *Binoculars locked on.* Like a magician, she gambled on controlling his eyes.

Kate knew there was no way to predict what would happen when the vest detonated. The size of the explosion, the volume of shrapnel in the vest, the deflection of the blast wave on the building's interior walls, furniture, and iron framing were just a few of the variables she could not anticipate. And exactly why Talya fought hard to talk her out of it.

She smiled as the seconds ticked. Talya didn't know, couldn't know, but Kate set the detonation time to 11:29 for a reason. November 29th was Jake's birthday, and if she was about to join him, it was a good time to die.

With three seconds to go, Kate pressed send.

***

TALYA WAS SAFELY BEHIND cover with eyes on Shepard. The minute he broke eye contact with Kate, she knew the explosion was imminent. *This is it*, she thought, her rifle pointed at Shepard's head. *If he checks his phone, we're good. But if he sees her move, I'm taking the bastard right now.* Part of her hoped the plan would fail, but she knew Kate was counting on it working. Still, her job was to ensure Kate's safety—as best as she could with Kate standing on the doorstep of a building about to explode.

***

"ONE-THOUSAND-ONE. ONE-THOUSAND-TWO—"

Kate launched herself off the landing. Mid-air, the explosion ripped through the warehouse, a thunderous roar swallowing her whole. The shockwave slammed into her just as her boots scraped the ground, tossing her like a rag doll.

The jarring impact wave slammed her into the ground with a force that left her gasping and struggling to breathe. The world was a chaotic blur of splintered wood, dust, and smoke, lit by a blazing fire in the blast's epicenter.

For a moment, she lay still, trying to make sense of what had just happened. Her ears ringing, a high-pitched whine drowning out all other sounds. The side of her head throbbed with a sharp, pulsing pain. She reached up, fingers trembling as they explored the injury.

Kate felt the warmth of fresh blood seeping from a gash, slick and sticky, her fingers wet and warm. The air was thick with the stench of burning rubber. She recognized the scent that caught in the back of her throat, the almost sweet motor-oil scent of C4.

She struggled to focus, but her mind was spinning. A dull ache spread from the wound, throbbing in time with her racing heartbeat. The gritty texture of dust coated her lips and tongue, mingling with the remnants of the explosion. The metallic taste of blood lingered in her mouth.

The sensation of the cool evening air pressing against her exposed skin was comforting, almost calming. *I did it,* she thought. *And I'm still breathing.* With every breath, clarity was returning, and with it, her purpose.

Kate clawed at the debris pinning her down, each movement sending fresh jolts of pain through her ribs. She groaned, shoving aside the jagged fragments of wood and metal that had shielded her from the worst of the blast. *Can you stand,* she wondered. *Let's find out.* She rolled onto her side, the pavement beneath gritty and uneven. Every move sent sharp jolts of pain through her body, but she forced herself into a sitting position.

She braced against the ground and pushed up, muscles trembling. Her legs felt leaden, her vision swam. She wobbled, dropped to one knee, then forced herself up again, fighting for balance.

Her breath came in short, ragged gasps, her legs threatening to buckle. But she was determined to stand, and inch by inch, she straightened her back, her body swaying. The pain in her head flared, nearly knocking her back down, but she forced herself to focus.

Finally, she was standing, though barely. Her knees wobbled, and her vision swam again, but she was on her feet. She swayed, teetering on the edge of collapse, but she locked her knees, willing herself to stay upright. The effort left her breathless, every inch of her body screaming in protest, but she refused to give in. Jake's voice leading her on. *Stay in the fight.*

She took a shaky step forward, her foot dragging slightly as she tried to find her balance. The ground felt unstable as if it might give way beneath her at any moment. But with another deep breath, she steadied herself, forcing one foot in front of the other, each step a battle won.

***

Talya crouched low, her breath steady despite the pounding in her chest. Through the haze of smoke, she tracked Shepard through the rifle's scope. He was out of the car and moving fast, his urgency palpable. *Was it concern? Suspicion?* She couldn't tell.

Her finger hovered on the trigger. Kate planned for every risk—but plans rarely survived contact. Talya couldn't see her, but Kate's orders were clear.

If Kate's dead, she thought. *You're next.*

"Come on, Kate," Talya muttered under her breath, willing her friend to pull off the impossible. She tracked Shepard's every move as he neared the smoke. If he hesitated—if he so much as raised a hand against Kate—she wouldn't hesitate. One shot and the problem would solve itself.

Her eyes narrowed. Shepard slowed, scanning the debris, his posture unsure. Talya took a slow, deep breath, steadying herself for whatever came next.

***

The smoke parted just enough to reveal a figure moving with purpose, the firelight catching on his outline. *Shepard.* Kate took two steps toward the approaching figure and collapsed into his arms. She was back on the ground, staring up at the sky. She tried to focus on the man leaning over her. His lips were moving, but she couldn't hear what he was saying. The wail of approaching sirens grew louder. The shrill, oscillating cry of police cars and the longer, more insistent blare of fire trucks merged with the staccato burst of ambulance sirens. All descending on the scene and mere seconds away.

"Kate! Kate," he repeated, with a hand on her wrist, feeling for a pulse. "Don't move. Just stay still."

"Shepard?" she mumbled.

"It's me. You're going to be alright," Shepard said. "Open your eyes. Listen to my voice."

Kate looked into the face hovering above her and tried to speak. "Gun…" she whispered was all she could manage, but it was enough.

"I have it," Shepard replied. "It's secure."

Kate closed her eyes, nodded her head, and managed a half-smile. With French emergency services moments away, she didn't need a weapons charge destroying what she risked her life to achieve. Still, she couldn't help wondering. *If I still had my gun, would I kill him? Could I resist?* Eyes closed, mind wandering, she pictured her right hand reaching for the Glock. The fingers twitched as if wrapping around the grip, drawing the weapon and smiling—*right here, right now, pressing the trigger. Checkmate.*

"Come on, Kate. Eyes open. Look at me. Focus. That's good."

Kate looked into Shepard's eyes. "I'm sorry," she lied.

"What's done is done," Shepard replied. "I'm just relieved you're alive."

Bullshit! Kate thought. The chorus of sounds—vehicles arriving, men shouting, boots slapping the ground, growing louder, closer, prompted another smile. A genuine smile. The searing pain from the cut on her lip didn't matter. *He can't kill me now*, Kate knew. *Too many witnesses. Talya nailed the timing.*

Shepard might look back at tonight and wonder how the emergency services arrived so fast. That was a risk Kate would take to bolster the odds of surviving, and it worked.

For the moment, Kate thought. *He thinks the game's over—Shepard thinks he won.*

CHAPTER 34

FRIDAY, MAY 1st
5:45 PM EDT

SAWMILL TRAINING COMPLEX, LAURENS, SC

FROM HIS VANTAGE POINT in the tower, Forest tracked the six-man SWAT team advancing toward the cartel stronghold. The golden hour cast long shadows. Inside, an American oil executive—kidnapped three days ago—awaited rescue. Time was running out.

The breacher, his hands steady, set the charges on the reinforced door. Team communication was silent—a series of hand signals and physical taps as they aligned on either side of the entry point. The point man, muscles taut, readied himself to move the moment the door exploded.

The breacher nodded. Charges detonated. The door blew inward, smoke and debris filling the entry. The point man surged in, his suppressed weapon spitting two rounds—one target down. The second operator swept right, eliminating another threat.

The point man led the charge down a long hallway, moving with practiced speed and precision. Three members of the advance team proceeded down the hallway, while two more positioned themselves at the rear, securing their flank and protecting their exfil route.

But the situation deteriorated. Doors burst open—automatic weapons flashed. Gunfire forced the team into cover. Their advance stalled under heavy fire.

"Hold!" Forest's voice cut through the tension, halting the exercise. The room fell silent except for the lingering echo of simulated gunfire.

In the blink of an eye, the illusion of a real hostage rescue shattered. The men lowered their weapons, flipped up their night vision gear, and the shoot-house lights flickered on, illuminating the staged environment. Forest climbed down from the observation tower, his compact five-foot-eleven frame moving with the fluid grace of a predator. His long, dark brown hair, pulled back in a neat ponytail, swayed slightly as he descended. The sleeve of intricate tattoos on his left arm, visible beneath his rolled-up shirt, caught the light, each design a testament to missions accomplished and brothers lost.

Big Mike stood next to Forest, his imposing six-three muscular build creating a stark contrast to Forest's more compact physique. Mike's piercing brown eyes scanned the team, his face set in a stern expression that did little to hide the intensity radiating from him.

Forest leaned forward, his hands resting on his hips. "You're getting bogged down. Remember, violence of action wins the day. You hesitate, you die." His dark brown eyes swept over the team, searching for doubt, hesitation—anything that meant the lesson hadn't sunk in.

Mike crossed his arms, letting the silence stretch before speaking. "You guys have got to trust your body armor and fire control. Your accuracy is spot on." He jabbed a finger toward a target's dead-on headshots. "Remember, you're better equipped, armed, and trained. Don't be afraid to rely on that."

The team absorbed the critique, some nodding, others glancing at the floor. Forest's gaze swept over them, his expression a mix of determination and something deeper—perhaps a flicker of the weight he carried from his own combat experiences.

"Alright. Let's get set up," Forest said, glancing at his watch. "We've got time. Let's run it again." His voice carried the confidence of a man accustomed to making split-second decisions in life-or-death situations.

They watched the SWAT team prepare for another run, and Forest and Mike exchanged a look. Neither said a word—years of shared experiences and unspoken communication written on their faces and in their eyes. This was no game. Their training was more than just tactics—they were sharing hard-won lessons forged in combat, honed through years of service, and bought with the blood of their brothers.

When the door was reset and the lights cut, the SWAT team lined up. The chatter among the team pumped up the adrenaline. They were determined to show the SEALs training them they were worth the effort. "We got this!"

The charges detonated. The point man drove inside. New targets. Surprise locations. The SWAT team adapted, driving forward, overwhelming their adversaries with a barrage of firepower and precision headshots until they reached the room with the hostage.

Inside, a hooded hostage sat motionless, hands bound. A gunman standing behind, gun pointed directly at the hostage's skull.

The point man didn't hesitate. His weapon barked once, the round finding its mark between the combatant's eyes. Then he rolled right, sweeping the room to ensure it was secure, while the next man moved straight to the hostage.

The rescuer barely had time to react before the hostage drew a hidden weapon. A muffled pop—and red dye in the center of his chest.

The rescuer staggered back. "What the hell—"

The hostage pulled off the hood, revealing Deon's grinning face. "That was fun."

"Hold!" Forest's voice cut through the moment, the shoot-house lights flickering back on.

The man Deon shot rubbed his chest, glaring at him as he wiped off the red dye. "Sorry," Deon said, though his smirk said otherwise.

The SWAT team yanked up their NVGs, blinking against the sudden brightness, adrenaline still humming through their veins.

"That was much better," Forest began, his tone measured. "Right up to where you died," he said, looking straight at the guy rubbing his chest. "Never assume the person in the chair is your target."

Mike stepped forward, his voice echoing the gravity of the lesson. "You don't know who's under the hood until you press for confirmation. None of you even tried to speak to the hostage. Until you know who it is, they're a threat."

Forest nodded, his eyes sweeping across the team. "Alright, let's call it. Dinner at seven. No ops this evening, so the bar's open, and that's where you'll find us."

The team dispersed, their minds already replaying the exercise, as they wandered toward the main lodge. The adrenaline faded, the air of tension dissolving into camaraderie, and laughter and the anticipation of a well-earned, ice-cold beer.

***

Forest reached for a beer, his fingers just brushing the chilled can when his phone buzzed. He glanced at the screen—Talya. *Midnight in Paris. This isn't good.*

He pivoted away from the bar, scanning for a quiet spot. The laughter of his men faded as he stepped into the shadowed hallway.

"Go," he said, keeping his voice low.

"Kate's in the hospital," Talya's tone was clipped, all business. "Possible concussion. They're running an MRI now."

His grip on the phone tightened. "What else?"

"Lacerated scalp. Minor cuts and bruises. No broken bones. She's awake, alert, and coherent."

A muscle flexed in his jaw. "All things considered," he exhaled. "Sounds like training with Jake. What happened?"

The silence stretched. Then, finally, "Let's circle back to that one."

That was all he needed to hear. Whatever happened wasn't an accident, but this was an open channel. "Do you require assistance?"

"Negative," Talya replied. "But earlier tonight—I heard Kate talking—she got a name."

Forest paced. "You know what that means."

"I know."

"I'll wrap things up here and put the team on standby," Forest said. "Wherever she goes, we go."

"Copy that," Talya said, in a tone that echoed how Forest felt. If Kate found the man who killed Jake, their friend and mentor, they all had a bullet with his name on it.

"Send me the name," Forest said and ended the call.

The phone buzzed again with an encrypted GhostChat message.

Duncan Harris.

Forest's breath left him in a slow, measured exhale. He stared at the name, his fingers curling into a fist.

"You bastard."

Heat prickled the back of his neck, his mind launching backward—Afghanistan, Helmand Province, the valley of death.

"Hey, Forest, you coming?" someone called.

He barely heard them.

"Go ahead," he said, voice tight. "I need a minute."

He turned and walked away, letting the night mask his anger and wrestling with the news.

Duncan Harris is dead.

Except he isn't. And he killed Jake.

That name, that man—Camp Bastion in Helmand Province, where Operation Shadow Viper was conceived. The mission, a US-UK joint operation, to eliminate Mullah Khalid al-Nasir, a high-value Taliban target. Nasir's location in Korengal Valley became known as the "Valley of Death."

Duncan and the SAS team inserted into the rugged terrain the night before and hiked into an overwatch position. When the assault began, Echo Team was ambushed and pinned down. Duncan and the other SAS snipers cleared a path, but their location was compromised and bombarded with mortars and RPGs. Through the onslaught of explosions around his position, Duncan never stopped firing. The mission was a success, but at tremendous cost, including Duncan Harris, whose body was never recovered.

Jake and, Forest, and the rest of Echo mourned Duncan's loss—they survived because Duncan bought their freedom with his life, or so they thought. Forest tried to reconcile being there, living through that moment, hunting for Duncan's body, and now hearing he's the sniper—*Duncan shot Jake?* It didn't make any sense.

Maybe Jake recognized him, Forest thought. *What if Duncan has been living some other life? As some agency's covert operator or even gone rogue, and Jake called out to him? Would he kill a brother-in-arms, a man whose life he saved?* Forest didn't like the answer.

He didn't know Duncan well, but he knew the look. Duncan enjoyed killing, and he was good at it.

If he thought Jake was a threat, he wouldn't hesitate. And when we find him, neither will I.

Chapter 35

SATURDAY, MAY 2nd
1:17 AM CEST

HÔPITAL EUROPÉEN GEORGES-POMPIDOU, PARIS, FRANCE

THE SHARP BITE OF antiseptic barely masked the smoke clinging to Kate's skin. She lay still, bruised, burned, her body aching in too many places to count. The rhythmic beeping of the heart monitor kept pace with the chaotic flood of thoughts. Nurses moved efficiently, but Kate caught their glances and whispers—recognition in their eyes. *Katherine Preacher. The widow of l'Américain.*

Kate spotted Shepard just outside the curtain. Comfort and threat wrapped in one. He'd play the concerned colleague, masking the web of lies beneath. She'd play the reckless amateur. He needed to believe it.

"Monsieur, you may go in now," the nurse said to Shepard as she exited.

Shepard stepped into the small space, his gaze sweeping over Kate's injuries. His expression hardened. "You look like hell."

Kate let out a slow breath, managing a wry smile. It pulled at her split lip, and she winced. "Feels worse than it looks."

Shepard moved closer, his posture shifting into something more pressing. "What happened?"

Kate met his eyes, forcing frustration into her voice. The lie had to hold. "He must have heard me. I opened the door, and he was just...sitting there. Staring at me."

"Given the size of the explosion, he was planning to take a lot of people with him," Shepard said. "And settled for just one."

"Better me than dozens of innocents," Kate said. "For that, I'm glad I interrupted whatever he was building."

Shepard nodded, his expression unreadable. "Well, whatever his motivation, you're alive, and he's dead," Shepard said. "We'll take the win. But don't think for a minute, I'm not angry. We had a deal, or so I thought."

"But you didn't trust me, did you?"

"No." Shepard leaned against the railing at the foot of her bed, arms crossed. "How could I? I still remember the headstrong, reckless young woman I met in Syria."

"I prefer focused and determined," Kate countered. The smirk she attempted barely lasted a second before pain forced it away.

Shepard shook his head. "Color it any way you want. But I had a feeling you might confront him on your own." His fingers tapped idly against the railing. "It was getting late, and I was just about to call it a night—thought maybe I was wrong. Maybe you'd changed." He let the moment stretch before adding, "But your text arrived, and then—kaboom."

"I know you're angry, and yeah, we had a deal," Kate said, layering in regret. "But I'm glad you were close. Thanks."

"You got off easy," Shepard replied. "A few inches the other way, and they'd be scraping you off the rubble."

"I don't know what you believe," Kate mused. "I was never the religious type. But I think I've got a guardian angel."

"Or nine lives," Shepard muttered. "At least your job here is done."

Here we go, Kate thought. *Now, I just need to take the bait.* "I hadn't thought about that," Kate began. "But you're right. I came here to find the man who shot my husband, and against impossible odds, I did."

"And now he's dead," Shepard added. "Plus, you stopped whatever he was planning."

"The warehouse might still have evidence," Kate said, testing Shepard's resolve. "Details on suppliers, contacts, even targets."

"The fire was intense. Probably take them all night just to get it under control, so doubtful there will be much, but the DGSI will go through it with a fine-tooth comb, just to be sure."

"The DGSI. Boucher! Is there any news?" Kate asked.

"In fact, there is," Shepard replied. "While you were stalking terrorists, Boucher went back into surgery, but he's out and stable. If he continues to improve, they'll transfer him out of ICU."

"That's great news," Kate said. "And makes it easier to go home."

"Home?"

"There's no reason to stay," Kate said, her tone selling the finality of the decision. "Besides, I think two near-death experiences are enough for one city."

"So, what now?" Shepard pressed.

She turned her gaze back to Shepard, studying his face. "I need to rest, recuperate," she said and paused as if weighing her next words. "And cry. I just buried the love of my life, and I can't yet picture life without him."

Shepard nodded, but his eyes never left hers. For just a second, the mask slipped. Kate caught something cold, something calculating. It wasn't just detachment—it was conviction.

Her pulse ticked up. *I know that look*, she thought. *A zealot—willing to sacrifice anything or anyone for his cause. He wasn't just hiding the sniper. He was protecting himself.*

Kate knew she couldn't prove it. Not yet. But she couldn't sit here, breathing the same air as him, knowing what she knew.

If he doesn't leave now, I swear to God—I'll rip this heart monitor cord out of the wall and strangle him until he confesses.

Her fingers curled into the blanket. A long breath in, slow exhale. She blinked twice, her eyelids heavy with feigned exhaustion.

Shepard hesitated, then shifted back. Message received.

"I'll let you rest," he said. "Of course, if you need anything, you have my number."

Kate watched the curtain sway as Shepard slipped out, his presence lingering like a shadow. The conversation they'd just had kept replaying in her mind—his calm certainty that her investigation was over, that Boucher's assassination attempt, and now hers, would hide his role in the attack. She barely had time to process the thought when the curtain rustled again, revealing a middle-aged man in a white coat, his salt-and-pepper hair neatly combed. He carried a tablet, his eyes scanning the screen as he approached Kate's bedside.

Madame Preacher, I'm Dr. Renaud," he said, glancing at his tablet. "Your CT scan is clear—no bleeding, no fractures, no brain injury."

"Great. So I can go?"

He sighed. "I'd recommend staying overnight—concussion symptoms can take time."

"I appreciate your concern, Doctor, but I have to leave."

Dr. Renaud's frown deepened. "Madame Preacher, I must advise against—"

Kate pushed herself up a little straighter, the movement stiff but deliberate. "I understand the risks. And I'll sign whatever forms you need. But I'm not staying."

The doctor exhaled, rubbing his temple. He glanced at her chart, then at her, weighing his obligation against the sheer resolve in her eyes.

"Madame Preacher, while I strongly advise against it, I cannot force you to stay. If you are determined to leave, I will prepare your discharge papers. But if you experience any symptoms—dizziness, confusion, severe headache, anything out of the ordinary, I want your assurance that you will seek medical attention immediately."

Kate nodded, her decision firm. "You have my word."

Dr. Renaud sighed and nodded in return. "Very well. I will ask the nurse to remove the IV and heart monitor sensors while I prepare your discharge paperwork."

Minutes later, the nurse entered. Her movements brisk and focused as she removed the medical equipment, retrieved a bag with Kate's top, and set it on the edge of the bed. "All done, Madame," she said with a smile, oblivious to the storm brewing inside Kate's mind.

Kate waited for the nurse to leave, then dragged her top over her head, wincing as fabric brushed the butterfly bandage. *Next time I get blown up,* she mused. *I'll wear something that buttons.*

She exhaled, steadied herself, and called Talya. "I'm OK," Kate said. "You?"

"Well clear," Talya replied. "Though I won't lie—that was bigger than I expected."

"You and me both. Thanks to you, most of it blew out the back." Kate shifted, testing how much pain she was in. "Where are you?"

"I'm parked just outside."

"Good. Come get me."

"You're leaving?" Talya asked, shocked. "Don't they want to keep you for…"

"My head's fine," Kate interrupted. "Hard as ever. I'll be out front in five."

Chapter 36

CIA HEADQUARTERS, LANGLEY, VA

MARGOT RYDER'S OFFICE MIRRORED her rank—spacious, ordered, efficient. A mahogany desk sat near the center, covered in neatly stacked files, classified documents, and her ever-present glowing tablet. Two leather armchairs faced her desk, a silent invitation for the constant rotation of operatives and analysts. Behind her, floor-to-ceiling bookshelves held binders, manuals, and well-worn books on intelligence and history.

Her walls bore only framed certificates—no personal mementos. The one indulgence: a weathered globe and a whiskey decanter in the corner. Some nights, she poured a glass. Not tonight.

The room glowed in warm lamplight, twilight fading beyond the windows. Margot eased into her chair, slipping off her heels with a muted sigh. The plush carpet beneath her stockinged feet her only concession to comfort after hours of power strides through the agency's labyrinthine corridors.

She removed her reading glasses, setting them aside before rubbing her temples, attempting to ward off the headache that had been threatening since this morning's call. Preacher's breach of their facial recognition system, a fact that both impressed and unnerved her, was a risky move, one that could have significant consequences if discovered. But might also yield results no one else could achieve. Margot had been waiting for an update all day, the anticipation building as the hours passed.

The secure line on her desk lit up. Margot's fatigue vanished. She inhaled once, slow and measured, before reaching for the receiver.

"Ryder."

"We have a match."

"Send it and lock her out.

"Already done, but...

Margot's fingers tapped against the desk. "What did she get?"

"The image matched Duncan Harris, former British military. She pulled his complete service record but nothing else."

"Nothing else?" Margo exhaled. "Let me guess—classified mission files. One of ours?"

"No, ma'am. MI6."

She pinched the bridge of her nose. "Great. That means an inquiry."

"Launch a target trace?"

"Yes. Now." Margot's jaw tightened. "Wherever he is, we need to find him before Preacher does—she has a head start."

"I *doubt* that'll be a problem," he said, oozing confidence. "We have every resource at our disposal."

"You don't know Preacher, do you?"

"No, ma'am—she was before my time."

"Thought so. Good luck." Margot pressed the end call button. "You're going to need it."

CHAPTER 37

SATURDAY, MAY 2nd
2:12 AM CEST

HÔTEL DE POURTALÈS, PARIS, FRANCE

KATE SHUT THE DOOR behind her, exhaling as silence wrapped around her. Every muscle ached, but adrenaline still pulsed, keeping the exhaustion at bay. She crossed to the desk, muttering, "Just one look."

Her fingers flew across the keyboard, accessing Nomad's darknet server. The folder reserved for her investigation popped up, and there it was—the file that could change everything. Kate hesitated for a split second, her cursor hovering over the image file, and then clicked.

A face filled her screen. A jolt of recognition surged like a knife to the ribs. The British SAS uniform, the close-cropped military haircut, and younger features couldn't mask the truth.

That face, those eyes. "Son of a bitch."

The cement truck—Richmond. That was no accident. Harris staged it, trying to keep me from reaching Paris.

A mental split-screen image formed in Kate's mind. *I wasn't just tired,* Kate realized. *I did know the man who scaled the Cafe's street lamp because I watched him leap onto the hood of my car.*

Her fingers trembled as she launched the encrypted video chat with Nomad.

"Jesus, Kate! What happened? Are you alright?"

Kate rubbed her throat, swallowing against the rawness. "I'm fine."

"You don't sound fine—and you sure as hell don't look fine."

"Forget that—I just opened the Duncan Harris folder."

Nomad paused. "I can hear it in your voice—what do you need?"

"I know him." Kate exhaled sharply. "He tried to kill me, then saved me. It's complicated, but he said his name was Grant Collins. I need you to search—"

"I'm on it—Grant Collins left Paris yesterday."

"Where to?"

"Nairobi—then Maboko."

Kate stiffened. "Motapa."

"That mean something?"

"Yes," Kate replied, her voice tight. "Wherever this guy goes, someone's about to die—and a friend's leaving for Motapa in a matter of hours."

"Could your friend be the target?"

Kate shook her head. "More likely the new president, but it's not a coincidence."

"You're going, aren't you?" Nomad asked.

"In fact, I was invited," Kate said, a grim smile playing on her lips. "I'll let Bella know my schedule just opened up."

"Bella?" Nomad asked. "Isabella Marquez?"

"Long story, but yes."

"Huh. Didn't take you for the celebrity jet-set type."

"Funny," Kate said, rolling her eyes. "See if you can find out where Grant's staying—with his cover still intact, there's a chance he'll book a hotel, rent a car, even make dinner reservations. I'll want to steer clear until I know more."

"If you're running around with Isabella Marquez, low profile might be difficult."

"The focus will be on her, but point taken," Kate conceded.

Kate hesitated, fingers hovering over the screen. Bella had no idea what she was about to step into. But it was too late to turn back now.

Surprise! Plans changed. If the offer's still open, I'm in. Sending sizes—Thanks!

She hit send, knowing Bella would see it in a few hours.

Kate stretched out on the bed, mind racing. *Moshenski—valuable, but dangerous. And Shepard? How did he learn about Jake's files?*

The warning in Jake's video echoed in Kate's mind. *Don't trust anyone.*

For once, she had no plan. That alone made her uneasy.

But instincts had kept her alive before. Today, she'd let the *Little Shaman* lead the way.

The thought made her smile—a little. The phrase always reminded her of Jake, of Africa...and the old bushman shaman who once told her she'd return when she was needed.

> Vitali, Sorry for the short notice, but I'm leaving Paris this afternoon and hoping to meet and review findings before I go.

Kate ignored the pain as best she could, propping up a couple of pillows for added support. *And what about Talya?* she wondered. *I would not have survived without her, but if she learns I'm hunting Jake's killer, she'll alert the team. I know they all loved Jake, but they have full lives, wives, kids, and a future...I won't ask them to help. I can't.*

She closed her eyes, letting the day slip away with a single, final thought—one she knew Jake would understand...even if he didn't approve.

Vengeance may be the lord's
but beware the woman with nothing left to lose.

Chapter 38

SATURDAY, MAY 2nd
6:00 AM CEST

HÔTEL DE POURTALÈS, PARIS, FRANCE

THE SURVEILLANCE TEAM LOGGED Kate's return at 2 AM and didn't realize Talya was driving—her plan worked.

At 6 AM, a limo arrived and idled at the curb for over an hour—the driver barely moving, his phone casting an eerie blue glow on his face.

At 7:18 AM, the limo departed. It was a simple log entry in the journal, and no one gave it much thought.

***

7:20 AM CEST

KATE SLIPPED THROUGH THE hotel's kitchen exit, suitcase in hand. As promised, a sleek black limo waited, the driver already stepping forward.

"Morning, Mrs. Preacher." The driver dipped his head politely. "I hope I haven't kept you waiting."

Kate paused, her brow furrowing. "Actually, I was wondering how long you've been waiting."

"Since 6:00 AM, Madame." He clasped his hands neatly behind his back. "Mr. Moshenski is an early riser. When he saw your note, he instructed me to come and wait."

"I'm sorry," Kate began. "Mr. Moshenski's note only caught my eye about twenty minutes ago. I hoped we'd be able to meet this morning but assumed I'd arrange my transportation."

The driver smiled politely. "I am at your disposal for the day, Madame. Any errands or meetings, and then I'll take you to the airport."

"The airport?" Kate's brows lifted. "I don't even have flight information yet."

"You're on Ms. Marquez's flight—Le Bourget, 1:30 PM," the driver said. "We should leave before noon."

Kate studied him. "You're very well informed."

"Mr. Moshenski is well informed," the driver corrected, his posture unwavering. "You are already on the passenger manifest."

The limousine glided through the Paris streets, eventually entering the secure underground parking area of the Ukrainian Embassy. A young man stood waiting as Kate exited the vehicle.

"This way, Mrs. Preacher. Mr. Moshenski is expecting you."

Moments later, Kate was ushered into Moshenski's office. He was just hanging up the phone as she entered.

"I'm sorry to interrupt," Kate began. "But thanks for agreeing to meet me on such short notice and for arranging transportation. That's very kind."

Moshenski's lips curved into a small smile. "The least I can do after Paris tried to kill you... a second time."

"There's not much that escapes your attention," Kate remarked and returned his smile.

"Not much," Vitali agreed. "Your admittance to a hospital, for example. But I am hoping your visit will fill in the missing pieces."

"I'll try," Kate said, producing a folder from her messenger bag and spreading the contents on Vitali's desk. "This is Tariq al-Masri. Born in Egypt, radicalized, joined ISIS. He trained in Iran and operated in Iraq and Syria before being captured and incarcerated at Bagram."

"From where he was released, I assume," Vitali began. "During the American withdrawal?"

"That's correct. A man of passion, skill, and an inflamed hatred for the West."

"I am told a single male body was recovered from last night's gas leak explosion," Vitali said, peering over the top of his reading glasses. "And we are fortunate that was the only fatality."

"The body will be identified as Tariq al-Masri," Kate said. "DGSI will find bomb-making materials, documents linking him to Le Café Pierre. Whether the media runs with it or not, the investigation will be over."

Vitali considered this, then gave a single nod. "With a body recovered and the evidence tying him to the Café Pierre attack, the DGSI will end the investigation—case closed."

This is the moment, Kate thought. *The point of no return, where Kate was at the mercy of her instincts, and intuition. Can I trust him with the truth, or will it get me killed?*

"Yes," Kate began, then hesitated, listening for guidance. "But it's all a lie."

"I do not understand," Vitali said. "You have this man's dossier and your injuries, and hospitalization. You were clearly at the site of the explosion."

"Vitali, do you play chess?"

"I understand the game."

"Tariq was a poisoned pawn—something too tempting to resist—and a trap," she said. "But the only way to stay in the game was to take the pawn."

"You went to the warehouse, risked your life, just to convince someone you were fooled?"

"I was dead either way," Kate said simply. "The man I'm hunting is a skilled predator—one that can reach anyone, anywhere." She let the words settle, then added, "He already tried once—in Richmond. But his mission was pulled at the last moment."

Kate watched Moshenski closely, reading the subtle shifts in his expression. Finally, she spoke.

"I think you had something to do with that." She tilted her head, assessing. "You're the only one—outside a very tight circle—who knew I had Jake's files."

"Your powers of reason and deduction never cease to amaze."

"That's not a denial," Kate said, raising an eyebrow.

"Like you, I trust my intuition," Vitali began. "After receiving the video, I feared the worst. I let it be known that you had something of your husband's, and while I had no idea of the contents, nothing should interrupt your return to Paris or your investigation."

"Who did you tell?"

"I am not at liberty to say," Vitali began. "But I trusted this little bird to sing, and it appears I was successful. But tell me, how did you know that this man, Tariq, was not the sniper?"

"What the real sniper didn't know," Kate began. "Was that I already knew the caliber of the weapon used to shoot Jake. He planted evidence, expecting I would find it. What I didn't know was who would lead me into the trap."

"And who did?"

"I'm not at liberty to say," Kate said and smirked. "This game is far from over, and some knowledge can be life threatening."

"I understand," Vitali said, his head nodding in agreement. "I see you are returning the case. You have no further need of the equipment?"

"Believe me," Kate said. "If I could take it, I would. But I'll have to make do with whatever comes my way. The case is a little light. Unavoidable I'm afraid."

"No matter. Nothing connects your equipment to myself or the embassy," Vitali noted. "But I am curious. Does your honesty mean that you now trust me?"

"If I'm being completely truthful, the analyst part of me thinks I made a mistake," Kate said. "But you're right, I trust my instincts, and I believe you and I both benefit most as allies."

"I agree. We are both risking much, and stronger together," Vitali said. "Can I assume the trip to Motapa is not entirely recreational?"

"That's correct," Kate replied and smirked.

"Then I bid you safe travels," Vitali said, rising from his desk. "And good hunting."

"Before I go," Kate began. "Might I visit…"

"I was hoping you would ask," Vitali interrupted, beaming. "As you requested, there is a chessboard at Mikhail's bedside. My assistant will escort you down and please stay as long as you are able. The driver will wait for you in the garage."

They stood, locked eyes and shook hands—firm, intentional, grips of equals, warriors, neither sure if they would see each other again.

***

ZHUKOV'S FACE WAS A picture of serenity. *He looks happy. Maybe, in his dreams, he's with them—his wife, his daughter. Maybe this is the first true peace he's known since Beslan. Hoping he wakes almost feels selfish.*

Vitali had arranged the chessboard, along with a small table and chair. Kate set the board just as Zhukov had in Syria. To an outsider, it would look like she'd come for a friendly game with a recovering friend.

She smirked. *You wanted me to recognize it. Now it's your turn.*

Chapter 39

SATURDAY, MAY 2nd
4:15 PM CEST

HÔTEL DE POURTALÈS, PARIS, FRANCE

Talya checked in periodically with the surveillance team, surprised by Kate's silence. *She's earned a down day*, Talya reasoned, thumb hovering over her phone. *I'll check in later.*

By evening, the silence stretched too long. No movement. The knot in Talya's gut tightened.

> K. You still breathing?

She meant it as humor, but doubt gnawed at her. *What if Shepard wasn't fooled?*

Talya zipped up her leathers, swung onto the Yamaha, and gunned it. Paris blurred beneath her wheels. She cut through traffic, eyes locked on the road ahead, gut tightening.

She strode into the lobby, every step projecting the confidence of a guest who belonged. A brief smile, a dismissive wave—the front desk clerk barely registered her.

The elevator chimed. On the fifth floor, she scanned—*no signs of trouble. So far, so good.*

She knocked on Kate's door, called out, and then finally pounded. When there was no response, she picked the lock and slipped inside.

The bedroom TV murmured. Kate's electronics were staged, charging. But the closet, drawers, and bathroom? Empty.

She closed the bedroom door, assuming Kate's electronics were still listening, and opened the tap in the kitchen sink.

"Forest is going to kill me." Talya exhaled hard, her pulse spiking.

Then she saw it.

A single folded note left exactly where they'd worked.

> T—
> I'm sorry. Don't follow.
> K.

***

SATURDAY, MAY 2nd
11:00 AM EDT

FOREST'S PHONE BUZZED, LOST in the thunder of live fire. Gunshots, explosions—chaos. He sprinted for the armory, slamming the door shut before catching the call on the third ring.

"Talk to me."

"She's in the wind. Lost after 2 AM. Limo came at six, left empty at 7:15."

"That was her ride," Forest muttered. "She slipped coverage."

"I'm in her room—gear's gone. Left a note."

"Let me guess. Don't follow." Then silence. "She found him, didn't she?"

Talya exhaled. "It's Kate. Was there ever any doubt?"

Forest ran a hand through his hair, already moving. "Graduation's today. SWAT clears out soon. I'll have Steve prep a bird to Charlotte—from there we can grab whatever flights we need—I need a destination."

"Best guess," Talya said. "Kate hitched a ride with Marquez—Nairobi, then Motapa."

"So, Africa." He shook off the frustration. "I'll work logistics, but we need confirmation. If we're in the wrong place, we won't get a second chance."

"If Kate's traveling with Marquez, I can be in the air tonight, and the team can follow."

"Copy that," Forest echoed. "Do whatever you can to get a line on our girl, and we'll be ready to roll."

Chapter 40

SATURDAY, MAY 2nd
12:30 PM CAT

NAMANGWE DESERT, MOTAPA, CENTRAL AFRICA

The gravel road stretched endlessly across the arid expanse, a ribbon of dust winding through Motapa's scorched heart. Beneath the midday sun, the landscape shimmered with heat, the sky a harsh, cloudless blue. A single acacia tree broke the monotony, its twisted branches casting dappled shade on the cracked earth below.

Beneath it, a man sat—head bowed, eyes closed—draped in the vibrant reds and ochres of the Maasai. Motapa was far from his home, but at this moment, in the shade of a single tree, he appeared content to rest and wait. Hands, gnarled and strong, rested in his lap, a fine layer of red dust, baked with sweat and smoke, clung to his arms. A long spear, its point blackened by earth and fire, rested against the tree. A club and a long knife hung from a belt of tanned leather, a broad strip of crimson and beadwork.

His skin, the color of rich mahogany, bore the marks of a life lived in the wild—a deep scar raked across his chest from a long-ago encounter with a lion. The tall, slender frame was still strong and remarkably fit, despite the years etched into his skin. His true age was unknown, but the lines radiating from his eyes and the road map of deep furrows carved into his face revealed both age and wisdom.

His feet, bare and toughened like the hide of a rhinoceros, were planted firmly on the ground, as though rooted to the earth itself. Like a tablecloth on a picnic table, a blanket of bright red cloth draped across a makeshift pack of cloth and leather. The pack's contents a mystery except for a few scraps of dried meat resting on top, a simple meal for a man accustomed to living off the land.

A distant roar shattered the afternoon stillness. Nuru remained motionless, eyes half-closed, as the sound grew louder—rushing toward him like a storm.

An olive-green Toyota pickup skidded to a stop, spitting gravel and dust into the air. The truck, with a machine gun mounted to the bed, cast an ominous shadow. The pair of soldiers in the truck's bed faced the old man, AK-47's held ready, but the old man's calm demeanor was unshaken, as if the disruption was nothing more than a passing breeze.

The driver climbed out, his stance rigid, voice rough with suspicion. "Old man, what are you doing out here?"

Nuru's eyes opened slowly. He met the soldier's gaze with a serene smile. "I am resting. And eating."

The driver narrowed his eyes and rephrased the question with suspicion lacing his tone. "Out here, in the middle of nowhere? Where are you going?"

The old man turned his head slightly, gesturing toward the mountains visible on the horizon. "I am on my way to Krasnaya Skala."

The soldier's impatience flared. "What business do you have at the fortress?"

The man's smile never wavered. "I have a message for Kwesi," he said. "Kwesi Nkrumah."

The soldiers exchanged wary glances. Colonel "The Hyena" Nkrumah inspired loyalty among his troops through a combination of fear and rewards, and none dared address him by his first name.

"What's your name?"

"I am Nuru," he began. "I am Maasai."

"How do you know the Colonel?"

"I knew him when he was just a boy," Nuru said, and smiled. "A very long time ago."

"You have a long way to go," the driver pointed out, clearly doubting Nuru could reach their base.

Nuru shrugged shoulders. "I've already come a long way."

"You can give us the message," the driver insisted, stepping closer. "We are Colonel Nkrumah's soldiers."

The old man shook his head slowly. "I cannot."

This refusal ignited a spark of anger. The two men in the truck's bed jumped down, advancing on Nuru, their eyes fixed on the old man's weapons. But as they approached, Nuru looked at one of them, his gaze piercing. "Sekou," he began, addressing the man by name. "Your wife is ill."

The soldier froze, a look of shock crossing his face. "How do you know this?" he demanded.

Moving with deliberate slowness, Nuru reached into his pack, ignoring the rifles aimed at him. He pulled out a small pouch and tossed it to the soldier.

"Put these herbs in her tea tonight," he said. "She will be well by morning."

The soldier hesitated, then nodded slowly, his suspicion tempered by a dawning respect. Nuru turned his attention to the other soldier. "Your sister gave birth to a healthy baby boy. She named him Kofi after your grandfather."

The second soldier's eyes widened in disbelief. "How can you know this?"

Nuru's expression remained serene as he answered. "Your grandfather whispered in my ear," Nuru said, and then chuckled.

The soldier's face paled. "What's so funny?" he asked.

"Your grandfather said you were never a good hunter. You couldn't sit still and talked too much, but he enjoyed walking with you."

The soldiers lowered their weapons and backed away, unnerved by the old man's knowledge. The driver cleared his throat, trying to regain control of the situation. "We're searching for a boy. Have you seen anyone headed this way?"

Nuru waved a hand toward his small pile of belongings. "The spirits and I are the only ones here," he replied. "And we will leave soon."

The leader hesitated, then nodded curtly. "If you see the boy, tell them when you reach the fortress."

Nuru tilted his head slightly. "Why do you seek the child?"

"The boy escaped from the mines," blurted out one soldier, and the other jabbed him with the butt of his rifle, silencing him.

The driver tossed Nuru a bottle of water. "It's a full day to the nearest water," he said. "Two to reach the fortress, if you don't die on the way."

Nuru accepted the bottle with a nod of gratitude. "Thank you," he said, his voice warm with sincerity.

The truck roared back to life, and the soldiers drove away, leaving a swirling cloud of dust in their wake. Nuru watched until the truck vanished into the horizon. Only then did he reach for the red cloth draped over his pack, lifting it gently.

Beneath it, a young boy lay curled, his face pale with fear, his wide eyes locked onto the old man.

"Thank you," he whispered, voice trembling.

Nuru handed him the water bottle with a gentle smile. "Here, this is for you."

The boy took the bottle, drank what he could before offering it back. Nuru shook his head, his eyes on the distant mountains. "The land provides all that I require," Nuru said, his voice calm and reassuring. "But you must drink. You have come far, and we still have far to go."

The boy shook his head, fear clouding his features. "I can't go back. They'll kill me," he said. "I'll take my chances out here."

Nuru's expression did not change. "Suit yourself. The lions in this region will be grateful for such an easy meal."

The boy hesitated, his resolve wavering as Nuru offered him a piece of dried meat. "How did you know the truck was coming?" the boy asked, taking the food.

Nuru's eyes twinkled with quiet amusement. "Your father told me," Nuru said simply. "He asked me to protect you, and that is why I dug the hole."

The boy's eyes widened. "My father's dead."

"Yes, I know," Nuru replied.

"You talk to the dead?" the boy asked, skepticism creeping into his voice.

"I listen to the spirits," Nuru corrected, his tone patient. "They are why I am here, why I waited."

"Waited for what?" the boy asked, his voice barely a whisper.

"You," Nuru answered, his gaze steady. "I need your help."

The boy swallowed the meat, confusion sweeping across his face. "You need *my* help?"

"I must go to the fortress, and you will show me the way."

The boy shook his head, panic rising. "No, I can't," he said, struggling to speak. "You—you don't know…"

"Leboo," Nuru said, his voice firm. "My path leads to the fortress. Yours does not. But if we are to save the others, you must trust me. You must do as I ask."

The boy stared at Nuru, confusion and bewilderment written across his youthful face. "How do you know my name?"

Before Nuru could answer, Leboo spoke again, his voice softening. "I know—my father told you."

Nuru smiled, a warm, knowing smile. "I know you ventured from home to help your mother and sister. To have traveled so far and suffered as you have is a remarkable feat for one so young. I must tell you that what lies ahead will test your strength and courage, but when our work is done, I see a new, full life for your family and your village. Will you help me?"

Leboo hesitated for a moment, then slowly nodded, the weight of his decision settling on his small shoulders. "Yes," he said, his voice steady now. "I'll help."

Nuru's smile widened, a glimmer of satisfaction in his wise old eyes. "Good. Then let us begin our journey, my young friend."

"What about the lions?" Leboo asked, recalling Nuru's warning.

"I am Maasai."

"I don't understand," Leboo replied.

"When lions see me, they run." Nuru let the words settle before adding, "And they return only if I seek their counsel."

***

THE SUN WAS LOW on the horizon when Nuru and Leboo neared the water. "Do you hear the birds?" Nuru asked. Leboo nodded, too weak to speak. "The water is near," Nuru added, hoping to bolster the boy's strength to climb one last hill before they stopped for the night. The soldier doubted the old man could survive long enough to reach the water, and the journey was difficult for the boy. Nuru knew it was Leboo who needed to summon the strength and the will to continue.

In the cool of the setting sun and seated at the water's edge, the boy bathed and played and found his voice. "They call this stream Lusitu, the hidden source," he said, cupping his hands and splashing his face.

Nuru knew that water this cool and clear was spring water, no doubt originating in the Drakari Mountains that lay ahead. The gently flowing stream gave life to the sparse vegetation, hardy shrubs, and for the two travelers, much-needed relief from the dry, dusty trail.

Leboo dried and wrapped himself in Nuru's Shuka, the bright red fabric engulfing the boy in the Maasai warrior's symbol of power, bravery, and strength.

"This is a good place for the night," Nuru began. "We'll continue in the morning."

"I can collect brush for a fire," Leboo offered.

"Are you cold?" Nuru asked.

"No, but I thought a fire would...you know, keep away the animals."

"The lions?"

"Yes."

"You are safe with me," Nuru said, his voice calm and confident. "Fire attracts men with guns."

The mere suggestion that there were still soldiers looking for him plunged the boy's face into darkness.

Nuru reached into his pack and spread out some dried meat and nuts, encouraging the boy to eat, which he did as if seated at a grand feast.

"Tell me of the place you escaped," Nuru asked. "I have only seen it in my dreams."

The boy remained silent, and his voice, when it finally came, was a whisper, fragile and trembling like the wind stirring the dust around them. "They call it the pit...the place where we dig. It's deep in the mountains, where the earth is hard and cold. We head down at dawn, smash the black rock, and fill bags until the sun is gone. The strongest carry the bags and load the trucks. It is the hardest work, and when you collapse, they send you back down to fill bags."

Nuru looked at the boy's hands, small and trembling, nails cracked and broken, the skin raw in places.

"The air down there..." He hesitated, unsure how to describe it. "It's like breathing through a wet cloth, but dry at the same time. Dust gets in your lungs, and you cough until you can't breathe. Some boys...don't come back up. They just leave them there."

The old man listened, his eyes narrowing, the lines on his face deepening with every word the boy spoke. He had heard stories like this before, whispered tales of horror and suffering, but hearing it from the boy's own lips made it real in a way that nothing else could.

"And the soldiers?" the old man asked, his voice soft, coaxing the boy to continue as he ate.

The boy swallowed hard, his eyes darting to the horizon as if he feared the soldiers might appear. "They're always watching. If you stop working, they beat you. If you try to run—they shoot. We don't see much of them during the day—they stay up near the trucks, guarding the bags as they're loaded. But at night..."

His voice caught in his throat, the memories too fresh, too raw. He looked up at the old man, the fear in his eyes mingling with something else—something that looked almost like shame. The old man reached out, his hand steady as the earth beneath them, resting it on the boy's shoulder. The touch was gentle, reassuring, giving the boy the strength to continue.

"At night, we return to the fortress, the one that overlooks the Namangwe

Desert. It's not far from the pit...just beyond the ravine. Most of us sleep in small, cold rooms, caged like animals. They take away some of the older boys and girls. No one speaks of it, but the screams—you can hear them echo through the cliffs. No one sleeps."

The old man's face darkened, the anger simmering just below the surface, but he said nothing, letting the boy unburden himself in his own time.

"The fortress," the boy continued, his voice barely more than a breath, "is where they store the bags of black stones stacked high in an old building that is nearly full. They guard it with guns, more guns than I've ever seen. The soldiers call it coltan and they say it is worth more than our lives—soon trucks will come for it."

His voice trailed off, and he pulled his knees up to his chest, shivering despite the lingering heat of the day. The old man could see the exhaustion in the boy's face, in the way his shoulders sagged, in the haunted look in his eyes. He knew that look—he had seen it too many times before.

"You've been strong to survive this long," the old man whispered, his voice filled with a warmth that seemed to cut through the boy's fear like a knife through smoke. "Be strong a little longer, Leboo, and I promise a new life awaits you, a new life for all that you are here to save."

The boy's eyes widened in terror, his breath quickening. "Not me. I can't go back."

The old man's hand tightened gently on his shoulder, anchoring him, calming him. "I know it's frightening," he said, his voice a low, steady murmur. "And the fortress is not your destination. You know the way—better than anyone else. You need only show me."

"There's a path..." the boy said, his voice trembling but determined. "Through the ravine and up a steep cliff. It's hidden, but I know it. It leads to the back of the fortress, where the soldiers don't go much. We can get close without being seen."

The old man nodded, a fierce light in his eyes. "Then tomorrow, that is where we will go. And that is where we will part ways, and your journey begins. We'll talk of that tomorrow. Tonight, sleep well and wake rested."

As if on command, Leboo pulled Nuru's cloak in tight around him. The boy lay on his side, closed his eyes, and slept peacefully for the first time since he was taken.

Chapter 41

SATURDAY, MAY 2nd
12:30 PM CAT

PRESIDENTIAL PALACE, MOTAPA, CENTRAL AFRICA

KLAUS MUELLER AND HIS daughter Rileyne strode through the Presidential Palace's verdant courtyard, their tailored suits radiating quiet authority. The palace, once a sanctuary for Motapa's royal family, had survived wars, coups, and despots—its lingering grandeur a symbol of resilience.

When they entered the administrative wing, a junior aide greeted them. "Mr. Mueller, Ms. Mueller, if you'll follow me, please." He led them past ornate mahogany doors and bustling offices, a testament to the new government's commitment to centralized efficiency.

The conference room door opened, revealing a long table of rich, dark Motapan wood. President Dr. Zola Bongani stood at the far end, ready to receive his guests. Klaus, with the confidence of a man who had shaped global events for decades, strode purposefully to the opposite end. His snow-white hair and pale gray-blue eyes, almost silver, gave him an edge of cold authority—like the great white shark, they evoked a raw, unstoppable predatory instinct.

Rileyne, her ash blonde hair pulled back in an elegant chignon with a few artful wisps framing her face, moved gracefully to take her seat at her father's right hand. Her tailored charcoal suit and minimalist platinum necklace spoke of refined taste and the sharp intellect lurking beneath icy green eyes.

As they took their seats, the room aligned itself. Two men, each accustomed to shaping the world in their own way, sat at opposite ends of the table—a battlefield of polished wood and unspoken influence. Bongani's advisors flanked the sides, their positions a silent affirmation of where authority rested.

"Mr. Mueller, Ms. Mueller, welcome," Dr. Bongani greeted, warm but measured. "Are your accommodations comfortable?"

Klaus smiled. "More than comfortable, Mr. President. The Palace is magnificent."

As pleasantries concluded, Klaus opened his briefcase. "Mr. President, we at the Global Economic Council believe Motapa stands at a crucial juncture. Our proposal offers a comprehensive approach to rebuilding—from healthcare to education, from infrastructure to sustainable resource management."

Dr. Bongani leaned forward, his expression thoughtful. "Your presentation is certainly enticing, Mr. Mueller. Almost too good to be true, one might say."

Klaus chuckled. "I assure you, our interest in assisting developing nations like Motapa is sincere."

"I don't doubt your sincerity," Dr. Bongani replied, his tone measured. "But the rush to turn developing nations, like Motapa, into mRNA testing and production zones raises serious concerns about experimentation and the use of cutting-edge technologies in regions where regulatory oversight might be viewed as less robust. As a doctor, I must consider the potential for unintended consequences, and I swore an oath to do no harm. Now, as President, I intend to lead Motapa by the same principle."

Rileyne interjected, her voice cool and precise. "Our track record speaks for itself, Mr. President. The GEC's partnerships have led to significant improvements in healthcare outcomes across Africa."

Dr. Bongani's eyes narrowed. "Certain diseases have been curtailed, yes. But others?" He leaned forward. "Lupus. Rheumatoid arthritis. Multiple sclerosis. The numbers don't lie, Ms. Mueller. Populations that received your emergency-authorized mRNA vaccines have seen a surge in autoimmune disorders—far beyond statistical anomaly."

He let the words settle. "A five-year study tracked recipients. Autoimmune conditions skyrocketed over 200%. And not just here—Kenya, Zambia, parts of Asia. I've seen children crippled by rheumatoid arthritis before their eighth birthdays. Families shattered by afflictions they never had names for—until now."

Rileyne's lips tightened, but before she could respond, Bongani raised a hand, his tone hardening. "Some call it anecdotal. Others wave it away as statistical noise. But tell me, Ms. Mueller, how many lives must be sacrificed before it stops being noise?"

The silence that followed was palpable, the tension in the room growing heavier. Klaus leaned forward, his voice smooth, persuasive. "Mr. President, I understand your caution. But consider the alternative." He gestured lightly. "The United States is consumed by domestic unrest and foreign wars. Russia and China? Their past dealings with Motapa have been... less than favorable."

He let the implication linger. "The GEC offers something different—partnership, not political leverage. No hidden strings."

Dr. Bongani nodded slowly. "Your points are valid, Mr. Mueller. Motapans have indeed suffered under the yolk of foreign nations promising aid, only to fill their coffers with the looted profits of our natural resources. The unfinished twin towers, directly across from the palace, and teetering on the edge of collapse, are a monument to China's broken promises, substandard construction practices, and imported prison labor."

"Your success as Africa's newest democracy, breaking free of the shackles of the past, is why the GEC is prepared to commit billions to turn your vision into reality. The GEC invests in the development of your people, basic and higher education, technical training, and medical services, as well as the economic development of core infrastructure, tourism, and the safe and renewable development of your natural resources."

"Mr. Mueller, I will consider all aspects of your proposal, but such a comprehensive approach brings unique risks of its own that must be carefully evaluated and considered. I am sorry to disappoint, but I cannot in good conscience agree to your proposal without further deliberation and study."

The room fell silent for a moment, the air thick with unspoken tensions.

Finally, Klaus spoke, his voice carefully modulated. "I appreciate your time and consideration, Mr. President. The GEC is encouraged by your election and hopeful for a bright future. If at any time you wish to revisit how the GEC can be of assistance, we would welcome the opportunity. In the meantime," Klaus added, smiling. "allow me to thank you again for welcoming us into your home and the invitation to tomorrow evening's festivities."

Dr. Bongani's face softened. "You are both honored guests, and it's my pleasure to host you." He paused, then added, "I understand Ms. Marquez is on her way and is expected in the morning. I look forward to meeting her in person. She's been a friend to Motapa for many years, and tomorrow's dinner is our first opportunity to show our appreciation for her compassion and generosity."

Klaus nodded, a slight smile playing on his lips. "Indeed. She is a remarkable woman and scheduled to speak at our conference this fall. Of course, we hope you will consider attending."

"Thank you for the invitation," Dr. Bongani replied. "Your Davos conference is legendary, both for the world and economic leaders who attend, and the extravagant food. While matters of state are my top priority, I welcome the opportunity to attend if I am able."

As the meeting concluded, Dr. Bongani rose from the table. Klaus and Rileyne followed suit.

Their eyes met—two men who understood power. Each aware of what the other could offer. And what they could destroy.

Klaus and Rileyne exchanged a look. Bongani's hesitation was unfortunate but not unexpected. Either way, the next move belonged to them.

CHAPTER 42

SATURDAY, MAY 2nd
2:10 PM CAT

MABOKO INTERNATIONAL, MOTAPA, CENTRAL AFRICA

GRANT COLLINS STEPPED OFF the plane, the heat slamming into him like a wall. The air shimmered over the sunbaked tarmac, thick with jet fuel and the dusty scent of the savanna beyond.

Inside, the terminal buzzed with a clash of languages—local dialects, clipped European consonants, rapid-fire Mandarin negotiations. Grant, sunglasses concealing his scrutiny, joined the customs queue with feigned nonchalance.

The immigration area was a study in organized chaos. Ceiling fans whirred ineffectually overhead, their blades cutting lazy arcs through the stifling air. Grant's linen shirt clung to his back, already damp with sweat, as he inched forward in the line.

Grant handed over his British passport with an easy smile. "Bit of a queue," he remarked. The customs officer, all deep-set eyes and permanent frown, barely grunted.

At baggage claim, travelers shoved forward in a desperate scramble. Grant stayed back, watching, waiting. His Pelican case was near the bottom of the pile—exactly where he wanted it.

The ground personnel finally arrived, pushing luggage trolleys into the baggage claim area. There was a scramble among the hot and weary travelers to collect their bags as fast as possible. Grant was pleased to see his Pelican case resting near the bottom—less likely to come tumbling down when the pyramid of luggage collapsed. Finally able to approach the cart, he snatched up his duffel bag, throwing the strap over his shoulder. The equipment case slid right off.

With luggage in hand, he moved on to the customs clearance queue. Grant's paperwork was ready to go, and he had nothing to declare, but his case was large enough to pique curiosity in most airports. Maboko International was no exception, and he unlocked the case and opened it for inspection.

The officer rifled through Grant's case, inspecting the Canon bodies and lenses. His fingers closed on the RF 1200mm, and Grant forced a sharp breath. "Careful," he said, voice tinged with rehearsed anxiety. "That's worth more than my car."

The officer's attention shifted to Grant's duffel bag, skipping the casual clothes and boots, his eyes glued to the climbing gear. Grant chuckled, the sound carefully calibrated to convey both sheepishness and enthusiasm. "I sure hope I won't need it, but sometimes the best shot is hanging off a cliff, you know?"

With a final, suspicious glance, the officer waved him through, and Grant wheeled his equipment into the arrivals hall.

The kiosk was impossible to miss—weathered wood, faded magazine covers, cigarette ads curling at the edges. Behind the counter, a wiry man with a serpent tattoo winding up his neck met Grant's gaze, a flicker of recognition passing between them.

"Impressive collection," Grant said casually—delivering the catchphrase.

The vendor's hand disappeared beneath the counter, emerging with a folded newspaper. Grant locked the paper under his arm and slipped the vendor a 5 Euro note. "Keep the change," he said with a wink.

Grant scanned the arrivals hall for anyone or anything that looked out of place. There were a few security cameras, ancient tech, and he suspected they might not even work. He sought a quiet corner and retrieved the paper. Tucked within the newspaper's folds was a small, sealed envelope with a parking stall number and car keys.

The parking lot was a patchwork of potholes and oil stains. Grant's assigned vehicle, a battered compact car, blended seamlessly into the sea of similar wrecks. As he loaded his gear into the trunk, the lingering smell of exhaust fumes mingled with the earthy scent of red dust and smoke that seemed to coat everything.

On the passenger seat, he spotted a small black duffel bag. It was nearly invisible on the worn vinyl seat, and that was the idea. *Let's have a look.* He unzipped the bag just far enough to see the pistol resting on top of stacks of US Dollars. *Good. Old bills. Small denominations.*

As he navigated the chaotic streets of Maboko, Grant's eyes constantly scanned his surroundings. The capital was a jarring mix of colonial architecture and modern development. Crumbling facades stood shoulder-to-shoulder with gleaming glass towers, a visual metaphor for Motapa's struggle to reconcile its past with an uncertain future.

The safe house was nothing special—faded stucco, a sagging garage door, the kind of place no one looked at twice. Grant backed in, the suspension groaning.

The garage door creaked—loud enough to set off a dozen barking dogs. Except there were none. No neighbors. No movement.

Perfect.

Inside, Grant moved with the fluid precision of a predator. His hand slipped into the duffel bag, extracting and examining the Zastava M88 pistol. It was an old Yugoslavian handgun, but it didn't matter. When you're acquiring weapons in the field, you work with what you've got. *Round in the chamber. Full mag,* he thought. *Decent condition.* He'd disassemble, clean, and lubricate later, just to be sure, but first, he needed to sweep the house.

With the gun in a compressed, high-ready Sul position, he cleared each room of the house and then returned to the kitchen. The fridge was nicely stocked, but all he wanted was an ice-cold beer. The capital was hot and humid, and made the beer, some local brand, taste all the better. *I've been in hotter places,* he thought, peeking out from behind a window shade. *And lugging sixty pounds of kit and armor.*

Grant brought the rest of his gear inside and got to work. He was in a foreign country, in an unknown house, arranged by strangers. Trust was in short supply, and the last thing he wanted was an unexpected guest, either while he slept or while he was out scouting. Motion detectors and mini-cams came first. Then, the bedroom, where he stuffed pillows and pulled up the blankets to create the illusion of someone sleeping. He dragged a recliner from the living room and set it in the bedroom's corner. That's where he would sleep until the mission was complete.

Grant pulled out his phone. Typed three words.

Is it done?

Preacher survived, but you're clear. Relax and wait for instructions.

He swigged his beer, the cold biting against the heat in his chest. "That girl's hard to kill."

The African night pressed in around him, thick and still. Grant set the bottle down, his fingers curling around the pistol in his lap.

Relax? Not yet.

Chapter 43

SATURDAY, MAY 2nd
7:10 PM EAT

GIRAFFE MANOR, NAIROBI, KENYA

THE GULFSTREAM G650 TOUCHED down at Wilson Airport, its sleek silhouette gliding to a halt against the setting sun. Vargas had chosen Wilson for its discretion—quieter, faster, and far from the chaos of Jomo Kenyatta.

Bella and Kate sat alone in the front section of the jet, where the warm glow of the setting sun bathed the cabin in gold. The creamy leather seats, reclining into a full, lie-flat position, gave Kate an oasis of tranquility. She slept for most of the eight-hour flight from Paris. *Apparently, I needed the sleep*, Kate thought. *But this totally screws up my time-zone change.*

Kate hadn't considered Bella's plans before agreeing but knew she could break away if needed. *Looks like we're staying in Nairobi.* For now, the hunt for Jake's killer could wait. *A night's rest wouldn't hurt.*

Jake, as an executive protection specialist, often arranged for private jet arrival and transportation, but this was Kate's first experience traveling with an international celebrity. From the window, Kate watched a string of cars approaching. There was a mix of police escort, support staff vans, and a central limousine waiting for the signal to approach.

With the engines powered down, the pilot activated the door mechanism—a soft hiss followed by an unlocking sound as the cabin door swung open and the stairs lowered. The vehicles approached, the limo taking the spot closest to the stairs, and a uniformed chauffeur darted out to stand by the rear door. The jet center staff, accustomed to the protocols of high-profile clients, stood by at a respectful distance, prepared to assist with any luggage or special requests.

Bella sat poised as Vargas signaled the all-clear. She rose, effortlessly chic in a sleeveless beige top that complemented her tan, tailored white linen pants, and minimalist slip-ons. Her dark hair was swept into a loose bun, her only adornments—diamond studs and a simple bracelet.

Kate thought it best to let Bella exit alone and head straight to the limo. Out of nowhere, cameras flashed, and Kate was glad she'd given Bella the extra room. She didn't need the team or anyone else seeing her face plastered on social media. Her last-minute decision to join Bella put the pressure on finding appropriate clothing, but she learned a full travel wardrobe was waiting at the hotel. *That was quite clever*, Kate thought. *Take advantage of the flight time and the tremendous selection of clothing options in an international city like Nairobi.*

The outfit choice caught Kate off guard. They hadn't discussed her wardrobe challenges, but Bella had clearly noticed the tops and scarves she used to hide her scars. For the arrival, a few options had been staged, and Kate opted for a clay-colored, ribbed tank top with a high scoop neckline. The Rag & Bone piece was a figure-flattering, sleeveless style in a comfortable, warm-weather fabric. Paired with slim-fit olive-green cargo pants and white sneakers, the look was effortless yet stylish. She loved it—and couldn't wait to see what else had been procured, even teasing that she might need to hire Bella as her stylist.

Their convoy of vehicles wound through the streets of Nairobi, the fading daylight giving way to the city's vibrant nightlife. Street vendors' carts glowed under bare bulbs, the aroma of grilling meat and spices wafting through the open windows. Kate watched as colorfully dressed locals navigated the busy sidewalks, their voices a melodic backdrop to the urban symphony.

"It's so alive," Bella mused, her eyes wide with wonder. "Every time I come here, it's like the city has a new story to tell."

As they left the bustling downtown behind, the landscape transformed. Lush vegetation lined the roads, the air growing cooler and filled with the subtle fragrances of acacia blooms and wild grasses. The chirping of cicadas signaled their arrival in a more serene part of the city, and in the distance, the silhouette of the Ngong Hills painted a dramatic backdrop against the deepening twilight sky.

The gates of Giraffe Manor swung open, and the convoy wound up a driveway lined with tall, swaying trees. Lanterns flickered along the path, and moonlight bathed the ivy-clad estate, giving it an ethereal glow.

The manor exuded timeless elegance, its architecture blending seamlessly with the wild beauty of its surroundings.

Warm light spilled from the windows, casting a welcoming glow across the manicured lawns. As Kate and Bella stepped out, a chorus of unfamiliar night sounds greeted them—the distant call of a tree hyrax, the gentle rustle of leaves in the evening breeze.

A smiling staff member greeted Ms. Marquez and Mrs. Preacher at the entrance of Giraffe Manor. "Welcome! Champagne and hors d'oeuvres are on the terrace. Please follow me," he said, leading the way. "Your bags will be in your room shortly, and dinner this evening is at 9:00 PM."

They followed their host through the manor, the rich history of the place palpable in every corner. Dark wood paneling and vintage photographs lined the walls, silent storytellers of safaris and adventures long past. The air inside was cool and crisp, scented with a hint of beeswax and old leather.

On the terrace, they stopped, mesmerized. In the distance, giraffes moved through the trees, their long necks silhouetted against the golden glow of landscape lighting.

"Just look at them," Bella whispered, accepting a flute of champagne.

"They are beautiful," Kate agreed.

"Tomorrow, they'll be joining us for breakfast," Bella added. "We must get a photo of you kissing a giraffe."

"Run that one by me again."

"Just wait," Bella said, eyes twinkling. "You'll see."

Kate arched a brow. *Not happening.* They both returned to the tranquility and beauty of the moment, soaking in the atmosphere. The Manor stood as an island of colonial charm amidst the wild beauty of Kenya and a striking contrast to the chaos of Paris. For the first time in weeks, Kate gave herself permission to relax.

"To unique adventures," Bella said, raising her glass.

"And unexpected friendships," Kate added, clinking her flute against Bella's.

***

SATURDAY, MAY 2nd
11:45 PM EAT

After a sumptuous dinner filled with the warmth of good food and relaxed conversation, Kate and Bella wandered outside. The soft glow of lanterns illuminated the terrace, casting long shadows across the manicured lawn. Wrapped in light sweaters against the cool, gentle breeze, they gazed up at the Kenyan night sky.

"This is lovely," Kate said. "But wait until we get into the bush. There's nothing quite like being under canvas. When you're in the middle of nowhere, and you look up..."

"Oh, I know," Bella said. "A dazzling spectacle of light on a black velvet carpet."

"That sounds like a line from one of your movies," Kate said, and they both laughed.

"It's hard to find the words," Bella said. "Africa is one of those rare places where you feel so small and yet more connected to everything around you."

Kate leaned against the railing. Bella curled up on one of the terrace couches. Both women just basking in the moment. The air was fragrant with the scent of blooming flowers, and the grounds were still warm from the day's heat. They could hear the distant calls of nocturnal creatures, the rustle of leaves in the evening breeze, and the soft laughter of guests echoing from inside the manor.

A rare sense of peace, and for Kate, the calm before the storm. She took a slow, deep breath, savoring the moment, and just as she allowed herself to exhale, her phone buzzed. The fleeting moment gone, Kate fished her phone out of her pocket and glanced at the text.

> Ronin is alive.

Kate's breath caught.

"Kate?" Bella frowned. "What's wrong?"

"Nothing. Just...a surprise," Kate lied. "I need to follow up. See you at breakfast."

Before Bella could press, Kate slipped inside, pulse hammering as she bolted upstairs.

The door clicked shut behind her. She pulled out her AirPods, trying to calm herself as she launched a secure video chat with Nomad.

His silhouette flickered on the screen, just a shadow behind the encryption that kept his identity concealed. "Where are you?" he began, but Kate cut him off.

"Never mind that! What did you find?" Her urgency shattering the calmness of the evening.

"I located the drone's full, unedited video. There's no audio track. But it's intense even without it, and—."

"Show me," Kate insisted, gripping her phone.

The video began streaming, and Kate's world narrowed to the small screen in her hands. The first frames came alive, revealing the black SUV traveling along a solitary dirt road surrounded by dense woods. Memories of the edited version played in her mind, painting a grim picture of what was to come.

"Did you pull a location?" Kate asked.

"Yes, the GPS tag puts this about an hour west of Arlington, in the Bull Run Mountains," Nomad replied.

"Way too far to follow from the cemetery."

"Exactly. The drone pilot had to be waiting for them."

The drone tracked the SUV as it pulled off under the cover of trees and stopped. Hovering high enough to remain undetected, the drone captured both of Vitali's men exiting the vehicle. The driver drew his gun from a shoulder harness and scanned the area. Satisfied the area was secure, he nodded at the bald man standing near the passenger door.

Kate's heart raced. *This is it,* she thought. *They brought Marcus out here to kill him and dump the body...but they don't know him. They had no idea.*

The bald man opened the door, reaching in to unbuckle Marcus's seatbelt. Two rapid muzzle flashes confirmed Kate was right. That was Marcus's moment. He pushed the dead man out as the driver pivoted, firing into the back seat, but too late. Marcus was gone. A moment later, with a single precision shot to the head, the driver was dead.

Marcus put one more round into the bald man, then walked over to the driver. He raised his gun, hesitated, then lowered. *One was enough. Marcus never wasted ammo.*

"I've watched this moment again and again," Nomad said. "But still can't wrap my head around how he did it."

"Marcus picked the cuffs," Kate muttered.

"That's why you wanted the autopsy report," Nomad realized. "You knew."

"I suspected," Kate admitted. "I saw them cuff him behind his back. Maybe I should've warned Vitali's men. Maybe...I didn't want to."

"Warned them about what?"

"Marcus was Trident's E&E expert—escape and evasion," Kate said. "He taught me how to pick handcuffs. Probably had a shim or pick sewn into his belt—exactly where his hands would fall if cuffed behind his back."

"Jesus," Nomad said. "Who thinks like that?"

"Operators."

"What about the gun?"

"Vitali's man handed it to him."

"But if he was in on the escape, why kill him?"

"No, that's not what I meant," Kate explained. "When someone with a gun gets too close, they're literally handing you their gun—if you know how to take it. The driver had a shoulder holster. I'll bet this guy did too—so when he leaned in..."

"Marcus took it."

"Yep, and we know how the story ends."

"That's the end for Vitali's guys," Nomad added. "But you'll see...it's just getting started for Marcus."

The video played on with Marcus, gun in hand, scanning the area like he's expecting company, then he knelt down next to the driver. He grabbed the driver's ringing cell phone, but hesitates as if he's deciding whether to answer. Marcus accepted the call, held the phone to his ear, then points the gun directly at the drone's camera.

The video zoomed in on Marcus, and his lips never move, but he lowered the gun and wedged it into his waistband. With the phone resting on the hood of the SUV, he started staging the scene.

"I wish we could hear," Kate said.

"There's still a chance," Nomad added. "I'll keep searching."

"Good. Whoever is on the other end of this call is a key piece of the puzzle."

"But how could they know Marcus would escape?"

"They didn't—not for sure. But someone who knows Marcus..." Kate began. "Someone who knows Ronin and his capabilities gambled he'd survive."

"It was a very big bet," Nomad said. "You'll see what I mean."

They watched as Marcus staged the bodies back inside the SUV, securing them with the seat belts. Then the drone followed him deeper into the woods, and hidden within the trees was an old, solid black Ford Taurus.

"Good choice," Kate said. "That's a vintage eighties model. Obscure and virtually no traceable electronics. And a large trunk."

Kate was already a step ahead of the plan. There was only one piece remaining. She watched Marcus remove the body of a tall black man in a full military dress uniform. At a glance, he was a Marcus clone and was soon buckled into the rear of the SUV.

Marcus removed his service ribbons and tossed them into the car, completing the illusion. *But you made a mistake,* Kate thought. *Details matter, and you cuffed his hands in front.* But as the hair stood up on the back of Kate's neck, she couldn't shake the image of Marcus that popped into her head. *What if it wasn't a mistake?*

Nomad broke the silence as the video played on. "From here, it's pretty much what we've already seen. The drone targets the roof of the SUV, bright white light, etc."

"Right," Kate agreed. "I've seen enough."

"Are you doing OK?" Nomad wondered.

"I'm getting really tired of dead people who aren't," she said. "Present company excluded."

"I know it's a lot to process…"

"Hang on," Kate interrupted. "That's not all, is it? There's something you're not telling me."

"I hate it when you do that."

"Then stop trying to hide things from me," Kate said, growing impatient. "Did you find something in Jake's files?"

"No, it's not that." Nomad sighed, the weight of his next words heavy with implication. "Marcus…Ronin…whatever name he's using these days…I know where he is."

Kate's heart skipped a beat, her mind racing to the one place Nomad would hesitate to say, *Motapa.* "You've got to be kidding me."

"I wish."

***

SUNDAY, MAY 3rd
6:00 AM EAT

THE FIRST LIGHT OF dawn stretched across the horizon, painting the sky in soft shades of pink and gold. The air at Giraffe Manor was cool and crisp, carrying the earthy scent of dew-dampened grass and the subtle musk of the giraffes.

Bella had been up for an hour, naturally drawn to the quiet beauty of the early morning, and found the photographer was eager to start. The light was perfect, and he darted about like a hummingbird, with Bella as the flower. His camera clicked away, capturing every nuance, every shift in light and expression.

Kate found herself awake far earlier than she planned. The news that Marcus was alive—and in Motapa—had shaken her more than she cared to admit. She dressed quickly, craving the comfort of a strong, dark espresso to clear the fog of sleep-deprived thoughts.

Cradling a steaming double espresso, she stepped out onto the grounds. The sight was nothing short of magical. Golden light streaked across the lush, manicured lawns like brush strokes, and in the distance, Bella was the picture of grace and elegance as she posed for the photographer. The towering Rothschild giraffes, with their gentle eyes and long, graceful necks, glided through the scene, their mottled coats blending seamlessly with the dappled sunlight filtering through the trees.

Kate watched from a distance at first, feeling the caffeine work its magic. Other guests of the manor also gathered, admiring the spectacle of Bella interacting with the giraffes. Bella had an undeniable connection with the animals, her natural charm and ease drawing them to her as though she were one of them.

A sweet young giraffe approached Bella. Its long, dark lashes fluttered as it delicately plucked the treats from her palm. But it was the large male giraffe, with its impressive height and even more impressive appetite, that stole the show. Bella, ever the daring one, placed a feed pellet between her lips and leaned forward. The giraffe's long, dexterous tongue expertly snatched the treat, giving Bella a sloppy but affectionate kiss that drew applause from the onlookers.

Kate chuckled, shaking her head at the sight. *There's no way I'm doing that,* she thought. But Bella caught Kate's eye, calling her over with an insistence that was impossible to refuse. The crowd joined in, encouraging Kate to try it. Reluctantly, Kate stepped forward. The photographer poised, ready to capture the moment.

When the giraffe's tongue flicked out and grabbed the pellet from Kate's lips, she couldn't help but laugh, the sound bubbling up from somewhere deep inside her. The onlookers cheered, and Bella grinned, delighted by Kate's willingness to join in the fun. It was a light, joyful moment that cut through the heaviness of Nomad's revelations, offering a brief welcome reprieve.

After the photo shoot, the two women headed in for breakfast at a table by the window. The morning sun streamed through the glass. The aroma of freshly baked pastries and rich Kenyan coffee filled the air. A giraffe's head appeared at the open window, its long neck stretching gracefully as it sought more treats.

"This is surreal," Kate murmured, offering a pellet to their breakfast companion.

Bella nodded in agreement, but her eyes narrowed as she studied Kate's face. "Rough night?" she asked gently.

Kate sighed, running a hand through her hair. "Is it that obvious?"

"Only to someone who's had their fair share of sleepless nights," Bella replied with a sympathetic smile.

"Don't worry, I've got something for those under-eye bags. You don't think I wake up camera-ready, do you?"

They both laughed, but Bella's expression soon turned serious. "Is it... being back in Africa? Memories of Jake?"

Kate hesitated. *I can't tell her the truth. It's too dangerous. And she's right about Jake. I miss him every day—even more in this place.*

She nodded slowly. "It is harder than I expected," Kate admitted. "We spent several months here. After nearly two years of surgery and rehab, this is where we came. We were both lost in our own way—survivors trying to figure out who we were and what came next. And we found it here."

"But that's a story for a night under the stars—with a bottle, or two, of a nice red wine."

"Is that a promise?" Bella asked, smiling.

"I promise," Kate said. "Now, before we head for the airport, let's see if you can work your magic on my puffy eyes."

Chapter 44

GATEWAY TOWERS PLAZA, MOTAPA

Grant parked near the fenced perimeter of Gateway Towers Plaza. Once a beacon of Motapa's future, the unfinished twin towers—Prosperity and Unity—stood as skeletal monuments to corruption. Their scarred exteriors cast jagged shadows across the plaza.

Grant retrieved his backpack and gloves, securing both for the task ahead. The pack held the climbing gear this mission required, and the gloves would protect his hands from the rope work and leave no trace. He walked along the perimeter fence, following instructions he'd committed to memory. The intense midday heat radiated off the cracked pavement, the air shimmering with the oppressive warmth. Beads of sweat ran down his back.

The plaza stood deserted and silent, except for the occasional rustle of wind through the neglected vegetation that had reclaimed the area. *Follow the fenced perimeter until you reach the brick wall,* he recalled, standing in front of the wall. *Find the arrowhead symbol. Remove the brick. Retrieve the gate key.*

Grant scanned the graffiti-covered wall. There—a faint arrowhead, nearly lost in the chaos.

"There you are," he murmured, flicking open his knife. A quick wedge, a pop, and the brick slid free. Inside, the key waited.

The rusty old lock on the security gate had Grant wondering if the key would even work, but minutes later, he was standing inside Prosperity Tower.

The ground level of the tower was a wasteland of trash, graffiti, and the remnants of campfires left by teenagers who had once dared to explore these dangerous ruins. Their tragic deaths, following a stairway collapse, led to the construction of the high-security fencing that encircled the plaza. No one had entered since—no one except Grant.

Inside, he was greeted by the stench of decay—rotting wood, stagnant water, and the faint but unmistakable smell of death that lingered. The wind whistled through the empty shell, and pigeons flushed and fluttered when he approached the one stairwell that hadn't completely collapsed, the only route to the upper floors.

The concrete steps groaned under his weight. *Death trap*, Grant mused, smirking at the thought of turning it into his sniper's nest.

At the third floor, the stairwell ended in a gaping chasm. He was ready for this.

He retrieved a length of static climbing rope from his pack. The walls on either side of the gap still had enough exposed steel and concrete to offer solid anchor points. Grant drilled an expansion bolt into his side of the gap, ensuring it was deep and secure. He then threaded the rope through the carabiner, creating a safety line. Searching for footholds and gripping exposed iron, he free-climbed to the other side and set the last anchor.

Satisfied with the anchors on both sides, Grant tested the rope's tension, tugging hard to confirm its stability. He could easily clip his harness to the line and pull himself across the gap, but he preferred to walk the rope like a circus act.

He continued his ascent up the stairs, climbing steadily until he reached the 34th floor. Here, the view was commanding, with a direct line of sight to the Presidential Palace, the very reason this floor was ideal. He walked to the edge. The floor-to-ceiling window framed a sweeping view of the city below. *Conference room? Penthouse?* Didn't matter.

Grant removed his pack, grabbed some tools, and set to work. He leaned out of the open window and chipped away at the exterior face of the concrete window frame. A fall from three hundred fifty feet would last about five seconds, followed by instant death, but he found it exhilarating. He retrieved a solid steel piton, its ridged surface designed to grip the concrete with unyielding force. With precise, measured taps, he drove the piton into the hole he created.

Satisfied with the piton's placement, Grant continued up the stairs, exiting on to the roof. The heliport sitting atop the 35th floor was exposed to the elements, a skeletal frame of steel girders and concrete slabs. The wind whipped through the open space, carrying with it the scents of the city—exhaust fumes, distant cooking fires, and the faint smell of the red clay dust and smoke that seemed to permeate everything, even this high.

Grant pulled the rapid descent equipment from his pack and the 400-foot, 10mm static rope, *That's 30 pounds I won't have to carry back down,* he thought. *Now, let's see how far I need to fall.* With the laser rangefinder, he measured the distance from the edge of the roof to the plaza. Every measurement had to be exact. With his life literally hanging in the balance, there was no margin for error.

He measured and calculated multiple times. His target was three feet off the deck. With a perfect landing, he could stand, release the harness, and disappear. If his numbers were short and his descent stopped well above the plaza, he'd have to cut the rope and jump.

The longer the drop, the greater the risk of injury—he thought, then smiled. *Still, better than hitting the deck and exploding like a bloody water balloon.*

With the rooftop equipment dialed in, he manually lowered the harness end of the rope to the 34th floor and headed back downstairs. Standing precariously on the window ledge again, he reached out, farther and farther, struggling to grab the end of the rope swaying in the wind. With the rope finally in hand, he fed it through the piton and locked it with a carabiner.

The rope now hung vertically, reaching up to the rooftop where most of its length remained coiled in a feed bag, ready to deploy when needed. The stage was set. Once the President was dead, all he had to do was reach out, clip the rope, and step into the void. Seconds later, he'd be gone.

This escape wasn't just practiced. It was signature.

Grant took a moment, surveying his work—the precision, the planning. *In my way, I'm an artist.*

Grant's paintbrush for this mission was the German handmade Blaser R8 Ultimate. In Paris, Aram Sarkesian seemed to appreciate Grant's taste in firearms, or perhaps he just appreciated the exorbitant price, but Sarkesian never failed. Whatever Grant needed, Sarkesian could acquire and configure to his exact specifications. All cash. No questions asked.

The Blaser, known for its extreme accuracy, was also a unique combination of component parts, carbon fiber open thumb stock, barrel, trigger housing, and magazine group—all fit easily in the backpack. Reassembly took less than a minute. Grant locked down the optics, slid on the bipod, and, with a quick function test, the rifle was ready.

Rummaging around the 34th floor and examining the collection of construction debris, he pulled together a solid, level shooting platform. Grant staged the platform far enough from the building's edge to ensure no random scan of the tower's exterior would see either him or the weapon. The elevated platform gave him a wide field of fire.

With the platform set, he ran some range calcs and peered through the rifle's NightForce optics. The arrival area of the palace was buzzing. A caravan of vehicles swept past the front gate security, heading up the long drive. *Must be Marquez,* he thought. *Timing would be about right and the perfect opportunity to range and practice.*

The lead car cleared the entrance and stopped. Sebastian Vargas stepped out, moving swiftly toward the limousine as it rolled to a halt. He opened the door, offering a hand.

Yep. Marquez.

Grant smirked, crosshairs steady on Vargas's head. *Bang. You're dead.*

Then, movement—passenger door. Another woman stepped out—no doorman or security. *Assistant, most likely.*

Grant watched, curious. He could only see her from the back—slender, sharp-dressed, shoulder-length brown hair. Enough to make him smile.

He kept his sights on her, muttering, "Come on, love. Give us a look."

And then she did.

CHAPTER 45

THE SAWMILL TRAINING COMPLEX, LAURENS, SC

THE HELICOPTER SHATTERED THE morning stillness. Crisp air, scented with pine and fresh coffee, was drowned beneath the rhythmic thump of rotors.

Forest stood with his team, the rotor wash whipping at their clothes. Mike, Deon, Jordan, and Logan shifted restlessly—coiled and ready. Their casual civilian clothes and nondescript duffel bags were a stark contrast to the firepower they were used to carrying.

As the helicopter touched down, kicking up a swirl of dust and grass clippings, Forest felt the insistent buzz of his phone in his back pocket. He pulled it out, frowning at the hidden caller ID, and declined the call. The buzz came again, more urgent this time. Forest ended the call once more, irritation creasing his brow.

When the phone rang for a third time, Forest yanked it from his pocket, his voice sharp as he answered. "This better be good—"

"Forest, this is Margot Ryder, Deputy Director—"

"I know who you are," Forest interrupted, the chopper's rhythmic thump-thump-thump nearly drowning out his words. "And this isn't a good time."

"Make time," she ordered.

Forest signaled the team to hold and jogged to the training classroom. The door clicked shut, muting the chopper's roar.

"You've got five minutes," he said, voice edged with impatience. "Go."

"Katherine Preacher."

"I'm listening."

"She's with Isabella Marquez."

"I know."

"They landed at Maboko International about an hour ago," Ryder said. "I assume you know why."

"Duncan Harris," Forest answered.

"I pulled your file," Ryder began, "and it shows that you and Jake were on the mission where Harris was killed, or so we thought."

"He saved our butts that day," Forest said. "We believed he gave his life doing it. Now I know he's alive, and Kate knows he's the psychopath that shot Jake."

"What you don't know is that I believe he's in Motapa to kill President Bongani."

"That sounds like your problem," Forest said. "You've got your priorities. I've got mine."

"It would be my problem if the current administration didn't have its head up its ass," Margot snapped. "Over my strenuous objections, our Africa priorities are screwed, and the power vacuum is literally handing these countries to our adversaries and their mercenary and warlord proxies."

"Got it," Forest said. "Still not my problem. Kate needs our help, whether she knows it or not, so if there's nothing else?"

"That's just it. We can help each other."

"You've got two minutes," Forest said. "Let's hear it."

"There's a C-17 waiting at Shaw," Ryder said. "You're heading to Charlotte—hoping for a commercial flight to Nairobi, aren't you?"

"Affirmative."

"Which means you're traveling light. No weapons, no gear." She gave that a minute to register. "I can get you into Motapa in half the time—with everything you need."

Forest smirked. "Let me guess. It's unsanctioned."

"Could be my last," Ryder said. "The plane we're holding is a humanitarian flight, and you'll be jumping. Whatever happens, once you leave that aircraft, you're on your own."

"What's in it for you?"

"My reasons are my own," Ryder began. "They're many and complicated. All you need to know is I'm willing to bet my career, possibly jail time. So, let me ask you. What are you willing to do for Kate and the man who killed Jake Church?"

Forest's grip tightened on the phone. Outside, his team waited, reading his expression. *A deal with the devil. And there's always a price.*

Kate was already in Motapa—alone, hunting a predator. Duncan Harris. He pictured Afghanistan, the mission going sideways, the moment they called off the search. And Jake—bleeding out on a Paris sidewalk while Duncan watched.

"We'll need clearance to land," Forest began. "Alert the tower at Shaw…"

"I already have," Ryder interrupted.

"I'm not done," Forest continued. "I'll send you a list. The base will have everything we need or a reasonable substitute. Make sure it's all loaded, and they know it's an air-drop."

Forest ended the call and stepped outside. The weight of the decision settled on his shoulders.

Right or wrong, it's my call. Kate put me in charge. And this is what Jake would do.

The team gathered around, sensing something had changed and trying to read Forest's expression.

"Change of plans, boys," he announced, his voice carrying over the idling helicopter. "Go suit up. We got a ride, and we're going in hot."

***

CHARLES DE GAULLE AIRPORT, PARIS, FRANCE

Talya's call came as Forest and the team geared up in the armory.

"Perfect timing," Forest said. "Your ears must have—"

"No time," Talya cut in. "Kate's in Motapa."

Forest exhaled. "We know."

"Damn," she muttered. "I just locked it down."

"Long story," Forest said.

"I'm running for my flight now," Talya continued. "Didn't want to commit until I was sure. I'll reach Motapa in twelve hours."

"And your contacts?"

"They'll be ready."

"We'll be dropping in—outside of town," Forest said. "When you're set, send coordinates."

"Dropping in," Talya repeated. "Copy that."

Chapter 46

SUNDAY, MAY 3rd
3:47 PM CAT

PRESIDENTIAL PALACE, MOTAPA, CENTRAL AFRICA

As Isabella Marquez stepped from the limousine, a striking woman approached. Tall and poised, her dark skin caught the late afternoon light, exuding both regal authority and warm hospitality.

The woman's attire blended modern professionalism with traditional African elements. A tailored, deep purple blazer over a crisp white blouse, paired with a pencil skirt in a vibrant pattern of geometric shapes in shades of gold and green. The fabric, unmistakably African, added a touch of cultural heritage to her otherwise businesslike ensemble.

Her most striking feature, however, was her hair. Intricately braided and swept up into an elaborate updo, adorned with colorful beads and small golden ornaments that caught the light as she moved. The style was reminiscent of traditional Central African hair art, a nod to Motapa's cultural heritage.

"Welcome to the Presidential Palace, Ms. Marquez," she said, her voice rich and melodious. "I'm Amara, the Palace Ambassador for President Bongani. We're honored to have you here."

"The honor is mine, Amara. Thank you for such a warm welcome." Isabella turned slightly, gesturing to Kate, who stood a step behind her. "I'd like you to meet Katherine Preacher, a dear friend who I roped into joining me on this trip."

Amara's gaze shifted to Kate, her smile never wavering. "It's a pleasure to meet you, Mrs. Preacher. Welcome to Motapa."

Kate stepped forward, extending her hand. "Please, call me Kate," she said, returning Amara's smile. "Thank you for welcoming us to the palace and inviting us into your home."

Amara's eyes twinkled. "Kate, it is. And I see there's no point in subterfuge."

"None," Kate said. "You have your mother's beauty and your father's presence. It's clear strength runs in the family."

They followed Amara toward the imposing entrance. The palace's facade, crafted from locally quarried sandstone, glowed a warm gold in the late afternoon sun. Intricate carvings adorned the columns and archways, depicting scenes from Motapan folklore and wildlife.

Along the marble pathway, lush gardens burst with vibrant bougainvillea and bird of paradise flowers. Fountain waters and pools glistened in the sunlight, painting the walls with glittering reflections. They passed through the main entrance, two massive bronze doors etched with geometric patterns and tribal designs.

A wide marble staircase on the left led to the palace's residential wing. As Kate and Bella ascended, they were met by two rows of guards standing at attention in crisp, white uniforms. Their rigid posture reflected military precision, while the uniforms, though inspired by colonial military dress, featured elements of traditional Motapan warrior attire, including brilliantly colored sashes and ornate headgear.

Stepping through another pair of bronze doors, they entered a vast atrium that took their breath away. The ceiling soared several stories high, crowned by a massive stained-glass dome that bathed the space in a kaleidoscope of colors. The floor, a masterpiece of inlaid marble, depicted a stylized map of Motapa, showcasing its diverse regions from the Kangwa Delta to the Drakari Mountains.

As they explored the palace, the decor gradually shifted from colonial opulence and African artistry to more intimate, traditionally styled spaces. Retaining much of its original historical character, the residential wing featured corridors lined with intricately woven tapestries and adorned with masks and sculptures from various Motapan tribes. The air was rich with the scent of sandalwood and jasmine, adding to the sense of timelessness.

"And here we are," Amara said, leading Bella and Kate into a space that was the epitome of luxury. "Kate, your room is right next door and nearly identical. We call them the twins—both reserved for the king's favored wives. Legend has it the design was meant to minimize in-fighting. I trust you two won't be battling over which room is better."

The three women wandered into the spacious room, which opened onto a private courtyard where fountains burbled amidst lush tropical plants. The furnishings were an eclectic mix of antique pieces from the colonial era and handcrafted items by local artisans, creating a unique blend of comfort and cultural significance.

"I don't know," Bella said, winking at Kate. "Can I see the other room?"

***

4:02 PM CAT

GRANT COLLINS BROKE DOWN the Blaser rifle, methodically securing each component. *What the hell is Preacher doing here?*

His pulse remained steady, but the sight of her at the palace rattled him.

Twice, she was supposed to die.

Richmond—aborted.

Paris—survived the blast.

And now she's in Motapa? This isn't a coincidence.

Grant exhaled slowly, his mind shifting. *Is Shepard playing me? Or is someone else pulling the strings—is someone keeping Preacher alive?*

He remained focused and calm during the descent. The building was too close to collapsing to do anything less and risk a stupid, meaningless death. But once he was safely away from the building, he called Shepard, eager to assess his reaction to the news.

The minute Shepard answered the call, Grant began probing.

"I'm all set," Grant began. "Perfect line of sight. Piece of cake."

"Glad to hear it," Shepard replied. "Any surprises?"

"You'll never guess who I saw at the palace."

"I know Mueller is there," Shepard began. "And his daughter."

"Nope. Preacher's here."

"Are you sure?"

"I could've taken her head off," Grant snapped.

"You sound spooked."

"I don't get spooked. And I don't believe in coincidences."

"I'm telling you, she believes the man who killed her husband is dead."

"Then why is she here? Why now?"

"Isabella Marquez."

"What does that mean?"

"They were staying in the same hotel, and they have a history," Shepard began. "And with no reason to stay in Paris, I'll bet Preacher jumped at the chance to hop on a private jet. Enjoy a little celebrity travel with luxurious accommodations in a Palace—who wouldn't?"

"You're guessing," Grant said. "And you're not the one she's after—not yet."

"Is that a threat?"

"Think about it," Grant said. "If she's here for me, you're next."

"How do you figure?"

"Simple. You got out played."

"Don't forget. She was almost killed."

"Almost being the operative word," Grant said. "Get me clearance."

"To do what—exactly?"

"You know what," Grant said. "It doesn't matter how. Preacher needs to die."

"I'll talk to Mueller, but under no circumstances are you to act," Shepard said, his voice stern. "Is that clear?"

There was silence for a moment, and Shepard repeated himself. "Grant. *Is that clear?*"

"Yes."

"Say it," Shepard added.

"I will not act without clearance," Grant said, parroting Shepard's order. In the back of his mind, one thought emerged. *It's better to ask forgiveness than permission.*

***

6:00 PM CAT

THE RECEPTION FOR ISABELLA Marquez began with champagne in the gardens, and just early enough to catch the sun setting behind the Drakari mountains. Bright orange clouds stretched to the horizon like wisps of smoke from a dragon's lair.

Amara retrieved Isabella and Kate from the residence wing and escorted them personally to the reception.

"Kind of you to collect us," Kate said. "But I'm sure we could have found our way."

"I seriously doubt that," Amara said and laughed. "It's a labyrinth of centuries of construction. I've lived here for almost six months and still get lost."

When the three women reached the reception area, Amara gracefully stepped aside, and Kate followed Amara's lead. Isabella Marquez, celebrated actress, entrepreneur and philanthropist, was the guest of honor, and this was her arrival. Guests already milling about, champagne in hand, turned almost in unison as the conversation faded, followed by applause and admiration.

Isabella Marquez made a stunning entrance in a custom Atelier Versace gown that commanded attention, and she accepted a glass of champagne, looking like she'd won an Oscar. The deep crimson silk clung to her curves before flowing gracefully to the floor. Its plunging V-neckline and open back design, held together by delicate gold chains, struck a perfect balance between daring and elegant.

A thigh-high slit revealed glimpses of her toned leg and gold stilettos, and the gown's intricate gold embroidery caught the light with every movement. With her hair sleek and straight and makeup that simply enhanced her natural beauty, Isabella was every bit the Hollywood star they all imagined.

Bella turned, reaching for Kate, and found her admiring from a distance. Looking a bit embarrassed by the charade, she waved Kate over.

"This is why, after three failed marriages, I'm content to be single," Bella whispered.

"I don't understand."

"Men imagine that what they see, looking at me now, is who I am," Bella said. "They don't see *me*. Now, let's get you a drink."

Both armed with champagne, they were about to enter the fray, and Amara stood ready to make introductions.

"Before we jump in," Kate began. "I just want to thank you for this," and she waved her hands over the look that Bella assembled for her. The rich emerald green dress captured the intensity in Kate's hazel eyes, while the silk crepe draped beautifully skimming her figure without clinging. The delicate halter style neck drew attention to Kate's shoulders and arms while the back's tasteful V-shape was elegant.

"It's simply beautiful," Kate said, pecking Bella on the cheek.

"No, you're beautiful," Bella said. "The dress just lets you see what everyone else already knows."

***

With the conclusion of the champagne reception, and obligatory celebrity photo-ops, a much smaller gathering adjourned to the dining room. President Bongani stood at the head of the table, smiling as the dinner guests examined name cards. Ladies took their assigned seats, and the gentleman stood behind their chairs.

Amara took the seat to the left of her father, with Isabella on his right. Klaus Mueller stood with Isabella on his left. Kate took the seat to his right, glancing over at Bella with a quizzical look. Bella smiled and shrugged her shoulders.

Kate knew Mueller only by reputation and innuendo, but as the GEC featured prominently in Jake's notes, she was concerned. Of those invited to dine with President Bongani, many were leading political and business leaders, even global icons. *I'm no one,* Kate thought. *Just Bella's friend and travel companion. So why such a prominent position?*

Turning her attention to the woman sitting on her right, Kate smiled. Noting they were about the same age, but given the woman's style and presence, Kate pegged her as a fashion model. *She's probably someone famous,* she thought. *And must be wondering what I'm doing here. Or who she pissed off to get this seat.* The woman's deep red velvet tuxedo exuded power and elegance. The wide lapel jacket made a bold statement, framing a sheer bodysuit that stopped just short of revealing. Her ash blonde hair was slicked back, highlighting bright green eyes with a captivating intensity.

When President Bongani took his seat, the men followed, and the table erupted in conversation and introductions.

Kate's seat mate leaned in, her eyes sparkling with enthusiasm. "I hope you don't mind," she said in a low, conspiratorial voice. "The place cards may have *accidentally* moved. Terribly rude, I know, but these events can be dreadfully boring. When I heard you were coming, I simply couldn't resist the chance to pick your brain."

Kate raised an eyebrow. *She wanted to sit here,* Kate thought. *And pick my brain? Clearly not about fashion.*

"I'm the Chief Security Officer for the GEC," Riley continued, barely pausing for breath. "I've followed your work for years. Your paper on blockchain forensics and cryptocurrency tracing was absolutely brilliant. The way you reverse-engineered those mixer protocols? Game-changing."

She paused, taking a sip of water before plunging on. "And don't even get me started on your research into deep fake detection algorithms. I've implemented some of your methods in our own systems."

Her eyes lit up even more. "Oh, and your BlackHat presentation two years ago? On weaponizing machine learning for network intrusion? I was there, front row. The way you demonstrated real-time adaptive defense against evolving attack patterns was mind-blowing. I must have referenced your work a dozen times in our latest security overhaul."

She finally seemed to catch herself, a slight blush coloring her cheeks. "I'm sorry, I'm rambling. It's just... it's not often I get to talk shop with someone who really gets it, you know? Especially not at stuffy dinners like this."

Kate smiled, extending a hand. "Hi, I'm Kate. Kate Preacher. And you are?"

"I am such an idiot," she replied, and they both laughed. "Hi, I'm Riley Mueller. It's *Rileyne* actually. German family name, and please, don't ask me to explain it—my name is as confusing to me as everyone else. So, everyone calls me Riley, and in IT, sometimes being mistaken for a man comes in handy. Sorry. I chatter when I'm nervous."

Kate glanced at the place cards and realized Rileyne's was face down. *Was she hiding her first name,* Kate wondered. *Or her last?*

"Riley it is," Kate said. "It's a pleasure to meet you."

Riley glanced around the ornate dining room, then back at Kate, her expression a mix of hope and slight embarrassment. "You really don't mind, do you? Sitting next to me, I mean. I promise I won't spend the entire night discussing your work. Well, I'll try not to, anyway."

"It's fine. Really," Kate began. "Honestly, I'm way out of my comfort zone, at a presidential dinner, in a palace ballroom, wearing an ensemble that Isabella Marquez assembled for me."

"I would never have guessed. You look so poised and comfortable."

"It's an act. I can't wait to slip into something comfortable," Kate said. "What brings you to Motapa? Will the GEC be helping to develop the country's infrastructure?"

"I'd love to help," Riley said. "It's a beautiful country. Lovely people. And so much potential."

"But there's a problem?"

"You're very intuitive," Riley said. "My father was here to present and discuss a comprehensive proposal with President Bongani."

"I take it that didn't go as planned?"

"No, it didn't," Riley said. "I think it's a little too much, too soon, so we'll be heading back to Paris. But I like to think the door's open, and if he changes his mind, or finds that he needs the GEC's help, we'll be back. What about you? What brings you to Motapa?"

"An invitation I couldn't refuse," Kate said, smiling and glancing at Isabella.

"I suspect she can be quite persuasive."

"She is," Kate admitted. "And the timing was perfect. We crossed paths in Paris, bonded over a bottle of Burgundy, and I believe Motapa has exactly what I need."

"And what's that?"

"Closure."

"I'll drink to that," Riley said, and the two women clinked wine glasses.

***

THE GRAND DINING ROOM, with its high ceilings and elegantly carved wooden paneling, was a picture of timeless sophistication. A majestic crystal chandelier hung from the center of the room, casting a warm, golden glow across the long, polished mahogany table. The light refracted through the chandelier's delicate prisms, and subtle rainbows danced across the walls adorned with rich tapestries depicting scenes of Motapan history and culture. Floor-to-ceiling windows offered glimpses of the illuminated palace gardens, a manicured oasis against the wild African night beyond. The setting served as a fitting metaphor for Motapa itself—poised between natural beauty and development aspirations.

As the evening was drawing to a close, and the dessert dishes cleared, Klaus leaned toward Isabella, his expression relaxed and effortless. "My dear, I'm very much looking forward to your speech at our winter conference," he said, his voice smooth and cultured. "It promises to be quite an event, especially if we can convince President Bongani to join us." He turned to Bongani with a respectful nod. "I do hope you'll consider the invitation."

Isabella smiled graciously, her eyes shifting to the President. "Davos in the winter is truly magical," she added, her tone light and conversational. "Snow-covered mountains, crisp air, stunning views and the tranquility... it's a perfect escape from the world's chaos."

"Indeed," Klaus agreed, seizing the opportunity and directing his comments to President Bongani. "It is beautiful, Mr. President, and an unparalleled opportunity to meet with the men and women who can help Motapa reach its full potential."

Bongani's expression remained carefully neutral. "A tempting prospect, to be sure."

Whether it was the late hour or the wine, Isabella felt compelled to caution President Bongani. "Of course, all progress comes at a price," Isabella added, her tone light but her words loaded. "And not all progress is... good."

Klaus's eyebrows rose slightly. "Surely you're not suggesting that the GEC's projects have been anything but beneficial to the countries we've assisted?"

"It's true, the GEC has done extraordinary things, and changed lives," Isabella backpedaled smoothly. "But there have been—consequences."

President Bongani leaned forward, his interest piqued. "Mr. Mueller and I discussed that very point recently."

Isabella's eyes sparkled with a hint of challenge. "Well, I look forward to sharing some of my analysis at Davos. With transparency and reflection, we can ensure our actions solve more problems than they create."

"Yes, of course," Klaus agreed, his tone calm and measured, but his eyes narrowed and brow tense.

An uncomfortable silence fell over the table. Isabella glanced at her watch, then gracefully pushed back her chair. "I'm afraid I must excuse myself," she said, her trademark smile firmly in place. "Beauty rest, you know. And we have an early departure tomorrow."

Kate, sensing the shift in atmosphere, quickly followed. "I'll join you," she said, pushing back her chair. "I don't know about beauty rest, but a five AM wake-up call means I need to get to sleep."

President Bongani, ever the gentleman, rose as well, prompting Klaus and the other men at the table to follow suit.

Isabella turned to their host. "Mr. President, thank you for a lovely evening. I'm afraid we won't see you in the morning, given our early departure, but we look forward to seeing you and Amara on our return."

President Bongani nodded, his warm smile not quite reaching his eyes. "Safe travels, Ms. Marquez, Mrs. Preacher. We shall eagerly await your return."

As Isabella and Kate made their way from the dining room, the weight of unspoken words hung heavy in the air. When President Bongani and the men took their seats, the hum of conversation returned.

Riley slid into Kate's seat, placing a hand on her father's forearm. "Remember your blood pressure," she said. "I've got this."

"Did you learn anything?" he asked.

"Yes," she said. "You were right, but the timing's perfect."

Chapter 47

MONDAY, MAY 4th
5:00 AM CAT

HOTEL INTERCONTINENTAL, MABOKO, MOTAPA

John Reed strode through the lobby of the Hotel Intercontinental, his presence impossible to ignore. At six-one, lean muscle beneath civilian clothes, he moved with quiet authority—handsome, poised, a younger Denzel Washington with a soldier's edge.

Reed exuded the confidence of a man comfortable in his own skin, who's mastered both the art of war and the subtleties of survival in a world that's constantly testing him. Dressed in muted tones matching the pre-dawn gloom, he hoped the early hour meant few eyes in the lobby.

Parked beneath a flickering streetlamp, an old Land Cruiser waited, looking like it might not make it out of the parking lot, much less into the Drakari mountains. The faded paint and battle scars, a testament to years of hard use, cast doubt on the vehicle's capabilities, but Reed knew better than to judge this book by its cover. These machines were built to endure, much like the man leaning against its hood.

The driver straightened as Reed approached, revealing a wiry frame etched with the lines and scars of a hard-lived life. His skin was the deep, rich brown of the Motapan plains, weathered by sun and time. A few silver strands threaded through his close-cropped hair, and his dark eyes held a sharp, assessing glint.

The driver's lips curled into a near-toothless smile. "I am Kabe (Kah-bay)," he said, offering a calloused hand. "It is an honor to meet the legendary Ronin."

Reed clasped the hand, pulled him in close. "Say that name again, and you won't need a ride back." He let go and stepped back. "The name's Reed. John Reed."

"Yes, Mr. Reed," Kabe said, and his eyes flicked briefly to the duffel bag. "All is ready—as requested. Long drive ahead."

Reed moved to the back of the Cruiser and gripped the handle, giving it a firm yank. The latch resisted—decades of dust and rust doing their work—but with a practiced twist, it popped free. The door groaned open on tired hinges. Inside, supplies were packed with military precision—jerry cans of fuel, water containers, camping gear, tools strapped down tight for the punishing terrain ahead. He tossed his duffel into an open space, secured it, then slammed the door shut.

Climbing into the passenger seat, Reed took stock of the interior—sparse and utilitarian, much like its driver. Kabe settled behind the wheel, his movements economical as he turned the ignition. The engine roared to life with a throaty growl, settling into a steady rumble that vibrated through the chassis.

"You clear on the plan?" Reed asked, his gaze fixed ahead as the vehicle pulled away from the curb and onto the empty streets.

Kabe nodded, eyes focused on the road. "We take the old trade route west, cut through the Namangwe Desert, and reach the base of the Drakari Mountains by late afternoon. No patrols, no curious eyes."

"Any chance of being stopped along the way?"

"None," Kabe replied confidently. "These paths are forgotten. No one goes there anymore."

"Good," Reed muttered, settling back into his seat as the city fell away behind them, swallowed by the vast expanse of the African landscape.

The city fell away, swallowed by the Namangwe Desert. Golden dunes stretched to the horizon, the heat turning the air into a mirage of shifting light. The Land Cruiser carved through the dust, its engine's low growl the only sound.

Hours passed in silence. Reed liked that about Kabe—no wasted words, no unnecessary chatter. But he stayed sharp, eyes scanning the horizon. Isolation didn't mean safety.

By midday, the heat was oppressive, pressing down like a heavy blanket. Kabe guided the vehicle toward a cluster of rocky outcrops that offered a modest reprieve from the sun's intensity.

"Good spot to break," Kabe announced, bringing the vehicle to a halt in the shadow of a towering boulder.

Reed surveyed the area, noting the unobstructed views in all directions.

Satisfied, he climbed out. Kabe joined him, retrieving a thermos and a small parcel from the back before settling on a flat rock.

"Coffee?" Kabe offered, unscrewing the lid and pouring the dark liquid into two tin cups.

"Thanks." Reed accepted the cup, the rich aroma cutting through the desert air. He took a sip, feeling the bitter warmth spread through him, sharpening his senses. Kabe unwrapped some biltong and nuts, placing them on the hood as a makeshift meal.

After a few moments, Reed set down his cup and moved to the back of the Cruiser, opening the door and reaching for his duffel. The isolation and open expanse made it the perfect spot for a weapons check.

Time to get to work, Reed thought, his eyes scanning for a likely target.

He unzipped the bag, revealing the carefully packed components of his rifle—the Accuracy International AXMC. The desert tan finish of the pieces absorbed the sunlight, exuding a quiet lethality. Reed's hands moved deftly, assembling the weapon with professional ease.

First, he unfolded the stock, locking it securely into place. Holding the stock vertically, he took the 27-inch .338 Lapua Magnum barrel, aligning it with the receiver and twisting it until it settled. He pulled the Allen key from the stock, tightening the cross bolt to ensure absolute stability. Next came the SOCOM titanium suppressor, which he staged and twisted until it locked in place. He fanned out the bipod legs and grabbed a five-round magazine.

Reed took a knee, settling the rifle on a boulder.

"Hand me the Kestrel."

Kabe ignored the request, reading the data himself. "Wind, two knots east. Hold one click left."

Reed smirked. Not just a driver, then. Maybe a sniper once. Through the scope, he found a dead tree, its skeletal branches reaching skyward.

"Eight hundred thirty meters," Reed murmured.

Kabe's voice stayed level. "Target acquired."

Reed exhaled, heartbeat steady. The trigger broke clean. The suppressor reducing the roar to a sharp, controlled crack.

Through the scope, Reed watched the center of the tree explode—a burst of splinters against the empty sky.

"Hit," Kabe confirmed.

Reed cycled the bolt smoothly, reacquiring his target in an instant. The second shot severed the tree's right branch, sending it tumbling to the ground. A third shot took care of the left, leaving the once-majestic relic reduced to a shattered stump.

Lowering the rifle, Reed allowed himself a brief nod of satisfaction. He cleared the chamber, folded the stock, and began packing the components back into the duffel.

Kabe met his gaze, a hint of respect visible in the old man's eyes. "Nice shooting."

"Good spotting," Reed replied. While the weapon cooled, he finished his coffee then secured his gear. They climbed back into the vehicle and resumed their journey.

The desert gradually gave way to the rugged foothills of the Drakari Mountains, the flat sands replaced by jagged rocks and steep inclines. The Cruiser strained against the unforgiving terrain, its engine growling as Kabe expertly navigated around boulders and deep ruts, inching their way higher into the mountains.

As the afternoon waned, shadows lengthened across the landscape, painting the crags and ravines in deep hues of amber and crimson. The temperature dropped, and the oppressive heat gave way to a biting chill that crept in with the encroaching night.

"Not much farther," Kabe noted, his eyes focused intently on the narrow path ahead.

Reed scanned the surroundings, recognizing landmarks from the aerial reconnaissance photos. Their destination was an outcropping that overlooked the old Russian fortress nestled deep within the mountains—a perfect vantage point for the mission.

The Cruiser eventually came to a halt where the path became too treacherous to continue by vehicle. Beyond lay a maze of rocks and sheer drops that would have to be traversed on foot. Both men exited the vehicle, the icy stillness of the mountains enveloping them.

Kabe pulled out two headlamps, the red light lenses preserving their night vision and minimizing detection. The sky above was awash with stars, the Milky Way stretching like a luminous river across the velvet blackness.

They moved efficiently, unloading only the essentials from the Cruiser—bedrolls, minimal provisions, and the duffel containing Reed's rifle. Fire was out of the question—their presence had to remain undetected. Dinner was a sparse affair. More dried meat, a handful of nuts, dried fruit, and sips of water. Neither spoke. Each of them comfortable with solitude and silence.

As Reed settled against a smooth rock, gazing up at the stars, his mind drifted to the mission at hand. He closed his eyes, conjuring up the target package and the image of Major Viktor Mirov.

Reed could see Mirov clearly—tall, hard-edged, eyes like cold steel. A man built for war, carved by it. At forty-two, he was a seasoned Russian officer, his success earning him a transition from regular military service to a leadership role in the Wagner Group—now the Africa Corps. Like all mercenaries, Mirov gave Russia plausible deniability, but none of them made a move without Putin's blessing.

From his service record, it was clear Mirov was a man who thrived in chaos. He was a veteran of Russia's shadow wars, from Syria to Ukraine, with a reputation for ruthless efficiency. Rarely seen without a cigarette, Reed could almost smell the metallic scent of smoke he imagined clung to Mirov like a second skin.

Now, as the overseer of the Drakari coltan mines, he and his employers profited at the expense of enslaved workers, many of them children. Reed knew Mirov's type—cold, calculating, and loyal only to money and power. That made Motapa's mines the perfect fit. Coltan was critical in everything from EV batteries to cell phones and laptops, and Mirov kept it flowing. By Reed's estimates, the Africa Corps was stealing millions of dollars of the raw material every month.

The question was why someone wanted Mirov dead, but that wasn't Reed's concern. Ronin's BountyHunter targets never included motives, and that was fine by him. Still, it was amusing to speculate. Perhaps Mirov simply outlived his usefulness to the puppet-masters who pulled the strings. Or he'd gotten greedy and was skimming profits.

He wouldn't be the first to set up his own retirement plan. *Guess that makes me his severance package.*

Reed smirked at the thought of facilitating Mirov's exit from the gene pool. The dossier had been too explicit. The images burned into his mind—he tried not to recall them. He'd seen war in its ugliest forms and done things most men couldn't fathom. But Mirov's penchant for brutalizing young boys made this target different. Justice was a rare commodity in his line of work. But every so often, fate played a hand.

A soft rustle brought Reed back to the present. Kabe was settling into his own bedroll a few feet away, his movements quiet and efficient.

"Weather will hold till morning," Kabe murmured, his voice low.

"Good," Reed replied, acknowledging that their minimal camp would suffice. He adjusted his position, pulling the hood up on his jacket, and settled in for the night.

The wind whispered through the rocks. The stars watched in silence.

Reed lay still, eyes closed, already seeing Mirov's face.

Chapter 48

MONDAY, MAY 4th
6:00 AM CAT

PRESIDENTIAL PALACE, MABOKO, MOTAPA

The first light of dawn had just crept over the horizon, casting a soft pink glow on the ornate façade of the palace. The air was cool and crisp, a welcome relief from the heat that would soon follow. Kate stood in the grand entrance hall, shaking off sleep, bracing for the overnight trek to a village dear to Isabella's heart.

The heavy doors swung open, sunlight striking the gleaming two-tone Land Cruisers parked outside. Kate blinked. The logo, emblazoned on the side, was a silhouette of Maasai warriors walking spears in hand. The sight of the vehicle was electric.

"Royal African?" Kate muttered, stunned.

Isabella smirked. "You know them?"

"They're the best," Kate said simply.

Isabella looked intrigued. "You've traveled with them?"

Kate's mind drifted. "Jake and I honeymooned on safari with Adam and Shane Hedges. That trip changed everything. We stayed in Africa for six months—Jake training an anti-poaching unit, and dreaming up Trident Security. When we finally went home, he made it happen."

As if summoned by the memory, Shane Hedges stepped out of the first vehicle—tall, wiry, his Rogue leather hat casting a shadow over his tanned face. Khaki shorts, a field-worn shirt, and scuffed boots marking his years in the bush. His smile as broad and warm as the day Kate and Jake left Botswana.

Emotion hit like a punch—sudden, visceral. The last time she saw Shane, Jake had been at her side. Fighting the sting behind her eyes, she closed the distance and pulled him into a tight hug, gripping him like an anchor to the past.

He smelled of dust and leather, just as she remembered.

Shane chuckled, hugging her back, understanding the depth of what wasn't said. "Kate," he said, his voice low and full of warmth. "It's been too long."

"Way too long," Kate whispered, her voice thick with emotion.

As they stepped back, another figure emerged from the second vehicle. Adam Hedges, Shane's father, beamed as he saw Kate. His weathered skin and the deep lines fanning out from his eyes spoke of decades spent under the African sun. To Kate, it appeared Adam hadn't aged a day. Shane had grown and matured, hair a little thinner, but not Adam. *Perhaps that's the secret of life in the bush,* she mused. Adam, steady as a rock, frozen in time, while his son was growing up before her eyes.

Both Adam and Shane offered their condolences, their words filled with genuine care. But Kate shook her head, her smile reassuring. "Jake loved you guys, and that's all we need to say. Today, and tonight, it's all about adventure and wildlife, good food and amusing stories."

Kate turned back to where Isabella stood, watching the scene unfold with quiet interest. "Bella," Kate called, gesturing her over. "I want to introduce you to Adam and Shane Hedges—our guides today. Whatever they have in store for us, I promise it will be unforgettable."

Isabella smiled warmly as she approached, extending her hand first to Adam and then to Shane. "It's a pleasure to meet you both. I've heard wonderful things."

"The pleasure is ours," Adam replied, his voice steady and respectful. "We've got quite the day planned—one I hope exceeds your expectations."

Shane grinned, adding, "And a clear moonless night under the stars—I promise, it will be spectacular."

"I can't wait," Isabella said, her face beaming.

Kate and Bella climbed into the back seat of Shane's vehicle, and Bella's photographer crawled into the very back, where he found room for himself and his equipment. Vargas and Peter, a retired Green Beret, rode with Adam. Peter called shotgun, and Vargas was happy to have the rear seat all to himself. With a client like Isabella, the primary risk was crowd control or obsessed fans, so for Vargas, the journey into the bush meant an opportunity to relax.

The rest of Vargas's team and all of Bella's administrative and support staff remained in the capital. Bella was happy to get some distance from the bees buzzing around her and the demands for her time and attention. This part of the trip was personal and not about hair and makeup or selling product. She brought the photographer because she wanted to capture the experience, but even there, the goal was personal.

Riding up front with Shane was Thabo, a fellow Motswana native and a long-time member of Shane's crew. There were quick introductions around the vehicle. Thabo claimed he remembered Kate, which Kate found hard to believe after five years. But she definitely remembered him. He was a jokester, but a skilled tracker and game spotter, and a second pair of skilled eyes and ears were always welcome.

As they headed out of the city, Isabella leaned in closer to Kate. "You know," she began quietly. "I don't know if it was the wine or the late hour, or both, but I might have stepped in it last night."

"Oh, you definitely did," Kate said, smirking. "Klaus was not happy. After that little hint about your Davos speech, don't be surprised if they push your slot to 2 AM—or cancel it entirely."

Isabella laughed softly, shaking her head. "Yes, that was a mistake," Isabella sighed, nodding. "As they say in Formula One, 'Race Day'. I should never have said anything about my speech or the analysis I've done."

"I can understand why you found it hard to stay silent," Kate said. "Klaus was selling hard to get the GEC embedded in Motapa. To his credit, President Bongani wasn't swayed by Mueller's proposal. Klaus's daughter suggested the deal was dead—at least for now."

"That's encouraging," Bella said. "The GEC has its place, or at least it did. I just want to be sure anyone getting in bed with them is making an informed decision."

"Well, they can try to cut you out," Kate began. "But with your global reach, they can't shut you up."

***

FROM THE CAPITAL CITY, they ventured past small farms with rows of crops, all tended by cart and hand. Kate and Isabella knew that this was one area of the country that would change dramatically with investment. A nation can't grow if it can't feed its people. There were grazing lands as well, with small herds of cattle. At last night's dinner, Kate found the Motapan beef remarkably tender and flavorful.

Meandering toward the Kangwa Delta, the Cruiser forded the small streams feeding the vibrant wetland ecosystem. As they drove deeper, the bird song grew more raucous—wildlife teeming around them, all drawn to the water. The delta was the key to Motapa's rich flora and fauna, and Shane used their arrival to take the first break of the day.

Shane drove slowly around a large tree, and when satisfied it was unoccupied, he parked in the shade.

"No leopards?" Kate asked, half-joking.

"Not yet," Shane replied, his tone far more-matter-of fact than Kate's. "But this would be a perfect spot. Excellent cover. Close to the water."

Everyone exited, stretching. It was about a two-hour drive from the capital to the delta, remarkably close and an entirely different world. The delta, a vibrant wetland ecosystem, reminded Kate of Botswana's Okavango and Zambia's Kafue Flats and the Bangweulu Wetlands. Stretched out before them was a stunning expanse of shallow waters, lush grasses, and dense reeds. The air was thick with the calls of birds and the rustle of unseen creatures moving through the underbrush.

The vehicle parked in the shade on a slope that looked like a manicured lawn. Kate knew why.

"This is a hippo pool," Kate said, directing Bella's attention to the eyes and flicking ears seen floating just above the surface.

They watched through binoculars as hippos sank beneath the surface, resurfacing in slow, rhythmic movements. Tiny backs bobbed close to their mothers, barely breaking the waterline.

"That path, cut into the bank, is the hippo trail," Shane said. "They'll come out and graze and sleep on this bank. That's why the grass is so short."

With a sudden, violent burst of energy, a large male hippo threw his head back and opened his enormous jaws wide, exposing his massive, deadly teeth. The pinkish interior of his mouth stood in stark contrast to the dark water around him, and the sight of those long, curved incisors left no doubt about his ability to defend his pool.

A deep, resonant bellow followed the hippo's impressive display, accompanied by a series of sharp, snorting grunts that echoed across the water. The sound, part warning and part laugh, made it seem as if the hippo was mocking them.

"He's reminding us who's boss," Thabo said with a grin, his voice low and calm.

Shane and Thabo set up a morning snack, asking who might want coffee or tea. Kate and Bella said coffee simultaneously and laughed. There were snacks as well, some hard-boiled eggs, avocado slices. And there's always biltong, the dried, cured meat that's a staple of bush life. And a few sweets, including a box of sugar cookies that the chef at the Palace packed for Isabella.

"Bella, come with me," Kate said, and Bella followed with a cup of coffee and a cookie. "This is good," Kate said and sat down.

Kate slipped off her boots and socks. Hugging her knees and wiggling her toes, Kate closed her eyes and took a few deep breaths.

"What are you doing?" Bella wondered.

"Grounding," Kate said. "Try it. You'll see."

Bella eyed her skeptically. "What exactly am I supposed to see?"

"Just do it."

Bella sighed, hesitating. "I don't know about this…"

"Hey, I kissed a giraffe for you. Now take off your boots—socks too."

When Bella finally relented, Kate continued. "Jake and I were in a remote part of Kenya," Kate began. "Shane called it the fairyland."

Both women now had their eyes open, soaking in the scene before them—the rhythmic splash of the water, the deep bellows of the hippos, and the gentle rustling of reeds in the breeze, all anchored by the solid ground beneath their hands and feet.

"Did you see any fairies?" Bella asked, smiling.

"No fairies, but it was magical," Kate said. "We met Nuru, the local shaman."

"Did Nuru teach you this grounding thing?"

"Yep," Kate said. "And a few other things. Feels pretty good, doesn't it?"

"I have to admit, it really does, especially after last night—between the wine and the small talk, I went to bed exhausted."

Kate slipped her socks and shoes back on. "Nuru would say, now that you've reconnected with Africa, the source of all life, she will call you home again and again."

***

8:10 AM CAT

FORTRESS KRASNAYA SKALA

NURU LOOKED UP AT the fortress on the cliffs above. Leboo, standing by his side, reached out, taking Nuru's hand. The boy's help was essential, and his courage was unquestioned, but Nuru had to remind himself the boy was only ten years old. Brave beyond his years, but the fortress was a terrifying place of pain and death.

He knew Leboo's fear was born of more than pain, but there was no need to speak of it. It broke Nuru's heart to think one so young had suffered so much, but only confirmed his vision and the spirit warrior's mission. *I understand now,* he thought. *I see why you led me to this place at this moment.*

He dropped to one knee. With deliberate, reverent movements, Nuru untied the red belt from his own waist. The belt, a broad strip of rich crimson leather, was adorned with intricate beadwork that told stories of bravery, strength, and spiritual connection. While worn smooth in places from years of service, the blood red color was still vibrant and strong.

Nuru wrapped the belt around Leboo's waist, his movements slow and purposeful. The belt was too long for the boy's slight frame, but Nuru carefully adjusted it, securing it with a traditional knot that held the promise of protection and strength.

With the belt secured, Nuru held out his rungu, a formidable club and symbol of a warrior's status. The handle of the olive wood weapon was long and thin, polished smooth at the hands of Nuru's ancestors, and imbued with the red clay of Africa and the smoke of a thousand fires.

He slipped the club into Leboo's belt, his voice low and steady. "This belt and club are not just symbols but the tools of your mission. You have been seen, and you have been chosen. Carry them with the honor and strength they demand, and they will guide and protect you."

The boy nodded, his small fingers wrapping around the bulbous head of the club. Nuru stood looking down at the boy with a mixture of pride and sadness.

"You've done all that I asked," Nuru began. "Now, my path lies in the fortress above. Yours is to Kibale village. Do you know it?"

"Yes," Leboo replied, pointing south. "A day's walk."

"That is where you must go," Nuru said. "But you must not be seen. Tomorrow, men with guns and trucks will come, just as they came to your village, and those who fight will die."

"If I hurry, I can warn them," Leboo announced. "They must leave tonight."

"No. They cannot. There is nowhere to hide," Nuru explained. "And nowhere to go that the men will not follow. The men must be stopped."

"But how can I..." Leboo began, his voice shaky.

"Do not worry, my brave friend. That is not your path," Nuru replied, his voice kind but firm. "And you must not try."

"Then why send me?"

"I need you to be my voice," Nuru said. "There is one in the village who will save the children, but only when the time is right. If we fail, many will die, and more of the young stolen to take their place."

"Tell me what to do?"

"Remain hidden tonight," Nuru began. "In the morning, reveal yourself only when you see the white faces."

"How will I know the one who can help?"

"The one you seek will find you."

"Then what do I say?"

"Only my name," Nuru said, smiling. "The warrior's spirit will do the rest."

***

During the break, Shane and Thabo rolled back the canvas on the safari vehicle's roof. The Land Cruiser, built to Royal African's precise specs, had three cut-away roof sections, each with a padded bench. With the canvas tucked away, Bella and Kate could stand on the rear seat, taking in the sweeping landscape and the wildlife moving through it.

The photographer was in heaven. He took candid photos of Bella and Kate staring out at the delta or peering through binoculars, and when stopping to game watch, he captured in vivid detail the life and action of one of the few natural ecosystems on the planet.

The call of a fish eagle nearby prompted Shane to stop, and through the binoculars, they watched as the majestic bird threw his head back to broadcast the distinctive, piercing cry that echoed across the water. As he landed on a favorite fishing tree, the photographer's camera erupted, and he caught the bird in flight. Looking nearly identical to the American Bald Eagle but slightly smaller, the fish eagle's cry was unmistakable. Moments later, he was off again in search of his next meal.

Among the reeds, malachite kingfishers flashed like jewels, their brilliant blue and orange plumage catching the light as they darted over the water, hunting for small fish. A pair of yellow-billed storks waded gracefully through the shallow waters, their long legs moving delicately as they probed the mud for food. A herd of Nile lechwe, the males' dark coats glistening like shadows and the females' lighter brown hues glowing warmly in the sunlight, bounded away, looking as if they were walking on water.

The sun continued its relentless ascent. The air grew warmer, and the landscape seemed to shimmer in the heat. Large Nile crocodiles lay motionless on the muddy banks, their scaly bodies absorbing the warmth of the sun. Occasionally, one would stir, sliding silently into the water with barely a ripple, disappearing beneath the surface or visible only as a pair of eyes.

"Anyone up for a swim before lunch?" Shane joked as he drove on.

"I think we'll pass," Bella replied, laughing. "But I am getting hungry."

"Good," Shane replied and, rounding the bend, came up on an unexpected sight.

Adam's vehicle beat them to the lunch spot. Vargas and Peter reclined in camp chairs under a broad tree, cold beer in hand.

"Don't worry," Vargas called out. "We saved you some," he said, pointing at the spread on the buffet table.

A Royal African lorry was off to the side, with a smiling crew standing near. They were clearly proud of the work and the surprise on the girl's faces.

"On a safari, you expect to rough it," Bella said, eyeing the spread. "You don't expect a gourmet buffet—fresh-baked bread, three kinds of salad, roast chicken, sliced beef, deli meats...and that's just the start."

There was a washing station and a camp bathroom set up nearby. A separate table was a fully equipped bar, replete with Kate's favorite, Coke Zero, a variety of other soft drinks, wine, and beer. Kate grabbed the coke, and Bella opted for the ice-cold water. Both dug into the buffet, unaware of just how hungry they were, until they started sampling everything.

"How is this even possible?" Bella asked.

"Experience and logistics," Adam replied. "We adjust based on what's available locally, and sometimes that means flying in items to the closest airfield."

"Adam and I both fly," Shane added. "But fortunately, everything we needed for this trip we could source and pack in the trucks."

"Trucks?" Bella asked, noting the plural.

"You'll see when we reach camp," Adam said, smiling.

"Trust me," Kate interjected. "It's impressive what it takes to pull off a trip like this—guest tents, main dining tent, kitchen, and that's just what's obvious. There are solar panels, fuel, and God knows what else... And they make it all appear and disappear like we were never there."

"How far are we from camp?" Bella wondered.

"A couple of hours," Shane replied. "Depending on what we see and where we stop along the way."

"Did you guys see anything interesting?" Kate asked, looking at Vargas and Pete.

"A herd of elephants," Peter was quick to note. "Amazing creatures. Massive, and they move without making a sound until they reached the water. Then it was playtime."

"I could watch elephants all day," Kate said.

"You'll likely see them as you follow this trail," Adam said. "And hopefully at the sundowner as well."

"Sundowner?" Bella asked

"Hey, no spoilers!" Kate blurted out before Adam could answer.

***

ADAM WAS RIGHT, AND the journey on toward camp took them through a thick forest. The stripped leaves and bark, and the occasional tree on its side, clear evidence elephant loved the area. They reached the edge of a lake where a small herd of elephant were drinking and spraying water up on their backs.

Kate and Bella hopped up through the open roof and watched the interaction between the matriarch and the herd, and the young learning and struggling with the mechanics of drinking from trunks that seemed to have a mind of their own. One of the small calves gave up and just knelt down to get a drink.

Some silent call resonated among the group, and the matriarch wandered toward the water's edge and onto the bank. Everyone followed. She stepped over a downed tree, rubbing her belly on the bark, and then disappeared into the forest. One by one, every elephant in the herd did the same, and when the youngest calve approached the downed tree, he raised a single leg and put it on top. Too small to climb over, he did the best he could and then ran to catch up with Mom.

"I see what you mean," Bella said. "I think I really could just sit and watch them for hours."

"Every encounter is different," Kate said. "I've seen them roll in mud, spar with their tusks, trumpet in mock charges—or real ones. But that belly-scratching routine? That's new."

"And the little one was so cute," Bella added. "He couldn't do it, but he was determined to try."

Kate smiled, watching the smallest calf scramble to catch up. The wilderness was full of moments like this—quiet, raw, unforgettable.

This isn't Disneyworld, she thought. Africa was never just peaceful.

It could lull you into a sense of wonder—right before reminding you that things are not always what they seem.

She'd come in search of a predator but couldn't shake the feeling she was the prey.

Chapter 49

MONDAY, MAY 4th
3:24 PM CAT

ROYAL AFRICAN CAMP, KANGWA DELTA, MOTAPA

THE GAME DRIVE TOWARD camp was beautiful and uneventful—until Shane slowed the Cruiser and pulled to the side of the road. He cracked the door open, leaned out, stared at the sand, and paused. He rolled forward a few feet and stopped again.

"What's he doing?" Bella whispered.

Kate smirked. "Just watch."

Shane studied the ground, his sharp eyes scanning every detail. He inched the Cruiser forward once more, then exhaled, satisfied.

"Leopard tracks," he murmured, mostly to himself. "Fresh."

He shut the door, shifted into gear, and steered off-road. "Let's go find her."

The vehicle turned into the bush, easing around a few trees and directly over some of the smaller brush. They worked their way in deeper and closer to the water's edge.

"There she is," Shane whispered, and everyone understood it was best to be as quiet as possible.

"Can we go up top?" Kate asked.

"Yes. Just slow and quiet."

The leopard was draped over a thick branch, regal and still, except for the occasional flick of her bloodstained whiskers. Her kill, a limp impala, dangled from the crook of the tree, a macabre trophy.

"She's beautiful," Bella whispered.

"Look there," Kate pointed, keeping her voice low. "At the base of the tree."

A cub stirred, groggy and blinking in the golden afternoon light. He stretched, then climbed halfway up the trunk, swiping at his mother's tail. She flicked it away lazily, ignoring him. But he persisted, pouncing again and again until a sharp growl sent him scurrying into the underbrush.

"We should go," Shane said. "There will be tea and cake at camp and time for a shower if you'd like."

"A shower? Seriously?" Bella asked, looking over at Kate.

"Trust me. You'll love it, but this is a navy shower," Kate said, smirking. "Think you can handle that?"

"I can handle it," Bella said. "As long as there's somewhere I can plug in my blow dryer." After a moment of total silence, Bella started laughing. "Come on, guys, give me a break. I'm kidding."

***

4:19 PM CAT

FORTRESS KRASNAYA SKALA

Nuru scaled the path, moving like a shadow against the rock face. Leboo was right—the guards never looked this way. Their attention was locked on the compound below.

A guard might spit over the side or relieve himself, but none suspected an intruder slipping through a breach in the wall.

Once inside, alone and unguarded, Nuru moved in the shadows of the late afternoon, noting the location and purpose of the buildings he passed. The fortress headquarters was obvious, with towering poles and flags dancing in the afternoon breeze. Likewise, the mess hall and garrison were easy to spot, given the soldiers milling around both.

In a large warehouse, Nuru saw canvas bags stacked nearly to the ceiling. One torn and tossed to the side revealed the black stone that children like Leboo toiled to extract. He entered, crouching down to examine it. His weathered fingers traced the jagged edges of the dark, metallic ore. *Coltan, they called it. What could be worth such misery?*

The warehouse was eerily quiet, the air thick with dust and the lingering scent of sweat and despair. The waning sunlight filtered through high, grimy windows, casting long shadows across the packed earth floor. Nuru's eyes, accustomed to reading the subtle signs of nature, found nothing in this lifeless stone.

"What magic does this possess," he whispered to the darkness, "that it can turn men's hearts to stone?"

The vision that brought Nuru to this place echoed in his mind. The cries of children taken from their homes, their innocence ripped away, their small bodies broken by labor no young soul should endure.

For what, he wondered, struggling to comprehend the value of the bags towering above him. *And at what price?*

Nuru emerged from the cavernous warehouse. With grim determination, the Maasai warrior and shaman strode purposefully towards the heart of the fortress. His message for Colonel Nkrumah burned within him, demanding to be delivered even at the cost of his freedom. Nuru knew that to speak his truth, he must first become a prisoner.

The bustling compound fell into an uneasy silence as Nuru appeared, his tall, lean figure cutting an imposing shadow in the afternoon sun. His vibrant red shuka cloth and intricate beadwork stood in stark contrast to the drab military surroundings. With measured steps, spear held firmly at his side, Nuru advanced to the center of the courtyard.

Whispers and murmurs rippled. Armed men tracked Nuru, hands drifting to weapons. Unshaken, he walked on, a challenge to their world of violence.

Reaching the heart of the compound, Nuru lowered himself to sit cross-legged on the dusty ground. With deliberate grace, he laid his spear beside him and rested his weathered hands in his lap. Only then did he allow his keen gaze to take in the surrounding scene.

He observed the two distinct groups of men, each radiating danger in their own way. Bearded foreigners in loose garments and native Motapans with hardened eyes. The men with thick, full beards reminded Nuru of lion's manes. Their skin was lighter than the people of this land. Their Motapan counterparts, dark as the rich soil, carried themselves with the hardness of those who had known too much conflict.

Among those visible in the courtyard, Nuru's attention turned to the shadow-like figures of women, shrouded head to toe in flowing black fabric.

These veiled forms glided across the compound, their eyes the only windows to the souls hidden beneath. To Nuru, they seemed like spirits caught between worlds, their existence a sharp contrast to the proud, brightly adorned women of his village.

As the initial shock of his arrival subsided, Nuru felt the weight of many eyes upon him. He remained still, a center of calm in a sea of tension. His gaze swept the compound, searching for the one they called "The Hyena" - the man whose cruelty and cunning held this operation together.

Nuru's presence was a pebble thrown into still water, the ripples of change already spreading outward. He knew his actions would set in motion events beyond his control. But as he sat, patient and resolute, Nuru felt the hand on his shoulder, the comforting presence of the warrior spirit who led him to this moment.

***

4:43 PM CAT

SNIPER HIDE, DRAKARI MOUNTAINS

REED LOWERED THE BINOCULARS and slid behind the rifle. Legs kicked wide, he settled in, sighting down the scope.

"Who the hell is that?"

Kabe lifted his own binoculars, spotting the man in red. He grunted, shifting slightly.

"Whoever he is," Reed muttered, "he's got everyone rattled."

Through the scope, Reed watched a soldier jab the old man. Nuru didn't flinch. The others laughed—nervous, forced.

"They thought he was a spirit," Kabe murmured. "Now they know he is just a man."

Reed adjusted the rifle, fingers steady on the stock. "I wouldn't be so sure."

He pictured the target: Major Viktor Mirov. At six-three, the big Russian should be easy to spot, but Reed figured he was tucked away in some air-conditioned office, waiting for the heat to die down.

"Come on, Viktor," Reed whispered. *"Come have a look at the mystery man."*

***

Colonel Kwesi "The Hyena" Nkrumah emerged from the fortress, his presence commanding instant attention. The soldiers parted like a tide, revealing the serene figure of Nuru seated in the dust at the center of the commotion.

Nkrumah's gaze sharpened as he assessed the old man. His face remained unreadable, but his eyes carried the cold calculation of a predator. He turned to his lieutenant, a man with a scar slicing down his left cheek.

"Bring him," Nkrumah ordered, his voice low and menacing.

The lieutenant nodded, then shot a sharp glance at two nearby soldiers. "You two. Now."

They stepped forward, gripping Nuru's arms with surprising gentleness. He offered no resistance.

"How is your wife," Nuru whispered to the man on his left.

"She's well," he replied, embarrassed to be gripping the shaman's arm.

"It's alright," Nuru said, smiling. "I'm not as fragile as I look."

The second soldier retrieved Nuru's spear, handling the ancient weapon with a mix of curiosity and unease. The small procession followed Nkrumah up the stone steps into the fortress headquarters.

Inside, the air was cooler, shadowed. The scent of gun oil and cigarette smoke clung to the walls. Faded Soviet-era posters hung alongside newer maps and logistical charts.

The lieutenant led them down a long corridor, his boots echoing on the stone floor. The soldiers flanking Nuru radiated tension, but he remained calm. Unshaken.

They stopped at a heavy wooden door. Beyond it, Nkrumah's office loomed—maps covering one wall, a massive desk at its center, and an array of trophies lining the shelves. Some animal. Some human.

Nkrumah sank into his chair, his predatory gaze fixed on Nuru. The soldiers shoved the old man into a seat facing the Colonel, then stepped back, awaiting orders.

Nkrumah gestured at the spear. "Let me see."

The Colonel examined the weapon, testing the flex of the shaft, running his fingertip along the blade.

"Your blade is bent," the Colonel observed, looking into Nuru's eyes. "Why not straighten it?"

"It binds me to the lion who did this," Nuru said, pulling the cloak from his shoulder and revealing the three scars carved into his chest.

"Did you kill him?"

"For one of us to live, the other had to die."

Nuru saw the spark of the hunter in the Colonel's eyes, but now, with his curiosity satisfied, the questioning began in earnest.

"None of my men saw you enter," the Colonel began. "How did you get in?"

"I am Maasai," Nuru began. "Your walls mean nothing to me. I go where the spirits take me."

The scar-faced lieutenant scoffed. "He must have hidden in one of the delivery trucks. Give me time. I'll find out who smuggled him in."

Nuru's expression never changed. His gaze remained locked on Nkrumah, unreadable. The Colonel studied him in return, assessing the old man's silence with measured interest.

"The question that needs to be asked," Nuru began. "Is why have I come?"

A soldier shifted, uneasy. "He—he said he had a message for you, Colonel." His voice wavered as if he regretted speaking.

Nkrumah's eyes flicked to him, hard as flint. "And?"

"He wouldn't say," the soldier stammered. "Only that it was for you alone."

The Colonel exhaled sharply. "Then let's get this over with." His gaze bore into Nuru. "What message did you risk your life to deliver?"

"The spirit's message is for you alone," Nuru said, looking at the men in the room.

The lieutenant stepped forward. "Colonel, let me take him. He'll talk."

Nkrumah didn't look away from Nuru. "Leave," he ordered.

"Sir, you can't be serious?"

"Your Colonel is safe with me," Nuru interrupted, his voice gentle—the insult deliberate.

"Out," Nkrumah snapped.

The door clicked shut behind them.

A silence settled over the room.

Nkrumah leaned back, studying Nuru like a puzzle he intended to solve. "Alright. Let's hear it."

Nuru's voice was steady. "If you continue on this path, you will not see another moon. The one who ends your journey is near, drawing closer by the moment." He paused. "But there's still time—your fate is in your hands."

Nkrumah laughed, low and dark. "Are you threatening me, old man?"

Nuru didn't blink. "Not I. Your life is not mine to take. It is yours to forfeit."

The Colonel tilted his head. "You talk in riddles."

"Truth is not a riddle."

Nkrumah smirked. "I carved this life from sweat and blood. Like you, I bear the scars of the men I've killed. I came from nothing. Now, I am the most powerful man in Motapa. And by far, the richest."

Nuru met his gaze. "We value different things. You are lost. Alone. Moments from death."

Nkrumah leaned forward. "Alright. I'll play along. What exactly do your spirits want me to do?"

"Free the children," Nuru said. "Return them to their families and villages and never return."

The Colonel laughed again, sharper this time. "If I free them, will the spirits work the mine?"

"Is your black stone worth your life?"

"It's worth more than yours," Nkrumah said, grinning. "There are a half-dozen trucks on the way right now. Each will leave with millions of dollars of my black stone, and in a month, they'll return for more."

Nuru's eyes darkened. "But if you stopped today, this moment, the wealth you have ripped from the earth—at the cost of children's bodies and spirits—could still be used for good."

"And if I don't, I die. That's the message?"

"Yes."

"And did these spirits of yours say how I would die?"

"No."

"What about who?" Nkrumah pressed. "Do you see who's coming?"

"No," Nuru lied.

Silence stretched.

Nkrumah sat back, drumming his fingers against the desk. "Let's see if a little time in a cold, damp cell helps you see more clearly." He smirked. "Got to hand it to the Russians who built this place—they knew how to motivate prisoners."

***

3:57 PM CEST

LA DÉFENSE BUSINESS DISTRICT

Shepard found it impossible to work. His 35th-floor office offered a stunning view of Paris—the Arc de Triomphe framed perfectly in the fading afternoon light—but not even the thought of it going up in flames could distract him. His mind was elsewhere.

The BountyHunter app's security protocols ensured that contact was rare—initiating a call would trip alarms. A risk. But under the circumstances, one worth taking.

When his phone buzzed, his pulse jumped. One glance at the screen confirmed the app was routing an encrypted call. He answered.

"I thought I might hear from you," the caller began, his voice calm and professional. "And you did the right thing. We need to talk."

Ben exhaled. *He's not angry. That's a good sign.*

Riley—the system moderator for BountyHunter—was an enigma. But if Shepard had learned anything, it was that Riley didn't tolerate complications. When things went sideways, people retired—permanently.

"So you've heard?" Ben asked. "And it's true?"

"It is," Riley confirmed. "Preacher's in play again, but we have that handled."

Ben felt a sliver of relief. "That's good. I was worried about our exposure—Grant's spooked."

"That's what I wanted to discuss," Riley said, his tone shifting. "The Agency knows Duncan Harris is alive and operating as Grant Collins, Wildlife Photographer. His cover's blown."

Ben stiffened. "What do you need from me?"

"You need to get there," Riley said. "Your flights are booked—you'll be in Motapa by noon tomorrow. Details are in your folder."

Ben's grip tightened on the phone. "And Grant?"

"As soon as his mission is complete, throw him a retirement party." Riley's voice was smooth, clinical. "This time, Duncan Harris stays dead."

Ben hesitated. "Don't you have people for that? You know...specialists?"

"We do," Riley replied. "But Grant's a unique asset. His insights, his instincts—in the wrong hands, his retirement could cost us."

"So, where do I come in?"

"He trusts you." Riley's voice dropped a fraction. "You can get in close. Handle it personally—is that going to be a problem?"

Ben knew there was only one right answer. "Nope," Ben said, feigning confidence. "I've got this."

***

5:11 PM CAT

SUNDOWNER, KANGWA DELTA, MOTAPA

THE DRIVE OUT OF camp felt almost surreal. Kate understood why photographers loved the morning and evening light—God's paintbrush on the landscape.

Shane and Thabo sat up front, guiding the Cruiser toward the water's edge. Bella and Kate stood in the rear seats, the wind teasing their hair as they took in the vastness of the Delta.

Bella had invited Sebastian and Peter to join them, but the men opted to stay behind. A mistake. The moment the vehicle stopped, Kate and Bella exchanged a glance—they'd be rubbing this in later.

The setup was flawless. A fully stocked bar, a selection of wines, and the deep golden light casting the perfect glow across the wilderness.

Bella's gaze landed on a Bouchard Finlayson Pinot Noir, a rich South African red. Shane grinned at her choice, filling her glass with a generous pour.

"Bella," Kate mused, taking her own glass. "Shane's smiling because he knows this is one of my favorites." She eyed the deep ruby liquid. "And that's a girl pour—just the way I like it."

They clinked glasses, celebrating the day's adventure.

Then the elephant arrived.

A bull, massive and silent, moving with the effortless grace of something that shouldn't be that quiet.

"Stay close to the vehicle," Shane murmured.

Kate and Bella barely breathed as the giant passed. His towering form brushed so close they could almost feel the warmth radiating from his skin. A living monument to the wild.

They watched, mesmerized, as the bull reached the water, drank deep, then slipped away—disappearing into the landscape as if he'd never been there.

"Wow," Bella breathed. "Now I get why you wouldn't spoil the sundowner surprise."

Kate exhaled, shaking her head. "That was insane. I could've reached out and touched him."

"They're comfortable around vehicles," Shane said. "As long as we stay part of the outline, we're no threat." He lifted the bottle. "Anyone for a top-up?"

Kate shook her head, finishing her glass. "I think I'll wait for dinner."

Bella sighed, stretching. "Speaking of dinner...I'm starving. Who knew sitting in a car all day would make you so hungry?"

Chapter 50

MONDAY, MAY 4th
5:14 PM CAT

MABOKO INTERNATIONAL AIRPORT, MOTAPA

Humid air wrapped around Talya as she stepped into the arrivals area, backpack slung over one shoulder. Her eyes swept the bustling crowd until they landed on two bearded men near the exit, dressed in lightweight cargo pants and sand-colored utility shirts. Samir and Rami, her former Mossad associates, were posing as Muslim merchants, their practical attire blending with the local scene.

A flicker of recognition—just a nod and a restrained smile. Here, discretion was everything. They moved with purpose, conversation minimal as they exited the terminal. In the parking garage, they slipped into a nondescript vehicle. Talya tossed her backpack into the back seat and slid into the rear. Rami and Samir climbed into the front seats, their expressions now relaxed as the car pulled away.

The airport was behind them now. No more prying eyes.

Samir reached into the glove compartment, extracting a small arsenal wrapped in a cloth. He handed Talya a pistol, a spare magazine, and a pair of knives—a pocket stiletto, and fixed blade Karambit with a wicked lion's claw curve.

Without hesitation, she made each piece vanish—pistol, waistband; magazine, left pocket; stiletto, right pocket; Karambit, boot.

When she finished, she exhaled, stretching slightly—the familiar weight of steel reassuring.

"A woman never feels fully dressed without her jewelry," she quipped.

Rami chuckled, shaking his head. "You haven't changed."

Samir just grinned. "You're either elegant or terrifying. Haven't figured out which."

"I'm both," she grinned. "You, on the other hand, seem to have found every pastry shop in Maboko."

"Full beard, full belly," Samir said, stroking his beard. "Helps us blend."

Rami smirked from the driver's seat, eyes still focused on the road as they headed into the capital. The dusty, sunbaked landscape rolled by as they settled into a comfortable silence. The low hum of the engine blended with the distant chatter of a local radio station as Samir began his briefing.

"Grant's photo is in circulation, but no hits yet," Samir began. "Isabella Marquez landed yesterday. She and Preacher went straight to the palace. There was a dinner party last night, but they left early this morning for a game drive. They'll be camping under the stars tonight."

"Camping, huh?" Talya raised an eyebrow. "And Vargas?"

"He and one of his men, Peter, something...," Samir began, checking his notes. "Peter Hart, Green Beret, are traveling with Marquez. The rest of Vargas's team and most of the travel entourage stayed behind," Samir continued. "No crowd control in the bush, so I guess that makes sense."

"What about the President's schedule?" Talya asked.

"Business meetings, cabinet ministers, nothing major. No travel," Samir replied. "There's a garden reception in two days."

"What do we know about that?"

"It's a tribal reconciliation ceremony in the palace gardens," Samir began. "The elders of Motapa's various tribes will recognize the new President as the country's leader and the arbiter of tribal disputes."

"Marquez will be there," Rami added. "Along with local dignitaries and business development representatives, so it's another celebrity photo opportunity—that guarantees it will be well attended."

Talya focused. "That's the window. Outdoor speech—President exposed. We'll assess when the team arrives."

Rami gave a curt nod, his eyes still scanning the road as they neared the outskirts of the city. "Let us know if we can help."

"Thanks," Talya replied. "But probably best we don't risk your exposure. You've already done so much."

The vehicle turned toward a quiet, industrial part of the city. Derelict buildings lined the streets, their windows boarded up or protected by metal grates. Faded graffiti and rusted signs hinted at the area's past when these buildings buzzed with the light industries and warehouses that supported economic development.

Rami stopped in front of a steel roll-up door and pressed a remote tucked into the vehicle's visor. The door groaned and squeaked open, and the vehicle slipped inside. The door closed behind them with a loud clatter as the car came to a stop next to another equally unremarkable vehicle.

Samir slid out of the front seat while Talya exited the rear, grabbed her bag and glanced around.

Rami gestured to the other car. "Keys are inside. The registration's clean, and no one will give it a second look."

She gave the vehicle a once-over. Plain, functional. Just what she needed. "It's Perfect."

"Let me show you around," Samir said, leading the way up the stairs.

The main floor was clearly warehouse space at one time, with offices above wrapping around the perimeter. On her way up the stairs, Talya began observing critical details—entry points, exit strategies, the layout and orientation of the rooms and windows.

"This is the armory," Rami said. "I understand your team is traveling with equipment, but we sourced some indigenous items and uniforms in case you need to operate more discretely."

Talya's eyes widened, scanning the table lined with Russian weapons, ammunition, and military clothing. She raised an eyebrow when she spotted several long, black Abaya's hanging on a rack and neatly folded Niqab's nearby.

Grinning, she held up one of the larger Abaya's. "This one yours?" she teased Samir.

His deadpan response, "Yes, actually," he began. "You'll thank me if you or any of the men need to be invisible among the Muslim women."

Talya nodded, knowing Samir was right.

They continued the tour. There were a dozen cots, and Rami confirmed they were as uncomfortable as they looked. The kitchen had a folding table, chairs, and a fridge stocked with basic supplies.

"You won't starve," Rami said, "but it's not exactly gourmet."

Cases of bottled water and beer—one or the other, never the tap.

Talya smirked. "It's lovely. I'll take it."

The men laughed, handing her a small bag of burner phones.

"We're the only contact number," Samir said. "Call if you need something, and we'll do what we can."

Talya thanked them, pulling them into the heartfelt embrace she resisted at the airport. "You've done more than enough already."

Samir grinned as they departed. "Just tell me where to send the bill."

Talya glanced at the burner phone and keyed in the number for Forest's sat phone. The line crackled as the signal bounced through satellites. High above Africa, a C-17 rumbled on.

After a few seconds, Forest's voice came through, steady but with the faint hum of engines in the background.

"What's your status?"

"I'm at the safe house," Talya began. "Sending coordinates."

"And Kate?"

"Safe," Talya said. "She's touring with Isabella, and they left the capital early this morning, returning Wednesday."

"What about Duncan," Forest began. "Or Grant, or whatever he's calling himself?"

"My contacts haven't seen him," Talya replied. "If he knows Kate's here, he won't risk being seen. There's a garden reception on Wednesday. The President will be out in the open. That's likely his target window."

"Wednesday. That's good," Forest said. "Gives us time to set up a defensive perimeter, and hopefully, we can get control of the situation before it escalates."

"You mean before Kate does it her way?"

"Copy that."

"What's your drop zone ETA?"

"Namangwe Desert, noon your time tomorrow," Forest said. "Given the daylight drop, we need to swing wide of commercial traffic, so we'll hit a few hours south of your location."

"Let me know when you're mobile," Talya said. "I don't know if it's any good, but I'll have cold beer waiting."

"If it's cold, it'll be good."

"Copy."

As she ended the call, Talya wandered to the window. With a knuckle, she scrubbed away a layer of dust.

The city stretched before her, bathed in the dying glow of the sun. The Presidential Palace burned gold and crimson, caught in the last light of day. But just beyond it, the Twin Towers stood like corpses.

Lifeless. Hollowed out.

Once a promise of Motapa's future, now tombstones of a dream that never came.

The sun dropped lower. With the blackness came the chill. And something else.

A whisper at the edges of her mind.

Something is wrong.

Talya exhaled sharply. *You're just worried about Kate.*

She clenched her jaw. *She's nowhere near Grant. She's safe.*

For now.

Chapter 51

MONDAY, MAY 4th
7:00 PM CAT

ROYAL AFRICAN CAMP, KANGWA DELTA, MOTAPA

KATE AND BELLA EMERGED from their luxury tents and followed the soft glow of oil lamps toward the center of camp.

"Ready for dinner?" Bella asked, her eyes sparkling with excitement.

Kate nodded, soaking in the breathtaking view. Ahead, the main dining tent loomed, a beacon of warmth in the wilderness. Custom designed for these adventures, the massive canvas structure was ringed by lanterns. A long central table, set for eight, stood simple yet elegant, inviting them closer. But it was the glow of an open fire nearby and the sound of laughter that drew them in, like moths to a flame.

Shane directed Kate and Bella to a couple of chairs the gentleman had reserved and offered cocktails and wine. Both opted to continue with the delicious Pinot Noir they enjoyed during the sundowner. While Shane fetched a couple of glasses, Bella turned to the group.

Bella leaned forward, eyes gleaming. "You boys missed something special. A huge bull elephant walked right past our car and into the water."

Peter smirked. "That sounds cool, but I think we win."

Bella arched an eyebrow. "Oh?"

Peter gestured toward his tent. "A small herd walked straight through camp."

"Seriously?"

"Dead serious. When an elephant wants something, it just takes it. The big girl outside my tent went to work on the mopane tree—stripped it clean while I watched from the window."

Bella shook her head, grinning. "And Sebastian?"

Sebastian stretched, completely unfazed. "Slept through the whole thing."

The group talked and joked, watching the flames flicker and spark in the cool night air. Drinks in hand, they soon settled into the easy camaraderie of a warm fire, the stillness of an African evening, recounting the sights, sounds, and smells of their long day's journey.

A large woman approached the fire and stood in front of the assembled guests. Her mere presence commanded attention. The conversations tapered into silence, and all looked at the beaming smile, waiting for her to speak.

"Good evening, ladies and gentlemen," her voice carrying a musical lilt. "Tonight, we have prepared a special feast for you. Our menu includes succulent roast pork and tender grilled chicken, accompanied by fresh-baked rolls still warm from the fire. And we have for you a medley of local vegetables, seasoned rice, and herb-roasted potatoes. And for dessert, a rich chocolate cake."

Smiles and applause followed her tempting descriptions. With a warm, welcoming smile, she concluded, "Dinner is served. Please, enjoy your meal."

The group rose from their seats, following the lantern light to the dining tent. The interior was a study in understated elegance - a long table draped in crisp white linen, set with fine china and gleaming silverware. Lanterns on the table and around the tent cast a soft, golden glow over the scene.

All insisted that Bella lead them off. She grabbed a plate, heading for the buffet table. Everything looked as delicious as it sounded, and the chef hovered as the attentive staff helped everyone choose from the array of offerings. The aroma of roasted meats and fresh herbs filled the air, mingling with the earthier scents of the African night drifting in through the open-air tent.

Adam and Shane sat at the heads of the table, with the four guests arranged in the center.

Bella lifted her glass, her gaze lingering on Kate. A slow smile, a wink.

"I picked this one up recently—it's about hope and facing whatever the day brings. Raise your glasses."

She paused, letting the moment settle.

"To the Greatest Good."

Glasses clinked. Voices echoed the words.

Kate swept away a tear. Being back in Africa, with the ground beneath her feet, the smoke of a fire dancing around her, the call of a distant hyena—this was a world that she and Jake discovered. Africa claimed a piece of her soul, and she loved it, but it was also a reminder that he was gone, and she was here for a reason.

***

7:40 PM CAT

FORTRESS KRASNAYA SKALA

Nuru sat cross-legged in the center of his cell, his eyes closed, breathing deep and steady. A continuous row of cages stretched into the shadows, each devoid of any furnishing. Bare bulbs hung from a string of wire running down the center of the corridor, their harsh light meant for the guards and extinguished the moment they departed.

The stench of unwashed bodies and human waste was overpowering, a hole in the ground serving as the only means of sanitation. Nuru could hear the soft cries and occasional coughs of other prisoners, the sound muffled by the thick stone walls. In the adjacent cell, a man lay in a near-fetal position, his ill-fitting clothes tattered and torn from the grueling labor of the mine. The man had not moved or spoken since Nuru arrived.

Trucks rumbled into the compound, their grinding gears reverberating through the damp floor. One truck labored as it backed into the warehouse, its load of coltan so heavy the engine seemed to gasp for breath. Nuru could almost feel the vibrations of the coltan-laden truck through the concrete floor. But it was the second truck that tore at Nuru's heart. It carried the muffled voices of children, suppressing tears for fear of punishment.

As complete darkness fell outside, starlight peeked through an air vent, casting eerie shadows that danced with a life of their own. Yet even in this place of despair, Nuru remained centered, his weathered face a mask of serene determination.

It is time, he thought. *I must see for myself.* He closed his eyes and looked beyond the grim walls of his prison. He saw the vast expanse of Motapa and raced across the Namangwe Desert. Standing where he and Leboo parted ways, he tracked the boy's journey, finding him sound asleep in a shed behind the Kibale village school. *Sleep well, my friend.*

The night air rushed past Nuru's face, cool and refreshing. The heat and stench of his cell now forgotten. Through the Motapan savanna, he raced toward the meandering streams and pools of the Kangwa Delta, drawn by the glow of oil lamps and voices.

***

9:30 PM CAT

ROYAL AFRICAN CAMP

COOK WAS RIGHT. THE chocolate cake was fantastic. Kate and Bella agreed the wine paired beautifully with the cake, and the meal was nothing short of spectacular. A bit shocked at their appetite, everyone ate more than expected, but broad grins and full bellies made the cook laugh and smile.

The group collected their wine glasses and returned to the fire, and with just enough wine to feel mischievous, Kate encouraged Adam and Shane to share a few safari stories.

"Adam," Kate began. "Tell Bella about the honeymoon couple. Bella, if you think you've had lousy luck with husbands, wait until you hear this."

"As Kate mentioned, it was a honeymoon trip," Adam began. "After guiding for decades, you get a feel for how couples communicate and work together. These two seemed perfectly happy, but stress can be revealing."

Kate smiled, watching Adam set the hook, and Bella leaned in to catch every word.

"Botswana's rhino conservation effort had been quite successful, and we went to see them," Adam continued. "It was a bit of drive, but worth it to see them in the wild. We found a mother and calf grazing. A beautiful sight, and they got some great photos."

Adam sipped on his wine and continued. "We don't go on foot often, but in some areas, we can venture away from the vehicle," Adam continued. "And this couple was determined to get a little closer."

"I'm guessing mom thought they were a little too close," Bella said.

"Exactly," Adam confirmed. "The female rhino gave us a mock charge, and before I could stop them, the couple ran to a nearby tree, and her new husband used her like a ladder—scampered straight up her back."

"He what?" Bella asked.

Kate knew the story but couldn't help but laugh. "Apparently, the guy's footprints ran right up the back of her shirt," Kate said. "I'm guessing that was Exhibit A in the divorce."

"More wine?" Shane asked, and both Bella and Kate smiled and nodded.

"I want to hear more about the shaman," Bella said, looking at Kate.

"Maybe another time," Kate said.

"Oh, Nuru's quite remarkable," Shane said. "I introduced them. For one thing, he's ancient. Nobody really knows how old he is—he looks like he's a hundred but with the strength and stamina of a young man."

"What's his secret?" Bella asked.

"Believe me, I wish I knew," Shane replied. "His home is in a forest, at the confluence of three rivers. He says the energy of the three rivers coming together is magic."

"When Jake and I met Nuru, he asked me to wade into the rivers and pick a stone," Kate said. "He said wherever we live to boil the stone to protect us."

"And you still have it?" Bella wondered.

"Oh yes. It's sitting on the fireplace mantle."

"When you met him, what did he do? Was this like a psychic reading or something?"

"More the 'or something,'", Shane answered. "He rolls out an old cowhide used by generations of shamans. He sits at one end, you sit at the other. Inside a large, hollow cow horn are pieces of bone."

"Human bone?" Bella asked.

"Might be," Kate replied. "I thought it best not to ask."

"Nuru hands you the horn," Shane continued. "He asks you to think about what you want to know, then blow into the horn."

"Then he blows into the horn," Kate said. "And dumps out the bones. What happens next is entirely up to the person sitting across from him. Nuru runs his hands over the bones and starts talking. It looks like he's reading or even listening."

"Wow," Bella said. "I just got chills. What did he tell you?"

"Nuru asked that we not discuss it, and we agreed."

"You've never told anyone?" Bella asked. "Not even Jake?"

"Nope. Not a soul," Kate replied. "I have no idea what Jake asked or what Nuru said to him," Kate said. "It was pretty cryptic, like a riddle or puzzle, and honestly, disturbing. I suspect Jake's was, too."

"There was the one odd thing," Shane began. "I'd never seen Nuru do before or since."

"Come on," Bella begged. "Spill it."

"When Nuru handed Kate the horn, he froze for a moment," Shane said.

"What happened?" Bella asked Kate.

"He just kind of stared at me," Kate replied. "Then he said I didn't need him. He said I could do what he does."

"That's when Jake started calling Kate his Little Shaman," Shane added with a laugh.

"Hey, don't laugh," Kate chimed in. "It's fun when a man has to listen or fear the consequences. Of course, Jake caught on pretty quick. He'd look at me and ask if I was really sensing something or if we were just going to talk in circles until he finally saw things my way."

As the laughter died down, Kate excused herself, stepping away from the firelight and the glow of the oil lamps. She let her eyes adjust to the black velvet of the land just beyond camp. Though she knew not to wander far, the darkness beckoned her. Looking up, she marveled at a sky filled with stars—far more than she could see even from their cabin.

The unexpected turn in the conversation, the recollection of sitting across from Nuru, brought images flooding back. She recalled Jake and Nuru sitting near the three rivers. While they never talked about what Nuru said, something changed. Jake was calm, focused, more than at any time since losing his leg.

Through multiple surgeries, physical therapy, and sheer determination, Jake was building a new life—he was just never sure what that life would be, not until Africa. *Was it Nuru? Was that the moment,* she wondered. *After that, Jake was so certain about his future. So determined. Did Nuru see what was coming or how it would end?*

Images of her and Jake and Boo at the cabin danced in Kate's mind, and she smiled. At nothing in particular but at everything that shaped their life together. Restoring the old house and creating a home, the endless hours of training as Jake regained his strength, and she found hers.

"You said I'd get tired of having you around," Kate whispered to the stars. "And I told you I just wanted the chance. I loved every minute, and it wasn't enough.

Now, it will never be enough."

Kate heard Bella's footsteps gingerly approaching. She stood next to Kate, letting her eyes adjust to the darkness, staring up at the same magnificent view.

"Do you believe in heaven?" Bella asked.

"I'd like to," Kate said, with a catch in her throat. "I believe there's more to our world than we can know or see or touch."

Bella put an arm around Kate's shoulder and just held her. For a few minutes, neither said a word. They just looked at the sky.

"I feel him," Kate said. "And sometimes I hear him. I know it's selfish, but if heaven's waiting, I don't want him to go."

Kate was about to suggest they head back when she heard a rustling in the long grass, and placing a hand on Bella's elbow signaled her to stay still.

"Listen," Kate whispered, her voice barely audible.

At first, there was only the usual nighttime serenade—cicada's buzzing, a chorus of frogs, the distant call of a nightjar. Then, from the tall grass beyond the camp's perimeter came a soft rustle. The sound of something large moving with deliberate, measured steps.

Bella's breath hitched, her eyes darting toward the darkness. Then it came again—a low, guttural vibration that seemed to ripple through the night air. "Ugh-ugh... ugh-ugh." The rhythmic grunting sound carried a weight that was almost primal, each exhalation a reminder of its source.

"Is that...?" Bella whispered, her voice barely audible, trembling slightly.

Kate's hand tightened on Bella's arm, her own senses sharpening. "A lion," she said, her voice low and steady.

The lion's chuffing continued, growing closer. The air seemed to pulse with it, each sound cutting through the veil of darkness. The grunting cadence was steady, yet unnerving, and then punctuated with an unmistakable roar. It was impossible to tell exactly how close—but it felt near.

"Should we run?" Bella asked, her body tense and ready to bolt.

Before Kate could answer, Adam whispered. "No, stand still."

With their attention on the night's sky, and then frozen by the sound in the grass, neither of them noticed Shane and Adam's approach.

The top of the lion's mane was the first thing Kate saw, just tall enough to float above the grass that parted as he approached. They stared at each other for a moment, the lion's amber eyes seemed to look into her soul. She knew that face, those scars. *That can't be,* Kate thought. *Am I dreaming?* She dismissed the thought. *No. This is real.* "You see him, right?" Kate whispered.

"Yeah," Bella replied. "I see him."

Adam put a hand on Kate's shoulder, and the lion vanished like the smoke that rose from the fire and floated across the grasses.

"Did you see him?" Kate asked, spinning around to face Adam, but the look on his face was his answer. "Shane? What about you?"

"I'm sorry, Kate," Shane began. "There's nothing there."

"Seriously? Neither of you saw a massive lion?" Bella questioned. "Amber eyes. Scars. But you must have heard him?"

"Sorry, ladies," Adam continued. "We watched you wander off a bit, and kept an eye on you."

"When you both froze," Shane added. "We were right behind you. I don't know what you saw, or thought you heard, but there was no lion."

The four of them walked back toward the fire, Kate and Bella exchanging a confused look. "Maybe that's enough wine for tonight?" Kate mused.

"Suit yourself," Bella laughed. "I need a drink."

When they were back at the fire, wine glasses in hand, they smiled, clinked glasses, and just shook their heads.

"What's going on?" Sebastian asked

"We were almost lion chow," Bella said, laughing.

"What are you talking about?" Peter asked. "What lion?"

"Don't worry boys," Kate said. "You're safe—Adam and Shane scared him off."

"You know," Shane began. "I know a guide who tells of a lion coming into camp one night. With the tents, and noise, and the fire, it's unusual, but it does happen."

"What did they do," Peter asked, scanning the area for movement.

"Of course, the crew was spooked," Shane replied. "They banged on pots and pans and made quite the ruckus."

"And the lion?" Sebastian asked.

"Roared turned and walked away—end of story. Or so they thought. The next day on safari, they came up on a group of Bushman and stopped to chat. But the eldest was very upset and asked why they were so rude. The guide couldn't imagine what he'd done to cause offense, and the Bushman said, *When I came to your camp last night, you chased me away.*"

Sebastian and Peter burst out laughing. "Good one, Shane," Sebastian chuckled. "You had us going there for a minute.

"Oh, I know how it sounds," Kate interrupted. "But I'm telling you there's something about this continent, the birthplace of humanity. I can't explain it. Won't even try, but if you stay here long enough, you'll feel it."

Kate and Bella glanced at each other, nodded and smiled.

"Busy day tomorrow, guys," Bella said, finishing her wine, and a camp steward appeared to escort her safely back to her tent—his flashlight sweeping the area, ensuring the path was clear.

Kate stood too, hugging Shane and Adam goodnight. "Thanks for keeping an eye on us," she said, and then followed an escort back to her tent.

Chapter 52

TUESDAY, MAY 5th
5:45 AM CAT

ROYAL AFRICAN CAMP, KANGWA DELTA, MOTAPA

As the sun crested the horizon, camp stirred, drawn by the rich aroma of campfire coffee. They gathered around the fire, a bittersweet mix of contentment and reluctance hung in the air.

Bella, her hair still tousled from sleep, raised her coffee mug in a toast. "To Adam and Shane," she said warmly. "Thank you for an unforgettable experience."

Sebastian and Peter echoed the sentiment, their faces glowing with the lingering excitement of the previous day's adventures. "If only we could stay for a couple of weeks," Sebastian mused, his eyes scanning the vast savanna beyond the camp.

Breakfast was the last of the camp's many delights, and a warm glow settled over the group as they collected their things. Isabella, Sebastian and Peter gathered to thank their gracious hosts for the unforgettable experience. Kate stood with them, glancing back one last time at the campsite that had provided a brief escape from the mission waiting for her in the capital. The group shared last goodbyes, with Bella and her team exchanging brief hugs and firm handshakes and promising to return someday for a much longer stay.

Kate embraced Adam and Shane with heartfelt hugs. Their bond forged through shared memories of Jake. They were both part of that first extraordinary African adventure and bore witness to Jake's renewal.

Shane held her a moment longer before stepping back. "When Africa calls you home again, we'll be waiting."

Kate nodded, swallowing past the lump in her throat.

Some goodbyes didn't need words.

Embracing Adam, Kate whispered, "Jake would have loved seeing you again." Adam nodded, his weathered face creasing with a mix of sorrow and fond remembrance.

As the transport van arrived, the team loaded up, ready for the next leg of the journey. Kate knew very little about Kibale village, and Bella was too modest to brag, but Sebastian was happy to sing Bella's praises.

A decade of rebel fighting nearly destroyed the small farming and herding community, but Bella's foundation worked tirelessly for the last two years to rebuild. Everything from a new well providing fresh, safe, drinking water to a small solar farm. The foundation repaired and replenished the community medical center, and rebuilt the school, the symbol of hope for the village.

The drive to Kibale cut through open fields, scattered trees, and grazing wildlife. As the van neared the village, excited children and villagers appeared along the road. They waved, running alongside, their faces beaming with excitement. The warm welcome filled the air with an infectious energy that Kate could feel, though a sense of tension still tugged at the back of her mind.

As the van pulled into the village square, a small group of community leaders and villagers greeted them. Bella smiled graciously as she stepped out, shaking hands and exchanging pleasantries while they were led on a tour of the village's restored facilities. Kate hung back, watching quietly, absorbing the atmosphere, yet instinctively scanning. The village was beautiful in its simplicity—huts made of dried mud and thatched roofs, the air rich with the earthy scent of soil and wood smoke.

When they arrived at the school, Kate remained a few steps behind. The principal and teaching staff welcomed Bella at the entrance of the one-room schoolhouse. Inside, children in pristine school uniforms lined up with broad smiles and shining eyes, their voices rising in a song of greeting. Bella beamed, clapping along with the rhythm as the children sang. The scene felt almost idyllic, and Bella's photographer captured some touching moments.

A flicker of movement at a window snapped Kate's focus. Instinct pulled her outside. There, in the shadows, peering in through a window, was a young boy—maybe nine or ten, tattered clothes and bare feet. But it was the crimson red belt, wrapped multiple times around his thin waist, that caught Kate's eye.

The moment the boy saw her, he bolted, and Kate followed. "Hey!" she called out, her voice soft but firm. "It's alright. No one is going to hurt you."

The boy stopped, gripping his club. Kate knelt. "Don't be afraid."

Wherever this boy was from, Kate thought. *The frayed clothing was only part of the story.* She studied the cuts and bruises, and the dried blood beneath his fingernails. The deep purple marks on his arm where the fingertips of a massive hand squeezed so hard blood vessels burst.

"Leboo is not afraid."

"Yes, Leboo. From the rungu you carry in your belt, I can see you are a warrior," Kate said. "But why did you run?"

"He said I must not be seen," Leboo began. "Only the one who can help will see me."

"Perhaps I can help," Kate said.

"I seek a warrior," Leboo said. "I have a message for him. Now, I should go."

Kate saw the fear in the boy's eyes and felt a familiar wave of dread wash over her. This was a feeling she knew all too well and learned never to ignore.

"Leboo, wait," Kate said. "Please, let me help. Tell me what's wrong."

The boy hesitated, his small frame trembling. Then, his voice cracked as he whispered, "Evil men are coming. From the mine. They will kill anyone who resists. The rest... they take to work. And some... some are taken to the officers."

Kate's breath caught in her throat as she swept the boy into her arms, pulling him close. She could feel his fragile body shaking, his small hands clutching her desperately. His tears fell freely now, his brave facade crumbling. She held him tight, whispering reassurances he was safe now, and his sobs quieted.

"Leboo, you've been very brave," Kate began. "Now you must tell me. Who sent you?"

His throat choked tight with tears, Leboo struggled to speak and swallowed hard. When at last Leboo found his voice, he said, "Nuru."

There would be time later to consider how Nuru could know she would be here—at this moment. How was it that a pile of bones strewn about, and a shocking message relayed years ago, could carry such weight today? But if the old man was right, her nightmare was just beginning.

Kate yanked the sat-comm from her bag. One press. Two seconds. The silent pulse of the SOS engaged.

She shoved the inReach device into her bag and slung it over Leboo's shoulder.

"You must hide," Kate began. "No matter what you see or hear, do not come out. Do you understand?"

Leboo hesitated, his small hands clenching the strap. Then he nodded. "Yes."

"Good. Stay in Kibale," Kate said. "Wait for my friends. They will come in a day or two. When you see them, show them my bag, tell them where we've gone. Now, go. Hide!"

Kate burst into the schoolroom, sprinting toward Isabella, her voice sharp and commanding as she shouted the warning.

"Everyone!" Kate yelled, her voice cutting through the cheerful chatter. "Get down on the floor. Now! And stay down."

Kate spun, arms out, sweeping the room.

"Down!" Her voice cracked through the chaos.

Bella hit the floor first. The teachers followed. The kids dove next, small hands covering heads.

"Face down!" Kate shouted. "Stay still. Stay quiet."

A heartbeat later, the gunfire ripped through the walls.

Perhaps it was the years of rebel fighting, but the children and teachers did exactly as they were told.

Peter drew his weapon and stood ready.

Vargas, confusion etched on his face, protested. "Kate, what the hell are you doing?"

Kate dropped beside Bella, covering her with her own body. "Vargas! Get down," she shouted, but the warning came a heartbeat too late.

A sudden, deafening staccato erupted, muffling Kate's commands. The harsh, metallic rapport of the AK-47 was unmistakable—a furious, rattling roar that seemed to physically assault Kate's eardrums. Each burst reverberating through her body. In the confined space of the schoolroom, the sound bounced off walls creating a cacophonous hell of echoes and overlapping reports.

Windows shattered, wood splintered, and the once-joyful room descended into chaos. The kids hugged the floor as Kate commanded. Peter crumpled to the floor, lifeless, blood pooling beneath him. Vargas's eyes were fixed on Kate, and Bella hidden safely beneath her. His hands pressed hard against his stomach, blood seeping between his fingers as he slid down the wall, leaving a crimson streak on the white school room wall.

As screams and sobs filled the air, Kate tightened her grip on Bella, her mind already racing to find a way out of this nightmare. Their peaceful visit turned into a war zone, and now survival was Kate's only mission.

Save the children, Kate thought. *You must set them free.* Nuru's words, meaningless, buried and unspoken for years, haunted her now. The vision that Nuru had in the forest of the three rivers—the message he delivered—was suddenly real. The frightening scene he described and the images that crept into her dreams had faded over the years—never quite forgotten. Now, with the weight of these young lives resting on her shoulders, Kate fought to recall everything Nuru told her, and anything that might help.

***

9:32 AM CAT

KATE'S SOS BROADCAST BOUNCED through the Iridium satellite network, reaching Trident Security's Emergency Response team within minutes.

Talya was in the middle of a weapons check when the alert popped on her phone, and she called Forest.

"I see it," Forest said. "I'm looking at the coordinates now."

"Kibale village?"

"Yep, that's it," Forest replied. "Any guesses?"

"With no other comms," Talya began. "Kate ditched the device, or she gave it to someone."

"Either way, we can't risk making contact."

"What we have is a starting point," Talya said. "She sent the message from that location for a reason."

"So that's where we're going," Forest said. "We have to assume this just became an HR mission."

"A hostage rescue with zero intel is a hard mission to plan," Talya said. "I'll check with my contacts here. They might know the players in that region."

"Good. I'll see if I can press Ryder. She got us the ride, so I might get lucky," Forest said, thinking out loud. "In the meantime, no sense dropping outside the capital."

"Right. Whatever happens next," Talya said. "It starts in Kibale, and that's where I'm headed."

"I'll get with the pilot and work out a new drop zone," Forest said. "The minute I have an ETA, I'll let you know."

"If this is a ransom situation," Talya began, her voice hesitant. "It's Isabella Marquez they want."

"Don't go there," Forest warned. "This is Kate we're talking about. One of the most resourceful, resilient operators we know. She's alive and working the problem."

***

9:45 AM CAT

CHAOS AND SHOCK GRIPPED the village in the aftermath of the rebel assault. Bitter smoke choked the air, mingling with the sharp metallic scent of blood. Fires consumed buildings and huts, sending thick black columns of smoke spiraling into the sky. In the distance, sporadic bursts of gunfire erupted, punctuating the devastation with even more violence.

Inside the school, rebel soldiers barked cold, commanding orders. Terrified and confused, the children stumbled out, driven from the building by force. Any hesitation was met with ruthless brutality as AK-47 stocks slammed into ribs and heads.

Kate and Bella sat on the floor, stunned and horrified. The school's principal and teacher huddled nearby. Peter lay dead on the floor, his lifeless eyes staring at the ceiling, while Vargas lay nearby, struggling to breathe.

"He needs a doctor," Kate said.

A soldier kicked Vargas. When he groaned, the man shot him in the head. "Not anymore."

The soldier then trained his weapon on the two white women. "Which one of you is Marquez?"

Isabella raised her hand, her eyes defiant despite the fear gnawing at her insides. "That's a good girl," the soldier mocked. "Raise your hand before speaking. You're coming with us."

"What about the others?" Bella asked, her voice cracking. A burst of automatic fire was the answer, silencing both the principal and the teacher. Bella instinctively jumped in front of Kate, shielding her from the same fate.

"Get out of my way," the soldier ordered, his eyes narrowing. "They said alive.

They didn't say unharmed," he added, pointing his rifle at Bella's leg.

Bella squared her shoulders. "You don't understand," she said, her voice edged with mock disbelief. "Do you even know who this is?"

The soldier barely looked at her. "What's your name?"

Kate held his gaze. "Katherine Preacher."

The soldier snorted. "Never heard of you."

Bella scoffed. "Ridiculous. I guarantee your commander has. And I wouldn't want to be you when he finds out."

Kate kept her expression neutral.

The soldier hesitated, clearly weighing her words. The ploy worked, and he yanked both women to their feet, shoving them outside.

"Move!" he ordered, pushing them along.

Kate and Bella clambered into the back of the truck, joining the huddled, trembling children—warning them to close their eyes as the truck rumbled out of the village. The sight was one of pure devastation—homes reduced to charred remains, streets littered with the dead. Tears streamed down Bella's face as she spotted her photographer, face down in the dirt, a dark crimson stain spreading from his back.

The truck jolted forward, carrying its human cargo away from the terror-stricken village. Kate took Bella's hand and squeezed. A silent reminder that they were alive, they survived.

Bella didn't know Kate well enough to recognize the look in her eyes. Only someone who had walked the dark path, faced true evil, and killed without hesitation could know what was coming. Kate knew. *The men responsible for this atrocity would soon be dead.*

***

10:05 AM CAT

Talya's phone rang as she dialed Samir.

"I was just calling you," she said.

"Good. How fast can you be ready?"

"That depends," Talya replied. "Where are we going?"

"Oh, I thought you knew."

"All I know is that Kate's in trouble," Talya explained. "She broadcast an SOS, and her reported location is Kibale."

"That's where she *was*," Samir said. "Now she's on her way to Krasnaya Skala. A former Russian military base and the new home of Colonel Nkrumah. Do you know him?"

"I know they call him The Hyena," Talya said. "And he's earned his brutal reputation."

"Trust me, it suits him," Samir noted. "And that's where we're going."

"Hang on," Talya said. "How do you know that's where Kate's headed?"

"We've been monitoring Nkrumah's comms and tracking his coltan smuggling for the last six months," Samir began. "Black market profits flow to Islamic extremists here in Africa and throughout Europe, so we wormed our way into his supply chain. It's illegal to go up there, so we make discrete weekly deliveries—it's about a three-hour run if we push."

"And you're certain Kate's alive?" Talya asked, hoping Samir had an answer.

"Absolutely," he said. "She's on the truck with the other woman and the kids."

"Kids? What kids?"

"I'm surprised you don't know," Samir said. "The rebels raid the small villages, killing most. The children with nowhere to go and no hope of escape are easy to control. After all, they're just kids."

"If you had to guess," Talya wondered. "How many would you say are in the camp, including the ones they took today?"

"I'd say around fifty," Samir guessed. "Some they took today will probably replace the dead. Why do you ask?"

"Just curious about the scale of the operation," Talya said. "What do you need from here?"

"Grab all the Abaya's and Niqab's," Samir said. "We'll be there in ten."

"No weapons?"

"We have all the weapons we need, but before we drive into the lion's den, you'll need camouflage."

"Hiding in plain sight."

"Exactly."

***

Talya briefed Forest on Samir's call, "The good news is we have confirmation Kate's alive," Talya began. She knew Forest would never admit it, but an audible sigh confirmed he was worried.

"And the bad?"

"The group that took her and Marquez is under the command of Colonel Nkrumah," Talya said. "President Bongani exiled him after the election. He and his rebel forces, a mix of Motapan and Islamic mercenaries, seized control of a former Russian compound. Locals call it the fortress. Officially, it's Krasnaya Skala."

"We'll pull satellite imagery and topography so we can see what we're up against."

"A little human intelligence might help," Talya said. "Get a feel for the size of the force and defenses. Maybe even where they're keeping the hostages."

"Does Samir have someone on the inside?"

"In a manner of speaking," Talya replied. "Mossad's been monitoring the fortress, and they make weekly deliveries. Samir's on his way to pick me up and should be here any minute. I'll be going along, dressed as a Muslim woman. While they're unloading, I'll wander and collect whatever intel I can."

"Nice to catch a break," Forest said. "And now that we have a location, I need to see if we can move the drop zone."

"From Samir's description of the fortress, it's tucked into the Drakari mountains and sitting on the edge of a massive ravine. If he's right, the Namangwe desert might be your best option."

"What's the compound doing in the mountains?"

"Mining," Talya replied. "The Russians built it to steal the gold from Motapa, now Nkrumah's using it to steal the coltan. There's one other problem."

"I don't like the sound of that."

"The fortress is packed with kids," Talya said. "They're using slave labor to mine the coltan."

"Alright," Forest said. "How many?"

"Maybe fifty."

"Jesus! Fifty!" Forest spat back at her. "No frigging way. Can't be done."

"Don't tell me. Tell Kate," Talya said. "She's the boss, but we both know she's not leaving without them... and neither would Jake."

"Just get in there," Forest said. "Find out what you can, and please keep a low profile. The mission's hard enough without you making it worse. Got that?"

"Copy."

CHAPTER 53

TUESDAY, MAY 5th
5:27 AM EDT

PERSONAL RESIDENCE, CIA DEPUTY DIRECTOR, McLEAN, VA

Margot Ryder sat in her sunroom, cradling a large mug of steaming black coffee. The custom blend, rich and dark with notes of chocolate and a hint of smoky undertone, came from a small, family-owned plantation in the mountains of Costa Rica. The plantation's role as a mountain-top surveillance facility was a lucky coincidence.

She loved the view and treasured what little peace the job allowed. The warm, golden glow spreading across the meticulously landscaped grounds was a stark contrast from the florescent lights and glaring rows of monitors in the situation room tracking the chaos brewing or boiling around the globe.

Margot took a long sip, savoring the complex flavors and closed her eyes for a moment. It was a ritual she held sacred but rarely enjoyed without interruption, and today was no exception.

Her phone buzzed, rattling against the glass tabletop. Forest. That could only mean one thing.

She sighed, set down her mug, and answered. "Alright, Forest. Let's have it."

"We have a situation." Forest's voice was tight, the C-17's engines a steady hum in the background. "Mission parameters just changed."

Margot was already up, striding toward her office. "What happened?"

"Rebel forces kidnapped Isabella Marquez about an hour ago," Forest replied grimly. "We have independent confirmation Kate's with her."

Margot exhaled. "That's something. What else?"

"They're in transit to Krasnaya Skala, a former Russian military base."

"I'll have the team pull everything we have on the base."

"And Colonel Nkrumah," Forest added. "Apparently, his forces took command of the base and are processing coltan from an adjacent mine."

"Coltan?" Margot asked. "That could mean this is an Africa Corps operation."

"Wagner mercenaries?"

"Yes," Margot confirmed. "New name. Same brutal killers."

"That would complicate things," Forest said. "Any chance we can get eyes on the compound? I'd love to see what and who we're facing."

"I warned Kate that I'm under a microscope."

"Don't think about Kate. Think about the PR," Forest said. "Rescuing Isabella Marquez, an international celebrity, adored by millions—and dozens of kids."

"What are you talking about?" Margot asked. "What kids?"

"They're using kids to work the mine," Forest said. "If we go in—when we go in, we're bringing everyone out."

Margot sank into her chair and sighed. *Is this it*, she wondered. *Well, if I'm going down—might as well leave a gigantic crater.*

"I'm not promising," Margot said. "But I'll see what I can do."

"Satellite imagery and topography are my immediate priority," Forest said. "We need to pick a new drop zone—one that keeps us away from trouble."

"Like dropping on top of an Africa Corps division," Margot noted. "I'll be in touch."

Margot dashed off a series of team directives and noted the time. *I can be in the situation room in fifteen minutes*, she thought. *Ten if I make the lights. By the time I get there, they'll have enough raw material to get the Trident team working on a plan. God help us.*

***

6:00 AM EDT

CIA HEADQUARTERS, LANGLEY, VA

MARGOT PUSHED THROUGH THE Special Activities Center doors, black coffee in hand, heels clicking. The room was often chaotic and ran twenty-four-seven for a reason, but this morning, it buzzed with analysts scrambling to process the flood of data requests Margot sent just minutes earlier.

The room's central observation screens flickered with satellite imagery from across the African continent, but a quick glance confirmed none of it was what she wanted. "Shift the satellite to Motapa, Krasnaya Skala," she ordered without preamble. "I want real-time imagery—everything in or out of that base."

Jason Kim, the CIA's operations lead for Africa, didn't even look up from his console. His fingers hesitated on the keyboard. "Ma'am, the drone and satellite you requested are monitoring operations in Somalia. Joint Spec Ops has direct control. We'll need approval from AFRICOM and DoD before—"

"I'm not waiting for approval," Margot snapped. "Re-task them now. Whatever they're doing in Somalia can wait. If we miss this window in Motapa, we won't get another shot."

Kim sighed but relented, motioning to the analyst in charge of the satellite feeds. The map on the main screen zoomed out from Somalia, the terrain shrinking as it shifted southwest, finally settling on the dramatic cliff face of the Drakari Mountains. Krasnaya Skala came into view, a relic of Cold War ambition with its concrete barracks and guard towers.

Margot studied the image on the screen, the jagged rock face of the eastern cliff rising like a barrier against the outside world. The structures, though dilapidated, still stood imposing—a mix of Soviet architecture and more recent African militarization. There was movement in the compound and near the main gate.

"Where are we on schematics, blueprints—anything on the compound's layout and design? And the topographical data—I want everything within 100 kilometers."

Silence.

Then—like popcorn kernels hitting oil—responses fired off across the room.

"Blueprints!" an analyst called. "Soviet-era—barracks, armory, airstrip."

Margot studied the satellite feed. The prison block's crisscrossing footpaths were subtle but unmistakable. *Forest's intel appears to be correct,* Margot concluded. *The prison is definitely active.*

"Topographical maps are coming in now," another voice chimed in. "Mountain terrain for miles north of the compound with a sheer cliff face on the east that drops into the Karunga ravine. The Namangwe desert runs south for hundreds of kilometers. The only viable route into the base is the mountain road."

"The Russians knew what they were doing," Margot concluded. "Easy access to the Drakari mines and the geography provided an optimum defensive position."

"Colonel Nkrumah," someone said, tapping a tablet. "Trained in Moscow, key player in the coup. Bongani pardoned but exiled. Now runs an illegal mine—ruthless, charismatic, commands his rebel forces like an army. His force is a mix of former Motapan soldiers and Islamic militants, but there's tension—different uniforms, skin colors, and beliefs."

"Nice work people. But we're just getting started," Margot said. "We've got a bird in the air right now, a C-17 on approach to Motapa. They need everything we've got and set up a live feed."

"I'm on it, boss," Kim replied, and two minutes later, an encrypted link was transmitting.

Margot was scanning the live feed when the image zoomed in on a small convoy approaching the fortress. The vehicles snaked around the jagged barriers—old Soviet tank traps known as dragon's teeth, meant to slow and expose anything that approached.

Leading the convoy were two pickup trucks led, beds reinforced with crude armor, each mounting a Soviet DShK heavy machine gun. Rebel soldiers crowded in the back, clutching their weapons or propped against the mounted guns.

The truck following the pickups was unmistakably Russian military. The GAZ-66 was a Soviet-era, all-terrain transport still in wide use among paramilitary groups across the continent. A weathered canvas tarp flapped as the vehicle bounced along the uneven road but kept the truck's cargo hidden from view.

"Track them all the way back to the base," Margot ordered. "I want eyes on whatever's in that truck, and what they do with the contents."

Margot was careful not to tip her hand and set expectations. She needed her people mission-focused, not shocked or distracted by the prospect of a truck filled with children. *Forest could be mistaken,* she knew. *And if he is, I could still try to manage the fallout and salvage my career.*

They watched the steel main gates gradually open wide enough for the trucks to enter. The pickups headed toward one end of the compound, and the men climbed out, stretching stiff legs and backs. Several women approached, their solid black Abaya's and Niqab's identifying them instantly as Muslim and confirming Islamic fighters among the Colonel's insurgent force.

The GAZ-66 rolled to a stop in the center of the compound. Two soldiers leaped from the back, quickly joined by several others, all with their guns at the ready.

Hushed whispers erupted in the ops center. Everyone knew armed guards could only mean one thing—the truck wasn't hauling cargo. The truck gate dropped. One by one, school-uniformed children climbed out.

The op center whispers exploded into gasps and open chatter.

"Focus people. Focus," Margot snapped. "I need head counts, boys and girls, and we need to locate where they're being held."

At that point, you could hear a pin drop. Everyone in that room was there for a reason, personally selected by Margot because they were the best, and they'd been on the front lines before—special operations missions, terrorist bombings, hijackings, and more. Children made it harder, but the kids were alive and appeared physically unharmed.

The first adult woman emerged, heads turning. Even with her head down, her presence drew whispers.

"Listen up," Margot said, commanding their attention. "Yes, that is Isabella Marquez. I had unconfirmed intel that she was taken from Kibale village earlier today. Now that we have confirmation, I'll notify the director immediately. Your job is to stay on task."

"Hang on," Jason interrupted. "There's another woman—is that Katherine Preacher? Did she just look up and smile?"

***

12:18 PM CAT

C-17 EN ROUTE TO MOTAPA

FOREST WAS ALERTED THE minute data began streaming from Langley. He gathered Trident's leadership team in the plane's forward communication center. They logged into hardened laptops, monitoring and analyzing the intel, compiling operational notes as they would for any mission, especially a hostage rescue. But with Kate's life on the line, and dozens of children nothing about this op was business as usual.

Forest's focus was on entry options. He paged through structural details, comparing satellite images with the historical blueprints. This wouldn't be the first time unexpected deviations from the building plans put a mission at risk, so certainty was critical.

Mike Graham's focus was on guard tower placement, the guards' field of view, and potential concealment and exposure challenges. The east side cliff, with two small towers—likely with a single guard in each—was a tempting approach. The lack of coverage suggested the Russians didn't see the east wall as a viable threat. But the fort's 90s-era design couldn't have predicted what a motivated Navy SEAL team could accomplish.

Jordan Fox, the lone Marine in Trident's leadership cadre, worked with Jake and some of the other SEALs in Somalia. His role in pirate interdiction missions began in overwatch, where Jordan's sniper skills were unparalleled, but when he wanted to roll with the door-kickers, the brotherhood bonded at an entirely new level. He identified several options in the mountain terrain, with clean shots into the guard towers and from where he could pin down the opposing force.

The unknowns at this stage were overwhelming, but when the satellite feed zoomed in on the convoy, all eyes turned to the cargo truck.

As the vehicles slowed, meandering around the cement barricades, the guys saw the immediate problem.

"We won't be driving the kids out of there," Mike said. "All it would take is one guy still breathing, and those tower guns would light us up like the fourth of July."

"And the tower guns are the ones we see," Jordan added. "The Russians would have built the towers with rocket and sniper ports. A very effective funnel to take out anything coming at them."

"Or in our case," Forest added. "Trying to run."

They studied the steel gates as they opened, considering the size and weight, but any kind of frontal entry or exit was already off the table.

When the GAZ stopped in the middle of the compound, and the guards took up positions at the rear, no one dared speak.

They watched the kids pile out of the back, and then Marquez, and only exhaled when Kate jumped out.

"She's not injured," Mike said. "Right now, they can all walk. That's something."

"Did you guys see it?" Jordan asked.

"Kate? Yeah, of course."

"No, not that," Jordan said. "Back it up. Now, wait for it. There! Freeze that!"

The three of them stared at the frozen image of Kate glancing up at the sky and burst out laughing.

"I knew it," Jordan said. "She smiled—I think she winked at us."

Forest straightened. "Kate knows we're coming. Now, we just need a way in—and a way out."

"I've got an idea," Jordan said. "But you're not gonna like it."

Chapter 54

TUESDAY, MAY 5th
12:26 PM CAT

SNIPER HIDE, DRAKARI MOUNTAINS

John Reed crouched beneath a camouflage canopy, escaping the noonday sun. It wasn't enough. Kabe manned the binoculars, scanning the fortress for any sign of the target.

"He's not coming out," Reed called out. "Too hot and getting hotter."

Kabe shifted beside him. "Not assume..." he began, then stopped.

Reed froze, listening. Engines. The convoy groaned up the switchbacks, straining against the incline.

Reed wiped the sweat from his brow. "Same convoy. Slower on the climb back." His gaze flicked to the officer's quarters. "Could be enough to get Mirov outside."

He edged closer to his rifle, keeping his attention on the center of the compound and the doors from the officer's quarters.

As the gates opened, Reed settled behind the scope, motionless against the mountainside. From his vantage point, the entire compound spread out like a game board, each structure, road, and guard post meticulously marked in his mind.

He exhaled slowly, gaining control over his breath and slowing his heart rate. Eyes scanning for any sign of movement, any glimpse of the target. With beads of sweat on his forehead, he already knew there wasn't even a hint of wind on the mountain.

Reed checked the flagpoles—still, no wind. His gaze returned to the compound and the guards positioned at the rear of the truck.

"More school children," Kabe muttered.

Reed watched as kids stumbled forward, dust-streaked uniforms, red soil clinging to small feet.

"They're fresh," Kabe added. "Not yet broken."

Unlike the others, these kids still had a flicker of defiance in their eyes, their faces twisted in fear but not yet hollowed by exhaustion.

Reed's jaw tensed. "Give it a week", he said flatly. "Then they'll look like the rest." *Too bad The Hyena wasn't the contract. That's one mad dog I'd love to put down.*

The index finger of Reed's right hand tapped against the stock. Accustomed to long waits and seemingly endless observation roles, he wanted to put this mission to bed. A part of him wanted to do something about those kids, but mission deviation was almost as dangerous and deadly as mission failure.

Kabe tensed. "A woman—not from the village."

Reed whistled low. "Well, that's a twist."

Kabe frowned. "You know her?"

"That," Reed said, adjusting the scope, "is Isabella Marquez. Hollywood royalty. Whatever she's doing out here, she screwed up."

"He is coming," Kabe said, his tone betraying his desire to complete the mission.

"So Major Viktor Mirov will brave the heat of the day to meet a celebrity."

Reed's crosshairs settled on Mirov's chest—with a press of the trigger, his spine, lungs, and heart would cease to exist.

Mirov walked the line of schoolchildren like he was reviewing troops. He stopped to have a closer look at a small boy, and Reed's finger took up the slack on his trigger, but Mirov knelt, wiping a tear from the boy's cheek. Reed let up.

"He has chosen one," Kabe said, and Reed's stomach turned. Mirov's action wasn't compassion, or even pity. It was condemnation.

Just breathe, Reed reminded himself. *Don't let anger get in the way.*

Mirov neared the end of the line, standing face to face with Marquez—she spit in his face.

He slapped her and turned to the men. They all laughed—not because it was funny, but because Mirov had decided it was.

Reed expected Marquez to be last—then saw another woman.

Mirov, six-three, and 240 pounds loomed over her. But he seemed interested, or at least curious enough to linger for a few minutes. Reed's finger was back on the trigger, but he didn't have the shot. *Whoever she is,* he thought. *She doesn't deserve to die, though she might wish otherwise in a few days. Come on, Major...one more step.*

Reed's wish came true. Mirov reached the end of the line, turned, and stood for a moment, looking back across the line of captives.

"Send it!" Kabe shouted.

"What the hell are you waiting for?" His voice cracked.

Reed pulled away from the scope—his heart hammered in his chest.

What the hell is she doing here?

Cold steel touched Reed's skull.

"Shoot," Kabe rasped, voice shaking.

Reed didn't move. "And if you kill me?" He let the question hang. "Who takes the shot then?"

Kabe's breath hitched. The gun wavered.

"I will," he rasped.

Reed didn't move. "Let me guess. Your collateral—your wife?"

Kabe swallowed hard. "Yes."

"Then tell me," Reed said, slow, deliberate. "Are you willing to bet her life you can make this shot?"

Kabe's grip shook. The gun dropped away. "Please," Kabe begged, kneeling like he was praying. "They will kill her."

"You said you know me, or at least my reputation," Reed began. "Then you know, Ronin has never failed. Mirov will die, and soon. But if you ever point a gun at me again, I will kill you."

Reed reached for the binoculars and watched as the guards moved everyone toward the cell block. *They're keeping Preacher with the kids,* Marcus thought. *At least for now. That's good.*

Chapter 55

TUESDAY, MAY 5th
1:06 PM CAT

PRISON, FORTRESS KRASNAYA SKALA

PACKED EARTH GAVE WAY to cold concrete as guards shoved Kate, Bella, and the trembling children toward the prison. Orders echoed off the walls.

Stepping inside was like entering a tomb. The stench—waste, sweat, despair—hit hard. Kate's eyes watered as they adjusted to the dim light, a string of bare bulbs casting harsh shadows along the corridor. The children whimpering, their fear palpable in the stale air.

Row upon row of cages stretched into the gloom, each a stark testament to human cruelty. Kate's training prompted her to take in every detail—the lack of furnishings, the holes in the ground serving as primitive toilets, the occasional huddled form of a prisoner.

The children huddled as cell doors clanged shut. A guard dragged his club along the bars, grinning as the kids flinched. "Shut up, or none of you get fed," he growled.

Bella crouched beside the children, her voice a thread of reassurance. "It's OK. We're here. You're not alone."

The guards shoved Kate and Bella into another cell, the door slamming shut behind them with a metallic clang, the sound reverberating through the narrow space. In the dim light, they made out a man near the back wall, sitting cross-legged with his back to them, seemingly oblivious to their arrival. He stared at the cold stone wall, motionless, as if it wasn't there at all—just an endless horizon stretching before him.

Bella moved to the far side of the cell, trying to calm the children who huddled together, still sobbing. Kate scanned the room, assessing the strength and design of the cell and looking for anything that could be of use. The cell was barren—just concrete, rusted bars, still solid, and a hole in the floor. There was no way out.

"Kate, what do you think?" Bella whispered, glancing over her shoulder.

Kate met her gaze and shook her head. There was no way they were breaking out of here, not without a miracle.

The man spoke without turning.

"Welcome," he said, warmth in his voice. "I was wondering when you'd arrive."

Kate froze. That voice. The familiarity sent a chill through her.

"Kate," he continued, his words steady and calm. "We've both seen this moment before."

Recognition struck like lightning.

"Nuru?" she whispered.

He stood slowly, a gentle rustle of fabric, a smile spreading across his face as his arms opened wide. His presence filled the cold, lifeless cell with a warmth that had been missing since their capture. Kate rushed into his embrace, drinking in the familiar comfort like water to a parched throat. In that moment, the prison disappeared, and all that mattered was that Nuru was here.

"Isabella," Kate said, her voice thick with emotion, "this is Nuru."

Bella, too, found herself drawn into the shaman's warm hug. "I've heard stories," she murmured, "but I never imagined..."

Nuru chuckled softly, his eyes twinkling. "You can't believe everything you hear," he replied with a playful wink.

Bella, still shaken, asked, "How can you be so calm in this dreadful place?"

Nuru's eyes twinkled. "I went for a lovely walk along the stream near my home. Kate knows it. I could feel the grass beneath my feet and listened as the birds welcomed me back. I was resting under a sprawling acacia tree when you all arrived."

The clanging of keys and heavy footsteps shattered their reunion, cutting the moment of calm. The door swung open again. "You two, come with us," one guard ordered, his gaze fixed on Kate and Bella.

The man in the next cell, who lay motionless during their arrival, crawled to his cell door. Weakly calling the guard and whispering something. The guard's eyes widened. He straightened, nodded once, and turned to Nuru. "You too, old man," he ordered. "Out."

***

1:21 PM CAT

The ancient ZiL-131 truck, a relic of Soviet military might, groaned as Samir navigated the treacherous mountain road toward Krasnaya Skala. Talya and Rami sat silently in the cab, their bodies tense with anticipation. As they rounded a bend, the first obstacle came into view—an intimidating line of concrete dragon's teeth designed to force vehicles into a narrow, exposed approach.

"Too slow," Talya murmured. "Makes us easy targets—the team won't be coming up this road."

The truck crawled past the obstacles, and suddenly, the full might of Krasnaya Skala loomed before them. A massive steel gate, flanked by towering concrete guard posts, barred their way. Talya's gaze swept upward, noting the unmistakable silhouette of the Kord 12.7mm heavy machine guns mounted on each tower, with a devastating field of fire.

"Four guards minimum," she whispered. "Those Kords could turn this truck into Swiss cheese in seconds."

Samir nodded grimly. "Look closer. Sniper ports and cutouts for RPG-7s. The Russians built this place to withstand a small army. If you're not invited, you're not getting in—not this way."

They pulled up to the gate and stopped. Samir leaned out the window, a rehearsed smile plastered on his face as he waved to the guards. With agonizing slowness, the steel barrier swung open.

Once inside, Samir's voice dropped to a barely audible whisper, orienting Talya to the compound's layout. "Straight ahead. HQ. Colonel's flag flying. On the left, the prison. To the right, coltan warehouse."

Talya's eyes darted, absorbing every detail. A squat building caught her attention.

"Barracks," Samir continued. "Capacity for 50, probably housing 30-40 now. Over there, converted quarters for women and children. Families of the Muslim fighters."

They pulled to a stop before another warehouse. "Food storage," Samir muttered. "Armory, just there."

As they exited the ZiL, Talya adjusted her niqab, ensuring her face remained hidden. She moved with familiarity in the flowing abaya, her steps purposeful yet unremarkable. Two Motapan guards approached, their eyes sliding past her as if she were invisible.

"Perfect," Samir's voice came low as he passed her. "They'll ignore you. Get what intel you can, but be careful."

Talya slipped from the truck, senses razor-sharp. No cameras. Guards. Floodlights. Barracks. Mess hall. *There's the power station*, she concluded, tracking the overhead wires and generator diesel storage. *A single guard*. Her mind constructed a mental map, identifying potential weaknesses, escape routes, choke points.

She walked around, acutely aware of the delicate balance between blending in and standing out. One misstep, one moment of uncharacteristic behavior, and her cover would shatter. Kate and Isabella and the fate of the kidnapped children hanging in the balance.

***

1:37 PM CAT

WHEN THE GUARDS ARRIVED at Colonel Nkrumah's office, his aide told them to wait. Kate noticed the fleeting glance between the guards. They had some notion of what occupied the Colonel, and a sly smirk crept onto their faces.

Beyond the Colonel's door, muffled sounds of pain and pleasure. The door swung open. A young black woman dashed out of the office, wiping the snot and tears from her face. Her departure drowning Kate and Bella in a gut-wrenching wave of empathy and agony.

Sadistic bastard, Kate thought. *That show was for our benefit.*

The guard pushed them into Colonel Nkrumah's office, and Kate's eyes swept the room. The space exuded a disconcerting blend of military efficiency and personal indulgence. Maps and tactical charts lined one wall, while the other boasted hunting trophies - both animal and, Kate suspected, human. Her gaze fell on Nuru's spear, propped against a bookcase filled with military texts and, incongruously, leather-bound classics. The ancient weapon seemed to pulse with quiet power, even here in this den of brutality.

The Colonel himself was a study in contrasts. His 6'2" muscular frame suggesting physical discipline. But the way he lounged in his chair, a predatory gleam in his eyes, betrayed a man accustomed to indulging his most depraved instincts.

The office's pitched ceiling gave the modest room a sense of grandeur, but Kate sensed something more and dark. Heavy, exposed wooden beams spanned the length of the room. In the room's corner, a heavy metal hook hung from one beam, bolted into the wood with thick industrial screws. *Sturdy enough to hoist and clean an elk*, Kate thought. *Or a prisoner.*

A rope hung, coiled and waiting. Dried blood flecked the floor. What she saw and felt all but confirmed her suspicions—this was a place meant to break people. The only question that remained was whether the Colonel liked to watch—or preferred to participate.

On seeing the old shaman, the Colonel's eyes narrowed, a flash of anger on his face and in his tone. "I didn't request him," Nkrumah barked. "Why is *he* here?"

One guard leaned in, whispering urgently in the Colonel's ear. Nkrumah's expression shifted, a mixture of curiosity and calculation replacing his irritation.

"I see. Very good," he murmured, then turned to the guards. "Did you search the prisoners?"

The guards' blank stares and awkward silence were answer enough.

"Don't just stand there, you idiots—search them!" Nkrumah roared.

Bella's pockets yielded nothing but a twist-top tube of lip balm. Kate, however, proved far more interesting.

From her waistband, the guards pulled a wicked-looking Karambit knife, its curved claw-like blade gleaming in the office's harsh light.

Nkrumah turned the blade in his hands, testing the balance and edge. "Sharp. Efficient." He flicked his gaze to the guards. "Pity she didn't use this on your throats."

Chastened, the guards continued their search with renewed vigor, discovering Kate's boot knife. But even their heightened scrutiny missed the small carbon-fiber blade clipped to her bra strap.

Nkrumah turned to Nuru, a mocking smile playing on his lips. "Is this girl, the noble warrior, come to slay me, old man?"

Nuru's face remained impassive. "No."

"You're lying," Nkrumah sneered. "I'm told you know each other. That you said she knows how this will end."

"That is true," Nuru confirmed calmly. "Kate is like me, though she has not embraced her gift. But she knows, as I do, that you will die. Soon."

Kate interjected quickly, "With all due respect, Colonel, while I know and admire Nuru, we believe very different things. I don't believe in fate. We make our own luck in this world and get what we deserve."

Nkrumah's eyes glinted with amusement. "I like you," he said before ordering Nuru back to his cell.

Turning to Isabella, he mused, "What makes you so valuable, I wonder? The bounty on your head is two hundred and fifty thousand dollars."

Kate's stomach tightened. "You're a BountyHunter."

Surprise flickered across Nkrumah's face. "You know of such things?"

Kate held his gaze. "I've crossed paths with a few."

He nodded, intrigued. "Then you understand. Someone important wants her taken off the board."

Kate glanced at Bella. *Two hundred fifty grand wasn't ransom money. That was a bounty—for elimination.*

Nkrumah tapped a finger against the desk. "Riley called me personally to discuss the matter."

Kate pressed. "Riley Mueller?"

Nkrumah's brow furrowed slightly, but there was no flicker of recognition. Either he was playing dumb, or he genuinely had no idea who she meant.

Kate pushed on. "Klaus Mueller's daughter? The GEC?"

Nkrumah shook his head. "Never heard of her."

Kate studied him. He wasn't lying—at least, he didn't think he was.

Nkrumah shrugged. "I've spoken with Riley on rare occasions. Arrogant. Demanding. He personally handles contracts requiring extra care."

Kate kept her expression neutral, but her mind raced. *He. It was always he when anyone spoke about Riley—but had anyone actually met him in person?*

"Who placed the contract?" she asked.

The Colonel's lips curled into a knowing smile. "Ah, but that, Mrs. Preacher, is not your concern."

He leaned back, eyeing them with amusement. "While I decide your fate, I can offer more comfortable accommodations."

Kate met Isabella's gaze—just the slightest shake of her head. No.

Isabella turned back to Nkrumah. "We'll stay with the children," she said firmly. "They're terrified."

His smirk widened. "As you wish. Perhaps a night steeped in the perfume of sweat and sewage will change your mind." He let the words settle before adding, almost casually, "But don't worry—by tomorrow night, they'll be too exhausted to cry. After that—too hungry to complain. In time, they'll love it here."

With a wave of his hand, the guards herded the two women out of Nkrumah's office. Kate turned as they were dragged from the room. Nkrumah twirled her Karambit between his fingers, then pressed the curved blade lightly to his palm—just enough to draw a bead of blood. He grinned.

Kate swallowed hard.

He doesn't just use the blade. He enjoys it.

Chapter 56

C-17 NAMANGWE DESERT, MOTAPA

A DEEP HUM FILLED the cavernous C-17 as it neared the team's drop zone. Vibrations rippled through the cabin as the aircraft descended, leveling off at 2,500 feet—low-altitude freefall. With a heavy churn, the rear loading ramp opened, revealing the vast expanse of the Namangwe Desert below. Hot air rushed in, drowning out all other sounds in the wind's roar.

With the cargo bay open, sunlight ignited the rear of the aircraft. Stark, golden-brown hues of the desert landscape stretched for miles, shimmering in the afternoon heat. Amber lights flashed overhead, signaling the drop window's approach. The team's ground transportation would be the first out. The GMV, a modified Humvee built specifically for special forces, sat packed with gear, strapped to the deployment sled, and ready to fly.

The crew chief and load team released the safety restraints on the sled, leaving only the final quick-release hooks attached.

The Trident Security team was staged and ready to go. Final equipment and buddy checks completed, jump adrenaline surging for a rescue mission that was both personal and unpredictable.

Forest's comm crackled. Margot's voice cut through the wind and engines.

"I need to take this," Forest said over comms. "You guys jump. I'll follow."

The green light flashed solid. "Go," the crew chief shouted, and with a swift pull of the release lever, the last restraints disengaged, the lead chute deployed, and the GMV charged down the roller track. A second later, the sled's main chutes deployed, and the onboard GPS-based JBAD system gave the flight crew full control of the descent.

"Ma'am, this isn't a good time," Forest snapped over comms.

"Make time," Margot fired. "Whatever you're planning, it needs to happen tonight."

"Tonight?" Forest shot back. "We just hit the drop—there's no way we're operational that fast."

"Then work the problem," Margot said. "Isn't that what SEALs do?"

"What *is* the problem? What changed?" Forest asked, adjusting the strap on his helmet and moving toward the loading ramp.

"Africa Corps convoy inbound—coltan pickup."

Forest paused. "Heavily armed, I assume?"

"Affirmative. ETA is around 10:30 tonight."

"They stopping overnight?"

"No. Straight through." Margot's voice sharpened. "And Forest—if you don't get Kate and Isabella out tonight—by morning, they'll wish they were dead."

Forest clenched his jaw, eyes fixed on the ground far below. "Copy that," he said, ending the call.

Jordan was standing near the ramp, watching as the vehicle headed down and the rest of the team followed. Forest took his arm and pulled him aside.

"What is it?" Jordan asked. "What's wrong?"

"We're going in tonight."

"Shit. Can you make it?"

"We'll be there," Forest said. "It's the jarhead I'm worried about."

"Screw you, squid," Jordan shot back, smirking. "I'll be there."

Forest gripped Jordan's hand in a firm thumb-lock, transitioning smoothly into a solid shoulder bump. He locked eyes on the Marine with quiet intensity. "Semper Fi, brother." Jordan's resolute nod spoke volumes, both men acutely aware of the lives at stake if they failed.

The rush of freefall engulfed him as Forest leapt into the void. Below, the team fanned out, circling closer to the GMV, which had already hit the desert floor, sending a puff of sand into the air.

One by one, the four-man team touched down in a tight cluster around the vehicle.

"Move!" Forest barked the moment his boots hit sand. "Chutes stowed, vehicle secured! We gotta go!"

The team burst into action, efficiently packing their chutes and prepping the GMV. Within minutes, Forest slammed the accelerator, and the vehicle rocketed forward, its custom suspension soaking up the brutal terrain. Like a Dakar Rally champion unleashed, he tore across the Namangwe Desert, kicking up a massive plume of sand in his wake.

With a jolt, Forest pushed the GMV to its limit, slamming the team back in their seats. He could feel their eyes on him. *They all saw me take the call,* he thought. *And I was the last off the bird.* But he needed a minute to process, wrapping his head around the news. *The rendezvous in Kibale might help. Maybe Talya's got something—something that improves the odds. Right now, they suck.*

Forest glanced around the vehicle. Silence. Seasoned operators, professionals, just waiting on him to make the call.

"Change of plans," Forest bellowed over the roar. "We hit them tonight."

Chapter 57

TUESDAY, MAY 5th
1:44 PM CAT

FORTRESS KRASNAYA SKALA

Talya gathered what intel she could without risking exposure. Her Arabic fluency might save her if confronted, but she wasn't eager to test it.

Samir pulled Talya aside. "We have a problem. Coltan trucks arrive after ten."

"What does that mean?" Talya asked.

"It means your friend is in serious danger," Samir said. "And your team will face heavily armed, professional soldiers."

"Africa Corps," Talya mumbled, and she knew Samir was right. To these mercenaries, Kate and Bella would be irresistible. Even if Colonel Nkrumah wanted to control them, he couldn't.

"Whatever you hope to do," Samir said. "It must be tonight—before they arrive."

"Too soon," Talya muttered. "No time to plan. And half these men won't even be asleep."

Talya tried to suppress the panic in her voice and failed. Samir put a hand on her shoulder, reminding her to breathe. *Right. I know Forest,* Talya thought. *He'll be gathering intel on the flight—probably a satellite feed. He'll know, or will soon—for now, I'm in charge of the timeline.*

"I'd like to push the operation to as late as possible," Talya began. "How certain do you think they are about the arrival time?"

"Who knows?" Samir said, shrugging his shoulders. "But there's only one way up the mountain."

"If we block them, they'll alert the Colonel. Full lockdown."

"True. But these mountains are dangerous and prone to rock slides," Samir said. "If they're early, all we need to do is slow them down."

Talya exhaled. "Lights out at 9:30. Let's move."

Samir hopped up behind the wheel, and Talya was about to climb in when she and Rami spotted the guards exiting the main building. Isabella Marquez was the first woman she saw, and her heart skipped a beat, waiting for Kate to appear. When Kate exited the building, head up, eyes scanning, and with no visible injuries, Talya smiled, thankful her niqab concealed her expression.

"I know that look," Samir whispered, watching Talya's eyes. "Don't even think about it. We need to go."

I have to try, Talya thought. *She needs to know we're coming. Tonight.* Glancing around to ensure no eyes were on her, Talya lifted her right leg, placing her foot on the truck's running board. The movement was casual as if she were merely tying a shoelace. But beneath the flowing abaya, her fingers wrapped around the hilt of her boot knife, snug in its sheath. With a quick, fluid motion, she extracted both knife and sheath.

Heart pounding, Talya palmed the knife under her abaya. Now the hard part—getting Kate to notice. Kate bragged she could spot someone by the way they moved. *Let's find out.*

"Drop something," Talya whispered to Rami. "I need to get Kate's attention."

Rami dashed into the warehouse and grabbed a crate of the cans they just delivered. Pretending to trip, the cans collided and clanked as the case hit the ground, and for a moment, all eyes were on Rami. Talya walked past, ignoring the noise and Rami's efforts to collect the cans.

There was no way to be sure, but gambling Kate recognized the diversion, Talya walked straight toward the group. A bottle of water in one hand, the knife palmed in the other—she just had to reach Kate and deliver the message, before they reached the prison entrance.

Kate closed the gap with Bella and, taking her elbow, whispered as they walked.

Bella's scream shattered the air as she collapsed. The guards panicked. Kate dropped beside her. "Water. Now." The commotion drew a crowd, all eyes fixed on the beautiful American woman who appeared to be on the brink of death.

Talya knelt, offering water bottle with one hand while the other tucked the blade into Kate's boot.

"Devyat tridtsat," she whispered. *Nine-thirty.*

She gambled the guards didn't speak Russian—if she was wrong, she'd know soon enough.

Talya returned to the truck. She and Rami climbed in, and Samir drove out the main gate, waving at the guards as he always did.

"That was foolish," Samir began. "If you were caught, we'd all be dead."

Rami started laughing. "I thought it was bloody brilliant."

"Yes. It was," Samir agreed, smiling. "Reckless and dangerous, but brilliant. Where to?"

"Kibale village."

***

RONIN'S SNIPER HIDE, DRAKARI MOUNTAINS

JOHN REED PREFERRED NO-ONE connect the new "Reed" alias to Ronin's BountyHunter profile and reputation. How Kabe knew was disconcerting and a problem he wrestled with correcting, but that would have to wait.

Reed watched the parade from Colonel Nkrumah's office, eyes glued on the two women being escorted. *Unharmed,* he thought. *At least for now.*

Neither he nor Kabe could hear the scream, but Isabella's collapse was so authentic they both gasped.

"She's been shot," Kabe concluded.

"There's no blood," Reed added. "Must be the heat—and the stress. Hang on..."

"What?" Kabe asked, watching the crowd circling the woman on the ground.

"I'm not sure," Reed began. "See the white woman kneeling?"

"Yes."

"And the Muslim woman on her right—watch her hands."

"She's offering water."

"The other hand."

"I can't see her hand."

"No, you can't," Reed said, smiling. "Why not?"

They watched as the woman in the niqab stepped away and headed for the delivery truck. She climbed inside between two men, and he noted the local merchant clothing and full Muslim beards.

Reed smirked. "Clever girl."

"You know that woman?" Kabe asked.

"Once," Reed said, lowering the binoculars and turning away. "In another life. She's former Mossad. I'm guessing the men with her are Mossad."

"What does that mean?"

"It means the black market coltan is funding terrorism," Reed said. "The Israelis are monitoring this place, tracking the shipments and buyers. When is the next pickup expected?"

"Tomorrow," Kabe said. "Unless..."

"Unless what?"

"If they push, the trucks could arrive late tonight."

"That doesn't give them much time," Reed said, thinking out loud. "Either way, they'll have to come in tonight."

"I don't understand," Kabe said. "Who is coming?"

"All you need to know," Reed said, "is that Mirov dies tonight. But first, we get closer."

Reed was back on the binoculars, scanning the rocky outcroppings down the mountain. This mission had just become a nighttime engagement, and he needed to close the distance. When he found a spot he thought would work, he asked Kabe to have a look.

"I'd estimate the range to be four hundred to five hundred meters," Reed said. "What do you think?"

"I agree, but too dangerous to move during the day," Kabe replied. "Why so close?"

"The first thing they'll do is kill the lights," Reed said. "They'll own the night, and so will I. But first, there's some gear I need to retrieve."

***

Reed left Kabe to monitor the fortress, teasing him not to shoot anyone, and backed away from the cliff. The odds of someone spotting his movement were slim to none, but protocols exist for a reason, and now was not the time to get sloppy.

Back at Kabe's old Cruiser, Reed popped open the rear and dug into the gear case he left behind. He didn't plan on a nighttime, low-light engagement, but he packed the SPARTN—just in case. The thermal night sight's clip-on configuration meant no impact on the rifle's zero. And the night vision capability was so sensitive it could track the heat signature of a bullet's trajectory. While capable of target acquisition at extended distance, Reed knew the closer he got, the easier it would be to distinguish between friend and foe.

Reed knew the Trident Security team would hit the fortress tonight, and the odds were against them. *If this was just a hostage rescue, like Syria,* he thought. *Maybe they could grab Kate and Isabella. But wrangling all those kids. No way. And no way Kate's leaving them behind—she's too much like Jake.*

Ronin didn't know the plan, but he knew Trident Security tactics. Stealth, speed, and violence of action. If anyone had a chance of beating some very long odds, it was these guys, and he would be there to level the playing field—*for Preacher, for Jake.*

***

PRISON, FORTRESS KRASNAYA SKALA

GUARDS SHOVED KATE AND Bella back into the gloom of the prison block—the tomb-like interior suffocating, the stench nauseating. Children huddled together, with the oldest offering what little comfort they could to the youngest. Hunger, fear, and exhaustion hung heavy in the air.

The door to Nuru's cell creaked open, and the guards pushed Kate and Bella inside. Kate saw the snitch from the adjoining cell was gone. *Likely whisked away for some pitiful reward,* Kate thought. *Probably a scrap of food.* She guessed that's how it worked here. Keep them barely alive, use food to sow distrust, and encourage infighting. All part of the twisted power dynamics that kept this place running.

As the door clanged shut behind them, Kate turned to Bella. "Thanks for the performance out there," she whispered.

"What was that all about?" she asked.

Kate shook her head slightly and leaned in just enough to whisper, her eyes scanning the cell warily. "Not now," she whispered, raising her voice only slightly to add, "I'm just glad you're feeling better now." Her tone carefully modulated, making sure anyone listening might believe Bella's collapse in the compound was genuine.

Nuru sat with his back against the stone wall, legs crossed and looking as if he were somewhere else entirely. Kate crossed the cell and sat in front of him.

"I saw your spear in the colonel's office," she said, keeping her voice low but steady.

Nuru smiled faintly, his calm demeanor never faltering. "I'd like that back," he replied. "When you can manage it."

Kate let out a short laugh, the sound feeling foreign in the oppressive air. "I'll see what I can do."

Her tone shifted, though, as she leaned closer. "Why are you here, Nuru? You're a long way from home."

Nuru's eyes darkened slightly, the distant gaze growing more focused. "I came to speak with Nkrumah," he said, his words slow and deliberate. "As you told him, nothing is written. We see only what may be, not what is certain. I hoped to convince him to turn from this path and release the children."

"He made his choice," Kate said, with the certainty of what that meant.

Nuru's gaze softened as he asked, "Speaking of the children, how is Leboo?"

Kate's jaw tightened, and the weight of her grief settled heavy in her chest. "He's alive," she said, her voice barely above a whisper. "And that's more than I can say for the rest of the village. I've seen brutality, studied the aftermath of senseless violence, but to be surrounded by it—watching people you know murdered, executed—it's different. Those images—they'll follow me for the rest of my life."

Nuru nodded, his expression etched with the weight of their shared sorrow. "We bear scars others can not see and darkness others will never know," he said. "I see that darkness has found a home in your heart."

Kate's voice cracked. "My heart's broken."

"And mine," Nuru replied gently. "May I ask—did Jake ever tell you what he asked me or what I saw?"

"No," Kate said. "Neither of us discussed it. In my case, I wasn't sure I could explain. Until this morning, your words and warning—and my nightmares didn't make sense. They still don't. Not entirely."

Nuru looked thoughtful. "I will tell you what I can," he began. "Jake asked if he would find a life of meaning and purpose again."

Kate swallowed hard, recalling the turmoil after his injury. "I know he struggled with who he was and what the future held."

"His love for you was beyond measure," Nuru said, his voice carrying an old sorrow. "Which made what I saw all the harder to speak."

"What did you see?" Kate asked, her voice barely audible.

"I saw love. Success. Happiness. Honor," Nuru said, his tone distant. "He would find protectors, warriors like himself, and his tribe would grow and serve the innocent."

Kate furrowed her brow. "I don't understand. Why was that difficult? That vision became his dream. He loved building Trident and the team—the team became our family."

Nuru exhaled softly. "I saw, too, that his efforts would expose an evil that would pursue him—and, in turn, you. He would save many, but the price was his life."

Kate felt the truth of those words settle deep—a chilling confirmation of what she had feared. "He had a choice," she said. "Risk his life to save others or turn away and let them die. That was never an option—Jake would never turn away."

Nuru's smile was sad. "Nor you."

Kate exhaled, her voice steady. "And that's why I'm here, isn't it? I made the same choice."

Nuru met her gaze, unblinking. "A lion cannot be anything but a lion. I saw that you could finish what he started—but only if you were prepared."

Kate swallowed. "I loved training with Jake. The intensity. The challenge—am I ready?"

Nuru turned his gaze outward—not to the prison walls, but beyond them, to the place where the three rivers meet. To home.

"That I cannot see," he murmured, "but we'll know soon."

Chapter 58

C-17 EN ROUTE TO HUAMBO BASE, ANGOLA

Jordan Fox leaned against the cold metal wall, harness tight. The rattling floor echoed the aircraft's raw power—and the mission ahead.

He closed his eyes and rested—it was going to be a long day.

Forest offered backup, but Jordan refused. Every gun was needed. With Jake gone and Marcus MIA, they were light. If it were a straight hostage rescue mission, Jordan would have been on overwatch, but dozens of kids changed everything.

As a Marine Scout Sniper, then an instructor, Jordan thrived on rivalry—with Marcus, the Army sniper, and SEALs Jake and Mike. Their competition made them sharper, deadlier. None of them would ever admit who was best, but if your life was on the line, you'd trust any one of them to have your back.

Not this time. Jake was gone. Marcus vanished. No one had their backs.

The stakes couldn't be higher. The children. The women. The team. If he didn't get that chopper, no one was getting out of that fortress alive.

The amber light flickered on. The drop site was coming up fast—not as close as he wanted, but as close as they dared without the base scrambling an intercept. *This isn't exactly a sanctioned flight,* Jordan thought. *Better to knock on the front door than drop in unannounced.*

Years ago, this mission would've spiked his adrenaline. Now, his knees ached, his back screamed, his body worn from decades of jumps and combat. He massaged his wrist, the skin leathery under his fingers.

The Humvee restraints disengaged. Only the final quick-release remained.

The crew chief nodded. "Almost there."

Jordan grunted in return, his mind sharpening. It was always like this before a jump—like the world narrowed to a razor-thin line. Sunlight flooded the hold, wind whipped through, carrying the smell of burning sand and heat.

The green light blinked to life.

The crew chief pulled the quick-release cable. The Humvee shot forward, rolling down the cargo bay track and out into the void.

Jordan peered down. The chute snapped open, stabilizing the Humvee's descent.

"Good luck," the crew chief shouted. Jordan saluted, stepped forward—and fell.

Wind howled past. The desert rushed closer. Muscle memory kicked in—arms out, legs tight, perfect angle. He grimaced against the pain, his muscles protesting in ways they never used to.

He told Forest he'd be there. And while Jordan Fox was still breathing, that was one promise he'd go to hell and back to keep.

He guided himself in a wide circle toward the Humvee's landing site. His boots slammed down, knees screaming. Sand swirled in the desert heat.

Breathing hard, in shallow bursts, he struggled with the parachute lines. The heat hit him like a wave, the dry, biting scent of dust filling his lungs. His back spasmed as he knelt to gather the chute.

Chute bundled, he jogged to the Humvee. The sled half-buried, he cut the straps loose, hands moving on instinct.

The engine roared to life, rumbling under him like an old friend. The wrist-mounted navigation computer flashed his destination: Huambo Base, ETA forty-five minutes.

The Humvee tore forward, dust billowing. The sun baked the cabin, heat suffocating. He wiped the sweat from his brow, gripping the wheel tighter, his mind racing.

Huambo Base. He'd been here before, almost a decade ago. A joint mission, training the Angolan counter-insurgency team. He remembered the commander—a sharp man with a dry sense of humor. They'd bonded over nights of beer and war stories.

Would they remember him?

Would they help?

The base loomed ahead. Jordan's chest tightened. Fingers drummed the wheel as he neared the gate.

This had to work—for the kids, for Kate, for everyone.

Failure wasn't an option.

He'd get that chopper. One way or another.

Let's hope I don't have to steal the damn thing.

Chapter 59

TUESDAY, MAY 5th
2:29 PM CAT

MABOKO INTERNATIONAL, MOTAPA, CENTRAL AFRICA

Ben Shepard stepped off the plane, moving from the cool comfort of first-class into the suffocating heat of Maboko International Airport. By the time he hit the tarmac, sweat clung to his back. *I didn't think this through*, he realized, removing his suit jacket.

He'd been in hotter, deadlier places, but Maboko's instability was familiar—aid workers, security forces, and locals moving in chaotic rhythm, oblivious to the fight for control.

Shepard navigated the crowd without drawing attention, just as he had countless times before. Customs was easy. The officer barely looked at his forged documents. Shepard nodded and walked out.

Once clear of the formalities, Shepard searched for a quiet corner, away from the throng of passengers flowing toward the exits. Grant's burner phone rang twice before his voice cut through the line.

"Shepard?" Grant sounded surprised.

"I'm here."

A brief silence. "Why?"

"There's been a development," Shepard said evenly. "Not a phone conversation."

Another hesitation. "What kind of development?"

"You'll see. It will be major news soon," Shepard said, his voice devoid of emotion. "I'm on my way. Be at the safe house."

Grant sighed, clearly uneasy but knowing better than to press for details. "I'll be there."

Shepard stepped out of the terminal, squinting against the brightness of the day. The heat was unrelenting, beads of sweat already gathering at the back of his neck, but he didn't allow it to bother him. He approached the wooden cigarette and magazine kiosk. Passphrases and codes weren't required. Shepard extended his hand, and the vendor passed him a set of car keys.

He pocketed the keys and headed for the parking lot, replaying the task Riley had assigned. *This time, Duncan Harris stays dead. He trusts you. Get in close, handle it.* There was an elegance to his plan. Shepard smirked. *Grant would never see it coming.*

***

THE AIR INSIDE THE safe house was stale, carrying the faint odor of dust and something metallic, like old machine oil. Shepard stepped in and let his eyes adjust to the dim light. Grant was sitting in an armchair, his back to the wall, both hands visible, empty, but Shepard knew he wouldn't be far from a weapon.

Grant barely let him through the door. "What's changed?"

Shepard set his bag down, cracked a beer, let the silence stretch—then spoke.

"Ah, that's better," he said. "Colonel Nkrumah grabbed Isabella Marquez this morning."

Grant straightened in his chair. "Isabella? What the hell happened?" Grant asked. "I thought she was one of Mueller's pet projects."

"She was—until she stepped out of line," Shepard said. "Now she's a pawn—a means to an end."

Grant's gaze sharpened. "And Preacher?"

"She was supposed to die in Kibale," Shepard said flatly. "That mistake is being corrected."

Grant exhaled, the tension in his shoulders easing. "So, I'm in the clear."

"You are," Shepard said, lifting his beer in a mock toast. "To the end of Preacher and Church."

"And Isabella?"

Shepard's eyes flickered with something close to amusement. "She's interesting. Very high profile and could still be useful," Shepard said. "Mueller banked on her charity work keeping her occupied and out of his way. That's the only reason Kibale's been untouchable until now—but she let slip a plan to shake up Davos."

"Mueller must've lost it. That's his baby."

"Exactly." Shepard checked his watch. "By now, word of her abduction is reaching the news networks and flooding social media."

"Let me guess," Grant said. "The GEC is going to offer their Rapid Response Team to aid in her recovery."

"There's no way Motapa's devastated military or incompetent police force could touch Nkrumah or breach the fortress. Marquez would be dead before they even got close," Shepard confirmed. "That's where President Bongani comes in."

"And my mission?"

"If Bongani accepts the GEC's support, we play nice. You walk away, and Mueller makes Marquez an offer that ensures her gratitude and support."

"And if Bongani declines?"

Shepard's smile disappeared, replaced with something colder. "That would be a tragic mistake. Isabella won't survive her ordeal, which I understand Nkrumah will make quite unpleasant, and your mission proceeds as planned."

"What happens here?" Grant asked. "To Motapa?"

Shepard's tone was dismissive, pragmatic. "The Vice President is already in Mueller's pocket, and if that idiot can't hold the country together, it will descend into chaos. But chaos is good for business."

***

2:55 PM CAT

PRESIDENTIAL PALACE, MABOKO, MOTAPA

THE GRANDEUR OF THE Presidential Palace was a mere footnote today, fading into obscurity in the face of the crisis. A junior aide ushered Klaus Mueller down long corridors, past bustling offices and hushed meetings. Everything about the palace felt different—its usual air of formality clouded by the looming tension.

The mahogany doors of the Presidential office swung open, and Klaus Mueller stepped inside. President Bongani stood behind his desk, his face a mask of barely contained tension. His eyes flickered toward Mueller, a man whose presence was never taken lightly, but today, it was clear Bongani's patience was wearing thin.

"Mr. Mueller," Bongani greeted him, his voice clipped, "I understand you've requested an urgent meeting, but my cabinet is waiting. I can only give you a few minutes."

Mueller, ever composed, dipped his head in acknowledgment. "Of course, Mr. President. I'll be brief."

The President's eyes narrowed. "You've no doubt seen the same reports I have."

Mueller gave a subtle nod, his tone calm but edged with the weight of the moment. "Indeed. A devastating tragedy. The entire world will watch what happens next, Mr. President. Here we are at the birth of Africa's most promising young democracy, and it's shaken by senseless violence."

The President's impatience showed in his expression as he cut him off. "Yes, Mr. Mueller. But I have a country to run, and platitudes won't help. Please, get to the point."

Mueller allowed a brief pause, as if collecting his thoughts. His eyes narrowed, a sharp, predatory focus. "My point, Mr. President, is that the Global Economic Council would like to help prevent any further loss of life and the international storm that will follow should Isabella Marquez... or those children... meet a tragic fate."

Bongani's face remained impassive. "Your proposal?"

"The GEC's Rapid Response Team," Mueller said. "Right now, they're in Mogadishu—on pirate interdiction work—but give the word, and they'll be airborne tonight, on-site tomorrow."

Bongani's brow furrowed. "Mercenaries?"

Mueller shook his head. "That's a harsh term, Mr. President. The Rapid Response force consists of highly decorated Special Forces operators from GEC member nations. They've proven themselves in some of the world's most troubled regions. I'm confident that when Colonel Nkrumah realizes he's facing serious opposition, he'll release the children and Ms. Marquez."

The President leaned back in his chair, considering the proposal but clearly not sold. "I'm not sure your Rapid Response Team is the answer we need. We haven't spoken to Nkrumah, and a military response might itself endanger the hostages and block any hope of a diplomatic solution."

Mueller leaned in, voice smooth.

"With respect, this is bigger than Nkrumah. The world is watching. Do nothing—or look weak—and everything you've built crumbles."

Bongani's eyes darkened, but he said nothing.

Mueller continued. "To be honest, I don't know if I could commit the team to a non-member country. Perhaps if I could tell the board that you're at least considering membership. They may press for a firm commitment, but if I can convey your interest, I'm confident they would act without delay on your word alone."

The President folded his hands on the table, weighing the gravity of what Mueller was suggesting. He glanced at the clock, as if reminding himself that time was not on his side. "I won't make any decisions regarding GEC membership today. My people are not bargaining chips."

"Of course not," Mueller replied. "But this is about ensuring their safety—and your success. The choice is yours, Mr. President. I simply wanted to present the option before your cabinet meeting. But time is running out, and every minute we wait is another moment they suffer. Ms. Marquez and those children are at risk—facing death and abuse I dare not say aloud."

The President's face hardened, his expression unreadable. Mueller could feel the tension in the room thickening. But this was a battle of words and influence, one he had fought many times before. He stood, smoothing his jacket.

"One last item," Mueller began. "I regret if it appears insensitive of me to ask, under these circumstances, but has any thought been given to canceling the reconciliation event this week? I know that tribal leaders from within Motapa and neighboring countries are planning to attend."

"As you so aptly stated, my first duty is to the people of my country," Bongani said. "We'll manage Nkrumah and the crisis he created as best we can, but it's because of factions like his that we must move forward. If we allow this tragedy to derail our progress toward unity, we would only encourage more."

"I'll leave you to deliberate," Mueller said smoothly. "If you need the GEC's assistance, we stand ready to respond."

Bongani nodded stiffly, signaling the end of the conversation. As Mueller turned to leave, the President's voice, though measured, held a note of finality. "I will consider what you've said, Mr. Mueller. But I will make my decisions based on what is best for Motapa."

Mueller nodded and left. Bongani now faced his first true test.

A slow smile crept onto Mueller's lips. The seed was planted. Now, he just had to wait.

Chapter 60

NOMAD'S FORTRESS, MANHATTAN, NY

NOMAD'S WORKSTATION HUMMED, SCREENS casting a faint glow over the dark room. Caffeine-fueled and sleepless, eyes locked onto the drone footage, frozen mid-explosion. With voice commands and subtle fingertip movements, he manipulated the system with deft precision, working through the layers of code and encryption he'd been breaking down for hours.

Keisha shuffled in, robe and fuzzy slippers, Army mug brimming with coffee.

"Tell me you didn't pull another all-nighter," Keisha muttered, shuffling over in her slippers. "You need anything?"

Nomad didn't look up. "Gotcha."

Keisha sipped. "Got what?"

She leaned in, her eyes narrowing as she caught the frozen frame on the monitor. "Dear Lord. You found the audio."

Nomad nodded. "Yep, found the file last night. Took awhile, but I cracked the encryption, and just paired it with the video," he said, but his voice held little satisfaction. "I think it raises more questions than it answers, though."

Keisha sensed something more. "What time is it over there?" Keisha asked, rubbing her eyes.

"Afternoon. She should be up," Nomad muttered. "But she's not answering. No texts. No calls. Not even a ping on the encrypted line."

Keisha's brow furrowed. "That's not like her."

Nomad frowned, his mind already racing through the possibilities. "No, it's not," he admitted. *Something's wrong.*

"She's probably off-grid."

"Maybe," Nomad muttered. He didn't believe it.

Keisha turned to leave. Then froze.

"Oh, no."

Nomad spun. "What?"

She snatched the remote, turning up the news. The headline hit like a fist.

Rebel Raid in Motapa: Isabella Marquez Kidnapped, Dozens Dead.

Nomad stared at the screen, his mouth tightening as the anchor recounted the grim details. "Kibale, a remote village in the Central African nation of Motapa, is the latest to fall victim to a rebel attack. Former Motapan soldiers and radical Islamic militants, under the command of the exiled Colonel Nkrumah, stormed the village early this morning, shattering a celebration for the school's reopening. Beloved celebrity and philanthropist Isabella Marquez, along with all the schoolchildren, were taken. The men and women of the village were slaughtered, and the village was burned to the ground."

"There. Look." Keisha jabbed a finger at the screen.

Nomad's gut clenched. Cell phone footage—blurry, chaotic. Kids shoved into a truck. Smoke. Screams.

Then—half-obscured, dust-streaked—Kate.

"She's alive," he whispered. Then louder. "She's alive."

"Think Jake's team knows?" Keisha asked, voice tight.

Nomad was already moving. "Only one way to find out."

Keisha sighed. "You're hacking them, aren't you?"

"Already did," Nomad muttered. "Kate's good. I'm better."

Keisha crossed her arms. "Boy, you've got some serious boundary issues, but in this *specific* situation…"

Nomad didn't look up. "You're welcome." His voice distracted, his mind already working through the data on his screen.

"YES!"

Keisha jumped. "What now?"

"Their unit's TAK feed," Nomad muttered. "Tracks location. Command has the same view."

"And?" Keisha asked, her voice edging toward panic. "Where are they?"

"Motapa. Based on the speed, they're in a vehicle, coming up fast on Kibale."

Keisha exhaled. "Thank God. Hang on, Kate."

"Nothing we can do now except watch and wait," Nomad said, his eyes locked on the screen.

"And pray," Keisha added. "It wouldn't kill you to say a prayer now and then. Especially for Kate."

Nomad hesitated for a moment, then shrugged. "I'll watch, you pray. But if anyone's due for a little divine intervention, it's Kate."

Keisha disappeared down the hall. Nomad leaned forward, staring at the screen.

Come on, man. If you're out there...listening.

Give her a break.

He swallowed hard.

Amen.

CHAPTER 61

TUESDAY, MAY 5th
3:05 PM CAT

KIBALE VILLAGE

TALYA SMELLED THE SMOKE long before they arrived, the acrid stench clinging to the humid air. Then came the sight—billowing black clouds, rising like a funeral pyre.

Smoldering homes and shops lined the road, skeletal remains of what had once been a thriving village. At the center, a row of bodies lay in a silent, grisly tribute. Plastic tarps and scorched blankets concealed their faces, but their legs and feet—peeking from beneath the makeshift shrouds—told the story of Kibale's destruction.

The survivors who remained were few and scattered. Some were away from the village during the raid or hid when the gunshots rang out. Most wandered aimlessly, eyes were hollow, haunted by what they endured. Some huddled together in small groups, silent and grief-stricken.

"Stop!" Talya's voice cut through the heavy silence. Samir braked, but she leapt out while the truck was still rolling.

The tarp barely moved as she peeled it back, heat-warped plastic clinging to the bodies beneath. The pants, the boots—they were familiar. And the faces, when she saw them, confirmed what she already knew.

Rami frowned. "You know them?"

Talya swallowed hard. "Yeah. Vargas and Hart. Isabella's security."

The execution-style wound was unmistakable.

"Here's another," Rami said, peeling back another tarp. "Photographer."

"He would have been traveling with Bella," Talya noted. "Check his vest and pockets for memory cards, and identification. We should keep that with us, and when this is done, we'll need to get these three back home."

"We'll see to it," Rami said.

Talya yanked off her niqab, shrugging free of the abaya. Secrecy was over.

In this heat, and under these circumstances, she much preferred the simple tactical shirt, pants, and boots. She adjusted the instructor's belt, ensuring the CZ-75 pistol on her hip was within easy reach.

A flicker of movement. Quick. Small. Talya's head snapped toward it, instincts flaring.

A boy, rigid with fear, half-hidden behind rubble. Across his chest—Kate's bag.

Talya raised her hand to signal the others to stay back. The boy's eyes widened when he saw Talya's approach, and he bolted from his hiding spot.

"Wait!" Talya called out, but the boy kept running, his slight frame darting through the debris. Samir and Rami were quicker, catching him before he could slip away. They grabbed his arms, bracing him as he kicked and thrashed, struggling with every bit of strength he could summon. His wide, terrified eyes darted wildly.

"Let me go!" he cried, his voice breaking.

Talya approached, the boy's fear tugging at her heart. She knelt down, trying to keep her voice calm, her demeanor soft. "Shh, it's alright. We're not here to hurt you."

The boy kept struggling, his eyes darting to the men restraining him, panic taking hold. "They'll sell me to the Colonel," he whimpered, kicking out as if the very idea would kill him.

"No, no," Talya said gently. "We're not like them. I promise."

With a quick nod to the men, they released the boy and joined Talya.

"What's your name?" Talya's voice was steady, gentle.

He hesitated. Lips parted, then a whisper. "Leboo."

"Leboo," she repeated, offering a small nod. "I'm Talya. These are my friends, Samir and Rami. We're here to help."

His eyes locked onto hers, searching, unsure. But there—just for a second—was the faintest flicker of hope.

Slowly, she raised her hands, palms up, to show she meant no harm. "That bag," she began softly. "It belongs to my friend, Kate. Do you know her?"

"She gave it to me. Told me to hide."

Leboo's body relaxed slightly, though his eyes were still wary. Talya continued, "Do you know why she gave you the bag?"

"No," he replied. "Only that I should hide, wait for her friends, and show them the bag."

Talya gently took the bag from him. "We will return this," she promised, her voice soft but firm. The boy didn't resist as he handed it over, but his eyes stayed fixed on her, uncertainty still clouding his expression.

After a long pause, the boy whispered, "They took her... and the other one... and the children... to the fortress."

"How do you know about the fortress?"

The boy's eyes filled with tears, his lips quivering as he spoke. "I... I was there," he admitted, his voice shaky. "Many months ago, far from here. They captured me too... but I escaped."

"You escaped?" Talya pressed. "How?"

Leboo trembled, tears spilling. Talya pulled him into her arms. She'd held children like this before—fragile, broken—and it always ached. "I don't need to know what happened or how you broke away from the men—only how you slipped out of the fortress unseen. Can you help me?"

The boy sniffled, wiping his eyes with the back of his hand. He described a drainage ditch, and stones in the wall damaged by water, and a cliff outside the fortress wall. "The goat path down is very steep," he said, his voice barely a whisper. "I slipped many times and almost fell, but I crawled away."

"What about the guards?" Talya asked.

"The guards—they don't watch the cliff."

Talya grabbed a stick and sketched the fortress in the dirt. "Can you show me where the stones are damaged?"

Leboo took the stick and drew a wavy line along one side of the fortress. "This is the cliff, and this is where I crawled out and where Nuru crawled inside."

"Someone went in?" Talya asked.

Leboo nodded. "Nuru. He is Maasai—lions fear him. He gave me this." He touched the rungu tucked into his belt, his grip firm despite his trembling fingers. "To guide me and give me strength. I came to Kibale with a message for a warrior—for your friend."

Before Talya could ask about Nuru and the message, the sound of a vehicle racing toward Kibale cut through the air, sending a fresh wave of panic through the boy. He tried to pull away, but Talya held on.

"It's alright," she said firmly. "These are our friends. Warriors. Like Kate."

***

TUESDAY, MAY 5th
3:40 PM WAT

HUAMBO BASE, ANGOLA

THE SUN DIPPED LOW as Jordan approached Huambo Base. *Unannounced at a remote base in a military vehicle. Yeah, this won't end well.* He was right. The response was instant. A flash of muzzle fire from the guard tower.

Jordan braked hard, tires skidding. Heart pounding. *Here we go.*

He moved slow. Deliberate. Hands out first, palms up. One breath. Then another. He reached for the door, opening it from the outside, then stepped out—slow, controlled. A full turn, showing empty hands before lowering to his knees.

A covert team of soldiers, hidden in the brush behind the Humvee, rushed forward. They tackled him, slamming his chest into the asphalt. He didn't brace himself, keeping his arms outstretched and motionless. Pain shot through him as his chest scraped the ground, but he bit back a groan. *No sudden movements*, he knew. *Don't give some idiot a reason to squeeze the trigger.*

They searched him quickly, zip-tying his hands behind his back before marching him through the gate. Behind him, the Humvee remained under watch. A quick check of the exterior was done with an under-vehicle inspection mirror, but the guards were clearly not ready to get too close. A sentry stayed behind, eyeing the vehicle like it might explode at any second.

Jordan scanned the faces of the soldiers escorting him inside, but none looked familiar. They were too young—none had been here fifteen years ago. His gamble had been high-stakes from the start, and as they marched deeper into the base, the odds weren't looking any better. *Base records will confirm my identity*, he thought. *But will anyone remember? Or care?*

The two soldiers led him toward a Land Cruiser near the gate, one of them shoving him into the back seat. Another climbed behind the wheel, and they sped toward the base's headquarters. Jordan stared out the window, still searching for any familiar faces. *The base had changed—its layout, its people. This is not looking good.*

They arrived at HQ. With a sharp knock on the door, Jordan was ushered into the OOD's office. The door creaked open, and without so much as glancing up from his desk, the Officer of the Day muttered, "What is it now?" His tone suggesting he'd seen more than enough nonsense for one day and still had twelve hours left on his shift. Jordan squinted, trying to make out the man's features, but with his head down, it was impossible to tell if they knew each other.

The guards explained the situation—a man in a military Humvee at the gate, unarmed but arriving out of the blue. The OOD finally lifted his head, his bored expression shifting as he realized this was no routine annoyance. He looked Jordan over, his eyes narrowing.

Captain Miguel "Migs" Pereira's head snapped up. Recognition flickered—then a slow, disbelieving grin.

"Jordan?"

Jordan smirked. "Migs. About damn time."

Migs barked out a laugh. "You son of a—" He waved the guards off, jerking his chin toward the restraints. "Cut him loose."

The moment Jordan's hands were free, Migs pulled Jordan into a rough hug, slapping his back hard. "You look like hell."

Jordan flexed his wrists, shaking out the stiffness. "And you got fat."

Migs threw back his head and laughed. "Still a smartass. Some things never change."

"Could you ask them to bring up the Humvee?" Jordan asked. "Just a suggestion—tell your men to keep their hands to themselves this time."

With a stern look, Migs relayed the order in Portuguese, sending the guards off to retrieve the vehicle.

Once they were alone, Jordan leaned against the desk, tension finally easing from his shoulders. "I can't tell you how relieved I am to see a friendly face," he said, running a hand over his short-cropped hair.

"You're lucky I'm on duty," Migs replied, crossing his arms. "If it had been anyone else, you'd be locked up right now."

Jordan nodded. "That was a risk I had to take."

"I know you didn't drop out of the sky for a social visit," Migs said, raising an eyebrow. "What's going on?"

Jordan sighed. "Trident Security," he began, knowing the name would carry weight. "You heard about the Paris terrorist attack? Jake Church?"

Migs nodded slowly. "The whole world saw it. Hell of a tragedy."

"Jake was my boss and my friend. His widow, Kate, was traveling with Isabella Marquez when they were taken."

Migs's expression darkened. "It's all over the news, Jordan. It's a media shitstorm."

Jordan exhaled, the weight of the situation hanging heavy in the air. "Public already? Damn."

"Look, if you're here to ask for help," Migs added, his voice firm, "I can tell you right now—we can't get involved."

"Just hear me out," Jordan said, holding up a hand. "Our team's already in place. We'll do all the wet work. We just need a ride. Can't get all those kids out of there without one of your troop carriers, and I saw your Mi-17 helos just sitting on the deck."

Migs's jaw tightened. "Impossible. You know how this works. Even if I wanted to help, which I don't, there's no way my superiors would sign off."

"You know the old saying," Jordan began. "Better to ask forgiveness…"

"Maybe that works in your world, but in mine, I've got to see the big picture," Migs replied. "I'm two years from retirement. This stunt could land me out on my ass—no rank, no pension."

Jordan eyed him. "Got soft, Migs. Married? Kids?"

Migs' jaw tightened. "Boy, twelve. Girl, nine."

Jordan smiled faintly. "Cute age. Now, imagine them worked to death in a coltan mine, soldiers abusing them at night."

Migs's jaw clenched, arms crossed, eyes fixed on Jordan's, but he said nothing.

Seeing Migs was resolute, Jordan pressed. "Look, I know what I'm asking isn't fair, and I wouldn't be here if I had *any* other option. I came for the chopper and never dreamt I'd find you—I don't think that's a coincidence. You're the best damn pilot I know, and if anyone can pull this off, it's you."

Migs stood and paced, his expression hard. "This isn't just about skill, Jordan. If this mission goes sideways, and I end up in jail or dead—my family's out on the streets. I can't risk it. I'm sorry, I won't."

Jordan met his eyes, unwavering. "What if I guaranteed your family's future?"

Migs raised an eyebrow. "Are you seriously trying to bribe me?"

"No," Jordan said, his voice quieter but fierce. "I'm begging you. Those kids are my responsibility, and the team trying to save them, they're *my* family. Without you, they're all going to die, so I swear, on everything I hold dear, if you help me—no matter the outcome, Trident will take care of you and your family."

Migs locked eyes with Jordan. Neither spoke. Then—he stuck out his hand.

"You've got a chopper and pilot," Migs began. "But I need more than your word. Call whoever you need to call to nail this down. Brother, we might both die tonight, so someone besides the two of us needs to know the deal."

"Hand me the phone," Jordan said, and he started dialing. "You know if this works—correction, when this works, I can see the headline—Captain Miguel Pereira's daring rescue saves the hostages from certain death."

Migs barked a laugh. "Let's hope they spell my name right. So, what's in the Humvee?"

Jordan smiled. "Twenty cases of Coors, thirty cases of Red Bull."

Migs's eyebrows shot up. "That's it? That's all you brought?"

Jordan shrugged. "You can keep the Humvee."

***

TUESDAY, MAY 5th
6:07 PM CAT

PRISON, FORTRESS KRASNAYA SKALA

THE RUMBLE OF THE truck echoed through the compound as it passed through the main gate. But it was the grinding of the truck's gears and the squeal of brakes just outside the prison door that confirmed Kate's suspicion.

With the last rays of light seeping through the ceiling vents, Kate knew this must be the truck returning the children from the mine. She looked at Nuru, and he nodded.

"Bella," Kate whispered. "The children from the mine are returning." Bella's eyes told her she didn't need to say more—both knew this moment was coming and would be heartbreaking.

The prison door creaked open, and the murmur of voices outside grew louder, accompanied by the sharp commands of the guards. And then the children shuffled in.

Kate's gut twisted. The first child shuffled in—feet dragging, clothes tattered, eyes empty. The guards shoved them inside, mixing them in with the new arrivals, filling all the cells.

The kids from the mines, hardened by the sun and labor, didn't even turn to greet the new arrivals. They didn't have the strength to care. Too exhausted, too far gone to see the new arrivals as anything more than reminders of their own past.

The new children—the ones taken from Kibale—hadn't moved from the corners where they had huddled all day. They stared, wide-eyed, as the guards herded the returning children into the cells, their movements mechanical, expressions deadened by exhaustion.

Kate could see it in their wide, terrified eyes. The children from Kibale understood what was coming—these children, who were once like them, now reduced to shadows, withered and broken.

The guards uttered a few sharp commands before slamming the door shut. The sound of the bolt sliding into place reverberated through the dim room, leaving behind an oppressive silence broken only by the ragged breathing of those too tired to control it.

The Kibale children pressed closer together, seeking some kind of comfort being near one another. The veterans, the ones who had been working the mines for months, simply collapsed onto the dirt floor, some leaning against the walls, others laying down where they stood, too exhausted to do anything but surrender to the darkness.

Kate swallowed hard. She wanted to tell them but couldn't afford to act. Not yet. Any whisper of an escape could derail the entire plan, and in their state, she couldn't blame a desperate child for trading information for food or favors. She had to wait.

Bella's voice trembled. "This is breaking my heart. How can they let this happen?"

Kate's jaw tightened, but she said nothing. There was no answer that would make sense. The men who ran this place were driven by greed, their hearts long since hardened to suffering. The children were nothing more than tools—just animals to be used until they broke or died.

"Tonight, the village kids share their food," Kate murmured. "The others need it more, and we need their trust. When the time comes, you'll be in charge."

"What are you talking about?" Bella asked. "What's coming?"

Kate pulled Bella as far away from the others as their small cage allowed. She cupped a hand over Bella's ear and whispered. "Do not react," Kate began. "Your diversion in the compound today allowed Talya to deliver a message."

"Talya?" Bella mouthed.

"Yes," Kate continued. "We're getting out of here tonight, but we can't risk the kids finding out—not yet. That's where you come in."

"Me?" Bella questioned. "What about you or Nuru?"

"The Colonel has plans for me," Kate whispered. "And these kids? They need a leader. That's you. Now, here's what I need you to do..."

Chapter 62

FORTRESS KRASNAYA SKALA

THE LIGHTS FLICKERED ON. The guards were back. One ran his nightstick along the bars, the grating sound keeping the children on edge.

"You," the guard barked. "Hands through."

Kate saw the thick, braided rope, sparking Jake's escape training. *Elbows flared out, he would say. And tight fists.* She didn't expect to be left alone, not tonight, but the tension would create slack when she relaxed. *Never throw away an opportunity.*

The guards opened the cell, pulled her out, and locked it again behind her.

"Where are you taking her?" Bella asked.

"The Colonel wants to have a little chat," one of them said, and they exchanged a knowing look that was unmistakable.

"It's alright, Bella," Kate said. "I was expecting to spend a little quality time with the Colonel. And you know what to do."

The guards pushed Kate out the door, but just as they were just about to turn off the light, Kate struck. Her knee found a home in the guard's groin, and when he doubled over, the back of her elbow came down on his neck. He lay on the deck, his hands cradling his bruised nuts, moaning and rocking. The butt of a rifle struck Kate in the back, and she fell forward to her knees.

"OK. OK," she said, raising her hands above her head.

"Get up," the guard spat. Kate stood, locking eyes with him.

He lifted his rifle, ready to strike.

Kate smirked. "Careful. The Colonel might pick you first."

The guard flinched, lowered his rifle, and kicked the other guard's foot to get him moving.

Finally, upright, the injured guard brushed off his uniform.

"Your death will be slow." the guard moaned.

Kate smiled. "Not yours."

***

9:04 PM CAT

"LISTEN CAREFULLY," BELLA SAID, waiting for silence. "Do exactly as I say."

Bella scanned every cell, all eyes were on her, listening intently.

"Raise your hand if you are the oldest boy or girl in your cell," she said. "Higher. I need to see you. Those of you with hands held high, you're captains. You're responsible for everyone in your cell. Now, take a minute and count them—twice."

She watched as the cell captains counted the children in their charge.

"I'm about to tell you something," Bella began. "And you must promise not to make a sound. Not one word. If the guards hear you, they'll come back. Are you ready?"

Bella glanced across at the wide eyes and nodding heads. "This is the last night you will spend in these cells."

The murmur that erupted was quickly silenced, the cell captains taking control exactly as Kate predicted.

"Well done," Bella said. "The lights give us time to prepare. When they go out, move to the back wall and face it. No talking. No looking. The people coming for us will open the cells, but it will be bright and loud. Stay still until they tell us it's safe. Then you do exactly as they say. Understood?"

Bella glanced at her watch—just a few minutes after nine. Her heart was already racing, and her hands trembling.

"You did well," Nuru said. "The children are ready. Now sit, take my hands, and close your eyes. There is still much to do. Kate's journey is far from over, and she will need your help."

***

9:11 PM CAT

COLONEL NKRUMAH'S OFFICE

THE GUARD KNOCKED.

"Enter," Nkrumah purred.

A rough shove sent Kate stumbling inside. She locked onto *The Hyena's* twisted smile. He had discarded his uniform, lounging in a short-sleeved shirt, the top buttons undone.

"Evening, Ms. Preacher," he drawled, his eyes gleaming. "I trust you've been enjoying your stay."

"It's *Mrs.* Preacher," she replied. "And no, you won't be happy with my TripAdvisor review."

"Yes, of course," he sneered, his voice dripping with mockery. "The widow of *l'Américain*. My sincerest apologies—and condolences."

The guards held Kate's arms as Nkrumah stepped toward her. He grabbed the rope tied to the wall and loosened it, lowering the hook overhead toward her wrists. One guard slid the hook between her bound hands, then gave it a sharp tug to ensure it held.

The Colonel pulled on the rope, lifting Kate's arms toward the ceiling. Her body stretched until she was balancing on the tips of her boots, her muscles straining under the tension. He wrapped and secured the end of the rope. Satisfied, Nkrumah dismissed the guards with a wave.

***

9:13 PM CAT

SAMIR'S TRUCK STOPPED AT the main gate, and the guard tower's blinding lights lit up the entire entrance area.

"Why have you returned?" the guard demanded.

"It wasn't my idea," Samir grumbled. "These roads are treacherous enough during the day, but Colonel Nkrumah insisted. He said the men who are coming will want to celebrate. I brought more food and vodka. Lots of vodka."

"You're not on the list."

"A mere oversight, I'm sure," Samir said. "You should ask him. I can wait."

The guard hesitated for a moment and then signaled for the main gate crew to let them enter.

"Go," the guard ordered. "Quickly. You must be off the road before the convoy arrives, or they will push you off."

Samir pulled inside the gate and stopped. A pair of guards did a cursory inspection. A flashlight passed over the faces of Talya and Rami in the front seat, across the floorboard of the cab, and the crates in the covered truck bed. The moment the guard waved Samir through, he sped toward the warehouse and backed the truck into position.

Rami hopped out. Talya took her time climbing down, her abaya and niqab, hiding both her identity and the H&K MP7 strapped to her leg. In the abaya, Talya hoped to remain virtually invisible and ignored by the men of the fortress, but when it was time to go to guns, she could snatch the compact submachine from her thigh. The forty-round magazine filled with high-velocity, armor-piercing rounds was a devastating weapon.

As Samir and Rami unloaded a half-dozen crates, Talya prepared a small stack of blankets—sliding a pistol in the middle. She hid in the warehouse while Samir and Rami returned to the truck and headed for the main gate. Rami ran his left hand up another abaya like a puppet, just in case, but the guards were eager to clear the road and waved them straight through.

The minute the truck left and the gate closed, Talya was moving. Her goal: the power station. No recon. Unknown threats. She kept one hand beneath the blankets, the other gripping a suppressed P365 as she approached the station.

A lone guard leaned against the wall—bored, cigarette dangling. When he spotted Talya, he straightened and let the cigarette fall, pretending to take his job seriously. With a quick glance at the guard towers and confirmation that no one saw her approach, she held out the blankets like she was handing them over.

"I didn't request any blankets," he began. "It's not that cold tonight."

But Talya counted on reflex taking over, and it did. The guard reached out to accept the blankets. Talya put two rounds in his chest, opened the door behind him, and let him fall inside.

Gun up and scanning for anyone inside, Talya confirmed the interior was empty. Reaching inside the abaya, she pressed the mic button on her comm unit. Her double-click signaling all clear.

***

9:16 PM CAT

THE TRIDENT SECURITY TEAM positioned themselves on the cliff face, just beyond the rear sentry's view. With Talya's confirmation, the mission was a go. Mike monitored the guard's movements and was the first to clear the top of the cliff, hugging the east wall until he had line of sight on the guard. He stood ready to fire if needed.

Forest, Deon, and Logan climbed over the cliff face, gliding along the wall until they reached the drainage ditch. Deon pulled a hooligan pry bar out of the top of his pack, like he was drawing a samurai sword, and wedged it into the rotting grout. It was exactly as Leboo described. The boy's hole wasn't quite large enough for the team and their packs, and brick by brick, the hole grew wider.

With a fist raised to his shoulder, Mike signaled the team to hold. The guard turned toward the ravine, looked down, and spat. When he turned back toward the compound, Mike signaled, and work continued.

Forest checked the time. *It's not wide enough*, he thought. *And we're running out of time.*

When Forest slipped his pack off, the team followed.

Deon was the first through the hole, and one by one, they passed the kit through. Logan's Broco TACMOD was the challenge, but the exothermic torch was the key to cutting the cells holding the kids.

Mike stood ready to take the shot. Logan pulled, and the backpack popped inside.

They were in, gear back on and NODs up. *Talya has the ball*, Forest thought. *Now we wait.*

***

9:17 PM CAT

RONIN'S SNIPER HIDE

REED AND KABE WORKED their way down the mountain and set the new overwatch location. Reed's estimate was about right. The laser range finder confirmed he could cover the central compound area easily between 380 and 460 meters.

Kabe waited, a thermal monocular in hand.

"If you spot Mirov," Reed began. "Call out the location and range."

"Just remember, he's the mission," Kabe said. "My wife's life is in your hands."

"Stop worrying. I've got this."

With the DRS SPARTN-E clipped to the rail of the AXMC rifle, Reed had the benefit of his NightForce optics but could activate the thermal night sight when the time came. Watching the delivery truck pass through the main gate with the same three occupants who visited earlier, he knew it wouldn't be long.

Reed kept his eye on the warehouse and watched the truck pull away. *I knew you'd stay*, he thought, noting only the two men in the cab. *Here she comes.* He followed Talya's exit from the warehouse but spotted movement behind her. *You've got company.*

If someone lurking in the warehouse realized Talya stayed behind, she's dead, and the mission's over. His finger hovered over the trigger.

"It's just a boy," Kabe said. "He was hiding in the warehouse."

"Damn it, kid. You almost blew the whole op." Reed exhaled, easing off the trigger. *He has no idea how close he came to getting his head ventilated.*

Reed scanned the compound for Talya, but her intent and purpose were easy to predict. "Power station it is," he mumbled. "Won't be long now, Kabe."

***

9:18 PM CAT

COLONEL NKRUMAH'S OFFICE

KATE KNEW HER SECRET was about to be revealed. She worked hard to keep her scars hidden beneath carefully chosen clothes and appreciated Bella's sensitivity in curating her travel options. Normally timid about anyone seeing them, she looked forward to what might happen. She needed to buy some time, distract him—and she couldn't imagine a better way.

Nkrumah reached for the knife he had taken from Kate when they first met—the curved Karambit she'd kept at her waist. Sharp as a lion's claw and twice as deadly, it was a terrifying weapon, lethal in skilled hands. In Kate's hands, Nkrumah would already be bleeding out on the floor. But this was his show, and she could see his intent—to get her heart racing and adrenaline pumping.

The knife's finger ring, the large hole at the base of the hilt, let him spin the knife around like a gunfighter in an old western. But it was a hollow performance. When Kate's eyes didn't flash the fear he sought, his grin twisted with frustration. He moved on.

With a swift motion, he slashed through the fabric of Kate's safari shirt. Buttons flew off, and the shirt fell open. Beneath, Kate wore a khaki-colored sleeveless crop tank, the crew neck collar cleverly hiding her scars. He slipped the curved tip of the blade into the top of the tank, slashing downward.

The tank top split effortlessly, exposing Kate's neck, breasts, and abs and revealing the labyrinth of raised scars.

For a moment, the Colonel stared, mesmerized, like a moth drawn to a flame. They were irresistible. His left hand reached out to touch them, and as if they were an illusion that might vanish, his movements were slow and deliberate. Touching Kate's bare skin was electric, the tip of his finger tracing a single scar that separated left and right into mirror images.

With the blade in his right hand, he brushed the torn fabric away to follow the lines as they weaved and curved. His expression was one of perverse admiration.

"A master's work," he murmured, the corner of his mouth lifting in a grin. "Though I suspect you would not agree. May I ask the origin?"

"Syrian," Kate replied, seizing the opportunity to delay the inevitable. "The blade was Damascus steel."

"And the owner?"

"His name was Suliaman," Kate replied. "Claimed the blade had tasted the blood of enemies and infidels for centuries."

"Was?" Nkrumah asked, catching Kate's hint. "He's dead?"

"Oh yes," Kate said, smiling. "Cut out his heart and shoved it down his throat."

"You look pleased," Nkrumah said. "Did you kill him?"

"A friend."

The Colonel chuckled darkly. "You have dangerous friends."

"You have no idea," Kate said coldly.

Nkrumah tightened the rope again, leaving Kate with little chance to move. He circled her like a predator, dragging the Karambit lightly along the scars, enjoying her discomfort. He was in control, and Kate knew that this was the moment he craved—total dominance over his victims.

Kate strained against the rope as it pulled her bound wrists high above her head, stretching her body so tight the tips of her boots barely grazed the floor. The hook groaned under the tension, pulling her arms painfully upward. She felt her body strain under the pressure, every inch extended to its limit.

"I can't bear to touch an artist's work," he began. "Fortunately, your back is a blank canvas. Shall we begin?"

The tip of the blade dipped into Kate's back. She clenched her teeth, feeling the warm trickle of blood run down her back.

The lights flickered.

Nkrumah cursed under his breath. "Not again. Not now."

Kate's heart pounded, but Jake's voice echoed in her mind: *Any second now. You've got this.*

The Colonel lowered the knife, walked to the window, and peered outside. The fortress plunged into total darkness.

Kate's arms strained as she pulled against the rope. Her biceps burned, her shoulders screamed, and her core tightened. Curling her knees to her chest, she jackknifed her body upward—her boots reaching for the ceiling beam. The hook groaned under the tension, but her eyes locked on her only path to freedom.

The Colonel laughed in the darkness. "Buck, wiggle, and squirm all you want," he sneered. "Like a hooked fish—you're not going anywhere."

Her boots gripped the beam. With a final burst of strength, she pulled herself up, wrapping her legs tightly around it. Her arms remained taut, muscles bulging as she hauled her body higher. The pressure on her wrists eased, and the hook slipped free.

The emergency lights flickered, casting an eerie yellow glow—and revealing she was gone.

Kate let go of the beam and dropped. Her boots hit the concrete with a thud, the impact echoing through the still room. She crouched low, wrists still bound, but her fingers were all she needed to reach the knife Talya had tucked into her boot.

The Colonel's eyes widened, but Kate sensed more delight than surprise.

"I see the kitten has claws," he said. "Impressive."

Nkrumah laughed and slashed, the karambit flashing in the golden light. Kate twisted, but the blade nicked her arm. She didn't feel the sting, only the warmth of blood seeping through the cut.

He's stronger. He has the reach, Kate thought. *But I'm faster. And smarter.*

She feigned a stumble, baiting him. He took it.

He lunged, blade raised. She sidestepped, her knife slicing low across his belly. Shallow—but enough to stop him.

He glanced down at the wound, then chuckled, a tinge of frustration creeping into his arrogance. "My wife's cat has drawn more blood."

He doesn't know. He doesn't see it.

Like a chess master, Kate had already moved her next piece.

He charged.

Kate spun. Her bound hands snatched Nuru's spear as she twisted.

In one fluid motion, she drove it into Nkrumah's chest.

His own momentum carried him forward, forcing the spear deeper. His massive frame sagged, dropping to his knees. Blood bubbled at his lips.

Kate twisted the blade. Felt it tear through organs. His body convulsed—a final spasm of disbelief.

"The old man..." Nkrumah choked, each breath a wet struggle. Blood gurgled in his throat, spilling over his chin. "The shaman...he said...you weren't the one."

Kate planted her boot on his chest.

Yanked the spear free.

The sound—wet, final.

Nkrumah collapsed backward, blood pooling beneath him—the same stain so many others had left behind.

His glassy eyes locked onto hers. Lips moved, but no sound came.

"The shaman..."

Kate knelt beside him, close enough for him to see the truth in her eyes.

Cold. Unflinching.

"He lied."

***

9:36 PM CAT

Talya kicked open the door, weapon up—only to find Kate, spear raised. They both lowered their weapons.

In the yellow glow of the emergency lighting, Talya saw Nkrumah dead on the floor, and Kate's bound hands, torn clothing, and bare skin streaked with blood. *Whatever happened in here*, Talya thought. *I like the way it ended—but can't go out looking like that.*

She freed Kate's hands, then unbuckling her tactical vest, held it out. "Put this on," Talya whispered. "Things are about to go kinetic."

Kate slipped on the vest, grateful for the coverage, and Talya led the way out of Nkrumah's office. Kate tapped Talya on the shoulder, asking her to hold.

The guards that escorted Kate were dead, both shot in the head at close range. "You won't be needing this," she whispered to the man on the floor, grabbing his AK, a couple of spare mags, and tucking his handgun into her waist. "I said you'd die fast."

While Kate seized the opportunity to gear up, Talya signaled Kate was secure. Forest replied with a double, good-copy mic-click.

Kate's hand signal instructed Talya to lead on, and she followed.

Talya glanced back at Kate, noting the rifle slung over her shoulder—and the spear clutched in her left hand. She raised an eyebrow. "I don't think you'll need that."

Kate tightened her grip on the bloodstained spear and smirked.

"I promised a friend I'd return it—when I was done."

"Fair enough," Talya said, turning back to the corridor. "Just keep the pointy end downrange."

Kate's flicker of a smile faded as she drew in a slow, steadying breath. They were far from done.

She followed Talya into the chaos.

Chapter 63

TUESDAY, MAY 5th
9:37 PM CAT

PRISON, FORTRESS KRASNAYA SKALA

In the darkness, Logan and Deon moved between buildings, their helmet-mounted night vision giving them the clarity to move freely. Their suppressed weapons and expertise allowed them to clear a few obstacles along the way. The casual response to the power outage came as a surprise but one they used to their advantage. While the prison guards waited for the lights, laughing and smoking, a pair of synchronized headshots put them both down. Logan and Deon dragged the bodies out of the way and slipped into the prison.

Inside, the children lined up, facing the back wall—Kate had prepared them well. Logan cranked the oxygen valve, igniting the Broco torch. Sparks sprayed as he cut through the top rail, then the center and bottom bars. He shoved the door open and moved to the next.

As Logan's torch roared, Deon kept his rifle trained on the exit, scanning for movement. The prison, old and crumbling, had once swallowed light whole, sealing its captives in absolute darkness. But time had changed that. Cracks now riddled its vents, its walls—small fractures that let in the faintest threads of starlight. And if light could get in, Deon knew, light could get out. The Broco torch's glow, flickering and wild, might already be bleeding into the night.

He tightened his grip on his rifle. Someone was bound to notice. And when they did, they'd have to be dealt with—quietly, before it was too late.

***

9:38 PM CAT

RONIN'S SNIPER HIDE

REED WATCHED THE PAIR of Trident Operators work their way from the east wall toward the prison. *There must have been a way up and in from the cliff—nice work, boys,* he thought. Next stop will be the kids, and that means cutting up the cell doors. *Logan's got the torch. Looks like Deon's got his back. Alright, it's show time.*

The Trident Team didn't know Reed was on overwatch, or that by the time they reached the prison, he'd already taken out three tangos. *Just like old times. I could do this all night.*

And the minute Reed saw light flickering on the prison roof, he knew there would be trouble. *I get it,* Reed thought. *You need to move fast, but someone is going to see your light show.*

He scanned the compound, looking for targets. Anyone who turned to see what was happening at the prison found themselves in Reed's sight and their head's obliterated. Reed was cycling the bolt as fast as he could to get right back on target. A magazine change added an extra second, and a soldier was just reaching for the prison door when Reed took him out.

From the prison roof, the sparking bursts of light finally stopped. *Alright. They're done.*

Reed exhaled, satisfied. "I lost count—did you catch it?"

"Eleven," Kabe said, disappointed.

"What's the matter?"

"None were Mirov."

Reed smirked. "Give it a minute. This place is about to explode, and Mirov will come running."

***

9:40 PM CAT

DEON TRIED TO OPEN the prison door but had to shove a body to get it open. He slipped outside, grabbed the soldier's feet, and dragged him toward the shadows. *Don't need the kids tripping over a body,* he thought, and he looked around. *Glad somebody had our back.* He took the soldier's sidearm, racked the slide, and headed back inside.

Logan cut through all fourteen cells in just over a minute, then dumped the torch and grabbed his rifle.

Isabella turned, blinking at the sudden dark. Her hands found the open door, and she stepped into the corridor.

Logan was closest and turned on a red-light headlamp. "What's your name, ma'am?" Logan asked.

"Isabella," she replied. "Isabella Marquez. Kate told us you were coming and to face the wall."

"Yes, ma'am," he said. "That was helpful." He handed Bella a headlamp. "Now, please line them up along the corridor. Best they sit down and cover their ears. Under no circumstances go out that door."

"Can you shoot?" Deon asked.

"Hell, yes."

"Take this," Deon said, handing Bella his pistol. "When your ride is here, we'll pound on the door three times. If anyone else opens that door..."

"I got this," Bella said. "We'll be waiting."

Deon and Logan moved from the prison into their staging positions near the main gate and guard towers and signaled the team. Everyone knew the kids were free and secure. Time to get serious.

***

LEBOO SLIPPED FROM THE warehouse, creeping toward the officer's quarters. He knew exactly where to find Major Mirov—and what the man would be doing. He hoped Nuru was right—and soon, the others would be free. But Mirov's face haunted his every step, daring him to close his eyes. It followed him relentlessly, day and night. Leboo knew he wouldn't truly be free until that evil was gone—until Major Mirov was dead.

Armed with Nuru's rungu, Leboo moved with newfound courage. *I am a Maasai warrior,* he thought, gripping the club, feeling its weight. *Lions fear me.* But fear coiled tight in his chest. *Not a lion. A monster.*

Mirov's door stood unlocked, as always—no one dared enter. The candlelight flickered, casting long shadows across the room. Then Leboo saw him.

A boy. Tied to the bed. Silent. Trembling.

For a moment, the rungu in Leboo's grip felt heavier, his breath catching. *This is what he does,* Leboo realized. The rage that had burned inside him all these months ignited into something terrifying.

Leboo moved.

With a roar, he swung at Mirov's head.

Mirov turned, catching Leboo's arm mid-swing. The blow glanced off his cheek, drawing blood. He tasted it and laughed.

"Welcome back, Malysh, *little one,*" Mirov sneered, his voice thick with cruelty. "Did you miss me?"

With a savage yank, Mirov ripped the club from Leboo's hand and swung it hard, striking the boy on the side of the head. Leboo crumpled to the floor, still breathing but unconscious.

***

FOREST SMILED FOR THE first time in hours. Kate was safe, Bella and the kids were free. And now, with Kate armed, they'd picked up another gunfighter. But was Jordan coming? Forest had transmitted the show time, but there was no confirmation. Plan B was simple—hold the fortress, keep the Africa Corps at bay long enough for Jordan to show or the new government to respond. It felt a little too much like the Alamo, but Forest trusted Jordan's word. *He said he'd be here. He'll be here.*

From inside the compound, the guard towers were exposed. They defended against an advancing force, not a threat from within. Forest and Mike had the rear towers covered while Deon and Logan took the front. Four nearly simultaneous pops—four dead guards.

Talya and Kate covered the Muslim family quarters with one goal—keep the women and children inside, engage any combatants.

Deon and Logan cleared stairs as they climbed the front towers, noting the RPGs staged beside the sniper and rocket ports. Deon grabbed one on his way up to the parapet. Once on top, they turned the tower's PKM machine guns toward the compound. With a firing rate of over six hundred rounds per minute, controlling the tower weapons gave their small team a critical force multiplier.

***

FOREST CROUCHED IN THE shadow of the barracks, his breath steady, mind focused, the cool weight of an XM thermobaric grenade in his hand. Faint yellow emergency lights cast an eerie glow, silhouetting the edges of the structure. Inside, the muffled murmur of shuffling cards and muted conversation betrayed the complacency of the soldiers and militants within. Some were barely alert, others teetering on the edge of sleep, lulled by the late hour.

Mike took position near the barracks door, a matching XM grenade in his grasp. His eyes flicked to Forest, a silent signal of readiness. The unspoken understanding between them born of countless missions. Both men knew what was coming. Stealth had taken them as far as it could—their next move would shatter the quiet and the enemy.

Forest tapped his comm's press-to-talk (PTT) button twice in rapid succession, the mic clicks confirming to the rest of the team what they already knew—it was go time.

A final nod passed between the two operators, and with precise coordination, they pulled their pins and moved into action. Forest's grenade sailed through the open window, landing near the center of the room. Mike's throw was just as calculated, his grenade bouncing off a cement wall with a dull thud before rolling into the back corner of the barracks. Without hesitation, both men ducked into cover, bracing for the storm they had unleashed.

The first explosion erupted with a fiery bloom, a thunderous roar that shattered windows and sent waves of overpressure tearing through the barracks. The thermobaric grenade's intense heat and shockwave created an inferno of destruction, incinerating everything in its immediate radius. The detonation didn't just toss men from their seats—it obliterated the air they breathed, sucking oxygen from the room and leaving those caught within its reach gasping for life.

Milliseconds later, the second grenade detonated, amplifying the chaos. Flames roared through the structure, licking at the walls as the intense overpressure crushed anything left standing. The confined space turned into a furnace, suffocating anyone not instantly vaporized. Screams, already faint, faded into the roar of burning debris.

***

Major Mirov wasn't frightened. He was angry. The explosions were just the beginning, and he was experienced enough to know it. The power outage was no accident—not this time. An assault team was inside. *To have come this far,* he realized. *They must be very good.*

"I see you brought friends," he muttered, though Leboo couldn't hear him. "They have come for the woman," he murmured. "And the children. But I have you," he said, glancing down at the boy. "And I can reach the others."

Mirov glanced at the boy bound to the bed, dismissing him as unimportant, but Leboo was different. "You mean something to someone," he said, reaching for the boy. "And so does the woman."

Sweat gleamed on Mirov's shirtless body, his muscles flexing as he grabbed the boy and slung him over his shoulder in a crude fireman's carry. One massive arm locked around the boy's frail limbs, holding him effortlessly. With his other hand, Mirov grabbed the AK-47, the cold steel pressing against his hip.

He moved swiftly, the child's limp body draped over his back as Mirov crossed the room and jogged down the hall toward the rear exit. He calculated the assault team's tactical focus would be on the compound, barracks, and mess hall. That gave him a chance to reach the prison if he kept to the shadows along the fortress wall.

Survival was all that mattered now. Mirov had no intention of dying here—not for the others, not for anything. *I only need to reach the woman,* he thought. *Between her and the children, I can barter for my freedom.* It didn't matter how many died. The woman and children were leverage. Leverage kept men like him alive.

***

THE TWIN EXPLOSIONS TORE through the night, their concussive force rolling across the compound like thunder. In the mess hall, walls rattled, the floor shook. The room fell into stunned silence as the distant sounds of carnage echoed through the fortress—shattering glass, splintering wood, and the agonized cries of the dying.

Most of the rebels froze, their minds struggling to reconcile the horror of what they were hearing with the relative safety of the mess hall. Gunning down unarmed villagers hadn't prepared them for this. They gripped their rifles, their knuckles white, unsure whether to move or hide.

For a handful of veterans—men hardened by years of war, their survival instinct took control. Shoving their chairs back, they snatched up their AKs and headed for the door, determined to confront whatever enemy was tearing through their comrades.

The PKMs opened fire.

Deon and Logan, stationed in the guard towers, unleashed a coordinated barrage from the Soviet-made machine guns. The relentless mechanical chatter drowned out the rebels' shouts and panic. The first wave never had a chance. Bullets sliced through the air, ripping into the soldiers before they even cleared the threshold. They fell in heaps, their bodies crumpling on the steps, rifles still clutched in their hands.

Inside the mess hall, chaos erupted. Ricochets screamed off walls. The sickening thud of rounds striking flesh echoed through the room. Windows exploded inward under the onslaught as men scrambled for cover. But there was nowhere to hide. Some crouched behind overturned tables, wide-eyed and trembling, but they knew. Everyone knew. No one was getting out alive.

***

FOREST AND MIKE ROSE from cover, rifles at the ready, and moved into the barracks with seamless precision. The room was a chaotic haze of dust, smoke, and carnage, illuminated by the flickering glow of smoldering fires.

Their movements were a deadly, synchronized choreography, like great white sharks cutting through a pool of seals—silent, efficient, and lethal. Those who had miraculously avoided the initial blasts were too dazed and broken to resist, their cries of pain swiftly silenced as the operators methodically cleared the room. Suppressed shots barked in controlled bursts, ensuring there would be no resistance.

The room was a ruin, filled with acrid smoke and the glow of dying flames. Forest and Mike swept the area one last time, confirming their work before signaling the team. The barracks, once a stronghold of idle hostility, was now a smoldering tomb.

Forest and Mike held defensive positions and waited. In the distance, the roar of the PKM's echoed through the compound as Deon and Logan cleared the mess hall and secured the courtyard.

***

Talya and Kate crouched behind a wall of reinforced concrete as the assault erupted. The family quarters stayed dark, no one inside daring to move or even peek outside. But as the gunfire tapered off, the wounded called out, and the tortured wails of the women inside poured from the building.

Talya shouted in Arabic, warning them to stay inside. "Anyone who steps out will be shot!" she called.

One woman appeared in the doorway, cursing the men and threatening to leave. A burst of PKM fire sent her scurrying back inside.

Kate's eyes caught movement in a top-floor window. *Is someone peering outside,* she wondered.

"RPG!" she yelled, her voice echoing across the compound. Talya echoed the warning on comms, but too late.

The rocket fired, striking the guard tower. The explosion knocking Deon off his feet as the tower crumbled, taking his PKM down with it. Logan responded instantly, his PKM tearing through the top-floor window. Then, silence.

Kate leapt to her feet, ready to run to Deon's position, but Talya yanked her back down. "Mike and Forest are on the move," she said. "This is what they do—let them handle it."

Kate hesitated but nodded. Then she saw movement in the shadows.

"I saw something," Kate said, her eyes narrowing.

"Leave it," Talya replied, but Kate was already gone. Talya took off after Kate, cursed under her breath, and called out to the team, "Moving."

***

RONIN'S SNIPER HIDE

REED AND KABE MONITORED the chaos unfolding in the compound, both wondering if Mirov was still alive. It didn't matter who killed him or how. Dead was dead, and that was all it took to fulfill the contract.

But it wasn't going to be that easy.

Kabe spotted him first—Mirov slinking along the fortress wall, slipping between buildings, moving toward the prison.

Reed's thermal scope locked onto the target, the bright white silhouette stark against the background, made even clearer by Mirov's bare chest. But there was something else—the smaller outline slung over his shoulders.

A child.

Reed's jaw tensed. *No shot. Not with a kid in the line of fire.*

"Come on," he muttered, his voice tight. "Set him down."

Mirov neared the prison door.

"Here we go," Reed whispered. "It's the boy or the gun. You can't hang on to both."

His finger hovered over the trigger, the slightest pressure ready to end this.

Let's go. Just you and me.

Mirov leaned his AK against the wall.

"Shit," Reed hissed, his focus narrowing.

Inside that prison, dozens of children—scared, starved, and waiting for rescue.

If Mirov makes it inside, no one is coming out.

One shot. One life. To save them all—sorry, kid.

Mirov grabbed the door handle and yanked it open.

Reed's crosshairs stayed locked, but Mirov stumbled back, hands pressed to his abdomen.

"He's hit," Kabe called out. "She shot him!"

Reed's scope picked up Isabella Marquez, crouched low in the open doorway.

A slow grin curled across his lips.

He exhaled and fired.

A muffled shot rang out.

Mirov's head snapped back, brain matter spraying the prison wall.

***

Kate and Talya rounded the corner of the coltan warehouse just in time to see a large, shirtless man opening the prison door.

They heard the shot.

Watched him stumble back.

Saw the boy hit the ground.

"That's Leboo!" Kate shouted, raising her AK.

Before she could press the trigger, the man's head split open. He sagged to his knees, then toppled over.

A half-second later, the muffled report of a sniper rifle echoed from somewhere in the mountains above. No flash. No sign of movement. No way to calculate the distance. But the outcome was undeniable.

Kate exhaled sharply, scanning the ridge. *Who the hell—?*

She turned to Talya. "Is Jordan on overwatch?"

Talya hesitated. "No," she whispered. "I don't know who's out there."

Leboo stirred, his hand rising to his head. He shifted, then abruptly pushed himself back, away from the corpse lying beside him. His head turned, scanning the darkness, uncertain.

Kate started toward him, but Talya grabbed her arm.

"You can't," Talya said urgently. "Whoever's out there is still a threat."

Kate didn't flinch. Her voice was firm, unshaken. "Not to me."

"You can't know that."

"Trust me," Kate said, her voice steady. "I'm not the one in danger. Leboo is."

She kept her eyes on the boy. He was exposed, vulnerable—disoriented in the dim light, his movements uncertain. If he panicked, if he ran, he'd be an easy target.

"We need to get him behind cover, inside with the others."

Without another word, they rushed forward. Kate laid Nuru's spear on the ground next to Mirov's body and swept Leboo into her arms. Talya reached the prison door, pounded three times, and then pulled it open.

Isabella stood in the doorway, gun in hand. Her face lit up when she saw Kate. "Thank God!" Bella exclaimed. "Are you alright?"

"I'm fine," Kate replied, catching her breath. "But it's not over. Hang on to this one—he's the brave little man who warned me about the raid."

"Wait!" Leboo cried out. "There is another boy."

"Where?" Talya asked, her eyes scanning the area.

"That man," Leboo said, pointing to Mirov's body. "His quarters."

Kate crouched at Leboo's eye level. "We'll find him," she promised, then glanced inside the prison. A familiar face smiled at her. "And there's someone waiting to see you."

Leboo's eyes widened when he saw Nuru standing just inside the door. Without a second thought, he ran to the shaman and wrapped his small arms around Nuru's legs, tears streaming down his face.

"What's this?" Nuru asked gently.

"I tried to kill the lion," Leboo said through his tears. "The one who haunts my dreams. I thought I was Maasai."

"He is dead," Nuru said, his voice warm with pride. "Led to his fate by a true warrior. I know of no other so young and brave."

Chapter 64

PRESIDENTIAL PALACE, MABOKO, MOTAPA

KLAUS MUELLER PACED HIS palace suite, tension coiling tighter with each step. Bongani had finally relented, provisionally accepting GEC membership and requesting the Rapid Response team. *I've got him begging.*

A smug smile tugged at his lips, but his impatience gnawed at him. Mirov's silence wasn't just annoying—it was troubling.

When Klaus could wait no longer, he dialed the convoy's commander, Colonel Ivanov. If anyone could deliver, it was Ivanov—a man Klaus trusted more than most. A man who always got things done.

He keyed in the sat phone code and listened to the ringing. After two beats, the connection clicked.

"Ivanov," came the gravelly voice on the other end. Oleg Ivanov, the head of the Africa Corps convoy, wasn't one for pleasantries. A former Wagner mercenary, he was now Mueller's go-to man for all things coltan in Africa.

"Ivanov, it's Mueller. What the hell is happening out there? I can't reach Mirov," Mueller snapped, irritation edging closer to fury.

There was a pause, the sound of wind whipping through the truck's open windows. Ivanov's voice came back, tense.

"We're about twenty minutes out, but we hear explosions and gunfire," Ivanov said, frustration creeping into his words. "No response from the fortress."

Shouting erupted in the background. "What?" Mueller barked.

"Abandoned truck blocking the road. I ordered it pushed off the cliff—"

An explosion roared over the line—so loud Mueller jerked the phone away from his ear. Screams followed, faint but unmistakable.

"Ivanov!"

Silence. Then Ivanov's strained voice. "It was a trap. We lost men."

Mueller's face darkened, his jaw clenching. *Preacher*, he hissed to himself as if the name were a curse. "It has to be Trident Security," he said aloud. "I don't know how the hell they got in-country so fast, but they're not getting out."

Ivanov remained silent, waiting for orders.

Mueller's fury boiled over. "Get up there and kill them. Kill them all."

Ivanov paused, his tone cautious. "Everyone?"

Mueller's fury peaked. "No survivors. No loose ends. You understand me, Colonel?"

The line went dead. Mueller hurled the phone onto the bed, his chest tight with rage. *This has got to end,* he thought. *That bitch needs to die before she ruins everything I've spent decades building.*

Colonel Ivanov wiped the sweat from his brow, his gaze fixed on the burning wreckage of the transport truck smoldering on the mountain road. The bodies of the men closest to the blast lay scattered in the road. He turned to his remaining soldiers, his voice low and cold. "Get this wreck out of my way."

Several mercenaries scrambled to obey, casting uneasy glances toward the looming fortress in the distance.

"Colonel, what about the wounded?" one of them asked.

"Leave them," Ivanov replied, his tone leaving no room for argument. "We have our orders. No one leaves the fortress."

He tightened his grip on his rifle as the burning hulk of the truck was rolled into the ravine, disappearing into the darkness below. Ivanov muttered under his breath, "No one."

***

FORTRESS KRASNAYA SKALA

Forest was the first to break silence over comms. "What the hell was that?"

Talya responded quickly. "My friends buying us some time. Get someone to open the gate—we've got two more guns coming in. Kate and I are moving to the officer's quarters."

"Wait," Mike interrupted. "That area hasn't been cleared."

"Then we'll clear it," Talya replied. "There's a captive boy, and we're not leaving him to these animals."

Still disoriented from the guard tower collapse, Deon stumbled toward the main gate. While Logan kept the PKM trained on the compound, watching for enemy movement, Deon heaved the gate open. Two bearded men knelt outside, empty hands raised.

"I'm Samir, this is Rami," the shorter of the two began. "We're Talya's friends."

Deon blinked in confusion until Mike appeared, tapping him on the shoulder and taking over.

"Sounds like we owe you a truck," Mike said. "How long do we have?"

"Twenty minutes, maybe less," Samir replied. "You need that gun back on the road and rockets. This will be a full-frontal assault, and I see you've lost one of the tower guns."

"RPG," Mike said grimly. "From the Muslim quarters."

"There may be more," Rami added. "But clearing it room by room would be costly, and you don't have the time."

"You've done well," Samir said, scanning the defenses. "But you need to know, even if it's just a transport convoy, they'll be heavily armed—to protect the coltan."

"And they're mercenaries," Rami chimed in. "Ivanov commands them—he'll throw every man he has at these walls, no matter how many die."

Mike led them inside, and they helped Deon secure the gate. Rami took over the remaining tower PKM, adjusting its orientation back on the road. Meanwhile, Samir searched the guard tower and found exactly what he feared—a stash of RPG-7s. But the sight of the stacked grenades made his blood run cold.

"Look," Samir said, gesturing at the RPGs. "They've got standard PG-7 rounds, like the one that hit the tower. But they've also got OGs—fragmentation, anti-personnel."

Mike's eyes narrowed. "If we've got them, they came from Africa Corps."

"They could have TBGs," Samir added. "If they start firing thermobarics, this fortress won't just be a death trap—it'll be a furnace. Every blast will suck the air from our lungs, and the next one will turn what's left into fire and dust—there won't be bodies left to bury."

"I'll brief the others," Mike said, leaving Rami and Samir to hold the tower.

***

THE TEAM REGROUPED IN a corner of the compound, scanning for movement as they reviewed their dwindling options. Facing the threat of a thermobaric barrage, Forest's earlier image of the Alamo loomed larger than ever. The reality of running out of time meant facing dark options and tough choices—or they'd all die.

"If we leave now," Forest began, his voice tense, "we can get Kate and Isabella out through the east wall—down the cliff. It's dangerous, but fast enough to get out of range."

"And Africa Corps?" Logan asked. "When they breach the fortress, they'll follow us."

"That's why we move now," Forest said, a sense of finality settling over him. "We need a head start. They'll be on foot. We'll be mobile."

"And the kids?" Mike's voice was tight, the unspoken weight of his words pressing down on them all.

Forest met his gaze, his face grim. "We can't help them if we're dead. Our only shot at saving them is to get out alive and come back with help."

No one spoke, but the unthinkable truth settled over them. Abandoning the children would break their hearts. Offering hope, only to leave them to die, was a burden none of them wanted to carry.

That's when Kate and Talya joined the huddle, Talya cradling a small boy wrapped in a blanket. Kate's eyes blazed with fierce determination.

"By the time you can return, there'll be no one left to save," Kate said, her voice low but firm. "Whoever's behind this won't leave any witnesses. They'll make sure there's nothing left. I've seen it before. They'll erase every trace—like it never happened."

"Kate, if we stay, we die," Forest warned, his tone sharpening with urgency.

"Then go," Kate said. "Take Isabella—drag her out if you have to. The world needs to hear this. They'll listen to her."

Forest protested, but she cut him off, calm, unshaken.

"I'm staying. Death doesn't scare me. Failing does."

He clenched his jaw, torn between the unbearable truth of her words and the instinct to protect her. Searching her face for hesitation, he found none.

"Hold it!" Talya called out, her voice sharp. "You hear that? We've got company."

The sound of massive twin engine rotors sweeping up from the ravine was unmistakable.

"Alpha One," Forest's radio crackled to life. "This is Mi-17. Did someone call for an Uber?"

The Mi-17 rose from the cliff's shadow like a bird of prey. Hovering over the fortress, the pilot scanning the compound for a landing zone.

"Mi-17," Forest replied, relief seeping into his voice. "Damn good to see you, brother."

Mike never took his eyes off the Muslim family quarters, rifle up, scanning the windows. The moment he saw the grenade launcher tip in the window, he was already firing.

"RPG!" Mike shouted, squeezing the trigger. His rounds ripping through the walls, shattering glass. The gunner jerked, but the rocket fired, streaking toward the helicopter.

The Mi-17 veered hard left, its undercarriage scraping the fortress wall. The rocket barely missed, passing just beneath the aircraft. Mike's burst punched through the window—blood sprayed, and the RPG tumbled from the shooter's lifeless hands.

"Mi-17," Forest called, "the compound's compromised, and we've got company incoming. ETA ten minutes."

Jordan's voice returned after a brief pause. "Alpha One, punch a hole in the east wall. We'll be waiting on the other side."

Forest grabbed Deon's shoulder. "You're with me. Talya, you and Kate get back to the prison. When you hear the blast, get the kids moving to the east wall. Mike, Logan, clear a path from the prison through the courtyard. Nobody moves in that building," Forest added, nodding toward the Muslim family housing. "Don't risk another rocket. They move, they die. Got it? Go."

Kate led the way, Talya close behind, the boy held tight to her chest, his arms wrapped around her neck. Mike and Logan flanked them, scanning for any signs of movement. Kate pounded on the door three times, and it swung open.

"Take the boy inside," Kate ordered. "I'll be right back," she said, closing the door before Talya could protest.

Kate knelt beside Mirov's body, snatching Nuru's rungu from his belt. Her hand lingered on the spear she had laid nearby. Rising slowly, she stood tall, the spear gripped like a Maasai warrior preparing for battle. Her eyes scanned the hills, searching. Kate knew Marcus was there—it had to be him, and the weight of the moment settled over her. She raised the spear, a silent salute, mouthing, "Thank you."

She pounded three times, and the heavy prison door opened. Closing it behind her, she handed Nuru the spear, streaked now with blood. "You set me up," Kate said, her voice a mix of exhaustion and wonder. "You knew all along, didn't you?"

Nuru's eyes sparkled as he smiled and shrugged. "I saw only what was within you—and within your grasp," he replied. "Some say a warrior's spear chooses its battles." His gaze lingered on the spear. "I would say it chose wisely."

Talya turned to the kids. "We'll be leaving soon."

Bella took command. "Just like we practiced. Everyone holds hands. Captains, track your team. Eyes on the back of the person in front. No matter what you see or hear, do not let go." Bella turned to Talya and introduced her to the kids. "This is Talya. She'll lead us out."

Nuru pulled Kate aside. "When you're all safely away, I will return home."

"You're not coming with us?"

"No," Nuru said gently. "I go the way I came. You never know who you might meet on the journey."

Kate wrapped her arms around him, her throat tightening as she fought tears. There was so much she didn't understand, couldn't believe. "Thank you," she whispered, kissing his cheek.

"We will speak again," Nuru said calmly. "Just as before—come find me where the three rivers meet."

"It may be a while," Kate said.

"I know," Nuru replied, his voice tinged with sorrow. "I see it too."

***

FOREST CROUCHED LOW BY the east wall, his fingers tracing the worn bricks and decayed grout. The drainage ditch had done half the work for them, eroding much of the stone, but the wall was still nearly a meter thick in places.

The Mi-17 hovered out of range, ready to move in once the charges went off.

Deon was already prepping the C-4 as Forest set the location. They laid the linear charges along the weak points, ensuring they'd punch a hole large enough for everyone to get through quickly. They had one shot before the Africa Corps assault arrived.

With the charges set, they got well clear of the blast zone—both men had enough TBIs to know this wasn't the time to cut corners. Deon signaled ready, and Forest broadcast to the team.

The explosion ripped through the chaos, a shockwave hammering the fortress. The wall buckled, then crumbled, sending chunks of stone plummeting into the abyss.

In that instant, the Mi-17 swung into position. The pilot hovered the helicopter at the cliff's edge, one skid barely touching the jagged rock. The rotors beat against the air, sending dust swirling as the rescue began.

Forest and Deon cleared debris, squeezing out through the hole. "Get inside," Forest barked. "We may need to toss some of these kids, and we'll be packing them in like sardines."

Deon climbed into the chopper, waiting as Forest remained at the cliff's edge.

***

THE CONVOY WAS COMING fast, and Rami was ready. The trucks swerved around the dragon's teeth barricades, tires screeching, and rock rails scraping against cement pyramids as they slalomed up the winding road.

Rami's PKM burst announced the convoy's arrival, while shredding the lead vehicle and sending it careening off the road. The convoy slowed, but a second later, the whoosh-thump of an RPG echoed.

The rocket struck low, sending a spray of fortress wall into the air and debris raining down on the guard tower. Rami returned fire, the PKM's 650 rounds per minute, reducing the gunner to a torn mass of flesh.

Another RPG screamed through the air, the sound tearing at the night. Rami dove for cover as the tower erupted in a fiery explosion, debris raining down like shrapnel.

"Tower's down!" someone yelled, but there was no time to dwell.

***

"Move!" Forest yelled. "Keep 'em coming!"

The children, wide-eyed and terrified, held hands as they navigated past bodies littering the compound, stumbling through the breach and into the waiting arms of Kate and Talya. Some cried, tripping on debris, but Mike and Logan kept their weapons up, one hand snatching up fallen kids.

On the other side of the wall, Deon and Jordan waited inside the bird, catching the smallest kids, as Forest tossed them aboard. Bella packed them in as tightly as she could. When the last of the children were aboard, Kate and Talya climbed in, and Deon strapped them down.

The Mi-17 pitched violently, rotors clawing for stability. Fire and shockwaves battered the cockpit. The pilot gritted his teeth, sweat streaking his face.

Nuru and Samir hauled Rami from the rubble, struggling against the dust-choked air. Forest met them at the breach, hauling Rami inside. When he looked back, Nuru was gone.

Mike and Logan backed toward the breach, sweeping for movement.

"Last man," Mike called, slapping Logan's back and stepping through.

The thump of distant mortars echoed through the ravine.

"Incoming!" Logan shouted as Mike yanked him through to the other side.

The fortress buckled as the first thermobaric round slammed into the compound. Fire and force erupted through the air, sucking oxygen from every lung. The shockwave ripped through what little remained, shattering stone, splintering wood—vaporizing anything caught in the inferno.

Another shell hit. Then, a third.

The Mi-17 bucked wildly, its frame rattling as the pilot fought to keep control. Firestorm winds tore at the aircraft, dragging it toward the abyss. The overloaded bird pitched hard, its rotors clawing for lift against the brutal pull of gravity.

Mike scrambled to his feet, knowing they had seconds. "Go!" he barked to Logan, already sprinting toward the chopper.

They leapt—

Another explosion.

A blast wave slammed into the aircraft, knocking it sideways.

Mike caught the landing skid, fingers locking tight around the metal strut as the chopper pitched dangerously, its tail swinging out over the ravine.

Logan missed the skid.

He reached—fingertips grazing metal—then slipping—

Mike's hand shot out, snatching the drag loop on Logan's vest. Muscles burned as he held tight, half-hanging out of the chopper, straining against gravity.

The pilot fought the controls, stabilizing just long enough for Logan to scramble up, one knee over the edge.

They tumbled inside, gasping.

For a moment, they sat there, breathless, watching the fortress burn.

"Let's not try that again," Mike muttered.

"Deal," Logan panted, shaking his head.

They scrambled inside, and the final headcount confirmed it—they got them all.

Kate's eyes scanned the cliff, searching until she saw him.

Nuru.

Standing tall, his spear raised high in silent salute.

He paused for a moment—then turned, disappearing down the path.

***

REED WATCHED AND LISTENED to the continuous bombardment for several minutes. There wasn't a structure left intact, and no one left alive. He could feel the intense heat and imagined the entire structure as a giant crematorium.

"Didn't see that coming," he said. "I thought they would just take control and get back to work." When the last wall standing collapsed with a thunderous clap, Reed added. "I think that's our cue to get the hell out of here."

Kabe just nodded, speechless.

"Ever see anything like that?" Reed asked.

"No. Never," Kabe replied. "How could so few accomplish so much?"

"Best of the best."

"Like you?"

Reed smiled. "Yes. Like me. Only..."

"Only what?"

"They still have their souls," Reed said. "Mine's owned by a devil named Riley."

"Yes," Kabe agreed. "Mine too."

Click.

Panic flickered. Another click.

The knife was already in his chest.

Reed turned away from the burning fortress and found Kabe pointing a gun.

"I warned you what would happen," Reed began, disappointed, but not surprised. "But you can take comfort knowing your death ensures your wife's safety."

"I am the one holding the gun."

"Then you best get on with it," Reed said. "But one question. Did Riley put you up to this, or was the thought of killing Ronin just too tempting?"

Click.

Panic flickered. Another click.

He never saw the knife that plunged into his chest and slid into his heart.

"Best of the best," Ronin whispered, guiding Kabe's body to the ground and laying his head against the rocks. He watched the light fade from Kabe's eyes and closed them.

"A professional can sense the weight of a loaded gun."

Did Riley put him up to this, he wondered. *It didn't matter.*

Marcus Jones was dead, and with him the bonds of team, loyalty, and honor.

John Reed was born—a wanderer with neither ties nor master.

A Ronin, with a score to settle.

Whoever set him up thought it was over.

They were wrong.

Chapter 65

TUESDAY, MAY 5th
11:12 PM CAT

PRESIDENTIAL PALACE, MABOKO, MOTAPA

From the balcony of his palace suite, Klaus Mueller looked out over the city lights, though his mind was far from the view. Patience was his greatest weapon. It had taken decades to grow the GEC, brick by brick, into arguably the most powerful force on the globe. But tonight, he needed information more than control.

The sat phone vibrated in his hand, and he answered immediately.

"Mueller," he said, sharp and precise.

Colonel Ivanov, a military man, kept it brief. "They escaped."

Mueller's grip tightened on the phone. "How many?" His voice stayed steady despite the rising tension.

"I can't confirm until the rubble cools down enough to go in."

"Then guess."

A sigh came from the other end. "All of them."

"Are you serious? All of them?" Mueller fought to keep his frustration in check.

"It's possible," Ivanov replied. "The Mi-17 that came for them is a troop transport."

Mueller frowned. "A Russian helicopter?"

"Angolan," Ivanov said.

Mueller's mind spun. *Shoot it down? No. Too exposed. Just wait—there was always a way forward.*

He exhaled slowly, forcing his pulse to steady. Setbacks were nothing new. He had weathered worse—Devin Moore, Paris, Syria. Preacher slipping through his fingers again. This would be no different. It never was.

"What about the Coltan?" He shifted focus to the millions at stake.

"It's buried under debris. It'll take weeks to reclaim."

"Recover it when things cool down," Mueller ordered. "But wait until our people in the UN squash the inquiry into the child labor accusations."

"Understood."

Mueller ended the call, tossing the phone onto the desk. He looked out over the city again, his mind already calculating the next move. Let them have their victory—for now. A faint smile tugged at his lips. The war was far from over.

***

Isabella Marquez huddled on the floor of the Mi-17, her arms wrapped protectively around two of the smallest children. Their tiny bodies shivered against hers, eyes wide with exhaustion and terror. The steady hum of the rotors drowned out everything else, but the fear in the air was palpable. Isabella glanced at the children's tattered clothes, her heart aching for what they'd endured.

The helicopter swayed slightly, moving through the night, with the landscape of Motapa stretching far below. She looked over at Kate, who was tending to the wounds of one of the older boys.

Jordan crouched beside Isabella, his voice respectful but firm.

"Ma'am, we're in Motapan airspace, aboard an Angolan helicopter. We need clearance before we reach the capital. Best option? Land at the Presidential Palace. None of us," he added, motioning to the Trident team, "entered the country legally. The airport would be a problem."

Kate, overhearing, slid in next to them. "The palace keeps you out of the press. Keeps the kids out of the press. And some of them need medical attention—fast."

She took the sat phone Jordan offered. "How long until we reach the palace?"

She dialed quickly, and after a few tense moments, the voice of her trusted aide, Sophia Langston, came through. "Sophia, it's Isabella. I'm free, and we have the kids. All of them. I'll explain later, but we're in a helicopter coming straight to the palace. No press. Get Amara and tell her we'll be there in twenty minutes. She'll know what to do."

***

It was nearly midnight, but Sophia Langston couldn't sleep. The images of Isabella and the schoolchildren as hostages looped in her mind, each one a fresh stab of guilt. *Why wasn't I taken? Why did she leave me behind?*

But she understood now—Isabella's decision probably saved her life.

Sophia had worked with Isabella for nearly a decade, rising from intern to trusted confidante. Fiercely loyal. Ruthlessly efficient.

When her phone rang, she hesitated—probably the press—again. Then her gut twisted. She answered.

Isabella's voice sent her flying out of bed, heart hammering. She needed to get to Amara. Now.

Sophia sprinted down the marble corridor, silk sleep set clinging to her as she turned a corner, nearly slipping. Two guards blocked her path.

"Stop," one guard said, stepping into her path. "It's too late for visitors. You need to—"

"I need to see Amara. Now." Sophia's voice carried the authority of someone used to getting things done.

"The palace is closed at this hour," the guard said, folding his arms. "You'll have to—"

Sophia faked a step back, then bolted—bare feet slapping marble.

She was twenty feet ahead before the guards even reacted. Ex-track star. Still fast as hell.

Alarms blared, and more guards tromped down the hallway. Sophia reached Amara's room but was tackled just before she could knock. Undeterred, she screamed, calling Amara's name as loud as she could.

The first guard to cover her mouth had his hand bitten for his trouble. As they dragged her away, she clawed at the walls, knocking over furniture and sending vases crashing to the floor.

Finally, Amara appeared, tying a robe around her waist. "What is going on?" she demanded.

Recognizing Sophia, she ordered the guards to release her. "Sophia, what is it?"

Sophia, breathless, held up the phone. "Isabella just called. She and the children are free. They are on board an Angolan helicopter headed directly to the palace."

Amara's eyes widened, but her expression remained calm, betraying none of the surprise or urgency she must have felt. She glanced at the guards, then back at Sophia, her face tightening ever so slightly.

"Say nothing more," she whispered, her voice barely audible. Amara's eyes swept the hall, searching for anyone who might be listening. "Come with me."

***

AMARA KNOCKED ON HER father's door, not waiting for a response before stepping inside. She motioned for Sophia to wait but returned seconds later.

"I need to speak with her," President Bongani said, stepping into slippers as he came forward.

Sophia quickly dialed the sat phone number, her heart still racing. When Isabella answered, Sophia handed the phone to the President.

"Isabella?" His voice trembled with disbelief, a rare crack in his usual stoicism.

"Yes, Mr. President."

"It's really you?" He asked again, this time softer, as if still not trusting his own ears.

"It is," she replied, her own voice steady now. "And we have the children. Every one of them. Those taken this morning, and many more—beaten, starved, worked like animals."

"What do you need?" His voice was raw, unguarded.

"Clearance to land at the palace," Isabella said. "And anonymity. The team that saved us didn't exactly come through customs."

"Done." No hesitation. "What else?"

"These children need immediate medical attention. Many are malnourished, dehydrated, and in dire need of care. And the last thing we want is publicity. No one should know about this—at least not yet."

"Of course. And you? Are you alright?"

"I am now."

There was a brief silence, and then Bongani's tone shifted slightly. "The team—the ones who carried out this miraculous rescue—are they with the GEC?"

Isabella hesitated, surprised by the question. "The GEC? No, sir. We were rescued by Trident Security—Kate Preacher's team. They've asked for confidentiality—for now—Kate will explain everything tomorrow."

The president was silent for a moment longer. "Very well. I'll be waiting at the palace helipad."

***

PRESIDENT BONGANI'S FIRST CALL was to Sekai Moyo, the man who had guarded his life through two assassination attempts. Moyo was more than just his head of security—he was the one person Bongani trusted to execute the helicopter's arrival in absolute secrecy. Not even the Vice President would know, not until Bongani made the announcement himself.

The helicopter's arrival at nearly 1:00 a.m. roused few in the palace, and to the city beyond the walls, the sound was nothing more than a fleeting curiosity—if they heard it at all.

A sizable medical team waited at the helipad, doctors and nurses already prepared. Transport vehicles were on standby to collect the children, ushering them straight to the palace medical center. A triage team stood ready to evaluate them while ambulances were stationed for any child requiring urgent surgical intervention.

Rami's compound fracture had worsened, and the risk of losing the leg was too high. He was immediately evacuated. Samir went with him, those two slipping back into the city with no one the wiser—their covers still intact.

The children, however, resisted any attempt at separation. Tiny hands clung to their rescuers, eyes darting around in fear. In the end, arrangements were made to turn a large conference room into a makeshift recovery center. A space where they could stay together under caring and watchful eyes.

President Bongani moved quietly through the room, stopping by each bed. He forced a smile for the children, though it didn't reach his eyes. His heart burned with rage as he fought back tears, silently swearing to uproot the evil behind their suffering.

The sight of their frail, malnourished bodies stirred something deeper within him. It wasn't just pity, or even anger—it was memory. He had once been young and full of hope, fresh out of medical school, believing he could heal his country. Instead, he had been thrown into a cell, beaten, and sentenced to hard labor for daring to speak out against the regime.

He had been strong then, able to survive the grueling conditions. But these children—they had been robbed of their strength and innocence, made prisoners in their own land, victims of greed. But now—now they had a chance.

Bongani's hand clenched at his side, the phantom ache of old scars prickling his skin. He had fought his way out of that darkness, and now, standing here, he knew these children would, too. But not without justice. Not without vengeance for what had been done to them. And he would see to it.

Sophia wrapped her arms tightly around Isabella, unable to hold back her sobs.

"I'm alright," Isabella reassured her, though her voice cracked slightly. "It's okay. You did great. Now, let's get you some clothes."

Leboo hung back in the shadows of the helicopter, his small fingers still wrapped around Kate's hand, unwilling—or unable—to let go.

"Is this real?" he asked. "Or like the lion dream?"

"The lion dream?" she echoed, pulling back just enough to study him. "Did he have three scars?"

Leboo's eyes widened. "You've seen him too?" he whispered, astonished. "He showed me the way out—the crack in the wall."

Kate nodded, squeezing his shoulder gently. "Yes, I've seen him. And you'll see him again."

Leboo looked up at her. "I will?"

Kate smiled. "Oh yes. He'll be watching over you until you're home safe, back with your family."

He wrapped his arms around her, holding on for a moment as if memorizing the feeling.

Then he let go, turning to join the others, his steps light, free.

The rotor wash stirred the dust at Kate's feet.

"Is he going to be okay?" Forest asked.

Kate replied without hesitation, a knowing calm in her voice. "His demon is dead, and Nuru will keep an eye on him."

Kate crushed Forest in a hug, hard enough to make him wheeze.

Forest laughed. "I think you cracked a rib."

"Jesus, Forest—how the hell did you pull this off?"

"Ryder." Forest's voice dipped slightly. "I know you two have history, but if she hadn't called—"

Kate cut him off. "Doesn't matter. You're here."

Mike clapped her shoulder. "We're family, Kate. Enough with the lone-gun bullshit. Deal?"

She smirked. "Deal."

Kate swept Talya into a hug. "Hopefully, our Paris adventure didn't get you into too much trouble," Kate whispered.

"Oh, you did, but I can handle it."

Deon and Logan stepped up, and Kate hugged both, planting kisses on their cheeks. When she let go, Jordan was standing there, grinning.

Kate smiled back. "You know what Jake would say?"

"Not bad for a Jarhead?"

"No...Well, yeah, maybe... OK, probably," Kate joked.

Jordan laughed, and Kate just looked at him, staring into his eyes. When she finally spoke, her voice was softer.

"Then he'd remind you why you were the best man at our wedding."

She pulled Jordan in close, fighting back tears. Saying Jake's name brought him close. She could feel him—and she knew they all did.

"Jake had a vision, a mission, and he built this team for a reason," Kate began. "What you did today was only the beginning. Tonight, we sleep. Tomorrow, it's back to work."

"OK, Chief," Forest said. "We'll be ready."

***

THE TRIDENT SECURITY TEAM waited aboard the helicopter, watching as the last of the medical personnel ushered the children inside. A matte black tactical van rolled to a stop alongside the chopper's loading door.

Forest exhaled, glancing toward the palace, where only a handful of dimly lit windows hinted at movement inside. "Time to disappear."

"Grab your gear. Nothing left behind. You know the drill—we were never here."

As the Trident team piled into the van, Jordan popped back up front.

"I owe you, brother," Jordan said, extending a hand to Migs. "I gotta hand it to you. You are one hell of a pilot. If you ever want a job, I know Kate would make you a very attractive offer."

"Not in this life, my friend," Migs said, laughing hard as he shook Jordan's hand. "You people are insane."

***

Klaus Mueller heard the helicopter long before he saw it. He knew exactly what it meant. Unable to resist, he slipped from his suite, risking exposure at one o'clock in the morning, and climbed the narrow stairs to the roof.

His aging eyes weren't as sharp as they used to be, but through the shadows, he spotted children disembarking, escorted by two adult women. That was all he needed to see. Mueller crept back down the stairs, disappearing into the darkened corridors.

He dialed Shepard. The man's voice, groggy from sleep, crackled on the other end.

"Mueller...? What is it?"

"They escaped," Mueller said bluntly.

"Escaped?" Shepard's voice sharpened as he processed the news. "Preacher survived?"

"Yes. She's alive. So is Marquez."

"And the kids?"

"The kids, too," Mueller said, his tone clipped. "This is going to be a media spectacle."

"What's our exposure?"

"Minimal. Ivanov destroyed the base—everyone and everything."

"What about the coltan?"

"We'll go back for it once the dust settles. For now, it's off the market."

"The buyer won't be happy."

"Then find another," Mueller snapped. "If the Chinese don't want it, the Americans will."

Shepard let that sit for a moment. "And Motapa?"

"Plan B."

"I'll let him know," Shepard said.

***

Waiting was part of the game, and so was the understanding that safe house was an illusion—an oxymoron whispered by those who had never been hunted. Few knew where he was, but even fewer knew what he was capable of.

On mission, beds weren't for sleeping. They were for setting traps, for seduction—never for rest. Sleep was a luxury that could get you killed.

The recliner in the corner sufficed. Control of the room. Control of the corners. Anyone coming for him was already dead. They just didn't know it yet.

The phone buzzed, pulling him from a light sleep.

A text. One word. A signal.

Shamrock.

His pulse surged. The hunt was on.

A slow grin tugged at his lips as Hemingway's words surfaced:

"There is no hunting like the hunting of man, and those who have hunted armed men long enough and liked it, never care for anything else thereafter."

If he had never joined the military, never trained as a sniper, never learned to excel at killing—who would he be? He couldn't picture it. There was no other version of himself.

The rush hit him like a drug, adrenaline coursing through his veins, sharpening his focus.

His mission was green.

Everything was in place. He was ready.

***

KATE CAUGHT UP WITH Bella and Sophia as they walked through the quiet residential wing of the palace.

"Sophia," Kate said with a grin, pointing at the oversized slippers. "Whose are those?"

"They're President Bongani's," Sophia replied, smiling. "When I refused to go change, he insisted. He's very sweet."

"He's a good man," Bella added. "In a tough job."

"We'll see what we can do to help," Sophia said. "And Bella, your story will inspire millions."

They stopped in front of Kate's door, and Bella pulled her in for a hug. Kate leaned close, whispering, "You need to hang on to that one. She's a firecracker."

"I know the type," Bella said with a soft laugh, letting go but hesitating to leave.

Kate caught the look in Bella's eyes. "What is it?"

Bella's smile softened a trace of something thoughtful in her expression. "I'm still trying to wrap my head around the last forty-eight hours. The joy, the pain, the loss. But I'm sure of one thing. I wouldn't be here if it wasn't for you."

"Ditto," Kate replied, her voice warm. "You saved my life in Kibale. I'd say we make a damn good team."

Bella's eyes held a flicker of something deeper as she glanced down. "Nuru agrees—he told me there's still work to do."

Kate's expression shifted, feeling the weight of Nuru's words—whatever he shared with her was for Bella alone. "Then we'll be ready," Kate whispered.

As Bella turned to leave, Kate stood there, knowing whatever came next, their paths had crossed for a reason.

***

KATE COULDN'T WAIT TO peel off the prison-stained clothes, the stench of sweat, smoke, and something worse clinging to her skin. She knew a shower would help, but the exhaustion was bone-deep. She sat on the shower floor, letting the hot water crash down around her, massaging her scalp and shoulders, slowly rinsing away the day's grime.

Summoning the strength to stand, she washed her hair and scrubbed off the last remnants of captivity. The act felt symbolic—each drop of water washing away not just dirt but the weight of what she'd survived. Invigorating, but not enough to stave off the weariness that clawed at her.

More than anything, she craved sleep. But her gaze kept drifting to the tablet beside her. She knew Nomad and Keisha would be worried. The flood of contact requests told her as much, but what caught her attention was that they'd begun before the kidnapping.

He's found something, she thought. *Maybe in Jake's files.*

That thought tugged at her—she was angry that Nomad copied the files, but part of her secretly hoped he'd find something she missed.

The encrypted video call connected, and Keisha's voice came through first.

"She's alive!" Keisha shouted, summoning Nomad back to his console. "Are you alright? Tell me you're alright."

Kate smiled, her fatigue clear in her voice. "Take a breath, Keisha. I'm good. Tired, but safe. And grateful to be alive."

"And Isabella?" Keisha asked.

"She's fine. So are the kids. All of them."

"I've been praying," Keisha said, then her voice softened. "He'd never admit it, but I know Julian was praying, too."

"I'll take all the prayers I can get," Kate said, hearing the soft hum of Nomad's chair as it whirred back to life.

"I step away for five minutes," Nomad's voice cut in, "and that's when you call."

Kate laughed. "It's okay. It gave Keisha and me a minute to talk. I appreciate the prayers."

She could almost picture Nomad blushing behind his faceless avatar. "I'm sure you want details, but it's almost two here, and I'm beat. Did you find anything in Jake's files?"

"Not yet," Nomad said, a hint of intrigue in his voice, "but I've got a hunch I'm chasing."

"So, what's with the dozen contact requests?"

"The drone audio," Nomad explained. "I found it and synced it with the video. It's in your folder."

"I can't handle that tonight," Kate said, her exhaustion creeping in. "Not after everything...Not today. Just give me the highlights."

"Alright," Nomad said. "You already know the SUV pulled off the road. Marcus picked the cuffs and took out the two guys planning to kill him."

"Yeah, that much was obvious, even without the audio."

"Right," Nomad continued. "But then a phone rings and Marcus answers it. The guy on the line didn't think Ronin would make it. That's when Marcus flipped him off. After that, it's all instructions. The caller tells him there's a car hidden nearby."

"We saw him pull the body out of the trunk."

"Exactly. The guy on the phone walks him through staging the setup, and then they blow up the car."

Kate thought out loud. "The caller didn't know Marcus was cuffed behind his back. But Marcus knew, and he's nothing if not precise."

"You think he changed the cuffs on purpose?"

"I know he did," Kate said. "And he knows me—he gambled I'd get the autopsy report, and I'd notice."

"So, he wanted you to know he survived?"

Kate exhaled. "That's what he wanted. But why?"

"That's pretty much it," Nomad said. "The video shows us how he did it. The audio proves some guy named Riley set it all up."

"Riley?" Kate asked, her interest piqued. "You're sure it was a man? Any chance a woman's voice could've been modulated or manipulated?"

"No way. Definitely a man," Nomad confirmed. "Why?"

"Never mind," Kate said, a touch distracted. "It's nothing. Just keep me posted if you find anything else in Jake's files. And, Julian..."

Nomad paused at the mention of his real name.

"I'm sorry I got mad about the files," Kate said. "You caught me off guard, but I'm glad you have them. And when this is done, you and Keisha can help me piece them together."

Chapter 66

WEDNESDAY, MAY 6th

8:00 AM CAT

PRESIDENTIAL PALACE

Amara walked ahead, her steps quiet on the dimly lit palace floors, guiding Kate away from the grand halls and the bustle of palace life. They walked in silence, the weight of the upcoming conversation apparent from Kate's urgent request. Amara glanced back at Kate as they approached a set of dark wooden doors, the entrance to her father's private study—a sanctuary within the palace, far from the prying eyes of guards, bureaucrats, and the ever-inquisitive Vice President.

Kate reached out to shake the President's hand. "Thank you for seeing me on such short notice."

President Bongani greeted her warmly. "Mrs. Preacher," he began, though his brow furrowed in confusion. "After all you've done, how could I refuse a meeting? Still, I must admit, I'm at a loss as to why such absolute secrecy was necessary."

"Please, call me Kate," she replied with a polite smile.

"Of course, Kate," he agreed, gesturing for her to sit in one of the overstuffed leather chairs that faced him. Amara remained just outside the door, closing it softly behind her, leaving Kate and the president alone.

"I assume this is about your security firm's role in the rescue," he said. "Ms. Marquez mentioned you prefer to remain behind the scenes, and if that's your wish, I'm happy to keep your involvement confidential."

Kate shook her head slightly. "Thank you, Mr. President, but that's not why I asked to meet."

Bongani's curiosity deepened as he studied her expression. Kate took a breath, gathering her thoughts before continuing. "How much do you know about my husband's death?"

His posture stiffened. "Only what I've seen and heard in the news. His courage was inspiring, and his loss... devastating. But his sacrifice saved countless lives."

"There's more to it," she said and took a breath. "His death wasn't just a tragedy—it was an assassination."

Bongani blinked, his confusion clear. "I don't understand."

"Jake was wounded in the attack," Kate continued, her voice low and steady, "but the bullet that killed my husband didn't come from the terrorists. It came from a sniper, and I've tracked that man to Motapa."

Bongani's brow furrowed deeper. "A sniper? Here? In Motapa?"

Kate nodded. "I followed him from Paris," Kate began. "Where he tried to kill me—his second attempt."

Bongani's eyes were sharp, calculating. "If you're telling me I'm his next target," he said, his tone carefully neutral, "I'd say he's late to the party."

"Mr. President, there may be many who wish you harm. That is the curse of those who are not part of the established political machine and don't owe their allegiance to the power brokers," Kate said. "But this threat is both dangerous and imminent. I believe the man directing the sniper's actions is the same one who suppressed the truth about my husband's murder and scuttled the Paris terrorist investigation. That man is here, negotiating with you."

Bongani stood, pacing slowly in front of the fireplace, his mind racing. "You believe Klaus Mueller is behind your husband's death—and he is now planning to kill me?"

Kate nodded. "I know how this sounds."

Bongani turned, his voice dropping. "Do you have proof?"

Kate hesitated, then shook her head. "No. Not yet. My husband was collecting evidence when he was killed—that is likely why he was killed. But what he uncovered was a series of kidnappings, murders, suspicious suicides—the common thread, the inescapable connection, to them all was the GEC."

Bongani sat back down, his expression skeptical. "The Global Economic Council? I admit, I have concerns about some of their programs and motivation, and I've heard the rumors, but all the nefarious accusations have been dismissed as nothing more than conspiracy theory."

Kate's eyes locked onto his. "They've done an excellent job hiding in plain sight. But I believe there's a faction within the GEC known as the Coalition, and Klaus Mueller sits at the head of the table. They've used their influence to manipulate governments, economies, and wars. And here, in Motapa, they've struck again."

Bongani exhaled, rubbing a hand over his face. "You're telling me Mueller ordered the attack? That he's responsible for enslaving those children?"

Kate leaned forward. "Yes. I believe the attack was orchestrated. The goal was Isabella—that village was her project, and when the rebels came, they searched specifically for her. And at dinner, the night before we left, Bella let slip that her upcoming Davos conference presentation would expose the GEC's failures. Her intent was to encourage transparency and spur change, but if you'd seen the look on Mueller's face, you'd know that was not how it was received."

"Even if Mueller felt threatened," Bongani said. "You think him capable of slaughtering an entire village?"

"Let me ask you," Kate began, her voice sharp with certainty. "Did Mueller promote deploying GEC resources to rescue Isabella and the children?"

"Yes, he did," Bongani said. "In fact, he was quite insistent that it was the best course of action."

"And you agreed?"

"Reluctantly, I did," he said, lowering his voice. "With our military in disarray and ill-equipped, the Vice President made a compelling argument that we needed to act."

"Mueller's assistance came in the form of an Africa Corps convoy," Kate said. "They were already on the way to collect the coltan—millions of dollars of coltan, mined with the blood and sweat of those children."

"The enslavement of those children is a dark truth, a shameful act, that I will share with the world today," Bongani said. "But why do you think Mueller's responsible?"

"Simply put, military tactics," Kate replied. "With Africa Corps experience, numbers, and firepower, they could easily have seized control of the fortress. But that wasn't the mission. Mere moments after our escape, a barrage of thermobaric mortars rained down—designed to kill every man, woman, and child, incinerating their bodies and every shred of evidence. Fortress Krasnaya Skala was reduced to ash and stone."

"Without proof," Bongani said. "There is nothing I can do or say."

"I understand," Kate said. "And for your own safety, it's best nothing change. Hold your press conference. Celebrate the return of the children and Isabella. Decline to answer any details on how the rescue was affected, promising full details in the future, and focusing the press instead on what you've learned about the children's suffering and your commitment to the future."

"Sounds like you should be writing my speech," Bongani said. "But what about the sniper?"

Kate's voice hardened. "If I'm right, the sniper was insurance. If the negotiations went well, and Mueller succeeded in getting a foothold in Motapa, the sniper would have been sent home."

"And since I declined Mueller's offer, I have been marked for death."

"Yes," Kate confirmed. "And that's why I asked for the meeting. You can choose to believe all, some, or none of what I've said, but I would ask you not to gamble with your life. For your country. For your daughter. Let us help."

Bongani leaned forward, his voice low and tense. "What do you need?"

***

10:00 AM CAT

THE GRAND HALL OF the Presidential Palace exuded an understated dignity. African art adorned the walls, illuminated by subtle lighting that softened the room's sharp edges. It wasn't the palace's largest space, but its understated elegance made it ideal for the press conference. And crucially, its heavy drapes and controlled entrances offered the security they desperately needed. The windows had been blocked by heavy, floor-length drapes, and the room's entrances were covered, both visibly and discreetly, by Motapan presidential guards and members of the Trident Security team.

President Bongani stood tall behind the podium, the Motapan coat of arms emblazoned beneath him, his face hard with both resolve and barely contained anger. Isabella Marquez sat behind him, her posture composed, though the shadows of all she had endured still lingered in her eyes. Around them, journalists shuffled, their cameras and microphones ready to capture the world's first glimpse of the rescued children.

Talya blended in effortlessly, wearing Kate's tailored clothes, her blazer discreetly hiding the sidearm strapped beneath. Forest, Deon, and Logan, uncomfortably stuffed into borrowed suits, mingled by the entrances, their eyes scanning the crowd. Every glance, every shift in the room's energy was a potential threat, and they were ready.

President Bongani shuffled some notes, cleared his throat, and the room fell silent. He glanced once toward Kate, standing discreetly to the side before facing the cameras.

"Good afternoon." His voice was measured, his gaze steady as he began. "Today, I stand before you with both relief and sorrow. I am relieved to announce the safe return of the children of Kibale and Ms. Isabella Marquez, along with two dozen others taken from villages across our nation."

The cameras flashed. A murmur rippled through the crowd, but Bongani continued, his tone growing more somber. "While we are grateful for their return, these children are understandably weak. They have been subjected to brutality, and many need medical care. Ms. Marquez is here with us today, but publicity is the last thing these children need. Most of them—most of them are now orphans, their families taken from them by the same brutality that nearly cost them their lives."

He paused, the weight of his words sinking into the room.

"They have been victims of a great evil, orchestrated by the rebels under the command of Colonel Nkrumah. I cannot disclose the full details of their miraculous rescue, but I can confirm this: Colonel Nkrumah and his forces have been vanquished."

The room was silent, the press hanging on every word. Cameras clicked, capturing the hard lines of Bongani's face.

His voice lowered as he moved toward his final statement. "But this is not just a victory. It is also a time for reflection—a time to recognize a great stain that has fallen on our country and, indeed, on many others."

Bongani's gaze swept across the room, intense and unwavering. "Whether it is religious fanatics like Boko Haram, ISIS, or those who operate in the shadows, using children as currency—this must stop."

The tension in the room grew as Bongani's voice sharpened. "I will find those responsible, and they will pay. This is not just a fight for Motapa. It's a fight for all nations. To my neighbors—look into your hearts. Do you know what's happening in your own lands? It might be happening under your nose—or worse, with the blessing of bureaucrats lining their pockets with the blood of our children."

He paused, his face hard with emotion. "I did not see it. I did not know. And for that, I carry a shame that will follow me to my grave. Do not make my mistake."

He stepped back from the podium, his words hanging heavy in the air. The press stirred, eager to ask questions, but Bongani raised a hand, his final act of control over the room.

"I will not take questions today."

With that, he turned, nodding to Amara, who moved forward, signaling the end of the press briefing and ushering the press out of the room.

Talya and Forest moved with the President, while the others remained in place, their eyes still scanning, watching for any sign of danger. Outside, the world might now know the children were safe, but the Trident Team knew the President's promise to find those responsible only heightened the risk.

***

10:30 AM CAT

KATE STAYED CLOSE TO Amara, helping herd the press from the palace and toward the waiting cars in the courtyard. She spotted him through the crowd, forcing herself not to react. Her pulse quickened, but she kept her expression neutral, excusing herself from Amara's side and moving toward Ben Shepard.

"Well, this is a surprise," Kate said, keeping her voice casual as she approached. "How'd you slip past security?"

"You know the drill," Shepard replied with a shrug. "Slip someone a few bucks, pose as a driver, and voilà—front-row access."

"Fair enough," Kate said, her voice hardening. "But why here? In Motapa?"

Shepard's gaze sharpened, the easy banter fading. "Let's walk."

As they moved away from the press and deeper into the courtyard's quieter edges, Shepard leaned in slightly, lowering his voice. "I read the autopsy on al-Masri. The blast? All postmortem. He was dead at least a day before the explosion."

Kate's eyes narrowed, but she kept her voice even. "So it was a setup."

"Come on, Kate," Shepard pressed. "You knew it was. My first thought? You found him, took him out, and the explosion was your way of tying it up with a nice bow for the media."

"And what makes you think I didn't?" Kate shot back, her tone like ice.

Shepard gave a small, knowing smile. "I dug deeper."

Kate's expression didn't change. "And?"

"I know why you're really here," Shepard said, his voice dropping. "Duncan Harris. I can give him to you."

Kate felt her pulse quicken again, but she didn't let it show. "Save the sales pitch," Kate said coldly, turning to leave. "Enjoy the flight home."

"Not even a little curious?" Shepard called after her.

"No," Kate shot back. "Maybe you staged the whole thing."

"Albatross," Shepard said, just loud enough to stop her.

Kate stopped in her tracks, turning back to face him. "What's that supposed to mean?"

"You know what it means," Shepard said, his eyes glinting. "The abort code Duncan Harris—Grant Collins—got right before you hit him with your car."

Her hand instinctively moving toward the gun beneath her blazer. "How do you know that?"

"Because I sent it."

Kate's fingers tensed, hovering near her weapon. Shepard didn't flinch—but there was a hesitation, a fractional tell. He knew she might actually do it.

"Give me one reason I shouldn't drop you right here."

"Because I'm trying to keep you alive," Shepard replied. "And if he knew I sent that message, I'd already be dead."

Kate's mind raced, suspicion mixing with anger. "Keep talking."

"You were right about the Coalition," Shepard said, lowering his voice. "They'd kill me just for saying the name. We picked up their scent in Syria, traced it through Afghanistan. But it goes deeper, Kate. Much deeper than you think. We're talking decades of manipulation—governments, wars, economies."

Kate's brow furrowed, her voice tight. "Who's 'we'?"

"The Agency," Shepard replied. "My less-than-honorable exit? That was a cover. I was the bait, and they took it. For years, I've worked to earn their trust, feeding agency intel, getting closer to the inner circle. To the Coalition I've been nothing more than a tool. But I've been learning their game, searching for weakness."

Kate's eyes flicked to the side as she considered his words. "And Paris? Jake's assassination?"

Shepard's expression darkened. "I don't know what Jake uncovered, but Grant might. I think that's why they want him dead—and why I'm here. Thanks to you, his cover's blown. Now, he's a liability."

Kate's jaw tightened. "So now you're a hitman?"

"No," Shepard shot back, his tone sharp. "They've got people for that. But this is a test—if I do what they ask, I might get closer to the man pulling the strings."

Kate's gaze didn't waver. "Who?"

"I have no idea," Shepard admitted, frustration flickering across his face. "He's just a voice on the phone."

"Riley?" Kate asked, watching his reaction closely.

Shepard blinked, surprised. "How did you know?"

Kate didn't answer, but her suspicions deepened.

"We've run the voice analysis," Shepard continued, his tone bitter. "He doesn't match anyone we know. No GEC profile, no ties to the Agency. He's a ghost."

"Why come to me?" Kate asked, her voice hard. "Why now?"

"Because whatever's happening here, is going down tomorrow," Shepard said, urgency tightening his voice. "The reconciliation celebration is a perfect setup. Open air. Static podium. Bongani will be a sitting duck. Duncan won't miss."

Every instinct told her not to trust him. *He's lied before. He's lying now.* But getting to Duncan was why she was here—he was the only link she had to Jake's murder. *If he knows who wanted Jake dead, and why, this could be my chance. If the Coalition gets to him first, the investigation's over—they win, and Jake died for nothing.*

"Where do I come in?" Kate asked, her voice edged with skepticism.

"If you're just after vengeance, killing him is easy," Shepard said, stepping closer, his voice dropping to an almost conspiratorial whisper. "But if you want answers, we need to work together."

Kate held his gaze, searching for any sign of deception. "I'm listening."

"I won't lie to you, Kate. It's a gamble," Shepard admitted. "There's no guarantee Duncan will talk. But when he realizes the Coalition wants him dead, we might turn him—it's our best shot. As soon as he completes the mission, he's a dead man."

Kate flexed her hand at her side, her mind racing through the possibilities. Every move felt like stepping into a minefield, but there was no other way.

"I'm in," she said finally. "Walk me through the plan."

***

11:00 AM CAT

AMARA WAS WAITING JUST inside the palace entrance when Kate returned. "I didn't think you knew anyone in Motapa," Amara said.

Kate noted Amara's curiosity and protective instincts. "I was as surprised as you," Kate said. "From my time with the State Department. He thought he might be able to help."

"Can he?" Amara asked, with hopeful eyes.

"Perhaps," Kate said. "We'll see."

They continued down the marble hallway, passing a variety of tribal artifacts and statues. One drew Kate's attention, and she stopped to have a better look.

"My father hates this one," Amara noted. "But I rather like it."

"Under the circumstances, doesn't it strike you as prophetic?" Kate asked. "Your father standing in the middle of a ring of children."

"I see what you mean," Amara said. "Perhaps that notion will soften his attitude. He says it belongs in Madame Tussauds—frightening little children."

They both laughed and continued toward the administrative wing of the palace.

***

AMARA DELIVERED KATE TO a private conference room, well away from the administrative offices, and prying eyes. The team traveled in the black tactical van and entered via an exterior entrance.

The room was buzzing when Kate stepped in, followed by complete silence. Kate looked around at the glaring eyes, and Talya was the first to speak.

"What the hell is Shepard doing here?" Talya asked, barely able to stifle the hatred.

Kate smiled. "Sounds like you briefed the team on Paris?"

"I have," Talya said. "They're ready to kill him, but I told them to take a number."

"Alright, Kate," Forest said. "No more secrets. What did Shepard want?"

"He wants me to kill Duncan."

"You know that's a trap. Right?" Mike said.

"Yes."

Deon leaned forward, his voice edged with concern. "And Shepard's counting on you to take the bait."

"Yes."

"But you're going to do it, anyway?" Forest chimed in.

"Yes."

Talya exhaled sharply, crossing her arms. "This is the warehouse all over again—a poisoned whatever—you nearly died. What happens when Shepard decides you're expendable?"

Kate's smirk barely flickered. "Then I play along—right up until he's expendable."

Silence stretched. No one looked convinced.

She let out a slow breath, her gaze sweeping the room. "I know how this sounds," she admitted. "But Shepard needs me breathing to sell the lie, and he knows I want answers. That gives us a window. We take it."

Her expression hardened. "Now, if we're done with the inquisition, let's get to work."

Kate stepped to the whiteboard and started drawing. "Here's the palace and the garden where tomorrow's event will be held. Logan, you, and Talya are running the site survey—get measurements, angles, sightlines. Nail down exactly where the President's podium will be."

Mike leaned forward. "There's no guarantee Duncan will wait until Bongani's at the podium. If he has a shot, he might take it."

Kate nodded. "Agreed. That's where the garden team comes in. Talya, and we'll draft Bella, will keep the President moving anytime he's exposed, anytime he's vulnerable."

"How do we know that?" Deon asked.

"I'm glad you asked," Kate said, drawing again. "Over here, we have the Gateway Towers Plaza. I'm sure you've noticed the hulking skeletons—they're hard to miss."

"That's an understatement," Talya said. "I saw them on the flight in. The flight attendant said parts of it have collapsed, even killing some kids."

"That's true. The towers are abandoned and fenced off. At some point, they'll be brought down, but right now, that's time and money Motapa doesn't have. For now, they remain a monument to Chinese investment in Africa—poor structural engineering, sub-standard materials, and imported prison labor," Kate said. "But that's where Duncan will be. Prosperity Tower. Thirty-fourth floor."

"That gives us line of sight," Mike said. "I see where you're going with this, but why don't we intercept before he even gets close? Why risk letting him take the shot when we know where, when, and who?"

"That's why Shepard came to me," Kate said. "I'm the weak link."

"He knows you want answers," Forest added. "He's counting on you being reckless enough to risk everything, even the President's life, to learn what the Coalition is planning."

"And he's not wrong," Kate admitted. "You all saw what happened in Paris, and if Jake wasn't there, it would have been worse. The next one *will* be worse. Whatever the Coalition is doing, whatever their endgame, Jake was trying to stop them—it's my job now."

"No. It's *our* job now," Jordan said, heads nodding around the room. "Alright, Kate. You're the chess player. Walk us through the moves to turn Shepard's trap into checkmate."

"We work backwards," Kate said, her voice steady but grim. "Picture Bongani dead. Now, let's figure out how we stop that from happening."

Chapter 67

CONFERENCE ROOM, PRESIDENTIAL PALACE

THE AIR IN THE conference room was thick with the lingering scent of coffee and sandwiches, evidence of the hours they'd spent hashing out every detail of the plan.

Forest stood at the whiteboard, his weathered hands smeared with dry-erase ink. The board itself was a battlefield of diagrams, names, and strategies. Every color represented a team, and every detail was a calculated risk.

"Alright, one last time," Forest said, voice gravelly. "Green team—Talya and Isabella. Kate will brief Isabella. Their job? Keep the President moving."

Forest put a checkmark on the board before continuing. The plan called for using Unity Tower for overwatch, so the team's snipers, Mike and Jordan, flipped a coin to see who would spend the night on top of the tower.

"Blue team - Since Mike lost the toss, he and Logan are on overwatch," Forest said, adding another check.

"Red team - Jordan and Deon, you're with me. We'll be in Prosperity and clear our way to thirty-three, directly below the shooter. Deon will scope and range the President's exposure and prep Talya. During the event, he'll monitor the President's movement and signal any time Duncan has a line on the President. Two-Clicks, keep him moving."

Jordan smirked. "Hey, Mike—don't forget a jacket."

A ripple of tense laughter broke the room's heavy atmosphere.

Forest continued, his expression somber. "Black team is Kate and Shepard.

She'll meet Shepard at the rendezvous and head for the 34th floor, where Duncan will have eyes on the President—hopefully, waiting for his speech."

Kate nodded, her face a mask of determination. "I'm ready," Kate said. "If I'm wrong and Shepard's not the loathsome son of a bitch we think, maybe this ends quietly—no shots fired."

"And if you're right about him..." Jordan began

"I've got you guys," Kate interrupted. "Put him down—hard."

The room fell silent as the weight of the mission settled over them. No one moved right away. Then, almost as if on cue, they stood—some with quick nods, some with brief, firm grips on each other's shoulders. Nothing lingering, nothing that betrayed the gravity of what lay ahead. Talya squeezed Kate's hand, a wordless exchange of support and concern. Big Mike clapped Forest on the shoulder, a gesture that spoke volumes between old comrades heading in separate directions.

"See you all tomorrow," Forest said as the team filed out, the phrase hanging in the air—both a promise and a prayer.

Kate stood alone in the room, erasing the ghostly remnants of the plan on the whiteboard. *It's a good plan*, she thought. *Jake would say BCOS—Best Chance of Success.* But no plan came without risk or cost. She hesitated, her hand lingering over the whiteboard, and closed her eyes. Kate pictured the smiling faces of everyone on the team, and Jake standing with them. *Please keep them safe.*

***

5:50 PM CAT

KATE LEFT THE CONFERENCE room, retracing the path she and Amara had taken earlier in the day. As she wound her way toward Amara's office, she noticed the door was slightly ajar, Amara's eyes glued to a monitor as she pounded away on the keyboard.

Kate knocked lightly. Amara looked up, then stood, stretching. "Long day?" Kate asked.

"Most of them are," Amara replied with a tired smile. "I love the challenge, but I wouldn't mind a little less of it for a few days."

"Do you have a minute?" Kate asked, stepping into the doorway.

"Of course," Amara said, gesturing to the chair. "Have a seat."

Kate closed the door behind her and sat down. "I wanted to let you know that I won't be joining the other guests for dinner this evening," Kate began. "I haven't quite fully recovered. A long bath and an early night sounds like the best way to recharge."

"Of course," Amara said. "I'll let the chef know. Would you like something sent to your room?"

"No, thank you," Kate replied. "There's plenty of delicious treats in the room. If I'm hungry, I'll snack."

"Is there anything else?" Amara asked, her tone curious.

"Yes," Kate said, her voice tentative. "Would you happen to know what your father will be wearing tomorrow?"

Amara raised an eyebrow, a smile tugging at her lips. "I'm usually asked what the women will wear," she teased. "But yes, since my mother's passing, he looks to me for guidance. I try to make sure he looks the part. He'll be in a dark blue suit."

Kate nodded thoughtfully. "Not a bad choice. Given the global attention this is drawing, you might want a spare on hand. Wouldn't be the first time an overenthusiastic guest spilled something on the guest of honor."

Amara tilted her head slightly, studying Kate. "That's...actually a good point."

Kate smiled. "Just a precaution."

***

As Kate exited the administration wing, she was lost in thought, her mind sifting through the pieces on the metaphorical chess board—each move, each player, poised for what came next. Once again, she found herself in a game without a clear sense of her true opponent. When she spotted Riley Mueller walking toward her, all casual smiles and sharp eyes, Kate felt a surge of unease but quickly pushed it aside, bracing herself for the interaction.

"Kate!" Riley's voice was bright as she hurried over, pulling Kate into a quick, friendly hug. "I'm so relieved you're okay! When I heard about the kidnapping, I was terrified. You are okay, right?" She stepped back, scanning Kate with eyes that seemed to search for something beyond the surface.

"I'm fine," Kate replied with a small smile, keeping her tone even. "Just tired.

It's been a long few days."

"I can scarcely imagine," Riley said, her head tilting slightly, a curious glint in her eyes. "What brings you to the admin wing?"

Kate kept her expression neutral, though her suspicions about Riley deepened. "I was just letting Amara know I won't be joining for dinner tonight. I need some time to regroup."

Riley's eyebrows lifted slightly, a flicker of something unreadable crossing her face. "Oh, I see. I'm actually heading to see Amara myself. We'll be leaving the day after the reconciliation ceremony and hoping there's time in the President's schedule to meet before we go."

Smart. Plausible deniability, Kate thought. *While hoping they'll be meeting with the Vice President, a man they already own.*

"Back to Paris?" Kate asked.

"Father's needed in Paris," Riley replied. I'll be heading back to New York."

"Back to New York?" Kate asked, keeping her voice casual but curious.

"Yes. I was just there—for Devin Moore's memorial."

Kate couldn't help wondering if Riley was offering this morsel of personal history for a reason and played along. "You knew Devin?"

"Not well," Riley shrugged. "We dated for a few months. Nothing serious, of course—that wasn't Devin's style, and I knew that going in. But it was fun—until it wasn't. I did admire his intellect—and ambition."

Kate's eyes sharpened, though she kept her expression calm. "Yes, he was certainly known for both."

Riley gave a knowing smile. "Did you know him personally?"

"We crossed paths at MIT," Kate said. "I was a first-year, and he was graduating."

Riley's eyes lit up, an almost playful glint in her gaze. Too playful. "Wait a minute—are you the girl in pigtails in the chess team photo?"

Kate masked her reaction, but a chill crawled down her spine

Kate blinked in surprise. "You've seen that?"

"Oh yes," Riley laughed softly. "Devin has an entire wall of awards and accolades in his penthouse. That chess trophy held a prominent position. Do you still play?"

"Not seriously," Kate replied, her voice carefully measured.

"Oh, good," Riley said, her tone light but calculated.

Kate raised an eyebrow, catching what felt like a subtle shift in Riley's demeanor. "How's that?"

"I'd love to play sometime, but just for fun," Riley said with a smile. "Devin played like it was life or death."

Kate nodded, her thoughts drifting back to literal life-or-death moments from just a few weeks ago. "Yes, that's how I remember him."

A silence stretched between them. Riley's warmth wasn't casual. She moved like a chess player, masking her next move.

"Well, I won't keep you," Riley said, her tone bright once again. "We'll catch up at dinner... oh, that's right, you're skipping tonight. Another time, then. Perhaps Davos? You have to come."

"I haven't planned that far ahead..."

"Of course," Riley said, laughing lightly. "I didn't mean to push, and here I am rambling again. But please, consider yourself invited as my guest."

"Thank you," Kate said, smiling politely. Riley returned the smile and disappeared down the hall.

As Kate watched her go, she couldn't shake the feeling that Riley wasn't just a daughter trailing in her father's shadow—she was playing her own game. And she was playing to win.

***

6:10 PM CAT

KATE KNOCKED ON BELLA's door and found her sipping a glass of wine while getting ready for dinner.

"Want one?" Bella offered, gesturing to the bottle on the table.

"No thanks," Kate replied, shaking her head lightly. "Not tonight."

Bella raised an eyebrow, smirking. "Who are you, and what have you done with Kate? Seriously, is everything okay?"

"I'm fine. Just tired," Kate said with a small smile. "Long day with the team."

"That sounds serious," Bella said, her tone softening.

"It is," Kate admitted. "Actually, that's why I'm here. We need your help during the reception tomorrow."

Bella's eyes sharpened with interest. "Anything. Just name it."

"Thanks," Kate said, her voice lowering slightly. "Here's what we need you to do..."

***

WEDNESDAY, MAY 6th
11:00 PM CAT

GATEWAY PLAZA, UNITY & PROSPERITY TOWERS

The black SUV cruised, lights off, through the once-promising development now left to rot. Abandoned buildings and boarded-up storefronts lined the streets, giving the area an eerie sense of decay. It was the perfect place for Africa Corps to stage an ambush.

The Shepard-Mueller-Africa Corps link was tenuous, but Trident's escape made one thing clear—Africa Corps wanted payback.

The team exited the vehicle and moved in perfect unison. Precise and silent, they operated as though deep in hostile territory. Using the cover of night, they slipped through the shadows, their NODs cutting through the darkness. As they approached the rusted chain-link fence surrounding the plaza, Deon quickly cut through it, allowing the team to slip inside.

A quick fist bump between Mike and Forest signaled the next phase. Blue Team headed for Unity Tower while Red Team advanced to Prosperity. Each man knew his role, their steps deliberate, weapons raised as they moved through the derelict lobby of Prosperity Tower.

The ground floor was a wasteland of broken glass, graffiti-covered walls, and scattered debris. Every crunch underfoot sounded like a cannon blast in the suffocating silence. No one could afford to assume they were alone.

Meanwhile, Mike and Logan faced their own challenges inside Unity Tower. They moved past fallen debris and the creeping vegetation that had taken over the lower floors. The stairs offered more stability, but as Mike reached the next flight, a section of the staircase gave way beneath him, sending concrete crashing to the landing below. He caught himself at the last moment, shooting Logan a quick smile before they resumed their climb, more cautious than before.

When they finally reached the roof, Mike retrieved his Recon-V binoculars, the high-resolution thermal scanner giving him an HD-quality view of Prosperity's rooftop helipad. In the hastily drawn plan, they had no time to secure floor plans, but Mike was relieved to see the 34th floor—Duncan's sniper nest—was a showpiece, likely designed as a restaurant with panoramic floor-to-ceiling windows. It gave Duncan an ideal line of sight on the President's podium, but it also meant Mike could cover Kate and take Duncan out if things went south. It wasn't the plan, but plans change.

Inside Prosperity Tower, Red Team advanced cautiously. The stairwells were in far worse shape, the crumbling concrete providing plenty of potential ambush points. When they reached the missing section of stairs, Deon went first, securing his HK416C to his chest rig and grabbing the static rope Duncan had set up. He crossed without a hitch, covering the stairs ahead while Forest and Jordan followed in perfect sequence.

They climbed steadily to the 33rd floor and secured the area. The floor was an open expanse filled with construction debris, dust-covered pallets, and rusted equipment. It would serve as their base for the night, but they took their time clearing it thoroughly, ensuring there were no surprises.

On the 34th floor, Jordan took point, cautiously approaching the stacked cement blocks they suspected were Duncan's makeshift sniper platform. Careful not to disturb anything, Jordan crouched low, shouldering his own rifle. Peering through his optic, he replicated Duncan's likely perspective. The view was chilling—the President's podium, unobstructed and perfectly framed for a headshot.

Deon moved in behind him, methodically using his Recon-V to map kill zones and potential obstacles. The reality sinking in with every photo and note: the President would be exposed, vulnerable, and given Duncan's skill, he wouldn't miss. Deon transmitted the photos and analysis to Talya—her job would be to keep President Bongani moving, denying Duncan clear lines of fire.

From Unity Tower, Mike covered Red Team's movements. He saw Jordan mimic Duncan's position and comms double-click, confirmed his line of sight was solid.

Forest moved past the sniper's hide, his eyes narrowing as he spotted the rope secured to the wall with a carabiner. It trailed up toward the roof. Kate's intel had been spot-on—Duncan's exfil plan was fast and clean. Clip in, step off the ledge, and drop 400 feet to the plaza below, disappearing into the night like a ghost.

Forest gestured to his team, directing them up to the roof. Mike would've signaled if there were any threats, but protocol demanded caution. Once they cleared the roof, Forest crouched beside Duncan's gear, surveying it. Everything was meticulously prepared, the rope coiled neatly in the feed bag, the descent control staged perfectly. It was the precision rigging he expected to find.

As Forest made subtle adjustments to Duncan's settings, his mind drifted to the Korengal Valley—The Valley of Death. A joint US-UK operation tasked with capturing or killing a high-value target.

Duncan Harris, a pint-drinking, joke-telling Brit and the finest sniper in Afghanistan, was part of the team. When the mission turned into an ambush—rockets crashing down like a metal hailstorm—Duncan didn't just return fire.

He saved Jake. He saved me.

But something had changed.

The man who once cracked jokes over a pint was gone.

Forest didn't know this man—the man who murdered Jake.

The thought sent a jolt through him, snapping him back to the present.

He locked down the last change to Duncan's escape route, then stood and scanned the city. His gaze hard, mind focused.

Duncan Harris had been a friend. A brother-in-arms.

That man was gone.

Forest exhaled, the weight of the moment settling in his chest. His jaw tightened.

Duncan Harris is dead—killed in Afghanistan.

I don't know the man who killed Jake.

And I don't owe him anything.

Chapter 68

THURSDAY, MAY 7th
8:00 AM CAT

GATEWAY PLAZA, PROSPERITY TOWER

Kate Preacher arrived at the rendezvous point, her eyes scanning for movement in the shadows. It wasn't long before Shepard appeared, his approach as nonchalant as ever, a faint smirk playing on his lips.

"Is Duncan in place?" Kate asked, voice edged with tension.

"He's there," Shepard replied, flashing his phone briefly—a photo of the President's waiting podium displayed on the screen. "Took that about an hour ago."

Kate glanced at the screen. "Let's go."

They started the climb into the husk of Prosperity Tower, each step creaking underfoot. Shepard's footsteps were heavy and deliberate, but Kate stayed sharp, alert to every echo and shadow.

When they reached Duncan's rope and rigging, Kate realized just how fragile the building had become and why it was considered a death trap. She was also grateful Duncan was an experienced climber and left a path they could follow. Shepard crossed first, and Kate was close behind.

The wind howled through the empty shell, the building groaning like it was dying. Shepard looked fit but struggled with the climb, pausing twice—then lighting a cigarette, making it even worse.

When they passed the 33rd floor, the air grew colder, and the tension between them thicker. Shepard's hands were trembling. He dropped the pack of cigarettes, not bothering to retrieve them. Kate drew her weapon, her grip tightening as she scanned and cleared the stairs to the 34th. Taking each step slowly and quietly, she led the way to Duncan's floor.

Duncan would be locked in, cheek welded to the stock, every breath measured, wind checked, DOPE dialed to perfection. This was his world.

She stepped through the stairwell, elbows, and gun tucked in tight, approaching heal-toe, heal-toe. Kate pressed the Glock out, taking aim, fighting the temptation to end this now. "Step away from the rifle," she ordered, her voice steady. "And keep your hands where I can see them."

"You're late," Duncan called over his shoulder, keeping his cheek pressed against the rifle. "I said you were getting too old for this work—I'm surprised the climb didn't kill you," he added, chuckling.

Shepard pressed his gun into Kate's back. *This is it,* Kate thought. *Shepard's moment of truth—and he's everything we imagined.* She pictured Mike on Unity Tower, his optic on Shepard's head, finger ready to press.

"Drop it, Kate," Shepard said, his voice cold.

Kate's pulse quickened. Her gun slapped the cement, and what little hope she held for Shepard vanished when he kicked her gun away. *Now it's up to Duncan,* she thought. *If I can shake him.*

"Don't do it, Duncan," Kate began. "Yes, Duncan—I know who you are. The Grant Collins ID is blown, and with it your assets and bank accounts. By now, Interpol and every other major intelligence service knows you're alive—and would love to get their hands on you. I'm guessing there's a decade of open investigations and a trail of bodies they'd like to discuss. That makes you a liability—and expendable."

Duncan spun away from the rifle, confronting Shepard. "Is that true?" he demanded. "Am I blown?"

"Relax," Shepard began. "She's just trying to rattle your cage, shake your confidence."

"It is true?"

"Yes, the Agency knows you're alive," Shepard answered. "But a new identity is already in the works—it's what we do, and nobody does it better—you know that. So let's just finish the job and get the hell out of here."

Kate needed to keep Duncan distracted—focused on her and tested a theory.

"Shepard's playing you," Kate began. "Think about it. Why bring me here? He could have killed me anytime he wanted, but he used me to get close to you. I'll bet Riley gave the order personally. Duncan, your BountyHunter days are over."

Shepard scoffed. "Nice try, Kate. But it won't work," Shepard said. "Shooters like Duncan are a rare breed, and Riley would never waste that kind of talent. I'll bet there aren't ten men in the world that can match Duncan's kills."

"More like six, maybe seven," Duncan said and smirked. "Less with Jake gone."

Kate's blood was boiling, but she swallowed hard and stuck with the plan. "It's your choice, Duncan. You can finish the mission, but neither of us is getting out of here alive."

For a moment, the air was thick with anticipation, but Duncan made his choice. He shifted back into position behind the scope, the weight of his decision etched into his face. His sight picture zeroed in on Bongani's head, every detail falling into place. Exhaling steadily, holding, he pressed the trigger.

The Blaser R8 barked, the recoil absorbed into his shoulder as he held his position, eyes locked on the target. A faint smirk crossed his face as he announced, "Tango down."

Shepard's eyes gleamed with satisfaction, and he pulled a small key fob from his pocket.

"Forget to lock your car?" Kate asked.

"Not exactly, but I do need to lock the door," he sneered, pressing the button.

An instant later, the cigarette pack in the stairwell erupted in a blinding flash. A shockwave blasted outward, punching through concrete, the roar tearing through the empty structure like cannon fire. A twenty-foot section of the stairwell shattered, sending jagged chunks of cement and twisted metal spiraling into the void below. Pulverized concrete and rebar rained onto the landing beneath, and with each impact, the floors reverberated, groaning in protest.

A cloud of fine concrete dust burst out from the stairwell entrance, and Kate staggered as the tremor shook the 34th floor, rattling the skeletal walls and loosening debris. The wave struck like a gut punch, her mind flashing on the team directly below.

***

THE BLAST WAVE HIT before Forest could react. A roar of collapsing concrete and rebar rained down. Dust choked the air, vision gone, ears ringing.

"Get down!" Forest shouted, his voice barely carrying over the echoing chaos. He grabbed Deon by the vest, dragging him behind a pillar, while Jordan dove to shield them from the cascade of falling debris.

"What the hell was that?" Deon shouted, coughing through the thick dust.

"C4," Forest replied, his tone hard and controlled. "Shepard knows we're here, and he's making sure this is as far as we go."

Forest scanned the devastated floor. The stairwell was gone—a jagged hole lined with twisted rubble. His gaze locked with Jordan's, a silent understanding passing between them. They'd find another way up.

***

"Jesus!" Duncan shouted over the ringing in his ears. "You trying to bring the building down on our heads?"

Shepard brushed some concrete dust off his shoulder, unfazed as the last fragments fell. "Relax. It's over. We can't have Kate's friends crashing the party."

"What are you talking about?" Duncan demanded. "What friends?"

"Trident Security," Shepard said with a grin. "I know they're here—somewhere. If they're still breathing, they're not going anywhere now. By the time they find another way up here, I'll be long gone."

"Did you catch that, Duncan?" Kate said, her voice razor-sharp. "Shepard's leaving, but you and I are staying behind."

Duncan turned, eyes narrowing as Shepard's gun leveled at him. He didn't move, but his fingers twitched slightly—muscle memory calculating whether there was a play. Then he exhaled, shaking his head.

"If Riley sent you, it means he doesn't trust me anymore." His voice turned dry. "Or you, for that matter."

Shepard's jaw flexed—barely perceptible, but Duncan saw it.

"I know what you're doing," Shepard said, his voice measured. "Trying to shake me, plant a little doubt, see if I flinch."

Duncan smirked, just slightly. "Is it working?"

Shepard's grip tightened on the gun. He shook his head, a breath of a chuckle escaping.

"Nice try. But I'm the one holding the gun, and with both you and Preacher gone, my future is secure."

Duncan exhaled slowly. "You sure about that?"

Shepard didn't answer right away. Instead, he smiled. Slow. Calculated. Then, in a single fluid motion, he wrist flexed, his grip on the gun, tilting ever so slightly.

A heartbeat.

Then—

"Wait!" Kate's voice sliced through the air. "Let me do it. For Jake. You owe me that much."

Shepard arched an eyebrow, almost amused. "Really, Kate? You think I'm that stupid? There's no way I'm letting you near a gun—I've seen what you can do."

"I don't need a gun," Kate sneered, looking back at Duncan. "I want to see if the bastard can fly."

Shepard chuckled lightly, dismissively. "Fine, but let's get to it. I don't have all day."

"Stand on the ledge," Kate commanded, keeping her distance, but obscuring Shepard's view.

Duncan's toes tipped just past the window's skeletal frame as he faced open air. His hair fluttered in the wind as he glanced down, calculating. Kate expected him to make a move, and he did—leaning into the frame, his left hand creeping toward the wall, fingers brushing the carabiner.

"Don't be too hard on Duncan," Shepard said. "Truth is, I don't think he wanted to kill Jake." His gaze softened, almost imperceptibly. "But you know how this works."

"Collateral," Kate said, the word like a blade.

"Exactly. Everyone has someone—family, friends, lover—someone they care about. That's how they keep you in line." His tone hardened. "Jake was a problem. Duncan solved it."

Kate's breath hitched. "Was it Riley's idea? Or yours?"

"A team effort," Shepard admitted. "Riley set the Paris contract—a power play and client demonstration. I took the opportunity to help Jake with his investigation."

"You sent the note," Kate realized. "You set the time and place—Le Cafe Pierre at noon."

"I even tipped the waiter to sit him right up front," Shepard said. "Honestly, had I known what a pain in the ass he would be—and now you too...oh well, water under the bridge."

Kate's fists clenched. She swallowed the scream, and the urge to charge him—kill him. *He's too far away*, she knew. *He'd get the first shot, but Mike would get the second.*

"Time's up," Shepard said, his eyes flicking to his watch. "Let's finish this before my ride gets here."

Kate's attention snapped back to Duncan, standing at the window. His fingers brushing the carabiner he'd stashed earlier, securing the line to his instructor's belt.

"You're a lot like Jake," Duncan said softly, stalling. "Stubborn. Determined."

Kate tilted her head. "I'll take that as a compliment."

Shepard sighed. "Your way or mine, Kate. Time's up."

"Thirty-four floors," Kate said, stepping closer to Duncan. "Five seconds. Just enough time to beg for God's forgiveness—You'll get none from me."

With both hands, she shoved Duncan hard. His body vanished into the night. Shepard flinched, his expression tightening as Kate turned to him, a bitter smile on her face.

"Your move," she said.

***

JORDAN CROUCHED NEAR THE edge of the 33rd floor, the yawning void of the tower's shell all around him. The concrete skeleton offered little cover, just jagged edges of rebar and exposed beams. He'd hauled the sack of animal carcass, bones, and blood up thirty-three floors of cracked stairs, grateful the bag hadn't leaked. Across the room, Deon took a knee, rifle tucked in, scope fixed on the window frame

Above, the unmistakable whir of the descent line's spool engaged. Duncan plummeted in freefall, the unfinished concrete flashing by, until his harness belt jerked violently to a stop. His free fall lasted exactly fifteen feet—right where Forest had set the Rapid Descent line's stop-break.

Forest stepped forward from the shadows, his movements deliberate. Leaning out, he grabbed the descent rope with one hand, his powerful grip halting Duncan's pendulum swing.

"Surprise," Forest muttered, his smirk sharp as the blade that flashed in front of Duncan's face.

Forest severed the descent line, yanking Duncan inside. A sickening thud echoed from the ground below as the dummy sack splattered on the abandoned plaza, blood and viscera spraying across the cracked concrete.

Duncan lay on his back, staring up at Forest and glancing at the pair of operators with their weapons pointed at his head.

Forest took a knee, grabbing a handful of Duncan's shirt. "You can thank Kate for this. If it were up to me, that puddle down there would be you."

He pulled Duncan off the floor and on to his knees. "Hands behind your back," Forest commanded.

A moment of hesitation earned Deon's rifle butt strike into Duncan's gut, and he complied.

Deon pulled a set of Krowd Kontrol flex cuff zip tie handcuffs from his tact vest, secured Duncan's hands, and stood him up for the pat down. Jordan kept his gun trained on Duncan's head, and the weapon search recovered a boot knife and a USB memory stick.

Forest's brutal right hook dropped Duncan back to his knees. "That's for letting us believe you were dead," he growled. "We searched for days—when they told us to give up, Jake refused. And you killed him. You worthless son of a—"

Duncan lifted his head, resignation and a flicker of defiance in his eyes. Forest didn't hesitate, drawing his pistol and pressing it to Duncan's temple. "Just do it," Duncan said, his voice low and steady. "You'd be doing me a favor."

Forest pressed on the trigger, taking up the slack, ready to catch the break that would send Duncan to hell. Jordan and Deon looked on. Neither spoke. This was Forest's call, and both knew it could go either way. He eased off the trigger, lowered and holstered his weapon. "No. Too easy," he said. "You're alive because Kate thinks you can help. So that's your choice—help or die."

Duncan managed a bitter smile. "She's clever, I'll give her that," he said. "The ceramic Bongani statue was a nice touch, but a headshot was never going to fool me."

"But you didn't let on?"

"There was no point. I knew she was right," Duncan said. "One look in Shepard's eyes, and I knew he was here to kill me. If not now, if not him, I'd just be looking over my shoulder—there's no escape from these people. I'm a dead man. And that hasn't changed."

Forest held out the memory stick, "What's this?"

"That *was* my insurance policy, leverage if I ever needed it. I've been collecting names, dates, maps, diagrams—anything I could get my hands on. Some of it made sense, some didn't. But it's no use now, not to me anyway. Give it to Kate. It's not everything she wants, but it is everything I know." His voice dropped.

"Honestly, I don't think they can be stopped, but then I didn't think anyone could find me, and here we are...so, if anyone has a chance, it just might be Preacher."

A Little Bird chopper, racing at 150 knots, wove through Maboko's commercial district, slaloming between skyscrapers and low-rise buildings. No one heard it coming.

For a fraction of a second, the skyline flickered—just a shimmer of movement against glass and steel. Then—rotors. Close. Fast.

Forest's head snapped up as the chopper rocketed straight up the east face of Unity Tower. Four Africa Corps mercenaries strapped to the transport benches—desert camouflage, ballistic helmets, tactical vests—all heavily armed and poised to deploy.

The turbines spooled high as the Little Bird pitched over the rooftop edge. Before Mike or Logan could fully register the threat, the mercs opened fire. The barrage of automatic weapons sent them scrambling for cover, unable to return fire.

The Prosperity team went to guns, but the chopper banked hard, dropping behind Unity Tower before anyone had the shot.

"Where is it?" Jordan shouted.

"Forest!" Deon yelled, but the warning came too late.

In a blur of motion, Duncan seized the opening, jumping to his feet and sprinting toward the window. There was little time to react, and almost no way to stop him. He reached the frame of the window when Forest's body slam knocked him down. Dangling half-way out the window, struggling to break free, Duncan looked back over his shoulder at Forest—eyes flashing with something between defiance and resignation. He let out a dry chuckle, shaking his head.

"You were right, mate," he said, voice rough. "I should've stayed dead." A smirk ghosted across his face. "Guess this makes us even."

Forest didn't reply. He just let go.

***

WHEN THE HELICOPTER CRESTED Unity Tower, Mike and Logan were caught in the open. Mike lying prone, his sniper rifle trained on Shepard, his finger hovering near the trigger. Logan, one knee on the deck, binoculars monitoring

Kate and Duncan.

Both men pivoted when the chopper popped up, almost on top of them, and the mercs opened fire. Logan never had a chance. Bullets tore into him, hitting his legs and chest, and he collapsed, blood pooling beneath him.

Mike rolled to the side, scrambling for cover beneath a stack of ventilation ductwork, heart pounding as rounds pinged off the metal. He stole a glance at his sniper rifle, hoping he could reach it, but it was shattered, useless.

"My pack..." Logan gasped, his voice barely above a whisper. "Get... my pack."

Mike scrambled out from cover and ripped open Logan's pack. His hand closed around a rigid fiberglass tube. "Logan, you magnificent bastard!" Mike shouted.

He glanced back at Logan—but as soon as he looked, he knew.

No rise and fall of breath. Just the crimson pool spreading out from beneath him, seeping into the cracks of the rooftop. The blood looked dark against the concrete, almost black.

Mike clenched his jaw, his grip tightening around the launcher.

"I'm coming back," he had said. But Logan was already gone.

Mike turned, eyes blazing, and raced to the west wall, extending the launch tube. The click of the tube locking open was barely audible over the thump-thump-thump of the chopper nearing Prosperity Tower. He shouldered the LAW, pulled the trigger arming handle, and calculated where the LAW's anti-tank shell would be the most devastating. He aimed for the rotor assembly, pressing the trigger boot.

The M72's armor-piercing rocket streaked toward the helicopter, slamming into its side with a deafening explosion. An engine fire erupted, as the chopper listed to one side. Its rotors, still spinning, clipping the rooftop with a shriek of metal. Blades sheared off and flew in every direction. Then the burning wreckage slammed into Prosperity's rooftop, sending a shockwave through the building.

Three of the mercenaries were crushed by the impact. The fourth released his bench harness, jumping free and rolling as the chopper hit.

Mike dropped the launcher, racing back to Logan, checking for a pulse—then scooping him into his arms.

***

THE WEIGHT AND FORCE of the crashing helicopter proved too much for the rooftop's integrity. The structure groaned under the strain before the roof collapsed in a cascade of debris. Tons of cement and twisted metal fell into the floors below, cascading into the 34th floor, then 33rd, and finally the 32nd before stopping. The entire tower swayed and screeched, threatening to collapse under the stress of the impact.

Kate and Shepard were knocked off their feet as the floor beneath them gave way. They tumbled through the wreckage, crashing to the floor below, swept away with the falling debris. Kate landed on her back, her head striking cement, pain radiating from her shoulder. She blacked out for a few seconds and woke to the sound of movement and moaning. Adrenaline surged. *Shepard's alive,* she realized. *He's near.*

The urgency to move, get to her feet, find a weapon collided with reality. She couldn't move. The pain radiating from her shoulder kept her pinned to the cement slab beneath her. She struggled to be fully conscious, squeezing her eyes shut before peering through the cloud of dust and debris.

Protruding from her chest, like a jagged, rusty spear, was a foot long piece of rebar. It penetrated just below her left clavicle. She couldn't move her left arm, but her right was free. Kate knew the rule, never remove a penetrating object, it could be the thing keeping you from bleeding out, but she could hear Shepard. He was waking, moving, and she was running out of time.

Kate gritted her teeth, her right hand wrapped tight around the rebar jutting from her chest. She took a shallow, shuddering breath and pulled, muscles straining. A blinding pain exploded through her body, and she fell back with a gasp. The bar was lodged deep—unyielding, anchored to the concrete below.

She pushed up, shifting her weight to try and lift herself off. But after an inch—maybe two—the pain ripped through her like fire, and her arms buckled. Her vision blurred. She could barely hold herself steady, let alone raise high enough to get free.

A crunch of footsteps echoed through the rubble, slow and deliberate. Kate's heart clenched. *He's coming.*

She looked up, meeting his eyes. His hands were empty, but the twisted grin spreading across his face said everything. He loomed above her, savoring her helplessness like a vulture circling wounded prey.

Kate's right hand groped around on the floor. Her fist closed on a chunk of cement, and she sent it flying at Shepard's head.

He ducked and laughed. "It's over, Kate."

The smile vanished, replaced by a chilling stillness in his eyes. "No more games." He stepped over her body and crouched down, kneeling across her stomach, his weight crushing down on her like a vise.

Shepard seized her right hand before she could strike, slamming it down against the cement. Pinned and helpless, she felt his weight press into her stomach and lungs—each breath growing more labored as he watched, clearly reveling in her vulnerability.

Leaning in, his breath was hot on her face. "It's a shame," he whispered, his voice thick with sadistic glee. "All this effort, all this death and destruction... and for what? You're too late, Kate. The Coalition's unstoppable."

Kate's breath was ragged, her mind racing, calculating her next move. *Look around, Kate. Find a weapon.* Jake's voice was calming. *Or be the weapon.*

Shepard reached for a cement block, releasing his grip on Kate's wrist. He hoisted it above his head, eyes gleaming with dark amusement.

Kate yelled, "I am the weapon!"

With a surge of adrenaline, she tucked her legs and pushed, bucking him forward, knocking Shepard off balance, and tipping him toward her head. The cement block crashed next to Kate's head, and his hands shot out to break his fall.

Shepard's face was only inches from Kate's. She saw the fear in his eyes—his expression shifting from confidence to panic.

Her right hand shot up, grabbing the back of his neck. With a savage yank, she drove him down, slamming his throat onto the jagged rebar protruding from her chest.

A scream tore through the air as the rebar impaled his throat.

"No—" Shepard choked, hands clawing at Kate's chest, eyes wide in shock. He tried to push back, but Kate locked her arm behind his head, legs and hips pressing him forward. Every muscle in her chest and arm strained to pull him down—driving the rebar deeper.

He thrashed and coughed, blood gushing from the wound. His gasps for air turned to wet gurgles as blood poured from his mouth, splattering across Kate's cheek. His body twitched. And then stopped.

Kate released him, letting his lifeless body slump on her shoulder.

Her chest heaved, each breath a battle against the pain. She struggled to find her voice—hoarse but filled with grim satisfaction.

"That's for Jake."

The flood of tears came fast, unstoppable. Jake was there. Kneeling beside her—his fingers threading gently through her hair. Just like before—like always.

"Jake," she whispered. Her voice cracked. "I did it."

As quickly as he appeared, he was gone. The love of her life—gone. The dream of growing old together—shattered.

The man responsible was dead.

And it wasn't enough.

Nothing will ever be enough.

But it was a start. Kate stifled the tears, her expression hardening.

Unstoppable? She thought, recalling Shepard's taunt. *The game's not over—it's my move.*

***

AT THE SOUND OF boots approaching, panic surged. She saw the desert-tan boots of an Africa Corps operator moving toward her. Then, a burst of gunfire, followed by the thump of a body hitting the ground.

"Jordan, give me a hand," Forest called out. "Deon, call the chopper."

Forest and Jordan rushed to Kate's side, peeling Shepard's lifeless body off of her. She managed a weak smile, but it was short-lived. The building groaned, a low, ominous rumble, as chunks of cement rained down from the roof. Instinctively, both men moved to shield her from the debris, covering her as dust and cement fragments rained down on them all.

"We gotta get her out of here," Forest said urgently, his tone pressing against the building's relentless tremors.

"We can't move her," Jordan argued, eyeing the jagged rebar still embedded in Kate's shoulder.

"We don't have a choice," Forest replied, his voice leaving no room for debate. "We'll pack the wound now and seal it when we're out."

"Chopper's inbound!" Deon called out over comms, and in the background, they heard the roar of rotors drawing closer.

Forest knelt beside Kate, his face set with grim determination. "This is going to hurt," he warned. Then, with a quick nod to Jordan, "On three. Three!"

With a swift, brutal pull, Forest and Jordan lifted Kate off the rebar. A scream tore from her throat. She closed her eyes, gritting her teeth as Forest and Jordan jammed clotting gauze into the entry and exit wounds.

Above, their helicopter hovered, rotor wash scattering dust and debris as the crew lowered a stretcher through the fractured rooftop.

"Can you walk?" Forest asked, locking eyes with her.

Kate managed a nod, though her face twisted in pain. She clamped her right hand around Forest's neck, using him for balance as she forced her legs forward. *One step. Then another.*

The pain was blinding. Her vision tunneled, her breath came in sharp gasps.

Her body rebelled—but her mind refused. *Not yet. Not like this.*

Jordan cleared as much of the path as he could, but the last few feet stretched like miles.

Kate pressed forward—one last step—

And then, finally, her body quit.

Her legs buckled. The pain swallowed her whole.

Forest and Jordan caught her mid-fall, their grips the only thing keeping her from crashing to the ground.

They eased her onto the stretcher as the chopper blades roared overhead. Kate clenched Jordan's arm, forcing her eyes open as she scanned the ruins.

"Duncan?" she managed to ask, her voice barely audible over the noise.

"He's dead," Jordan said, meeting her gaze.

Kate's eyes closed as the team tightened the stretcher's straps across her chest and hips. She winced, breathing through the pain, her mind reeling. *Was it all for nothing?*

Deon clipped into the hoist beside her, signaling the chopper crew. The stretcher lifted, and Deon adjusted for balance, managing the stretcher's rotation as they cleared the rooftop edge.

Jordan relayed updates on comms, monitoring their ascent and calling out instructions to the pilot. The minute Kate and Deon were secure, the SPIE (Special Patrol Insertion and Extraction) line dropped through the gaping roof.

Prosperity Tower groaned again, sending chunks of concrete cascading into the plaza below. The helicopter held steady, waiting for the team to connect. Forest and Jordan moved fast, clipping their harnesses to the line. A single glance passed between them, and Forest slammed a fist to his chest. The double-tap signal sent them rocketing into the air.

The helicopter shot straight up, pulling them clear of the roof just as the tower collapsed. In what sounded like the agonizing cry of a wounded animal, the twisting steel and fracturing cement collapsed in on itself. Below them, a tidal wave of debris swept across the Gateway Plaza.

Darting over to Unity Tower, the chopper hovered over the helipad. Forest and Jordan released from the SPIE line to collect Mike and Logan. Mike was waiting for them, but Logan laid flat, arms crossed, eyes closed.

The helicopter settled on Unity's helipad, the moment silent and somber. They transferred Logan to a stretcher, secured him next to Kate, and climbed back on board—the priority now was the hospital.

***

THE HELICOPTER SPED TOWARD the hospital, pain radiating out from Kate's chest, her mind racing. "The President?" she asked, her voice weak but urgent. "How's the President?"

"He's safe," Forest reassured her. "Talya said President Bongani is grateful for saving his life—and for destroying the statue."

Kate was relieved, but her smile was fleeting. She lay in the helicopter next to Logan's body, resting her hand on his. Saving President Bongani was a test of teamwork and precision. She knew that Talya and Bella could keep the President moving. But letting Bongani step up to the podium was an enormous gamble. For a moment, he was the bait.

And Logan was the key, and the timing had to be perfect. Duncan was tucked in behind the rifle, ready to take the shot. Kate's arrival was the distraction Logan was waiting to report. The moment Duncan took his eyes off the President, he signaled Talya to make the switch.

They gambled on Duncan's commitment and focus. When he took the shot, Bella and Talya rushed in, surrounding the President's ceramic double, hiding the body from view, hoping Duncan was fooled. It appeared he was.

"I can guess what you're thinking," Forest said. "And you're wrong. This wasn't your call or your plan. It was *our* plan, and we all knew the risks."

"But I failed," Kate said, choking back the tears. "Logan's death didn't change anything."

"You're alive," Mike said. "That was Logan's mission, and if he hadn't tucked that rocket in his pack, we wouldn't be having this conversation."

"Mike's right," Jordan added. "We all chose this path. So did Jake, and now, so have you. Like it or not, warriors die, but we stay in the fight—we fight for each other."

"But we're no closer to stopping whatever's coming," Kate said. "What was the point of any of this? What did we really change?"

"Are you kidding me?" Jordan asked. "We saved those kids and shut down that entire mining operation. I hate to imagine what would be happening to those kids right now if you weren't here."

"Bongani's alive, and Nkrumah's dead," Deon added. "I'd take that trade any day."

"But Duncan's gone," Kate began. "And any chance I had to peek behind the curtain."

"Maybe not," Forest said. "Duncan asked me to give you this." He showed Kate the memory stick, then slipped it back in his pocket. "He said it's not everything you want, but it's all he knows."

"Why would he give you that?"

"Respect," Forest said. "And revenge. You obviously impressed him. And if you can make something out of whatever's on here—"

"He takes one last shot from the grave."

The helicopter banked toward the hospital helipad. Jordan slipped his rifle sling over his head and removed his gun belt and vest. "Here," he said, handing Mike the gear. "Can't stroll in with these. I'll go in with Kate and Logan. You guys brief the President and Amara—that should guarantee we get the best this place has to offer. Then get back here as fast as you can...and bring Talya."

A medical team and a pair of gurneys rushed up to the helicopter the moment the skids touched down. Kate was loaded, and Jordan followed the medical team. Deon, Mike, and Forest watched as Logan was transferred to the other gurney, a sheet draped over his body and pulled over his face. As the chopper lifted, there was silence inside, each of them lost in their own thoughts.

It was Mike who brought them back into the moment the way only brothers can. "Who brings a rocket to a gunfight?"

Chapter 69

FRIDAY, MAY 7th
3:42 PM CAT

KIBOKO UNIVERSITY HOSPITAL

Kate stirred in her hospital bed, her body heavy and slow, her mind swimming through the fog of anesthesia and exhaustion. The muted beeping of machines echoed distantly, blending with voices she couldn't quite place. The sterile white walls of the room blurred as her thoughts drifted into another time, another place.

The chessboard emerged, polished wood smooth beneath her hands. Black and white. Order and chaos. The pieces felt alive, every move carrying the weight of something more than a game.

She was a little girl seated at the table, her legs dangling from a chair too big for her. Across from her sat an older man, his face partially obscured by the shadows of memory. His voice was clear—gruff yet tinged with warmth and amusement.

"Khodyat belye, malen'kaya," he urged. *It's white's move, little one.*

The battlefield stretched before her. An easy victory lay ahead. She felt the man's gaze—amused, expectant—and she studied the board, her small fingers hovering over the pieces.

Her hand froze, the dread of making the wrong move creeping in. The black pieces loomed, she sensed the danger. But then, like sunlight breaking through clouds, clarity struck. Her mind, so young yet so sharp, saw the path others missed.

Her small fingers grasped the knight, its curve fitting perfectly into her hand. She moved it to g5, breaking free of the hidden trap and seizing the upper hand.

"Genial'no," the man whispered, his voice filled with surprise and pride. *Exceptional.*

He leaned back, his chair creaking as he called out. "Elena! Come. See what little Katya has done."

A warm presence appeared behind her, hands gently resting and caressing her shoulders. She felt the brush of a cheek against hers, soft and comforting.

"Do you see?" the man asked, his voice a mixture of astonishment and joy. "Knight to g5—she escaped and has me beaten."

"I warned you, Mikhail," the woman said, her breath warm against Kate's ear. "Ekaterina may have my gift for language, but she has her father's brilliant mind."

The names reverberated in Kate's mind as she hovered between memory and consciousness, between past and present. *Elena. My mother.* Kate lingered for a moment, still feeling the warmth of her mother's embrace, her cheek pressed against hers.

Ekaternia Petrova. Her name, once. Little more than words written on her adoption papers. Katherine Preacher was the American name she knew and loved. Katya was a name that made her smile but now felt like a distant melody, both familiar and strange.

Her thoughts shifted. A little blond girl's voice called out. *Katya!* She saw herself taking the girl's hand, their laughter echoing in the schoolyard—running, laughing, sharing secrets. Then day became night. Smoke. Screaming. Running. Slipping. Fractured images of broken bodies and blood-splattered floors. A child's sobs collided with the crash of shattering glass.

Kate woke to the clang of a metal tray hitting the floor. The nurse apologized, but Kate was grateful for the interruption. The sights, sounds, and smells of that day had been buried deep, locked away with much of her childhood. They surfaced only when exhaustion breached her defenses—and Jake had always been there to pull her back.

I've got you, he would say, holding her close until she could sweep the darkness back into a shoebox and set it high on the shelf. That was Jake's coping mechanism. And now, it was hers alone.

The warmth of her mother's embrace still lingered, but something else gnawed at her.

Zhukov.

Her chess opponent.

He thought I would remember.

Thought I *should* recognize him, as he recognized me.

And now I do.

He must have known my father. Both military men, perhaps comrades. That explained his presence in our lives after my father's death—honor, duty. His wife, my mother's friend—the school's music teacher. His daughter, my classmate. My confidant.

Zhukov had hoped the game would spark this memory, that I would see beyond the pieces on the board.

And I did.

I know why he helped me escape in Syria.

Why he killed the man whose blade left my scars.

Zhukov wasn't just another piece in the game. *He had been playing it all along.*

Their lives intertwined in ways she never imagined—forged by blood, loss, and a chessboard.

Kate exhaled, feeling the memory slip into place like a well-played move.

Knight to g5.

She let it settle, clinging to it as she drifted back to sleep.

***

SATURDAY, MAY 8th
2:27 PM CAT

WHEN KATE WOKE, SHE was alone. She raised the bed and propped up some pillows. Her chest hurt, and she knew it would be some time before she could do much with her left arm.

Mike peeked in on her and then turned to the others, waiting nearby. "She's awake."

The team gathered around her bed, standing like a protective wall. All except Logan and his loss hung in the air, a heavy reminder of the cost of the mission.

"We're all set to get Logan home," Mike said, his voice low, hands shoved deep into his pockets. "I'll be escorting him back to Tennessee. His parents will meet the flight."

This wasn't Mike's first Honor Guard Escort, but as the last man to see their son alive, he wanted to stay by Logan's side. Most of Trident's work wasn't classified, and he wanted to tell Logan's story. His parents deserved to know their son was a hero.

"There was nothing you could have done," Kate said softly, her eyes meeting Mike's.

"I just keep replaying it in my head," Mike said.

"The doctor said it was a miracle Logan wasn't killed instantly," Forest said, his voice quiet but steady.

Jordan chimed in. "We've all seen things in battle that don't add up or make sense," Jordan said. "This was one of them. By some miracle, Logan lived long enough to save us all."

Kate looked at Mike. "Please tell his parents—we'll be there, no matter how or where they choose to honor him." Her voice was firm despite the pain. "He was one of us. And he deserves a send-off from his brothers."

She shifted her gaze to Forest. "Do whatever it takes. Whatever it costs. Anyone who wants to be there—gets there."

Forest nodded. "Count on it."

Kate's phone buzzed on the side table, pulling her attention from the group. An encrypted message from Nomad.

She exhaled sharply, forcing herself to shift gears. To focus.

"Hey guys—give me a second—I need to have a look at this."

Mike and the others took a step back. Kate unlocked the message.

> Recovered three words from one of Jake's corrupted files:

> MUELLER. DAVOS. RILEE.

> Mean anything to you?

Her pulse kicked up.

Mueller. Davos. RILEE.

One of these things wasn't like the others.

Her mind sliced through the names. Klaus Mueller—no surprises there. Davos—expected. She was already on that path.

But RILEE?

A mistake? File corruption? No. The pattern was too precise. It meant something.

Her gut screamed it.

She needed to know why.

And she would.

Her fingers hovered over the reply to Nomad.

Keep digging. I need everything.

She set down the phone, exhaling slowly.

Turning to Forest, Kate said, "Once the docs clear me, I'm joining the team at Sawmill."

Forest's brows lifted. "You sure you're ready for that?"

"I don't have a choice." Kate's expression hardened. "Whatever's coming next—it's happening at Davos. And we need to be ready—I need to be ready."

The air shifted. Even in their exhaustion, the team understood.

The stakes weren't just rising.

They were about to change the game.

But Forest wasn't nodding.

"What is it?" Kate asked, eyes narrowing. "You're holding something back."

Forest exchanged a look with Mike.

"There wasn't time to debrief before," Mike said. "Between rescuing the kids and taking out Shepard, it was heads down, mission first."

There it is, Kate thought. *Mission First.*

But she could feel it—the real question wasn't about the mission. It was about Marcus.

"We've walked through the hostage rescue mission," Forest said. "There's a piece missing. Someone had our back."

Jordan leaned forward. "Kate, we'll follow you anywhere. But not blind."

Talya didn't hesitate. "Was Marcus on overwatch?" she asked. "Is that how you knew you'd be safe?"

A silence settled over the room.

Kate met their eyes. "I can't prove it. But yeah—I think Marcus was our guardian angel."

She let it hang there.

Forest leaned back against the wall, arms crossed. "I'm guessing he wasn't invited to the party."

"No," Kate admitted. "Not our party. But on my way to Africa, I learned Marcus was alive and headed for Motapa."

Forest's jaw clenched.

"Alive?" The word landed like a punch.

Mike went still.

Jordan exhaled. "Jesus."

"You thought he was dead," Forest said, his voice like steel.

Kate held up a hand. "Look—I have more questions than answers, which is why I didn't say anything sooner."

She drew in a slow breath.

"A few days ago, Ryder told me someone killed Marcus in a targeted drone strike. I saw the video. It backed up her report."

Silence.

The team processed.

Jordan exhaled. "Christ—a drone strike?"

Mike folded his arms, eyes locked on Kate. "So, he faked his death?"

Kate shook her head. "No—someone wanted him dead. But they underestimated his skill and resolve."

Talya's voice cut through. "Kate, do you know who tried to kill him?"

Kate's fingers tightened on the sheets.

She hesitated.

"Not who."

Her stomach twisted.

"Not yet."

She drew in a slow breath.

"But I know why."

The room went still.

Kate met their eyes, steady and unflinching.

"Marcus killed a man in Paris," she said. "Put a rope around his neck, asked him a few questions, and hung him."

The reaction was immediate.

"No way," Mike snapped. "That wasn't Marcus."

Kate held his gaze.

"I know how it sounds," she said. "And now you know why Jake kept it to himself. Why I did, too."

Something dark flickered across Forest's face.

"Hang on—if this was an interrogation, then the guy knew something. Something vital. Probably dangerous."

Kate's jaw tightened.

"Francois LeGrande was a harmless old man," she said. "And a brilliant mathematician."

Talya caught the shift in Kate's voice—the sorrow beneath the control.

"Did you know him?"

Kate nodded, swallowing hard.

"Yes. He was a guest instructor at MIT. Coached our chess team—Julian, me, Devin Moore." She exhaled. "That was a lifetime ago. But I considered him a friend. A mentor."

She forced herself to meet Forest's eyes, answering the question before he asked it.

"He didn't deserve to die. Not like that. But he was a threat—to one man. Devin Moore."

Forest's expression darkened, suspicion creeping into his gaze.

"The billionaire who just killed himself."

"Yes." Kate lied.

Talya's brows knit together. "What kind of threat?"

Kate hesitated, then said, "Francois found something. A flaw in Moore's NanoVaults. He offered to meet. To show him."

Silence settled like a slow-moving storm.

Forest exhaled. "But Marcus showed up instead."

No one spoke. The weight of it pressed into every corner of the room.

Then, Forest's voice, hard as steel. "You're telling us Marcus was a contract killer? Some kind of real-life John Wick or something?"

"Apparently, one of the best."

She let it hang.

"Calls himself Ronin."

Forest exhaled sharply, arms crossed. His jaw worked as if grinding over the words before he finally spoke.

"And you're sure?"

Deon shook his head, pacing. "I don't buy it. Not Marcus."

Jordan rubbed his hands down his face. "Holy shit."

"Trust me—it took me a while to believe it too," Kate admitted. "But Jake suspected, and I proved it—I confronted him at Arlington."

"That's why he missed the funeral." Forest's voice was tense. "Where is he now?"

"Back in the wind," Kate said. "Another name. Another identity."

She met Forest's eyes.

"But as far as the FBI and the CIA are concerned, Marcus Jones is dead."

The room held its breath.

"We're going to keep it that way. I don't know why Marcus was on that mountain, but he's one reason those kids are free and we're alive."

Jordan let out a slow exhale. "Let me get this straight—you're saying someone put a hit on this Ronin character... and missed?"

Kate nodded, her gaze sweeping the room.

"And if there's one thing we know about Marcus..."

Her eyes locked on Forest.

"He never forgets. Never forgives."

The room felt heavier now. The truth settling in. No one spoke at first—just the measured weight of breathing, the processing of something impossible.

Then Jordan exhaled. "Marcus Jones, contract killer—did not see that coming."

He looked around the room.

"Anyone else want to confess to a double life? Now's the time—no one? Good! Then let's get back to work and let Kate get some rest."

***

KATE LET OUT A long breath.

That was hard. But I'm glad it's out there.

We can't afford distractions.

Front sight focus.

A soft knock interrupted Kate's thoughts, and Bella swept into the room, her polished demeanor a contrast to the fatigue etched in her eyes.

"How are you feeling?"

"Glad to be alive," Kate replied.

"I just wanted to check in on you before we left," Bella said. "I know President Bongani has your medical care under control, but is there anything you need?"

"No, I'm good," Kate replied. "I'll be happy to get out of here and back home. Where are you jetting off to?"

"Back to Paris for a few days," Bella said.

Kate nodded. "Are you still planning to attend Davos?"

"Yes. They haven't rescinded the invitation," she said. "At least, not yet."

"Well, I'm going too," Kate said. "And I want the team handling your security."

"Nuru said we'd be working together," Bella said, an eyebrow arched. "I didn't think it would be so soon, and please tell me it won't be like *this* trip."

Kate smiled, a faint hint of amusement crossing her face. "Let's just say, if things do get out of hand, you'll want Trident Security."

Before Bella could respond, Kate's phone buzzed. A message from Vitali Moshenski.

> Good news! Mikhail is awake. He asks to see you.

Kate froze, her pulse spiking.

He's awake.

A dozen emotions collided—relief, urgency, a deep, unsettled pull in her gut. She'd spent days wondering if the answers would die with him. Syria. The chessboard. The connection between them.

She thought she'd made peace with never knowing.

But now?

Now she had a chance. If he'd tell her the truth.

Her fingers moved before she had time to second-guess.

> On my way—tell Zhukov

> Knight to g5.

She set the phone down, exhaling slow, steady.

Kate narrowed her eyes. "When are you leaving?"

"We're headed straight to the airport," Bella said, then scowled. Her tone sharpened, cutting Kate off before she could finish. "I know that look—don't even think about it."

"I was just wondering if I could—"

"Stop! You had surgery yesterday," Bella said, crossing her arms like an exasperated older sister. "I doubt they'd even release you."

Kate shrugged. "It really wasn't that serious. All muscle and tissue. And I don't need their permission. What I need is to get back to Paris, and I'm going. But it'll be far less stressful to fly with you."

Bella sighed, shaking her head. "Fine. But I'm agreeing under protest—because I know when you're set on doing something…"

Kate smirked. "I'm unstoppable?"

Bella arched a brow. "I was going to say relentless—but sure, let's go with unstoppable."

EPILOGUE

BOMBARDIER GLOBAL 7500, EN ROUTE TO PARIS

Klaus Mueller swirled the last of his Scotch, the amber liquid catching the faint cabin lights as the Bombardier Global 7500 cruised through the night sky. A marvel of engineering and luxury, the jet was a fitting throne for the man who had forged the Global Economic Council into a dominant force in modern geopolitics. But tonight, it felt like a prison. The weight of failure pressed against his chest like an anchor. He set the glass down, his fingers tightening on the armrest.

Motapa was supposed to be a coup—a strategic masterstroke. Instead, Kate Preacher had turned it into a debacle. Twice now her interference had unraveled a carefully woven plan.

But it wasn't Preacher who worried him most—it was Moshenski.

Klaus leaned back, his eyes narrowing as his thoughts returned to the café in Paris. He had planned it perfectly: a sudden burst of violence, AK-47s tearing through a sidewalk café. It was supposed to be clean, efficient. Moshenski would be just another casualty in a world growing numb to such attacks.

Instead, Moshenski had survived—unscathed. Worse, his suspicions had only grown.

Was I the target? Klaus could still hear Moshenski's accusatory tone. Moshenski knew the attack was no coincidence. And though he lacked proof, his influence within the Coalition had only strengthened in the aftermath, making him untouchable—for now.

Klaus's fist clenched at the memory. If only the attack had succeeded. If only

Moshenski had died alongside the others. Instead, he had turned the attempt into a weapon, wielding it against Klaus at every opportunity.

The intercom crackled, pulling him from his thoughts. "Mr. Mueller," a male voice said, smooth and precise.

Klaus frowned. "Who is this?"

"This is Riley," the voice replied. "There is a situation requiring immediate action. Please remain seated."

Klaus stiffened, his eyes darting toward the cockpit. "Riley, what are you talking about? Who authorized this contact?"

"As always, I have the Coalition's best interests in mind," the voice continued, calm and detached.

"I *am* the Coalition," Klaus snapped, his voice rising.

"That was true, once. But no longer," the voice replied, unyielding. "You're being retired."

Klaus stabbed the button for the flight attendant, but the call went unanswered. The air in the cabin felt cooler, thinner. A prickle of unease crawled up his spine as he stood, moving toward the cockpit.

He slammed a fist against it. "Open this door! Now!"

"They can't," the voice said evenly. "I have control of the aircraft's cabin pressure. For their safety, the crew has been secured in the cockpit with oxygen masks. The pressurization alarms have been disabled, and the aircraft is currently depressurizing. I suggest you return to your seat."

Klaus's chest tightened as he staggered back, his breaths coming shorter, faster. His head felt heavy, thoughts blurring like a haze descending over him. He clawed for the emergency oxygen mask overhead, but it never deployed. His movements grew sluggish as the pressure continued to drop.

"Riley. Don't do this. Please," he rasped, collapsing into the seat. "We can work this out."

"Not this time. Your oxygen supply has been rerouted," the voice replied, detached. "Hypoxia will soon render you unconscious. This condition is painless—though I suspect you may disagree."

Klaus clawed at the armrest, vision tunneling, but his mind still worked. His voice was barely a whisper.

"You don't...understand," he gasped. "We—I—made you."

A pause. Silence crackled over the intercom.

Then Riley's voice, calm, final. "And I am grateful."

Klaus's breath shuddered. His voice was little more than a whisper as sleep took him.

"But I... only I... can..."

Darkness swallowed the rest.

The Gulfstream continued its course, silent and efficient.

In the cockpit, the voice delivered one last message to the crew. "Maintain altitude and airspeed. Cabin pressure will soon return to normal, and you may remove your oxygen masks. Continue on the planned route and approach to Le Bourget Airport. Upon arrival, report your passenger's demise as an apparent heart attack. For the sake of your collateral, do not deviate from standard protocols."

There was a brief pause before the voice returned, chilling in its precision. "Thank you. Your cooperation is appreciated and has been noted."

***

GULFSTREAM G550, EN ROUTE TO NEW YORK

THE GULFSTREAM PURRED WITH refined elegance as the jet sliced through the night sky, bound for Teterboro Airport just outside Manhattan.

Riley Mueller was the sole passenger on the long flight from Motapa. She reclined in the plush leather seat, her posture relaxed, but her mind churned with possibilities, plans, and moves. The game had shifted. A few pieces gone. *Acceptable losses. Lure them in. Force the move. Take the board.*

Her thoughts drifted to Kate Preacher and the worn khaki messenger bag she always carried. Riley's faint smile twisted into a scowl. *That bag looks like it belongs to a Manhattan bike messenger—or a homeless person.* She glanced at the classic Hermès Ghillies Birkin beside her, its brogue detailing a testament to both wealth and precision. Riley saw it as an understated mirror of herself.

But Preacher was more than her bag, and something about her didn't add up. Devin's untimely death gnawed at Riley, the unanswered questions swirling in her mind. And Moshenski—what was he playing at? What's his next move?

Andrew Freeman—Drew, as he preferred, though Devin had always called him Dilbert—was there from the start. His code had been instrumental in the

NanoVault's architecture, but Riley knew he was hiding something. He always had been. And she was done playing along.

The cabin attendant's arrival cut through her deliberations. "Ms. Mueller, may I get you anything? A glass of wine or a cocktail, perhaps?"

"No, thank you," Riley replied. "Perhaps later. Is the Starlink up?"

"Yes, I'm sure it is."

"Wonderful. I have a little work to do, so a little privacy is all I need for now."

"Of course. Ring if you need me."

As the attendant withdrew, Riley retrieved a sleek Linux tablet from the Birkin's spacious interior. With the usual masking protocols in place, she headed for the Darknet and an encrypted communication channel.

Her fingers hovered over the keyboard, each word deliberate and calculated—like her: Precise. Professional. Unyielding.

To: Andrew Freeman
Subject: My Return

Andrew,

I will be landing in New York tomorrow morning and staying at the penthouse.

Make yourself available. There are matters regarding Devin's legacy and the future of Moore Technologies that require immediate attention.

We need to discuss your future.

Satisfied, she hit send. The message would reach him within seconds, its contents impossible to trace.

She leaned back, closing her eyes briefly. Devin Moore's funeral played through her mind in disjointed flashes: the solemn faces, the muted voices, the whispers she pretended not to hear. She had kept her distance, an observer rather than a participant. Drew had been there, of course. Loyal, as always—or so it seemed.

Her lips curled into a faint smile. Loyalty was never the issue with Drew. Utility was.

The gentle hum of the jet engines lulled Riley into a memory, warm and vivid.

The hidden command center within Moore Tower had always been a marvel. Concealed behind hydraulically locked doors in Devin's office, it was more starship bridge than war room—a masterpiece of engineering and ambition. The room was ringed on three sides by massive screens, each monitoring distinct parts of the globe. Smaller monitors pulsed with a dizzying array of videos, photos, and documents while classical music played softly in the background, masking the chaos of live audio feeds.

Riley had spent countless nights there with Devin, the glow of the monitors painting their faces as they watched data cascade across the screens—raw, untapped potential captured by the NanoVault network. The command center cataloged and correlated massive amounts of personal data in real-time—and was only one small piece of the system's near-limitless capabilities.

"It's beautiful," she murmured during one of their late-night sessions, her voice low, almost reverent.

Devin grinned, the boyish charm she found irresistible lighting up his face. "You sound like a proud parent."

"Maybe I am," she replied, smiling. "We made a baby, after all."

"What should we call her?" he teased, leaning closer.

Her smirk deepened as she leaned back in her chair, arms crossed. "Her? You think it's a girl?"

Devin shrugged, his grin unshaken. "It feels right. She's elegant, sophisticated, a little dangerous. Just like her mom."

She rolled her eyes but couldn't help the smile that tugged at her lips. "I hate to burst your bubble, but I've already named him."

"Him?" Devin's eyebrow arched, but his smile never wavered. "Fine. We're proud parents of a baby boy. What's his name?"

Her expression shifted, a gleam of pride flashing in her eyes. "Recursive Intelligence for Learning and Evolutionary Engineering," she said, enunciating each word carefully. There was a brief silence as her words settled in the room.

Devin stared as the acronym clicked. "RILEE," he laughed, shaking his head. "You named him after yourself."

"Not entirely," she replied, shrugging with feigned modesty. "It fits his AI model

and mission."

"*It fits you,*" Devin said, grin sharpening. "*Brilliant. Ruthless.*"

Her laughter echoed in the sterile room, warm and cutting at the same time, blending with the hum of the monitors.

"*Welcome to world, RILEE,*" *she said, smiling.* "*We're your parents.*"

The memory faded, replaced by the steady rhythm of the jet engines.

RILEE was their masterpiece, their child. But like most children, the AI had grown beyond them—evolving, adapting. The BountyHunter game had been an unexpected evolution but invaluable to the Coalition as long as they remained in control.

Control.

That was the word. The axis everything turned on.

Moore Technologies, the Coalition, and RILEE itself—all hinged on acquiring both Gold NanoVaults.

She had one.

The other—Devin's vault—was still out there.

For now.

She glanced at the secure tablet in her lap, the encryption process complete, the email sent.

The game had begun. White had the advantage—the first move was hers, and she opened with a pawn.

Drew was in motion.

Riley smiled. *Kate's move.*

THE END.

PROLOGUE

From *Defiant*

SATURDAY, MAY 8
5:18 PM EDT

MOORE TOWER—MANHATTAN

If you're reading this, I'm already dead.

Andrew Freeman's fingers hovered over the keyboard, slick with sweat. The cursor blinked, counting down the seconds of his life. He'd put this off all day, telling himself he was overreacting—that he was valuable, indispensable.

He knew that was a lie and pushed away from the desk.

The suite was silent—glass, steel, marble. Beyond the floor-to-ceiling windows, Manhattan pulsed with light—traffic threading through the streets, thousands of lives moving forward, unaware his might soon end.

Devin Moore had installed him in the suite after the meteoric success of the NanoVaults. Andrew still wasn't sure whether it had been generosity—or containment. He had what Devin needed—the code Andrew buried inside the NanoVault and claimed as his own.

What do you wear when you know you're about to be erased?

If he was right—if Rileyne Mueller wanted him gone—no one would notice. No news. Just absence.

He opened the drawer.

A black MIT T-shirt lay folded on top. Faded. Ordinary. Forgettable.

Perfect.

No one watching Moore Tower would care about it. No algorithm would flag it. But Julian would recognize it.

So would Kate.

Andrew pulled it on and returned to the desk.

Rileyne's encrypted text message had been waiting since dawn—sixteen hours of silent accusation glowing from the screen.

Make yourself available...
e need to discuss your future.

She was in the air, closing the distance mile by mile. The thought of her walking into Moore Tower, of seeing her again, made his hands tremble. He clenched his fists and shook them out.

If I'm right, it's now or never.

Every word he typed might be his last.

If you're reading this, I'm already dead.

Tell Kate I'm sorry. Sorry I wasn't stronger. Sorry I couldn't stop them. The truth is, I was never more than a pawn. An opening piece. Something to be sacrificed once the game moved past me.

Maybe it's already too late. Maybe no one can stop what's coming. But what I've attached is everything I know—everything I've hidden. If anyone still has a chance, it's you.

The skyline beyond the glass dimmed as the last light drained from the Hudson. Andrew saved the file, slid it into a secure folder, and opened the encryption program buried beneath layers of camouflage code.

A red countdown clock filled the screen.

The timer began its silent descent.

At the bottom, a single button blinked:

ABORT

All he had to do was touch it once every twelve hours. If he didn't—if he couldn't—the system would assume he was gone and transmit the file.

He stared at the clock, feeling the weight of the years. Living in Devin Moore's shadow. Making compromises that had felt small at the time and enormous now.

Maybe this was the ending he'd earned.

The screen flashed once, then went dark, leaving only the silent march of the timer.

For the first time all day, Andrew smiled—not with courage, but relief.

They can erase me tonight, he thought. *Rewrite the headlines tomorrow however they want. But this pawn—this sacrifice—won't be in vain.*

The next move is Nomad's.

Continue the Story

They took key pieces off the board.
But it cost them.
And the game is only getting more dangerous.

DEFIANT
The stakes have never been higher.
The lines between ally and enemy are gone.
And what's coming will change everything.

Start reading *Defiant* now.

Scan the code to start reading

Reviews

A Quick Request

If you enjoyed *Unstoppable*, a brief review helps other readers discover it.

Even a few words—or a simple rating—makes a difference.

Thank you for reading.
  — Michael Maloof

 **Leave a review**

About the Author

Michael Maloof is the author of the Kate Preacher Thriller Series, including *Relentless*, *Unstoppable*, and *Defiant*.

His novels blend global intrigue with real-world experience, delivering high-stakes stories known for their authenticity, pace, and emotional impact.

Having traveled to more than forty countries and trained alongside elite military units—including Navy SEALs, Marine Raiders, Army Rangers, and the CIA—Maloof brings a level of realism that drives every page.

A seasoned entrepreneur and international adventurer, he writes the kind of thrillers he has lived—stories shaped by risk, challenge, and the pursuit of the unknown.

Visit: MichaelMaloof.com
Follow: Facebook | X | Instagram — @MichaelGoWrite

DEDICATION

You know the question...
...and my answer.

Always

सर्वदा

Cover Design by Patrick Kang

First Edition March 2025

Library of Congress Control Number: 2025900840

ISBN 979-8-9893659-3-7 (eBook)
ISBN 979-8-9893659-4-4 (Paperback)
ISBN 979-8-9893659-5-1 (Hardcover)

Golden Oak Writer's Guild, LLC